THE FORGOTTEN HOME

Katie Coyne

Contents

Chapter 1

Ordinarily I would have been thrilled to move to a beach house along the beautiful coast of North Carolina. Maybe a cute place to spend summer vacations away from our life in Bedford. Providence was where I was born, after all. It might have been nice getting to know my home town a few months out of the year.

I could see myself relaxing on the beach with a book and attempting to tan my pale skin. Learning how to cook the fish I could buy at the local markets. Maybe meeting a handsome stranger I would never see again once I returned to New York.

I mean, the latter was almost laughable. I had never really spoken more than three words to a cute boy in my life, and one had certainly never gone out of his way to speak to me.

I blended into the crowd at my high school in Bedford. I was one of seventeen hundred students. Nobody noticed me and I quite liked it that way. I was a good student, and I got good grades, and so I liked to keep my head down. I didn't bother myself with teenage drama, and I never had to worry about boyfriends.

Not that my mom would let me have one anyway.

But now that my mom's job had taken us to Providence, North Carolina, I was sure I was going to stick out like a sore thumb. How could I not with only five hundred students in the school.

And I was starting late. It was October, after all. If a teacher made me stand up the front of the class and spout fun facts about myself I was sure I would die of embarrassment.

Maybe I should think up some just in case.

My name is Sara. I'm a Virgo. Why would I bother with that? I don't believe in astrology.

"I got nothing," I sighed. I looked at myself in the mirror and wished that I knew which box my makeup was in. All I had was a crusty, old concealer that I had found in the bottom of my purse. I used it to cover my eye bags and the few red unmentionables that seemed to enjoy popping up right when I didn't want them to.

I ran my brush through my brown hair and when I realised it wasn't going to cooperate, I pulled it up into a messy bun. It was still quite warm in Providence, so I had dressed in a plain white t-shirt and some ripped skinny jeans.

After checking over myself one last time, and realising this was as good as it was going to get, I grabbed my book bag filled with all new supplies and left my barely unpacked room.

My mom had moved us into a really nice little house on the beach. It was just the right size for the two of us. It was newly remodelled, but still had the character and charm of wainscoting and hardwood floors.

My mom was in our little kitchen, pouring a green smoothie into a travel cup for her to take to work. Mom had been really young when my parents had had me. She was only twenty and my dad had been a couple of years older.

After he passed away in an accident when I was two, she moved us away from Providence to New York, where she completed college and medical school as a single mom, eventually settling us in Bedford.

My mom and I had a really special relationship. It had been just us for so long, and so we had learned to heavily rely on the other person. She relied on me most of the time. With her hectic work schedule, I helped to look after the house, the grocery shopping, and most importantly, myself.

If I had been a difficult child, I don't think my mom could have been as successful as she is.

My mom, Dr Amanda Bryant, is a paediatric oncologist. People travel from all over the country to have her treat their kids. Kids who are going through the fight of their lives. I honestly don't know how she does it. All I could really do to help her was reduce the stress she had of having a daughter at home by looking after myself.

"Hey, hon," my mom greeted me when she noticed me entering the kitchen. She smiled at me warmly as she screwed on the lid of her travel cup. Mom was dressed for work. It was her first day, too. She had been headhunted to a specialty cancer clinic about a half hour drive from here. She never talked numbers, but I was certain the salary had to be good to take us away from New York.

She was dressed in a plain, long sleeved t-shirt and leggings, and was no doubt going to change into scrubs when she got to the clinic. Her hair, the same brown colour as mine, was slicked back into a neat pony tail, and she had effortlessly applied a nice amount of makeup to her ageless skin. Clearly she hadn't misplaced her makeup bag in the move.

"Morning," I mumbled as I went over to the coffee pot and poured myself a cup. My mom then hugged me from behind and rubbed my upper arms comfortingly. She could sense my nerves. I turned around to look down on her. She was a couple of inches shorter than my five six.

"Sara, you have nothing to be nervous about," she promised, her green eyes looking upon me sympathetically. "So what it's a new school? You will get the same wonderful grades you always do, and I'm sure you'll make some great friends." Bless her, she was trying to be supportive. I knew she felt guilty for pulling me out of my old school. "I lived here for a lot longer than you when I was younger. I always liked this town. The kids here were nice."

We shall see.

"You look beautiful," she added earnestly, brushing some hair out of my eyes. "Now, come on. Chin up. I've got to get to work and you've got to get to school," she urged. "I'll have my cell on me all day. You have the number of the clinic and I've given all my phone numbers to the school already. But I'm sure you won't need them." Mom took my coffee from me and tipped it into another travel cup before handing me the keys to my 'Please don't hate me gift'.

I had to admit, it wasn't so bad driving down from New York in my own Jeep.

Mom kissed me on the cheek as she ushered me out the door. She locked it behind us and blew me a kiss as she backed out of the driveway in her silver Mercedes.

I took a deep breath as I climbed into my Jeep. It was black and all leather inside. It still smelled brand new. I forgot my nerves for a second as I started the engine. I plugged my phone into the AUX port and found a song to drown out my thoughts as I started my drive through the town.

Providence was a really small town. Much smaller than I was used to, though I was used to weekend trips into Manhattan and anythingwould seem smaller than the Big Apple.

There were several streets of houses like ours along the beach, and a main street of stores and businesses serviced them. As I drove down the main street I could see there was one of everything. A grocery story, a post office, a hair salon, a book store. Near the end of the street, and feeding directly out onto the beach was a diner. Sally's, it was called. I wondered if they were hiring.

I drover further inland, only ten minutes or so, and Providence began to seem a little more suburban. The houses were larger and secluded by trees. Providence High School appeared soon after. The school was on a huge, flat acreage, with its football stadium appearing to be the main attraction. The scoreboard looked new, and as I drove past, I could see that "Donated by the Eckhart Family" was printed below the scores.

"Home of the Mighty Vikings," I read as I pulled into the school driveway. Students were streaming into school, and I was following other cars, attempting to find my way to the student parking lot.

The school building looked quite weathered and dated, and it was obvious when looking at the football stadium where most of the budget went. I supposed if I wanted to make friends at this school then I would have to get into football.

I nabbed the first spot I could see and shut off the engine. Before getting out of the car, I double checked that I had everything in my book bag, knowing full well I had triple checked last night. When I no longer had any excuses, I got out of my car.

I felt like I was sweating bullets. What a way to make a first impression than with pit stains. I tried to put blinkers on as I made my way towards the main school building, following the crowd. The school office had to be in there.

But my blinkers were failing me. I could see that people had already started to notice me. People were staring, assessing me, and making their judgements. I seemed to attract eyes like a magnet as I sped towards the main building, a new pair on me each second that passed.

I felt embarrassed and self-conscious as I looked down, attempting to avoid any awkward eye-contact. I thanked God when I made it to the front door, and I practically pulled it off its hinges in an effort to get inside.

Not that inside was any better. I just found another hundred people to stare at me. Were new students this rare in Providence? I really wasn't fascinating. I wished that I had the courage to shout that out.

"I really am ordinary!" I felt like telling them. "I do my homework early and watch reruns on Friday nights instead of going to parties!"

Instead I turned right and followed the signs to the school office. There were two desks behind reception. One in front of the other. The lady at the back, Glenda, according to her nametag, was tapping away at her computer, while the lady at the front, Cherie, was on the phone. By the sounds of the conversation, she was talking to a parent about an absence.

She smiled at me when she noticed me, and was the first one to do so at this school. She held her finger up, indicating for me to wait a moment. I fidgeted with the zipper on my book bag as I did so.

When Cherie hung up the phone, she smiled at me kindly. "You must be Saraphine," she deduced. "You look just like your mother," she gushed. "Oh, Amanda was so pretty, and such a good student. I understand she's a doctor now."

It hadn't occurred to me that seeing as my mom had grown up here, she had in all likelihood attended this school.

Glenda abandoned her computer to stand with Cherie at the front desk. "Saraphine?" she gasped. "You're right, Cherie, she is justlike Amanda."

"Sara," I corrected awkwardly. "And yeah, my mom is a doctor. She works at the cancer clinic not far from here, in Newtown."

Cherie and Glenda exchanged a glance. "Well, Sara,welcome to Providence High," Cherie greeted warmly. She retrieved a packet from her desk and started to flip through it. "I've got here your class schedule, your school map, locker number and code, a cafeteria menu, school calendar, and a list of our extra-curricular activities. Are there any clubs you were thinking of joining? Never too early to start padding that resume for college."

Cherie handed the packet to me. "Uh, I hadn't thought," I replied. Joining clubs had not been in my plan to try to be anonymous at this school. But she was right. I needed more than just good grades to get into a good college. "I'll look over the information. Thank you," I said gratefully.

"Of course, dear," nodded Cherie. "Now, your first class is Spanish. I've asked Señora Gomez to send a student down to collect you and show you where you're going. Ah, here she is."

At that moment, a cheerful blonde entered the school office. She looked really excited to see me, and I immediately felt bad for being so sceptical about the students here.

"Saraphine?" she queried animatedly, her brown eyes darting over me.

"Sara," I corrected. Only my mom called me Saraphine, and only when she was mad, which was hardly ever.

The blonde grinned happily before pulling me into a surprise hug. "Oh, Sara! I am so glad to meet you!"

I hugged her back, startled. I had not been expecting this greeting. "Same here," I managed to say.

"Go on now, Cece. You don't want to be late," urged Cherie.

Cece grimaced, though humorously. "Oh, of course not." To my surprise, Cece took my hand and dragged me from the office. She actually had a really firm grip. When were clear of the eyes and ears of the office ladies, Cece stopped. "I'm Cece Braverman," she introduced herself.

"Sara Bryant," I replied.

"I know!" she chirped happily. "Come on, Spanish awaits!"

I followed along behind Cece. Watching how she bounced, skipped and ran along the school corridors with ease reminded me of just how unfit I was. Perhaps track was one of the extra-curriculars I should investigate.

Cece did look really fit, though. Even though she was small, perhaps five four or so, she was toned, muscular, and her legs were defined and on show as she wore a pair of super cute denim shorts.

Perhaps I ought to ask her what gym she went to. I was slender, but weak as anything.

Cece brought us to a numbered classroom in a sea of doors that looked identical. She opened the door to a low hum of noise which quickly silenced as soon as I walked in.

"Señora Gomez, this is Sara," introduced Cece.

I could barely register was Señora Gomez said in response. All I could take in was the fact that I had twenty-two pairs of eyes on me, appraising me. I had never been the new kid before. Were we always this interesting?

"Welcome, Sara. Please, tell us all a little about yourself," beckoned Señora Gomez.

Crap. I paled. I did practice this. I searched my brain for fun facts but was coming up with nothing.

Cece, bless her, seemed to sense my terror. "You're from New York, right?"

"Yeah," I stammered, nodding.

"Have you been to Manhattan?" she continued, winking at me.

I relaxed a little. Cece had my back. "Yeah, loads of times."

This seemed to get the class talking, and their eyes off of me momentarily.

"Alright, alright, settle down," called out Señora Gomez. "We have a lot to get through and we're already a quarter of the way into the hour."

Cece led me to a table down the back of the classroom and we sat down next to each other. I dumped my book bag and my information packet underneath the table. I would need to locate my locker soon. I would ask Cece to show me.

"Thank you," I said to her gratefully. "I'm not quick on my feet."

Cece laughed. "Lucky for you, I am." She winked again. As she slouched down in her chair to begin listening to the lesson, her tank top shifted, and it was then that I noticed a tattoo on Cece's chest.

It was unlike anything I had ever seen. The ink was white. The writing was fine, so fine that it was hard to believe an artist had such control to ink such text. But it spelled out a word: Jamie.

"I love your tattoo," I remarked without thinking, not realising that at this moment I looked as though I was staring at her breasts.

Cece looked down and smiled. "Thanks. I got it a few months ago."

I knew my mom would kill me if I ever got a tattoo, but seeing such fine work was astonishing. Maybe just for future reference. "Where did you get it?" I asked.

Cece frowned. "I forget where," she replied. "Jamie and I were kind of out of it. We found a random place. I don't remember the name."

"Oh," was all I said in reply. I said nothing further. I then tuned into Señora Gomez's lesson.

Chapter 2

Cece and I then found out that we had the same English class.

English was a breeze. I was worried I would be behind, but they were studying "To Kill a Mockingbird" and I had already read that at my old school. I collected the essay prompt and made a mental note to start it tonight. I didn't have plans.

While I was jotting down ideas for the essay, Cece remarked, "As if you're starting already."

I just smiled. Cece showed me to my Algebra classroom before she darted off to Gym.

I liked math, as well. I was a strange specimen. I listened intently, trying to appear unaware that two girls behind me were speaking about me, or how the boy sitting next to me was trying to subtly look down my t-shirt. I 'accidentally' stabbed him with my pencil and that was that.

Cece found me after Algebra, her face flushed and her hair damp after showering. I was taken aback by how pretty Cece was. Without a speck of makeup, her skin was clear and glowing. She looked bright and healthy. I was only grateful that I had managed to find that old concealer this morning or else people would be saying other things about me.

Cece had changed into a cheer uniform, and I suddenly realised why she was so fit. Her flat and toned stomach was on show in the tight little number and I was a little envious.

"I'm starving!" Cece cried as she bounced over to the lunch line in the cafeteria.

I was, too, admittedly, though once again, all eyes were on me in this cafeteria. All three hundred pairs. Cece hadn't seemed to notice that the room had gone silent.

I felt weird and self-conscious. This was too much attention for just the new girl in school. I dared to look up again, to try and appear as though I had an ounce of confidence, and I immediately found a pair of chocolate brown eyes.

His stare was different. It wasn't one of curiosity or teenage lust like I had been experiencing from boys all day. His stare wasintense. As he looked at me, I felt everyone else in this cafeteria disappear. His eyes captured me and held my focus and I felt seen for the first time today.

He wasn't just seeing me, he was seeing into me. How was this possible? With one look he had made me feel completely transparent. What kind of supernatural bullshit was this?

"Sara?" Cece shook me.

My gaze snapped away from his eyes and went onto Cece. "What?" I gasped.

Cece smiled and furrowed her eyebrows. "I said, do you want pizza or lasagne?"

"Oh, uh, pizza," I said breathlessly. Somehow we had moved up to the front of the line. A kindly looking lunch lady placed a piece of cheese pizza on my plate and placed it my tray. I hurriedly collected some fruit and a water and paid for my meal.

To my surprise, Cece led me directly over to the table where the brown eyed boy was sitting.

Boy really was a poor choice of words. He didn't look like he had been a boy in a long time. He either worked out a lot or was on steroids because I have never seen someone so large in my life. He was sitting down, but with the width of his shoulders, the length of his strong arms, and his legs that I could see underneath the table, I would wager that he was about six and a half feet tall.

Every inch of him was taut, toned, and tanned. He looked a lot like Cece in that respect. And then, as I noticed the guys, and girls, that he was sitting with, they all looked as fit as each other. I paled in comparison.

He hadn't stopped looking at me since I had first noticed him. He was completely ignoring the conversation on his table as we walked over.

His eyes were beautiful. His face was beautiful. Was it weird to describe a man as beautiful? No other word seemed appropriate. His hair was the feature I noticed next. It was a russet brown colour, perfectly tousled and styled. The colour went impeccably with his olive skin. His skin was flawless, his jaw was strong and defined, and as we arrived at the table he smiled.

My heart stopped. His smile only grew wider. It was like he knew.

"Guys, this is Sara," introduced Cece. She sat down on the lap of another genetically blessed man and began to tuck into her pizza. I wagered he was Jamie. They held my attention momentarily. Jamie wrapped a large arm around Cece's waist and she nestled into his chest comfortably. He kissed her bare shoulder and she offered him a bite of her pizza. They were actually really sweet together. "Sara," Cece said once she had swallowed her pizza, "this is my boyfriend, Jamie." She gestured to the man behind her. "Liza," she pointed to a beautiful brunette who was also wearing a cheer uniform, "Zoey," a blonde in a cheer uniform, who, to my surprise, was glaring daggers at me, "Francesca," who was currently whispering something to Zoey that I couldn't hear, "Matt, Lucas, and my big brother, Shea."

Shea. He was the one who was staring at me. The one who had not stopped staring at me.

I felt nervous and vulnerable. I didn't like those feelings. Being seen so transparently by someone you don't know is something so completely foreign to me. I couldn't maintain eye contact with him. I felt like he could read my mind. He could hear how nervous and pathetic I was at having the attention of someone as beautiful as him.

We sat next to each other, though I dared not look at him for the entirety of the lunch hour. Instead I answered question after question about my life in New York, and how I was settling into Providence High School.

Shea didn't ask me any questions. He didn't speak. He just continued to stare. I knew because I could feel it, and the intensity of his gaze made me stumble on my words more times than I could count.

Zoey was the only person on the table that didn't seem interested in getting to know me. In fact, she seemed seriously put out that I was there. Seeing as I had only been at the school for five minutes and hadn't had the chance to piss her off, I could only imagine that she had a pretty big crush on Shea, and was now realising that it wasn't reciprocated.

What I didn't understand was my own feelings. How could this boy affect me so without even speaking a word to me?

I thanked God silently when the bell rang and it was time to move on to my next class. I moved faster than I probably ever had before to return my tray and I flitted off to Gym.

Apparently, someone in my Gym class did something to piss off the teacher last week, which meant the entire class was running laps for the hour. This gave me an awful lot of time to be alone with my thoughts.

What was wrong with me? I had never particularly noticed boys back home. I wasn't blind. I could tell when they were cute, but I had no desire to be with them. But one look from Shea and I was damn putty. How did he have that power over me? Did I want him to have that power over me?

"Hell no," I huffed on my third lap around.

No sooner had I said the words, though, I looked up to see him leaning against the bleachers, watching me run. He was smiling, though his gaze was just as intense as ever.

I gasped, my foot catching the other as I managed to do a clumsy pirouette before falling crash bang on my ass.

I was so embarrassed. I seemed to have a sea of well-wishers though, who were by my side in seconds. Cece, Liza, and Francesca had even run over from their cheer practice to see if I was okay. Zoey remained behind.

"I'm fine, I'm fine," I huffed as people tried to help me up. As I tried to get myself up though I realised just how hard I had landed on my tailbone. I think my ass was bruised. I winced in pain.

All of a sudden, my well-wishers parted like the red sea and Shea strode through confidently, an amused smirk on his face. If I wasn't so bewitched by that damn smile I would have slapped it right off his face.

"Something tells me you don't have a future career as a ballerina," he teased.

I glared at him.

That only made Shea laugh. "Are you okay?" he asked in all sincerity.

"I'm fine," I said through gritted teeth, except for the fact that my coccyx was throbbing.

He arched an eyebrow. He didn't believe me. He could see through me. "Alright everybody, leave her alone. She's okay."

People scattered and Shea extended his hand out to me.

Out of stubbornness I looked away.

Shea chuckled. Before I could say anything, his hands were under my arms, lifting me to my feet in one smooth move, as if I didn't weigh a hundred and fifteen pounds. He took the breath out of me as I stared up at him. I had been right, six and a half feet tall at least.

As he looked down at me though, all humour left him, and all stubbornness left me. My breath caught in my throat. I could see in the intensity of his gaze that he wasn't breathing either.

Holy crap. What was happening to me? Was he going to kiss me? Did I want him to kiss me? In all this flustering madness, I was certain that I did want him to. But that surely couldn't be a good idea.

"I'm sweaty," I said shakily. Why did I just say that? I slapped my forehead in embarrassment.

Shea cracked. He started to laugh again at my expense.

"I meant that I need to finish my laps and shower and ..." Oh, just shut up, Sara. I sprinted away from Shea, still hearing him laughing behind me.

In and amongst the pool of shame I found myself swimming in, I still felt so strangely towards Shea, as if there was something undeniably strong pulling me towards him.

What was even scarier, was that I felt like I was powerless to stop it. I just didn't understand what it was.

CHAPTER 3

I managed to avoid Shea for the rest of the day. Though, as he was senior, it was simple to avoid him in my classes, but I was terrified that I would run into him in the halls and have an overwhelming desire to make out with him in front of fifty teenagers.

I dumped my things in my newly located locker, put my homework for the night in my book bag, and sprinted out into the lot. I was able to get into my car and start it without seeing Shea again.

As I drove back towards my house, I found myself back on the main street of Providence. It was there that I saw Sally's diner once more, and I was reminded of my thought to ask if they were hiring.

I parked my car in one of the spots in front of the diner and went inside.

Sally's was a cute diner which clearly used their beachside location as inspiration for décor. Driftwood, seashells and jars of sand and starfish were scattered about the walls and tables. The smell in the air was delicious. Coffee and fresh baking.

I walked up to the counter confidently and smiled at the woman who stood at the coffee machine. She was an older woman, probably in her fifties, with perfectly styled red hair and a bright red lip to match. She wore a pale blue uniform with a cute white apron, and a name tag that said 'Sally'. She was the owner.

When she noticed me, she smiled, the skin around her blue eyes crinkling. "What can I get for you, sweetheart?" she asked kindly. "I've just made a fresh pot."

"Hi, thanks, yeah, coffee would be great." Though after the day I've had, caffeine probably wouldn't be advisable. I fished out my wallet from my bag and pulled out some cash to pay her. "I was also wondering if you had any jobs going?" I asked. "My name is Sara, and my mom and I just moved to Providence, so I am looking for some work if you have any shifts."

Her eyes saddened. "Oh, honey, tourist season is over. I'm really not that busy," she said regretfully.

Crap. Was it only possible to find work in this town in the summer? I never took money from my mom. I liked to be self-sufficient. I would hate to ask for twenty bucks if I wanted to go to the movies.

"Can't you swing something, Sally?" came a voice from behind me, a voice that sent shivers down my spine. "Show the new girl in town Providence hospitality."

Sally beamed a wide smile when she saw Shea come up behind me. "Oh, now Shea, you know I would help out if I could ..." Sally looked like she really didn't want to disappoint Shea.

"I would consider it a personal favour," Shea pressed.

A personal favour? I frowned. Exactly how much influence in this town did this eighteen-year-old kid have?

Sally seemed to concede. "Okay, then." She nodded. "Do you have any experience, Sara?"

I was still in the midst of my astonishment when I realised that Sally had directed that question at me. "Oh, yes," I confirmed. "I waitressed for two years at a restaurant back home in New York. I'm a hard worker and I always show up for my shifts." I glanced up at Shea beside me. "I didn't ask him to do this, either. I'm really sorry if this has put you on the spot."

Sally smiled. "If Shea vouches for you, honey, then that's good enough for me. I'll tell you what. Why don't you come in after school tomorrow for a trial shift and we'll see how we go. I can't promise you a lot of hours but the folks in this town are pretty good with their tips."

I smiled gratefully. "Thanks so much, Sally. I won't let you down. I'll see you tomorrow." As I was about to hand over the cash for my coffee, Shea beat me to it. He paid for my coffee and handed it to me, giving me a dazzling smile and an intense gaze while doing it.

We walked out of Sally's together silently. I saw that a black Chevy truck was parked next to my Jeep and I assumed that was Shea's car.

"Why did you do that?" I asked him, rounding on him with my question.

Shea shrugged his shoulders. "You needed my help. Sally is a family friend."

"I feel bad," I admitted. I almost wanted to work exclusively on tips if Sally couldn't afford to pay me.

"Don't," he urged. "Sally would have told me where I could put my nose if she really couldn't take you on. She already told you there wouldn't be much work so she's fine with giving you a couple of hours a week."

I pursed my lips. "Well, thanks, I guess."

Shea chuckled. "Don't sound too happy."

I pursed my lips. I was being rude. "Sorry," I apologised. "There probably aren't a lot of jobs for teenagers in a small town. I appreciate your help."

Shea smiled a smile that made me lose all coherent thought for a few moments. How was it possible for one man to be so gosh darn handsome? And why on earth was this attention being directed at me? Me? And why did I want it so much? I could pretend to be frustrated with Shea but something inside me wanted this attention.

"How's your butt?" he then asked suddenly, causing and embarrassing blush to fill my cheeks.

Bruised. It hurts when I sit down. Why did you have to distract me while I was running? "Fine," I grumbled in response. Well, perhaps I could be frustrated with Shea and still want his attention.

Shea smirked. "You're cute when you're flustered."

"I'm not flustered!" I exclaimed. I totally was. "You're just pissing me off."

He didn't buy it. "Can I piss you off some more this weekend?" he asked confidently. "We could get some dinner. A welcome to Providence type thing."

Huh. Was that a weird way of asking me out on a date? Or was he just some sort of strange eighteen-year-old mayor that could call in special favours with vendors that really wanted to welcome me to his town?

My girlish tendencies wanted it to be a date. Every other logical part of me resisted what I was feeling. It didn't seem natural, normal, to have such strong feelings for someone so quickly. I think I was just physically attracted to him. He was really good looking. Maybe it would pass, and I could get back to my plan of blending in at Providence High School.

"No," I forced myself to say, though I'm certain I could hear my ovaries screaming in protest. "I've got plans, sorry."

Shea looked truly shocked, as though a girl had never said no to him before. Though, with his face, I doubt they would say no. In that split second of imagining him propositioning other girls, I felt such an overwhelming sense of anger and sickness. Jealousy. I needed to get away from him. What was he doing to me?

"Plans," Shea repeated. "You don't want to spend time with me?" he asked in disbelief.

Wow, was he really that cocky?

"I've got plans," I repeated my lie.

"Um, okay." Shea scratched his head, but in doing so, tensed his large bicep. I wonder what it would feel like to have him ...

Nope, I need to go. "Okay, well, bye. Thanks for your help with the job." Quicker than anything, I jumped into my Jeep and started the engine, pulling out onto the street while Shea still stood there dumbfounded.

When I pulled into my driveway, my mom's car wasn't there. I didn't know what time she would be working to. But if it was anything like the hospital back in Bedford, she could be really late. I shut off my engine and carried my things inside the house.

Dumping my book bag and keys on the kitchen counter, I went over the events of the day. School had been good. I wasn't overwhelmed in my classes. The content seemed easy enough to catch up on. Señora Gomez had been my only teacher to try to get me to introduce myself in front of the class. I had made a friend. Cece seemed really nice, and she had been kind enough to include me at her table of friends at lunch. I had a job, even though Sally was coerced, or charmed by Shea, into giving me a shot.

Everything had gone pretty well. With one exception.

I was completely and utterly lusting after a guy I knew nothing about.

Well, I knew a couple of things. He was Cece's brother, which was weird in itself. I'm not sure how Cece would feel if she knew I had a thing for her brother. Secondly, he had a weird amount of influence for an eighteen-year-old in this town. At school, it was one thing. He was popular, people followed him. But in town? For Sally to just do what he said? I don't know. Something about it was odd.

I needed a distraction. I threw some popcorn in the microwave and then fetched my laptop from my room. As I got set up to start my English essay, I found myself on Facebook.

I had a few notifications from people back home wishing me a good first day. I stuffed some popcorn in my mouth as I replied to them quickly, before I clicked onto the search bar.

My fingers had a mind of their own as they typed Shea Braverman. His profile was the first one that came up in the results and I couldn't help myself. I clicked on it and saw this his profile picture was a glorious image of him shirtless, standing on a rock on the beach.

My heart literally skipped a beat for the second time today. Why was I so unbelievably attracted to him? Why me? What was going on inside me to create this almost magnetic pull I felt towards him?

I scrolled down his profile and noticed that it was not set to private. Shea seemed to have quite the social life ... and quite the collection of girlfriends. There seemed to be a different girl in every picture, and he seemed to have his arm around an awful lot of them. One girl that appeared quite often was Zoey Eckhart. She was tagged in the images she was in. Zoey and Shea looked quite close, which explained the animosity she was directing towards me at school today.

But I didn't feel badly for Zoey. Instead I felt awkward and angry, and absolutely jealous of each one of these girls that Shea had been photographed with. It was like I felt a sense of entitlement over Shea which was just nuts. I wasn't entitled to him and he certainly wasn't entitled to me.

"Stop it, Sara," I hissed at myself. As I made my way to close the window, I accidently clicked on the touch pad of my laptop. When I saw what I had clicked on, I just about wanted to die.

I had gone and liked his profile picture from 2015.

I screamed with embarrassment as I rushed to unlike the photo. But would that remove the notification? Would he know that I was Facebook stalking him?

But it was too late. My laptop chimed with a new Messenger request.

It was Shea.

I half covered my eyes as I opened the message.

I always liked that picture too :)

I cried out again and leapt away from my laptop, in doing so I spilled my popcorn all over the floor. Shame and humiliation filled me. I could feel my blush all over my body. I could not go to school tomorrow.

I needed to go back to New York. If I got in my car now, I could be in –

My laptop chimed again.

Did you see anything you like?

I gagged. I could practically hear him teasing me through the computer.

Just as I had just about made the decision to leave my mom a note to let her know I was leaving the state, he messaged again.

You're probably freaking out. You seem the type. It's okay. I was checking you out, too.

And just like that, a notification popped up. Shea had liked my very first profile picture from when I joined Facebook. Why was that picture still up on the internet?

You look cute in braces. Not everyone can pull them off.

I huffed and settled into typing. I started to type something sassy in reply, but I deleted it. Shea was trying to make me feel better for doing something embarrassing. In and amongst the girlfriends and the teasing, he seemed sweet.

Everyone has an awkward phase.

I wasn't entirely sure I had left mine. And from the looks of Shea's pictures, it didn't seem as though he had ever had one. He was a little more baby faced when he was younger, but always good looking.

Do you really have plans this weekend or are you just playing hard to get? I can deal with either.

My eyes widened as that message appeared on my screen.

Hasn't a girl ever told you no before? I shot back.

You didn't answer my question. If you really have plans, that's okay. I just get the sense that I make you nervous.

I wasn't about to let him get inside my head so quickly, even though he had hit the nail on the head exactly.

I have plans.

Okay.

I stared at my computer. That was it? Okay? I was disappointed. I expected a bit more of a fight from him. I wanted a bit more of a fight from him.

I quickly logged off and opened up a new document to start my English essay. I would try to keep my mind off of him for the rest of the evening.

My mom walked in the door with Chinese food just after nine o'clock. I had been diligently writing since I logged off of Facebook and had ignored social media since then. It was actually excellent timing. I was just putting on the finishing touches and I was freaking starving.

When I shut my computer, I looked at her properly and saw that she looked wrecked. "Are you okay, Mom?" I asked.

She smiled tiredly. "Long day, hon," she replied. "Lots of kiddos." She didn't elaborate, but I knew that was never, ever a good thing. Lots of patients. Lots of sick kids. My mom loved her job, and the wins made it worth it, but the losses cut you. I knew she carried around each and every loss.

She came over to me and kissed the top of my head. "You didn't want to eat the popcorn?" she asked, gesturing to the mess I had made on the floor. I had been so focussed that I had forgotten to clean up the popcorn I had spilled.

"I'll get the broom."

"Don't bother, Sara. Let's eat. I'm starved." She went left the plastic bag of food on the counter and went to the cabinet to get plates and cutlery. As she began dishing up the food, she looked up. "How was your day?"

Um. "Good," I replied. "My teachers are nice."

Mom smiled. "Yeah? Make any friends?"

"One." I nodded. "Her name is Cece. She seems really sweet."

"Oh, good, I'm glad."

It wasn't odd for me not to dump my crap on my mom. When she was like this, when I could tell she had had a day, she didn't need drama from me. Besides, what was I supposed to tell her? That her seventeen-year-old daughter was crazy hot for a senior boy for some unknown reason ... apart from the fact he was built like a freaking demigod.

Mom piled sweet and sour chicken, special fried rice and a couple of fortune cookies onto my plate before handing it to me with a fork.

"Thanks," I said gratefully, before hungrily tucking in. The batter was nice and sticky, which was my favourite part, and probably the unhealthiest part. It got me thinking about how fit Cece and her friends were. They probably didn't inhale take-out food like I did.

We sat in the living room and Mom switched the TV onto some mindless reality show. We watched and ate in silence. I was actually semi into the show when I had finished my dinner. We were about to see who was getting kicked off that week when I opened my fortune cookie.

I had to read it twice.

Your true love is closer than you think.

What did these dumb things know anyway? I would have won the lottery three times now if they were always right.

I opened my second cookie.

Take heed. Love can be dangerous.

What the hell? What sort of fortune cookie was that? They're supposed to be happy and optimistic.

Just as I was about to speculate as to whether Shea had somehow managed to play a trick on me, my mom said, "Hey, look. I've got great financial luck on the horizon. I better buy a lottery ticket this week."

I shook off my suspicions. Fortune cookies were light entertainment. They didn't mean anything.

We packaged back up the leftover Chinese food and put it in the refrigerator. By then it was nearly half past ten, so we both wandered upstairs to get ready for bed.

Before letting me go off to my room, my mom hugged me on the landing. I felt as though she needed it more than me. I hugged her tightly.

"I'm glad you had a good first day, Sara," she said quietly. "I know this move has been difficult, but this was a big opportunity for me, so I appreciate you being such a trooper about it."

My mom had worked hard her whole life to support me. Caring for a baby, working two jobs to pay rent, and somehow graduating medical school was no easy task. I aspired to be as badass as my mom.

"It's okay, Mom," I replied in the same tone. "The school is great. There are nice kids. I think there is even a football game on Friday night that I might make an appearance at." Might being the key word. And I was assuming there was a game. The stadium was grand enough for football to be a weekly production.

"That's great, hon. I would like you to get out of your comfort zone more often and widen your circle," she urged. Mom smiled at me and wished me goodnight before going into her room.

I closed my bedroom door, put all my devices on charge, and put on my pyjamas. When I checked my phone just before I went to sleep, I saw that I had missed a message from Shea.

I'm nothing if not persistent. See you tomorrow, Sara,

I found myself smiling and looking forward to it. I fell asleep easily.

Chapter 4

S hea wasn't lying. He was making it no secret that I was the subject of his attention.

Every guy in school had stopped staring at me and I knew that Shea had something to do with it. I received no more curious looks, no more lustful gazes, not even a side glance. The only guy who looked at me was Shea.

I wanted to enjoy it. I wanted to accept it. I wanted to leap into his arms and do something entirely inappropriate for a school hallway. But still, every fibre of my being, well, at least the sensible, coherent fibres were keeping me from doing that.

I shouldn't feel this way about Shea. He shouldn't excite me the way he did. He shouldn't suck me in the way he was. It was like I was in his orbit, he was a black hole and it was only so long before I disappeared inside him.

That thought frightened me. Disappearing inside of a relationship just seemed insane to the logical part of my brain. Especially since I had only met him the day before. This connection I felt was unnatural.

And I really had no one to talk to. I couldn't talk to my mom about it. She would probably freak out and call Shea's mom to tell him to leave me alone. I couldn't talk to Cece. Shea was her brother after all. Aside from that, there weren't really any people that I even knew in Providence, let alone people I could confide in.

Cece was just as nice as ever, though. We quietly chatted through Spanish about normal, teenager things. It turned out there was a football game on Friday night. Cece and her friends were on the cheerleading squad. After the game there was a party at the Eckhart's. I recalled the name from the scoreboard donation mention but hadn't made the connection that it had been Zoey Eckhart. Apparently, they were one of the richest families in town, and owned a ridiculous mansion on the beach, perfect for parties. Zoey's parents were always out of town anyway.

"Would Zoey even want me there?" I asked, concerned. Zoey was still glaring daggers at me. She had made a point to hang out near my locker this morning for the purpose of wishing me dead with her eyes.

Cece rolled her eyes. "Zoey will get over it," she assured me. "She's had a thing for my brother for years, but Shea was never serious about her."

I frowned. I mean, Zoey wasn't exactly the nicest person that I'd encountered but she didn't deserve to be treated like crap by Shea.

It got me thinking. Was this how it happened? Did he reel girls in with his good looks and charm, screw them, screw them over, and then move onto the next new face that wanders into his circle?

Would I be like Zoey in a few months, or even weeks?

Thinking about the possibility of Shea's dishonesty physically hurt. Considering that he didn't really like me, that he only wanted me for one thing, it felt like ... betrayal.

Betrayal! I was in way too deep.

"Do you want to hang out after school today?" Cece asked in the midst of my internal panic. "A bunch of us are going to go down the beach. I think Shea is coming," she hinted.

Oddly, that didn't encourage me. "Can't, sorry," I apologised. "I have my trial shift at Sally's after school."

"Oh, right. Shea mentioned something about that. You'll love Sally. She's so sweet. She's been really good to us." Cece didn't elaborate as Señora Gomez began to set the homework.

I made it to lunch without running into Shea in the hallways again. But of course, I couldn't avoid him in the cafeteria. Cece hadn't waited for me today. She was already at their table, sitting on Jamie's lap, and eating what looked like carbonara.

I looked for Shea, but I couldn't see him sitting with his friends. Zoey was there, glaring at me like usual. I felt a mixture of relief and disappointment. Relief that I wouldn't be feeling any overwhelming emotion, and disappointment for exactly the same reason.

"Looking for me?"

I jumped. I hadn't realised that he had been waiting near the cafeteria door. I looked up at Shea and stopped breathing. Was it possible for him to be even more good looking than this morning? His hair was damp, as though he had showered after Gym. He had styled it away from his face, leaving every gorgeous inch of it on show.

What was even more embarrassing was that Shea knew exactly how he affected me. He knew I had a big old crush on him.

"No, Cece," I lied. "She's over there." I pointed to their table.

Shea grinned, seeing through my farce. "How's your day been so far?" He led me over to the food line. He grabbed a tray for me and then a tray for himself.

Every event from the day so far suddenly left my head. I was blank. "I have Spanish homework," I replied, remembering something incredibly dull.

"Sounds interesting," he joked, nodding along.

No matter how confused Shea made me feel, the one thing he didn't make me feel was embarrassed for my gaffe the night before. He was genuinely interested in me, me, for some unknown reason.

"Now listen, I know you have plans this weekend, but does that include Friday night?"

We were both served a plate of carbonara for lunch. Shea paid for us both.

Would this be about the football game? I suddenly got the urge to ask him about Zoey, but I held my tongue. "Why?" was all I said.

"There's a football game on this Friday night. We're playing Newtown High –"

"Do you play?" I suddenly asked. Of course, he had to. He was built like a tank. Footballers looked like him, didn't they?

Shea chuckled nervously. "Uh, no. I don't play. But I like the sport. And there's a party after, at Zoey's. You should come. I'll introduce you to a few people."

We stood at the end of the lunch line with our trays as I stared up at him. Emotions crossed his face quite quickly, almost too quick for me to determine what they were.

He'll introduce me to a few people? I wasn't sure what I didn't like about that invitation, but it reminded me of a damn pimp searching for clients.

"Zoey won't want me there," I replied, instantly cursing myself. I should have just said I was busy.

"She'll be fine," Shea insisted. "Zoey's just being dramatic. I'll get her to be nicer. She'll do whatever I tell her to do."

I was taken aback by that. Did he seriously just say that? I wasn't Zoey's number one fan, but he was really treating her like crap. No matter how Shea made me feel, I couldn't excuse a guy that behaved disrespectfully.

"I can't go," I said firmly, staring up at him with all the confidence I could muster. "And you are the one who ought to be nicer to Zoey. I've heard it from a couple of people now. You don't treat her very nicely and she obviously has feelings for you. You can't tell her what to do any more than you can tell me what to do." With that, I turned on my heel and took my lunch outside into the sunshine.

Shea wisely didn't follow me.

And he wisely didn't try to speak to me for the rest of the day.

I managed to make it to the final bell having a reasonably normal time. I felt empowered, as though I had done the right thing. I wasn't going to allow myself to forget the things I cared about, or the values that I held deep in my heart, for a cute guy.

I expected to be treated a certain way. No amount of flattery would change my mind.

I drove to Sally's straight after school. I was excited to be working, to be earning my own money. I really hoped that Sally liked me enough to keep me on, and not just as a favour to Shea.

As soon as I walked in the diner, Sally greeted me with a warm smile. She beckoned me behind the counter and brought me into the back room with her. It was a small store room that housed metal shelving containing coffee and non-perishables that didn't need refrigeration. There were two hooks behind the door. One held a dark leather purse, and the other, a small blue uniform on a hanger. She had already made me a nametag!

"You can leave your things in here, Sara. I'll give you a moment to get changed and then I'll show you around the diner and let you know how things work."

Sally left me. I quickly stripped off my jeans and t-shirt and slipped into the blue dress. I buttoned the buttons and straightened my nametag. I hoped Sally didn't mind that I was wearing Converse sneakers with her uniform. I would have to find a store to buy some practical work shoes.

My shoes from my restaurant days were in a box somewhere.

I left the store room and looked over the diner from behind the counter. There was a mixture of different sized tables with an eclectic collection of chairs. There were two groups in the diner enjoying coffee, and Sally was serving one of them.

She looked delightful and friendly as she stood there chatting with her coffee pot in hand. Once finished, she made her way back to the counter to meet me.

"Okay, so welcome to Sally's." She laughed, clapping her hands together. "I bought this diner with my husband twenty years ago.

It's my baby, and I like to treat my customers like family. I will expect the same from you."

I nodded obediently.

Sally showed me how to work the coffee machine, the cash register, and then showed me where everything I might need or be asked for was stored.

After my tour, she sighed, and said, "Gosh, you look so like your mother."

"Did you know her?" I realised if Sally's had been here for twenty years, she would have crossed over with my mom's time in Providence.

Sally nodded. "Oh, yes. She was a frequent visitor in my early days. Lived on coffee that girl, helped her get through her studies." I noticed that she didn't speak of my mother in the tender way that Cherie and Glenda had the day before at school. She had a tone, but I couldn't quite put my finger on what it was.

Had my mom been rude? Maybe she was cranky while studying?

"Did you know my dad, too?" I asked curiously.

I didn't know much about my dad. Only that he died when I was two, and that he had been a few years older than my mom. Truthfully, I didn't even know what he looked like. Mom never displayed pictures of him, and I wasn't even sure if she had any. She never spoke about him, and I didn't want to upset her by asking.

I could make informed guesses. I mean, if I had lived here until I was two, he had to have lived here as well. Maybe I could find out some more about him now that we were here.

"No, I didn't," was all Sally said in reply.

Oh, there went that plan.

"Your first customer. Grab the pot and go and take the order," Sally encouraged, directing me towards the tables.

When I registered who had walked in and taken a seat at one of the empty tables, I frowned. What was Zoey doing here? Cece gave me the impression that they were all going to the beach after school.

Nonetheless, I walked over with the coffee pot, turned over one of the cups on her table, and filled it.

Zoey was very intimidatingly beautiful. She gave off the impression that she knew she was attractive, as well. Her blonde hair was perfectly highlighted, makeup was effortlessly applied to her well-proportioned face, and she had changed into clothes that looked designer.

"Can I get you anything?" I asked politely.

Zoey looked at me grimly, as though she was in pain. It was ... weird.

"I'm sorry I've been such a bitch," she apologised forcefully. "You're welcome to come to my party on Friday night."

She didn't sound sincere at all.

I dropped down into the seat opposite her. "Did Shea put you up to this, Zoey?" I asked quietly.

Her blue eyes narrowed. "You don't get it, do you?" she snapped. "You've won. Claim your prize. He's yours for the taking!" she exclaimed.

No, I didn't get it. Zoey did not seem like the person to just do as she was told. So why would she do what Shea told her to do? And why would she put up with Shea treating her like crap?

I needed to open my mouth. "Why do you let Shea treat you like this, Zoey? Don't you think you deserve better?"

Zoey laughed. "Don't pass judgement over something you clearly know nothing about," she retorted. "Shea and I were never serious, that doesn't mean I don't get to be pissed when he finds his –" She stopped herself and rethought her sentence.

"Finds his what?" I pressed.

Zoey glared at me. "Come to the party or don't, I don't care. But you're stupid if you deny your feelings for Shea. Everyone knows already." She hurriedly pulled some cash out of her wallet and left it on the table next to her untouched coffee.

As soon as Zoey had left the diner, Sally flitted over and collected the bill she had left behind. "Eighty per cent tip. Well done, Sara," she commented cheerfully. "Nice girl, that Zoey. Good family."

Well, I wouldn't exactly label Zoey nice, but she had certainly given me food for thought. Had I misunderstood the situation?

I mean, it was 2019, after all. Girls could enjoy casual relationships, too. Maybe I had been a bit quick to judge. Maybe the only issue was Zoey was jealous of me. Maybe, in his own weirdly worded way, Shea was only trying to do the right thing.

I found my thoughts drifting to Shea throughout my shift. There were still so many question marks there. I really didn't know him that well, after all. But I couldn't dismiss him altogether based on my own ill-informed presumptions. He deserved a chance.

The girly, giddy, pathetic part of me was suddenly ecstatic that I had given in.

When I took a quick bathroom break, I took my phone in with me. I put the seat down on the toilet and sat on top of it, opening my Facebook app and clicking on my conversation with Shea from the previous night.

I finish at 7, I typed. Will you meet me at the diner then?

Almost instantly his reply popped up on my screen. I rolled my eyes.

It's a date ;)

I was a mixture of nerves and excitement as the minutes of my shift ticked away. The work wasn't hard, and it was nice getting to know my customers. Almost all of them recognised me as Amanda Bryant's daughter. I didn't ask anyone again if they knew my dad. I realised that my mom was bound to come into the diner and meet these people around town and I didn't want it getting back to her that I was asking questions about him.

Sally paid me for my shift at seven and then gave me my share of tips.

"Now, I did tell you I wouldn't have many hours," she started seriously. For a moment I thought she was firing me. "But you seem very popular with my customers. They haven't tipped this well in a long time!" she remarked. "How about we start with six hours a week, two after school shifts? Six seventy-five an hour plus your tips?" she proposed.

Hours were hours. "Yes, thanks so much, Sally. I'm so grateful for you giving me a chance." I accepted my pay and left the diner, telling Sally that I would see her after school on Thursday.

No sooner had I crossed the threshold, I noticed Shea leaning against my Jeep. I nearly coughed up my tongue.

He had changed after school. Perhaps a better word to use would be undressed after school. He stood there only in a pair of board shorts. His large, toned arms were folded across his taut chest, giving me full view of his sculpted, tanned abs. He didn't look real. Only men on the covers of my mom's romance novels looked like him.

I felt my cheeks blushing, much to my humiliation. And to make things worse, he seemed to be enjoying my reaction.

When I regained a little composure I managed to snipe, "You know, steroids are bad for your health. The make things ... small." Why did I say that? It only made me feel more embarrassed.

Shea burst out laughing. "Well, lucky for me hard work and a good metabolism keeps me in shape. As to the other issue, well, you can check to see if everything's alright, if you want."

I knew he was teasing me. I slapped his arm as I unlocked my Jeep to put my things inside. God, he was firm.

"Zoey came by," I murmured.

"Was she nice?" he asked.

"In her own way," I replied. "She was really cryptic about you. There are things that I'm not so sure about, things that seem strange to me. But Zoey told me not to pass judgement over something that I know nothing about. And she's right. I have been judging. All I know for sure is that something is going on here that I can't describe."

Shea smiled, warmly this time. "I hope things will make sense for you in time. But for now, if it helps, something is going on for me as well. You're in my head, Sara. I'd like to know you better, if that's okay." He sounded so sincere, like he really cared.

Maybe he was just as confused about me, too. It was a comfort to know I wasn't the only one going insane.

"Do you want to walk down the beach?" he asked hopefully.

"Is everybody else still down there?" Truthfully, I was too shy to parade myself around with Shea so soon after meeting him. And after Zoey's dig about everyone already knowing, it made it all the more embarrassing.

"No, it will be just us," Shea replied, shaking his head.

I nodded. "Sure." Shea didn't offer me his hand, which I was glad about. It was too soon, too new. Instead, we walked side by side.

Shea matched his pace with mine. My legs were much shorter than his, and so I knew he would be able to march on ahead, but I was grateful for this small gesture. We crossed the main street and walked down onto the beach. As soon as I hit sand, I stopped to take off my Converses. Shea immediately took them from me and carried them for me.

"Are you a gentleman?"

"Just trying to impress you," he replied honestly, grinning.

I kept my eyes on the sand in front of me. If I let my eyes wander, I knew they would find his taut chest and I didn't need a second round of embarrassment. I had had enough for today.

"Tell me about New York," Shea began as we walked. "What was your life like there?"

"I didn't live in the city," I replied. "We lived upstate in the sub- urbs. But we would venture down into Manhattan frequently for weekends away. If there was a new show opening, or I got a good grade, my mom liked to take me into the city. Even if it was just for a sundae at Serendipity." I smiled nostalgically. I would miss the rhythm of the city. The noise to most was distracting and annoying. To me, the city just felt alive. So many people going so many places. New York City reminded me of most airport departure terminals. I hoped we would still visit, even though we were farther away now.

"I'd love to go," Shea commented. "I've never left Providence. This town is the only place I know."

"You should," I encouraged. "Maybe it could be a graduation gift from your parents next year?"

Shea's face softened. "I won't be leaving town any time soon," he said quietly.

"Not even for college?" I frowned.

He shook his head. "Not even for college. I might take some classes locally, but I can't leave."

"Why?" I demanded to know, then quickly realised my tone sounded forceful. "Sorry, it's none of my business."

"No, no, it's okay," he assured me. He sighed. "My dad died," he said bluntly. "Really unexpectedly. He had a heart attack three years ago surfing with Cece and me. We got him to the hospital as quickly as we could but there was nothing they could do. He was gone."

I felt goose bumps cover my body. Oh my God, that was absolutely awful! What a thing for a young brother and sister to go through! "Oh, Shea, I'm so sorry," I said tenderly.

"Thanks." He smiled down at me sadly. "I'm okay, but I'm not. When people say they had the greatest dad, they never met mine. My dad was a good, strong man, who did anything and everything for his family. He loved Cece and me fiercely, and we weren't prepared to be without him. Cece and I have learned to cope. Mom hasn't. She barely functions. She won't ever get over it."

That was so sad. The way he talked about his father was so admirable. Shea respected and loved his father deeply. But his mother? To still be so unreachable after three years?

"Mom needs me to take care of her. Cece needs me. I can't leave her alone with Mom if I go off to college. Cece has Jamie, thankfully, but I still can't leave her in that house alone during her senior year. Besides, I have to run the ... family business."

Shea wasn't talking like the cheeky, teasing eighteen-year-old he was at school. He was a young man with the weight of the world on his shoulders. What burdens he had at such a young age? To have so few options?

"Has your mom thought about seeing a therapist?" I asked quietly.

"Nobody can help her. The only thing that could would be to have my dad back and that's impossible," Shea said, defeated.

I wish I knew what to say. I knew what it was like to be without a dad, but I suppose I was fortunate in never having to grieve for him.

"I think you were very lucky to have such a wonderful father, even if you were only allowed such a short amount of time with him." I hoped my words could offer him comfort. It hurt my heart to know that he had experienced, and was still experiencing, a level of pain I did not understand.

"I know, I was," he agreed. "What about your dad?" he asked, turning the conversation back onto me. "You've mentioned your mom but not your dad."

"Oh, well, my dad passed away, too," I confessed. Shea had a look of shock and sympathy about him. "A long time ago. I don't remember him. I was actually born in Providence. My parents met here, got married young, had me. But he died in a car accident when I was two. I suppose my mom didn't want to be here anymore, so we packed up and left for New York. And now it's fifteen years later."

We had been walking for a while, so long that we had now come to the pier that harboured the dozen or so boats belonging to Providence residents. Shea made the move to sit down in the sand by the pier and I sat next to him.

The sand was warm from the sun. I buried my toes in it.

"What was it like?" Shea asked. "Growing up without your dad."

I pondered the notion for a moment. "I suppose I don't know any different," I replied honestly. "It's always just been Mom and me. I think I noticed that I didn't have something that other kids had on Father's Day. Mom would always try to distract me, but I didn't have anyone to make a card for. I often wonder what it would have been like to have a dad around. I often wonder what my dad was like. I know nothing about him." That was what happened when you had a mother who never spoke about him and a daughter who was too worried about stepping on eggshells to ask.

"Your mom never talks about him?" Shea asked in disbelief.

I shook my head. "Never. I mean, she doesn't have any pictures. She doesn't talk about him. I think, maybe like with your mom, it's too hard for her. Maybe this is how she's learned to cope."

Shea didn't say anything for a minute. He just looked ahead at the ocean. The tide was coming in and was almost touching our toes. We would need to move soon.

"These types of behaviours don't make sense to me. But then, I don't know what I would do if I ever lost my soulmate," Shea finally said. "Maybe I would be the same way." He turned his head to look down at me. His eyes looked almost hazel in the sunset, and I could see the honest truth in them.

I wasn't sure I believed in soulmates, but that definition could almost certainly be a possibility for the feelings I was experiencing. "I think we need to learn from our parents and endeavour not to repeat their mistakes," I offered quietly.

"That's a good way of putting it." Shea smiled slightly. "Come on, I better get you home." Shea jumped up to his feel and then helped me to mine. His large hand enveloped mine, and I was reluctant to let it go. "I enjoyed our date," Shea said, without letting go of my hand.

"That was a date, was it?" I asked vulnerably.

Shea leaned in and planted a kiss on my cheek, lingering for a moment. I felt my pulse quicken as I held my breath. "Doesn't it feel like one?" he whispered. I could feel his warm breath on my cheek. I shivered.

Oh, yes it did.

Shea walked me back to my car and opened my door for me. I climbed into the driver's seat and Shea leant on the door. "Can I have your phone number?" he asked hopefully.

I pulled my phone out of my pocket, unlocked it, and handed it to him. "Put your number in and I'll text you, so you have mine, too."

He smiled devilishly. "Or maybe I'll text myself, so you don't chicken out."

"Hey!" I snapped.

Shea laughed as he typed in his phone number. I could see by the screen that he had indeed gone and texted himself. "Can I call you later?"

What would my mom say if she knew a boy, a senior boy, was calling me late at night? Would she put a stop to it? Would she make me stop whatever this was? I felt like I was too far in to stop.

"I'll call you," I decided. It would be safe to call once Mom had gone to bed.

"Do you promise?"

I offered him my pinkie finger. "Pinkie swear." I smiled as he linked his finger with mine.

Shea then closed my door and let me pull out of the parking space. I noticed my car was the only one parked for a while. Looking at the clock on the dash I could see it was nearly eight-thirty, so the majority of businesses were shut. I wondered if Shea lived near me, near enough to walk home.

As I drove, I thought about what Shea would be going home to. I felt so sorry for his mom. To still be in such a deep depression after the loss of her husband was devastating. What was even worse was that Shea felt it was up to him to hold up the rafters of his home. It was his responsibility to look after his mom, as well as Cece. He couldn't go away to college because he felt that his home couldn't function without him. And by the sounds of it, he was right.

How was that fair?

One thing I knew for sure, Shea had honour. He respected and loved his family more than himself.

Zoey was right. I shuddered at that thought. I was too quick to judge Shea.

I was looking forward to our phone call.

CHAPTER 5

I had once again beaten my mom home. I grateful for that fact. There was no doubt that she would have bombarded my phone with messages and sent out a hunting party if I was this late getting home.

I quickly shut off my engine, grabbed my book bag, and ran into the house. I dumped my homework on the kitchen counter and ran upstairs. I changed into my pyjamas and grabbed my laptop and went back downstairs, opening it up onto my essay from the day before to make it look like I had been working.

I then went to the refrigerator and grabbed last night's Chinese and put it in the microwave. No sooner had the microwave finished heating our food, my mom walked in the door.

She looked decidedly less upset today. It must have been a better day at the clinic today. She smiled at me as she dropped her keys and purse on the counter next to my things. She kissed my cheek and smelled dinner hungrily.

"I've been hanging out for this all day," she said gratefully. "Did you have a good day, Sara?"

"Yeah." I nodded. "I had my trial shift at Sally's after school. She gave me a job."

My mom's eyes lit up. "Oh, Sara, that's wonderful!" she exclaimed. "Sally was always lovely to me when I was younger. I'm glad she's still in business."

"How was your day?" I asked.

As we ate, my Mom discussed the clinic more animatedly. She liked the other doctors, and she already had her favourite nurses. She told me about some of the children she had seen today. She was always careful not to go into specifics so as not to break doctor-patient confidentiality, but she told me if she was optimistic or not.

I was listening, but I was also watching the clock. As the minutes ticked on, I knew it would be nearly time to call Shea.

"How would you like to go and see a movie this weekend?" Mom suggested. "Check out the local theatre. Maybe get some dinner afterward? Really settle into Providence."

I was supposed to have plans this weekend. Who was to say this couldn't be it? "Sure, Mom," I agreed, smiling. I would have to look up online what was playing.

At ten-thirty, Mom took both of our plates to the sink and began to switch off the lights ready for bed. She hugged me on the landing and I had to stop myself from skipping to my room. I quickly jumped on my bed with my phone and opened up to the text message he had sent himself. I tapped on the number and pressed call.

The phone barely had a chance to ring before Shea answered.

"Evening," he said suavely.

"Good evening, yourself," I replied quietly. Oh my God, I felt giddy! My emotions couldn't pick a lane. I went from hating him this morning, to practically falling over my feet to talk to him. This was some messed up voodoo I was getting myself into.

"What have you been up to tonight?" he asked in an equally quiet tone. I wondered if he was hiding in his bedroom like I was. Though, Shea didn't seem like the kind of guy who would hide anything. With how open and honest he had been with me this afternoon, I felt like he would never hide anything from anyone.

My evening really wasn't that exciting. "Had leftover Chinese food." Counted down the minutes until I could call you. "Hung out with my mom." Until it was acceptable to go to bed and call you.

"Does your mom know you're calling me?" he wondered.

I resisted laughing. "Uh, no. Guys are kind of a touchy subject with my mom. I'm not allowed to date. Well, that was the rule when I was fourteen and I haven't really brought it up again since. I think she's afraid I'll wind up in too deep too young like she was and risk my future." Wow, that was unnecessarily heavy. "Sorry, that was probably too much information."

"No, no. I guess it's good to be across the rules of the parents. So, you haven't really dated?" He seemed really interested, and happy, at this notion.

I shook my head, then realised he couldn't see me. "No," I replied, smiling at myself. "I've never really met anyone I wanted to date."

"Interesting," he mused.

"What about you?" I turned the question around on him. There really wasn't a lot to my romantic history so it kind of was a dead end topic. "Have you dated a lot?" After stalking his Facebook profile, I felt like I already knew the answer to this. Either way, it made my stomach turn uncomfortably as I waited for his reply.

"Uh, yeah," he replied honestly. I felt a spark of jealousy. "I've dated a bit. Honestly, I just needed to get out of my house. Hanging out with cool people allowed me to do that."

I felt my heart soften at that. I hoped he was telling the truth. I doubt he would lie about something so serious as his home situation. Those girls in the pictures were distractions from what he had to cope with at home. I could understand that.

"But I never wanted to get serious with anybody." I felt like he was omitting an "until now" from the end of his sentence. Or at least my crazy brain was hoping he was.

I hated myself for asking but I couldn't help myself. "So, Zoey ...?"

I heard him sigh. "Zoey is ... complicated. Her family is close with mine. We were friends as kids. I think our parents always hoped there would be something between us but there wasn't. Zoey is ... well, you've met her. She's one of a kind. She was a lot to handle which made her a great distraction. But Zoey knew we were never serious, and she knew our thing wasn't going anywhere. Zoey used me, too. She's under a lot of pressure from her parents, you know."

I didn't think that explanation made me any more comfortable with the situation. So, were they just friends with benefits? That thought intimidated me. I had never even kissed a boy. Shea had so much more experience than me.

I was just flirting! Enjoying hanging out. Maybe we would get to dating. Was this what he would expect from me?

"Sara?" his voice brought me out of my panic. "What are you thinking?"

And Zoey wasn't the only one. How many girls had he been with to distract himself? I was clearly the next girl he wanted to distract himself with. What would happen when he realised that I wasn't going to jump into bed with him?

Would he move onto the next girl who would? That thought was actually devastating.

"I'm sorry," I said breathlessly. "I have to go." I then hung up the phone abruptly, throwing it away from me as though it had burned me.

It immediately started to vibrate as he called me back. I threw my robe on top of my phone. To get away from it, I went into my bathroom and brushed my teeth and hair. I fixed my hair in a braid and then got into bed, though I knew I wasn't going to be getting any restful sleep.

I dozed in between my phone vibrating. Shea was texting me every five minutes. By the tenth message I switched my phone off. Mom would check on me in the morning to make sure I was up.

I was awoken some time later by a tapping sound on my window. I didn't know what time it was as my phone was off, but my bedroom was pitch black. I almost went back to sleep, but I heard the noise again.

Someone was throwing stuff up to my window.

I got out of bed and opened my curtains. In the illumination of the street lights, I could see that Shea was standing down on the ground with another pebble in his hand ready to throw.

What if this had been my mom's window?

I slid my window up and stuck my head out. "What are you doing?" I hissed down at him. "Do you have any idea what time it is?" I mean, I didn't know, but that was beside the point.

Shea dropped the pebble. "You hung up on me and then didn't return my messages!" he hissed back at me.

"So, you thought you'd stalk me in the middle of the night!" I cried, and then covered my mouth. I could not wake my mom up. There would be no good way to explain this.

"I had to make sure you were okay! For all I knew you could have been a victim of a home invasion and that's why you didn't return my messages."

I rolled my eyes. "Right, so your first conclusion for a girl not texting you back is murder at the hands of a burglar?" I retorted sarcastically. "Not merely that perhaps she doesn't want to talk right now."

"Well, when you put it like that ..." he said sheepishly.

"Shea!" I snapped.

"Sara!" he shot back. "What did I do? Is it Zoey? Please, that's nothing."

I was not about to have this conversation. I went to close my window, but Shea immediately leapt onto the trellis. I watched in awe as he performed some serious parkour as he scaled the side of my house. He appeared at my window in seconds, holding onto the window sill with one arm, which was supporting his entire body weight.

Oh my God, he was strong.

"Sara," he said softly. I could see the earnest in his eyes. "I freaked you out. I'm sorry. Please, tell me how I can make it better. I don't want this to stop."

Could I tell him? This was so embarrassing. I really didn't want to admit this, but here he was, hanging off the side of my house. He wasn't going to leave until I told him. "Shea, I'm not like other girls!" I hissed, humiliated, my cheeks blushing. I was so glad it was dark.

Shea frowned. "Okay ...?"

"I can't be a distraction. I'm not going to sleep with you!" I slapped my hands over my face to hide my embarrassment and stepped away from the window.

Now he was going to leave. He was going to drop down and run off to find Zoey or one of the other girls in his pictures. He now knew he wasn't going to get what he wanted from me.

Do it quickly. Break my heart quickly.

But he didn't leave. The next thing I knew Shea was peeling my hands away from my face. He was inside my room, looking down at me tenderly. He placed a finger under my chin, forcing me to look up at him.

"Sara, the feelings that I have for you go way beyond using you for a simple distraction. I don't want you for two weeks in the summer. I want you for a hell of a lot longer than that. I don't expect anything from you that you're not comfortable with."

He spoke so sincerely. My legs felt like Jell-O, as though I was going to collapse on the floor right in front of him. But how could he mean that? How could he be satisfied with handholding and maybe, maybe, my first kiss when I wasn't so insecure and nervous.

"But you're just going to leave when you get bored of me," I worried out loud.

Shea exhaled in frustration. "Goddammit, Sara. I wish you could understand. I wish you knew ..." he trailed off. He grabbed my hand and placed it on his chest, right over his hard, left pectoral. But once I had got through the muscle, I could feel his pulse. His heart was racing. "You've got no idea what you do to me," he said intensely. "I hope you can trust me. I won't break your heart. Do you promise not to break mine?"

His question was so serious, but the idea seemed ludicrous to me. As if I could ever break his heart, or anyone's heart! "How could I?"

"Trust me, you could." His head suddenly perked up. "Your mom's awake," he whispered. "I'm guessing she wouldn't want to find a guy in your room." Quicker than anything, Shea was out the window, having closed it behind him.

I couldn't hear anything!

But suddenly I could hear movement. Mom was up, and she was crossing the landing to check on me. I launched into my bed, throwing my blankets over me and feigning sleep.

I closed my eyes tightly as I heard my bedroom door open. Mom lingered there for a moment before closing it again. Had she heard? Would she ask me about it in the morning?

I prayed she wouldn't. I honestly would have no idea how to explain this.

CHAPTER 6

Mom didn't say a word the next morning. It was just like every other morning. We ate breakfast got ready, and then got in our prospective cars for work and school.

When I pulled into the lot, I noticed that Shea was waiting for me, leaning against his truck. He didn't look like he had been out half the night. I, on the other hand, looked a wreck. I was still yet to find my makeup and so my under-eye bags were on show today.

I parked in the spot next to Shea's truck and shut off the engine.

He beat me to my door, opening it for me and helping me out. I didn't need help, but it was sweet of him to offer.

"Did your mom find out about last night?" he asked me quietly.

"No, you were lucky," I replied in the same hushed tone.

"And are you okay?" he checked.

I felt the blood rush to my cheeks again. I looked down at my feet and fidgeted with the zipper on my book bag.

"No, come on," Shea encouraged. He placed a warm hand on my cheek and brought my eyes to his. "Sara. You don't have to be embarrassed while you're with me. You don't have to be anything but yourself."

I couldn't understand his sincerity, just like I couldn't understand anything else that had happened over the last few days. But against my better judgement, my gut was telling me to trust him.

"Are you sure you don't mind?" I whispered. I felt naked in front of him asking these questions. The epitome of vulnerability.

Shea pulled me into a hug, and I relaxed in his strong arms. "I can't wait for you to understand," he murmured into my hair. He released me after a minute and took my hand in his. "Let me walk you to your first class."

I thought that Monday had been ridiculous with all the staring and the whispers, but today was worse. I was walking hand in hand with Shea Braverman and everyone's eyes seemed glued to our connection.

I was very aware of it. Shea seemed oblivious. Or maybe he was just that confident and comfortable. I tried not to notice but it was hard when every man and his dog seemed absolutely intrigued by you.

I mean, what was so interesting? Were there not couples at the school? I had not been here long enough to really know many. But I knew for a fact that Cece and Jamie were together. Cece had his name tattooed on her left boob, for Christ's sake! Was that not stranger than me holding Shea's hand?

"Shea, everyone is looking at us!" I finally hissed at him when we reached my locker. I punched in the combination for my lock and opened it, using the door as a sort of shield to protect me from the prying eyes.

"Well, if it makes you feel any better, they're not looking at me."

I slammed the door of my locker once I had my Spanish book and stared at him, deadpan. He was teasing me and was trying not to laugh at my expense.

"You're cute when you're angry," he commented, tapping my nose with his index finger infuriatingly.

"Trust me, you won't think I'm very cute for long. I can hit hard," I threatened. I had never hit anything in my life, but I had the urge to wipe that grin off of Shea's face. He was enjoying this too much. Perhaps he enjoyed being the centre of attention, but I certainly didn't.

And what would happen if this got back to my mom? A small town like this, there had to be gossip.

Shea softened then. He caught a stray piece of hair that had fallen from my ponytail and he tucked it behind my ear. That small affectionate gesture had suddenly wiped away all my hostility. I wanted him to touch me again. How was he doing this?

"You want them to stop staring?" he asked seriously, in a voice so low it was just for me.

I nodded. I didn't know how he could achieve something like that, but then again, he had gotten Zoey to apologise to me. Shea did have a certain talent for getting what he wanted.

"Okay." He smiled slightly and leaned in to kiss my forehead. I closed my eyes, enjoying feeling this close to him. If I wasn't so aware of the fifty or so people watching us, I would have wanted that kiss a few inches lower. "Get your butt to class. I'll see you at lunch." He winked and retreated off down the hall.

I shook my head as I moved off in the opposite direction.

I wasn't entirely sure how he'd done it. Not five minutes since Shea and I had parted, and people seemed to be minding their own business. I walked into Spanish and no heads turned to me.

Well, none except for Cece, who was practically bouncing in her seat in the back row. I hurried towards her and dumped my books on the table.

Cece was wearing her cheer uniform again today. She wore it so well. I wished I was as lean and toned as her. I probably seemed like such a pervert. Both Shea and Cece were fine physical specimens. Looking up at her face, I could see that she only wore mascara on her fair eyelashes. Her skin was so perfect that she didn't need concealer or foundation. Another reason to envy her. Cece was smiling widely, grinning like a Cheshire cat, exposing her perfect, white teeth.

"Tell me everything!"she whispered excitedly, though Cece's idea of a whisper was more like a quiet shriek. I knew others could hear us, though they didn't turn their heads.

How had Shea achieved this?

"I don't know what you're talking about," I mused, opening my exercise book to a new page and filling in today's date.

Cece huffed and snatched my pen from my hand. "My brother left the house in the middle of the night and he came home pretty satisfied. Come on!" she begged. "Details!"

What did Cece think happened? Was she assuming something happened? I mean, from the level of her excitement, it seemed like she thought that something had happened between us.

Shea would never have said anything. I know that. Did others assume? Did relationships go from 0-100 in this town?

"Cece, he's your brother," I reminded her.

Cece rolled her eyes impatiently. "And you're my friend. Come on, you've got to be able to talk to someone about these things."

That stung a little bit. I've got to be able to talk to someone about these things. Could I tell her? Could she comprehend that the connection that I felt with her brother was more than just physical? Could she understand that I felt something that could only be explained as beyond natural comprehension? That it felt like damned witchcraft? This need I had to be with Shea had started the instant I had laid eyes on him. It just wasn't normal.

Cece was willing me to confide in her. And I really needed to talk to someone. I couldn't talk to my mom. What I was feeling went way beyond the "no boys" rule.

"I didn't sleep with your brother if that's what you're thinking happened," I started quietly.

Cece did look surprised. "Really?" she asked in disbelief.

"I've only known him for three days!" I retorted. Was it really that much of a shock?

"Oh, I get that, but when I met Jamie, I think we lasted about three hours before we fell into the supply closet on the second floor." She blushed at the memory.

I gaped at her, my eyes bulging. "Three hours?" I gasped.

"Hey, we don't slut shame in this family," she scolded.

"Sorry, I'm not slut shaming, it's just …" What was it? Cece seemed to understand this connection if I was interpreting her correctly. When she met Jamie, she felt the same indescribably chemistry. It was so strong that they had … done the deed … within three hours of meeting.

Cece made a small noise as she smiled. "I guess it really is different for you," she decided.

"What is?" I asked.

Cece shook her head. "Don't listen to me. Look, what you're feeling, what you're experiencing with my brother, it's all good!" she assured me. "Shea is just crazy about you. So, trust him, trust your instincts, and go at your pace."

I appreciated her attempt to reassure me, but all she did was just further solidify my fear that Shea wanted more from me than I was prepared to give. He said he didn't mind, he wanted me to trust him, but how was I supposed to feel when Cece was telling me that she had consummated her relationship within three hours!

I didn't want to let my anxiety ruin this, but it was hard to ignore. Trust him, trust Shea, I kept telling myself.

I made it to lunch without a single person staring at me. And even if they did look, it was only for a split second before their eyes went elsewhere. Had Shea personally gone around and told everyone not to stare at me? Why would they do what he told them to?

But the not staring quickly became worse than the staring. I knew they were all thinking about me. I knew they all wanted to stare. I felt like some paranoid crazy person!

I was not paranoid! I had never been anything other than ordinary, going about my business and getting good grades. I stood outside the cafeteria, but I couldn't bring myself to go inside. I couldn't eat lunch, knowing that everyone in that room was thinking about me, thinking about Shea and me, and wanting to stare at us, but they couldn't because Shea said so!

I had too many questions! Too many things didn't make sense. My head felt like a multiplex, a thousand different screens, each playing a different scene of my paranoia. Shea leaving. Shea pressuring me. Shea cheating.

Cheating! He wasn't even officially my boyfriend.

What is going on with me?

I put my hand on my chest and I could feel my heart racing against it. There was condensation on my forehead and I couldn't breathe.

I think I was having a panic attack.

I ran from the cafeteria and into the girl's bathroom, locking myself in a stall. I put the seat down on the toilet and sat down, putting my head between my knees. I had never had a panic attack before, but I could remember my mom describing them to me. She had helped her patients through them multiple times before.

I focussed on my breathing. If I could get my breathing under control, then my heart rate would lower. I knotted my fingers in my hair as I breathed, my ponytail a thing of the past.

"Sara!"

My heart rate quickened again, increasing my stress and anxiety. "Go away!" I cried out in a laboured voice.

"Sara!" Shea banged on my toilet door, my voice giving away where I was. "Sara, let me in. What's wrong?"

I didn't answer him. I closed my eyes and tried to concentrate on my breathing again. In and out. In and out.

I was startled by the sound of metal snapping. The door to my stall suddenly opened, the lock on the inside completely ruined. Shea had broken it with his bare hands.

I looked up at him and met his concerned gaze. He looked terrified as he took in the sight of me. He immediately knelt down in front of me, cupping my face in his hands. "Sara, what's going on?" he begged me to know. "What's wrong with you? Are you hurt?" What was insane was that I felt concern for him when he spoke in this tone. My nut job brain didn't want him to be afraid when I was the one who was about to earn a one-way ticket to the psych ward.

"I have no idea what's wrong with me," I managed to blubber. "I feel like I'm going crazy!"

He looked at me with such empathy, and such compassion. He knew exactly what I was talking about. I could see it in his eyes. "There is nothing wrong with you," he told me seriously. "I promise. Come on, let me take you home."

Shea helped me off the toilet, which in any other circumstance would have been questionable, but I really needed it. My legs were like lead.

We didn't go by the school office to get an early dismissal. I hoped they wouldn't call my mom if I was absent for my afternoon classes. But that anxiety felt small compared to what I was currently feeling. Shea took me directly to his truck.

"I'll have Cece bring your Jeep home before your mom gets back," Shea promised as he opened the passenger door for me.

His truck was huge, and it required a significant step up to get inside. Before I had a chance to even attempt it, Shea's hands were on my waist, lifting me up into the seat. He closed the door behind me and jogged around to the driver's side.

The scent of his truck was comforting, and it oddly helped to calm me. One would assume a teenaged boy would smell quite gross, but Shea smelled warm and comforting. Whatever his cologne was, I liked it. The scent enveloped me and I settled into the cushioned seat.

Shea started his powerful engine and backed out of his parking space. I closed my eyes, focusing on my breathing as my surroundings helped me. Before I knew it, we were driving down the main street, mere minutes from my house.

Shea parked on the curb, leaving the driveway empty. He helped me down from my seat and we walked together to the front door. I did feel significantly calmer. Whether it was the fact that I was away from school, or the fact that I could practically feel the waves of concern and protectiveness radiating off of Shea, I couldn't put my finger on what had helped me more. My head said the former, but everywhere else thought the latter.

I unlocked the front door and let Shea into my house. I was immediately a little embarrassed. We hadn't tidied up from last night or this morning. There were dishes on the counter, my mom's blender was still half filled with green smoothie, and in addition to the boxes everywhere, we didn't look the neatest.

"Sorry about the mess," I murmured.

"Sara, I don't care about that," Shea replied, the worry evident in his shaky voice. "You need to tell me what you're feeling. I want to help you."

I dropped my bag at my feet as I turned around to face him. "What I'm feeling?" I repeated. "How can I tell you that when I don't even understand it myself?" I exclaimed. "All I know is I met you three days ago, and suddenly my life has gone to crap." I threw my hands up in the air. I felt my drama was justified. "I am not this person," I informed him firmly, gesturing to myself. "I don't catch feelings. I don't get jealous. I don't Facebook stalk! I don't have boys in my room in the middle of the night! And I certainly have never had a damned panic attack before!"

I could feel the tears coming. I hated that I cried when I was angry. It made me feel as though people didn't see the justification in my arguments. They only saw the hysteria.

Shea was taking it, though. He was listening to every word.

I took a few deep breaths, attempting to calm myself and to keep the tears away. "I don't understand why you're so important to me, Shea," I whispered. "But you are. And it scares me. It scares me so much because I am not the kind of girl someone like you would go for. I am not like Zoey, or any other girl so confident in herself that she can have casual relationships. And I'm scared that when you realise this, that you will dump me and run off with one of them. Which is why I feel so stupid and ridiculous because we're not even together." I practically collapsed into the sofa. "Three damn days. How is this happening?" I felt like I needed some ice on my forehead or something. I closed my eyes and rubbed my temples.

"Can I talk now?" Shea asked quietly, sitting down beside me on the sofa.

"Mmhmm." I nodded, not opening my eyes.

"Sara, do you believe in love at first sight?"

My eyes shot open and I was suddenly sitting bolt upright. My posture had never been this good. I stared at him like he had just announced he was an alien, or that he was from the future.

He had to be an alien or something. Why was he saying such a thing to me?

Shea's brown eyes were so comforting. So warm, and so full of truth. There had to be an explanation that helped to make sense of all of this.

"No..." I replied, though my answer sounded more like a question.

His face fell a little. "Well, I do," Shea insisted. "I have a belief that there is one perfect person out in this world for everybody, and when you see them, you just know. And when you meet that person, nothing makes sense anymore. Nothing but them. The world is a mess, but you make everything better. And it can feel crazy, and sudden, and completely foreign. It can feel like you're literally having an out of body experience. Logic and reason have no place in matters such as these. You've got to stop panicking with your head and listening to what your heart wants. It's called falling in love for a reason. You fall right out the life you knew and into a newer, better one."

Call me crazy ... which I had done multiple times today ... but it sort of made sense in a weird way. Love at first sight ... was that what this was?

I mean, I had never been in love before. I didn't know what it felt like. I only had movies and books as my reference material. But maybe it was like this. Maybe it was like literally falling. Falling out of your old reality and into a life led by two.

Love at first sight. Could this really be it?

I stared at Shea. He never wavered. I did have such strong feelings for him. Feelings that I couldn't explain. Feelings that shouldn't be there after only three days. Was I falling in love with him?

But why? Why me, and why him? What made us special?

"Why me?" I managed to ask.

Shea smiled. "Because you're perfect. I don't understand it exactly either. I guess the fates, or God, or chance, whatever it is that exists, decides just who our perfect half is, and when we find them, we need to realise just how lucky we are." Shea pulled me close and I found myself snuggling into his chest.

It was crazy how safe I felt. Crazy was my new favourite word.

Shea rubbed my back soothingly. "You aren't some fling for me, Sara. This is serious. I've got a history. Everyone does. But what I want to focus on is my future. Ourfuture."

I felt the screens of the multiplex in my head shutting off one by one. The warm feeling of security filled me, and it was this feeling that carried me off to sleep, right there in Shea's arms.

I awoke suddenly to the sound of the front door opening. I jumped, fully awake, and realised that I was alone on the couch. Shea was gone, and my mom was home.

She looked at me strangely. "Were you napping, hon? Big day?"

"You could say that," I murmured to myself. I wondered how I was going to tell my mom about this. How could I tell her I had a boyfriend, let alone that I was falling in love with him after three days of knowing him.

My mom launched into telling me about her day as she started to pull a few random things out of the refrigerator to turn them into something edible.

I half listened as I saw the clock and realised that it was a few hours later. I quickly looked out the front window to see that Shea's truck was gone and my Jeep was in the driveway. The key, which had been in my pocket, was now hanging on the hook by the door.

How had he managed to get the key out of my pocket without waking me up?

"Sara?"

"What?" I asked, spinning around at the sound of my name.

Mom was smiling. "I just said thank you, hon. It's always nice to come home to chores being done that I don't have to do." She winked.

I then noticed that the kitchen was spotless. The dishes were done, Mom's blender was clean, and everywhere else was straightened up. Shea was a regular house elf.

"Hey, Mom," I called out. "I'm not feeling that great. I might head to bed early. I'm not hungry."

Mom immediately came towards me from behind the kitchen counter, a look of concern on her face. She placed her hand on my forehead and looked me over. "What's wrong? You don't have a fever."

The downside to having a doctor for a mom was that it was nearly impossible to fake being sick.

"No, it's not that. Just cramps," I lied.

"Oh, okay. Well, there's Tylenol in the bathroom cabinet and I can bring you up a wheat bag if you want," she offered.

"No, that's okay. Thanks, Mom." I smiled at her reassuringly and hurried upstairs. I nearly had a heart attack as I entered my room as Shea was lying on my bed, reading one of my books. He had fished it out of one of my boxes.

I was glad he hadn't found a pathetic romance. Instead he had found one of my books from English last year. It was a novel about a man infected by a curse that turned him into a monstrous creature. It was all about inner turmoil, conscience, and truthfully, a little horror. My teachers had found tonnes in the books to have us churn out dozens of papers.

"This seems really inaccurate," Shea commented casually, as though it wasn't weird for him to just be hanging out in my room.

I snatched the book from him. "Of course it is. It's made up fantasy." I placed the book on my nightstand. "What are you doing in here?" I demanded to know.

"Just wanted to make sure you weren't running off back to New York or something while I wasn't looking," he murmured in reply. Shea rolled onto his side, facing me. He looked so comfortable.

I wanted to sit down beside him, lay down beside him, but I was too nervous. Instead I awkwardly chose to sit on the stool in front of my dresser.

Shea seemed to think this was an odd choice, too. He sat up on my bed and cocked an eyebrow. "Won't you sit by me?"

"I don't want you to get the wrong idea," I confessed quietly.

I heard Shea sigh exasperatedly, and quicker than anything he was kneeling in front of me. We were at eye level. He was mere inches from my face. I stopped breathing. My stomach lurched, and my heartbeat took off.

"Sara, I am capable of having things on my mind other than sex," he said firmly, but I could sense in his tone that he was getting frustrated with me. "You've told me that you're not ready for that kind of relationship and I accepted it. Were we having the same conversation? Was I speaking German?"

He was frustrated with me. He didn't like repeating himself. I pushed him away from me, and action which startled him, and I stood up and crossed the room to my window, the furthest place in my room from where he was standing.

"Don't be a jerk, Shea," I willed. "I'm an insecure person, I'm sorry. I've never had a boyfriend before. I've never even had a boy have a crush on me before! This is all new. And this," I motioned between the two of us, "isn't normal. You've established that. You need to cut me a little slack. I mean, Cece told me that she had sex with Jamie within three hours of meeting him! How is that supposed to make me feel?"

Shea exhaled. "I'm sorry. You're right," he conceded. "I have a tendency to expect that whatever I say is accepted."

"I noticed," I replied sarcastically. "Why is that? Why do people listen to you like they do?"

Shea shrugged his shoulders. "I don't know. Charisma?" He seemed genuinely bemused which was weird. "I'm good with people, I suppose. I'm influential. People listen to me. So, I guess it's different for me when I say something and you don't accept it."

Was he really so popular that people just followed him and obeyed him? I had seen people with popularity bully before, but I didn't think that was Shea's agenda.

Shea got up from the floor and opened his arms, displaying transparency. "I told you the honest truth, Sara. I don't care if you want to move at a snail's pace. I don't care if all you want to do is hold my hand. So long as it's my hand your holding, I'm okay with that." He came towards me slowly, like a man who was trying not to spook a horse. "I can't be away from you. This connection between us is the realest damn thing I have ever felt."

I felt the exact same way. Since Shea had offered me the love at first sight explanation as to what I was feeling, things were rapidly becoming clearer in the foggy mess that was my brain.

All I knew was that Shea was important to me. It was important that he was in my life.

I closed the distance between us and wrapped my arms around his waist. He reciprocated immediately, holding me tightly. Goddammit, this felt natural. "I can't promise I won't ever be insecure again. You have really pretty friends."

Shea laughed. "Have you looked in a mirror lately?" he retorted. "You are beautiful, Sara. You are not of this world."

I could have literally choked on my own tongue, I wanted to cry. Nobody had ever said that to me before. I wasn't sure if Shea had blinders on or not, but he believed what he was saying, and it meant a lot that he saw me that way.

His grip on me tightened. "And I find it utterly impossible that no guy has ever had a crush on you. I think you'll find that any guy with working eyeballs is well aware of you, believe me."

I laughed.

"And, just quickly," he added. "Please, never mention my sister's sex life to me again. I like to live in a pretend land where I believe that nothing but homework happens in the bedroom down the hall from me."

Chapter 7

I woke up to the sensation of being crushed. I would have been alarmed were it not for the sound of quiet snoring in my ear.

Shea was sound asleep, laying on top of me. His arms were strewn across my torso, unconsciously holding onto my waist. His left leg was likewise laying across me. He had somehow made it onto my side of the bed during the night, and we were sharing the same pillow. He really was a hog.

He looked younger when he slept, which was crazy to think seeing as he was only eighteen, but he did. I hadn't noticed just how much he carried when he was awake. The stressors of the day left his face when he was sleeping.

As I woke up properly, I felt something hard poking me in my stomach. I wondered for a split second before I realised what it was. I had read enough books and seen enough movies to know what happened to guys in the morning. I blushed crimson red and was thankful that he was still asleep.

Shea and I had spent the night talking. Just talking. He talked a little more about his family. He told me his mom's name was

Karen, and that she had been an elementary school teacher before his father had passed away. He then spent the next few hours practically grilling me about my life in New York. My school, my job, my friends, and any guys I had been interested in. He still found it impossible that no guys had ever asked me out.

As the night went on, I felt more and more reluctant to let Shea leave. I wanted him to stay. And I didn't have to repeat myself, or my fears. He knew it what capacity it was, and he didn't say a word to pressure me or make me feel uncomfortable.

Shea hid in the closet when my mom came to check on me, and then Shea climbed into my bed beside me and just held me as we both went to sleep.

Shoot! I resisted gasping. Whatever concealer I was wearing yesterday would have most certainly rubbed off during the night. I hadn't taken my makeup off so as to look as clear skinned as possible while he was here.

Very carefully, I reached my freehand out to my nightstand. I kept a small hand-held mirror on top of it. When I felt the cool metal of the mirror, I brought it back towards me slowly.

Shea was still snoring peacefully.

I held the mirror up to my face and almost said "Ew" out loud. My concealer had most definitely rubbed off in its entirety. My dark circles stood out like bruises no matter how much sleep it got. Red pock marks in the way of acne scars from my puberty years dotted my oily areas and a new friend was started to pop up on my forehead.

I wondered if I could somehow get out of bed without waking Shea up so that I could get to my dresser to clean myself up. No sooner had I started to formulate a manoeuvre that could get me out of my bed, my phone started blaring with my alarm tone. It was six-thirty.

Crap.

Shea jerked up, raising his head, his eyes still glazed with sleep. His hair was perfectly mussed. He probably wouldn't need to do a thing before school. God, he was handsome.

He yawned and then looked at me.

Double crap.

"You're so pretty," he croaked in a morning, sleep voice.

My heart softened, and I felt my insecurities fade. I switched my alarm off and pushed back the covers.

Shea groaned and pulled them back over himself. "Five more minutes," he grumbled.

"I have to get ready for school," I hissed, though I couldn't hide my smile. "And so do you!"

Shea stuck his arm out and grabbed my leg, pulling me back into bed. I tried to muffle my yelp and subsequent giggles. Mom would definitely be awake. Shea cuddled me into his chest and inhaled. I think he was smelling my hair. "Was last night okay?" he asked. His voice was still thick with sleep, but I knew there was no humour in his voice. He almost sounded vulnerable.

I nodded. "Yeah, it was okay," I whispered. Be vulnerable, Sara. I kissed Shea's cheek, resulting in him smiling so damned sweetly. I started to blush and lost my nerve. "But you snore, and you hog the bed."

Shea laughed. "Well next time I'm going to tie your damn legs together. You're a freaking starfish. You kneed me in the crotch at like three am. I nearly cried. I do actually want to produce a kid one day, you know."

Again, I was at ease. And I couldn't help but notice that he mentioned next time. I wondered if he would stay again tonight.

I quickly showered and Shea watched me get ready. He seemed to watch me with fascination as I covered my blemishes and brushed my hair. I changed in the closet and was ready to go downstairs for breakfast while he was still lying in my bed.

"School starts in thirty minutes," I reminded him. "You can't shower here. Mom will know it's not me and I'll be grounded until I'm thirty."

"I'm fast," he assured me. "I won't be late for school."

I didn't believe him. I wasn't even sure his car was here. Was he planning on walking? Did Uber pick up in the middle of nowhere North Carolina?

Shea freaking beat me to school. He was showered, changed, and looked like a damn Greek god. When he saw me climb out of my car, he just grinned and winked at me.

School went relatively quickly. I sat with Cece in the classes that I had with her, and other girls started to talk to me with interest now that I had been spotted with Shea. I sat with Shea and his friends at lunch and listened while the discussed tomorrow's game and the party at Zoey's house afterwards. I got through my afternoon classes, went to Sally's after school for my shift, and then went home and did my homework.

In the middle of my English essay, my laptop pinged with a messenger notification.

Hey, so I never officially asked you to be my date tomorrow night.

I frowned. Was Shea just stating a fact?

Is that your backwards way of asking me to be your date?

The little dots came up that told me he was typing, but there was a knock on the door.

Be right back. Door, I typed.

I wasn't expecting anyone. It might be a charity. I had some cash in my purse from work if it was. I pulled open the door to see Shea standing under the eave with a bunch of Gerber daisies in his hand.

One of the million questions he had asked me last night was my favourite flower. But I had answered lilies. Gerber daisies were my mom's favourites. That had been one of his questions, too.

"Are flowers enough to grease your mom up?" he asked.

Oh my God, Shea was wearing a pressed shirt. The gesture would have been really sweet if the white fabric didn't hug his perfect torso so well.

"Perfect for your funeral," I teased. "But Shea, seriously. My mom is really against me having anything to do with boys. She got pregnant young and she's terrified that I'm going to get knocked up and not go to college. All she'll see when she looks at you is a giant sperm producer."

Wow, Sara, that was graphic and gross.

Shea held his hands up in defence. "I know. But I plan on hanging around for a while, you know. She's got to meet me sooner or later. The quicker she sees that I'm not a serial killer out to impregnate her daughter, the quicker she'll like me. I hope."

I knew he was right. If Mom didn't meet him now, we were just going to have this conversation next week, or the one after. And I wanted her to know. I didn't want to lie to her.

"Okay, well, just make sure there's at least three feet between us at all times," I cautioned, taking the flowers and inviting him inside.

I made spaghetti for the three of us while we waited for Mom to get home from work. Shea sat at the kitchen counter watching me cook, or rather watching me try not to burn anything.

"Don't be expecting anything gourmet," I warned. "I was raised on take-out. I speak fluent Chinese food menu." I dumped a jar of tomato pasta sauce on the spaghetti and stirred it through.

Shea laughed. "You'll have to let me cook for you some time. My dad was a great cook."

I smiled. "I'd like that."

Just as I was dishing up the spaghetti into three bowls, the front door opened and my mom came in.

"Oh, God bless remission, Sara," she cried. She hadn't noticed Shea at the counter, but she was in a good mood. She'd had a good day thankfully. "One of my babies from New York flew down specifically to see me. He's going to be okay, thank God."

No sooner had she dumped her bag and keys, she noticed that I was not the only one in the room. Shea climbed off the stool immediately.

Mom frowned as her eyes flitted between Shea and me.

"Uh, Mom, this is Shea, my ..." We hadn't really discussed labels yet. I couldn't call him my boyfriend before he asked. "Um, and Shea, this is my mom, Dr Amanda Bryant."

Shea crossed the room to my mom with his hand extended. "It's a pleasure to meet you, Dr Bryant. Sara's told me so much about you," he said politely. He was trying to be charming. That wouldn't work on Mom.

Mom looked him up and down suspiciously. "Really? Sara's told me nothing about you." She then eyed me, giving me a look that told me we'd be having a chat later.

Shea laughed nervously. "Yeah, well, it's all new. I guess she hasn't had a chance yet. But I wanted to come over and meet you. Introduce myself ... and ask your permission to take Sara out tomorrow night."

Permission? No! She might have let me go to the game if she thought I was being social with my new friends. But now that she knew it was for a date she would say no!

"Shea brought you flowers, Mom," I offered half-heartedly, holding up the bunch of Gerber daisies on the counter.

Mom barely looked. "I'm sorry, how old are you?" she asked Shea accusingly. "You look too old to be at Sara's school."

"Eighteen, ma'am," he replied. "I'm a senior. And, uh, as to my appearance, I guess that's just genetics."

"Eighteen?" she repeated. "And how many sexual partners have you had?"

Shea choked on air and I just about died from humiliation. "Mom!" I cried.

Mom gave me a look that said, "What?".

"Shea, you don't have to answer that." I wasn't sure I wanted to hear the answer to that.

"One in four teenagers contract an STD in the United States every year," Mom said defensively. "And three in ten American girls will get pregnant before they're twenty. Fifty percent of those mothers never finish high school."

Where was she pulling these stats from? Did she just have them on file on the off chance that I brought a guy home?

"Mom," I said again firmly. "You're embarrassing me."

Shea just looked shell-shocked.

"Better you're embarrassed than me becoming a grandmother before I'm forty. Or me having to write you a prescription to treat chlamydia," she snapped.

I wondered if I prayed hard enough if the floor would open up and swallow me whole.

Shea seemed to regain his voice after the shock of my mom's medical jargon. "Dr Bryant, I care about your daughter very much. We aren't doing anything irresponsible, and I would never put her in harm's way. I'm not some sycophant out to impregnate Sara. I just want to be with her. I get good grades, and I look after my family. I just wanted to ask as a courtesy if I could take her to the game tomorrow night and a friend's party afterwards."

Mom pursed her lips. "What's your surname, Shea?"

What? That was random. Didn't she hear all the sweet things that Shea said?

"Braverman," Shea replied.

Mom nodded slowly. "How are your parents?"

Wait, did Mom know Shea's family from before?

"My dad died three years ago. Mom took it pretty hard," Shea replied glumly.

Mom seemed a little shocked. She had known them. Had they gone to high school together perhaps? "Oh, well, I'm sorry to hear that."

Shea managed a small, polite smile.

"Shea, let me speak with my daughter. She'll see you at school tomorrow, I'm sure."

I knew that tone. My heart sunk.

Shea didn't approach me. He offered me a small smile and his eyes flashed up, gesturing to my bedroom upstairs. He would be waiting for me after I was done speaking with Mom. Shea left and shut the front door behind him.

Mom's eye's followed Shea out before she rounded on me. "Saraphine Jo Bryant, you will not see that boy again, do you understand me?"

Chapter 8

I stared at her, bewildered. I couldn't have heard her correctly. She did not just tell me that I was never to see Shea again based on two minutes of conversation. Two minutes in which he had composed himself pretty well considering she had all but strapped him up to a polygraph machine.

"I'm sorry, what?" I had to have heard her wrong. She would clarify.

Mom's eyes narrowed, and she held her index finger up to me, as if I was a naughty child eating candy before dinner. "You are never to see that boy again," she repeated sternly. "He is not good for you. I forbid it."

My mother had never spoken to me like this before. She had scolded me, of course, but this was something else. Her tone was fierce, yet fearful. Her eyes were wild, and full of apprehension. Her entire body was rigid. It was as if flames were about to erupt from her ears any moment. She sensed danger, but why?

"You ... you forbidit?" I managed to choke out. I was in utter disbelief. "What are you afraid of? That I'll get pregnant? Come on, Mom. You know me. You raised me better than that."

"You heard me, Saraphine," she hissed, once again using my full name. "I made it clear from the start. No boys. Not until you finish high school. Especially not that boy." She pointed at the front door, as if Shea was still standing there.

Little did she know, Shea was probably already in my bedroom, listening to the hellfire that my mother was spitting at him.

She was making me angry. I was not stupid. I wasn't going to get pregnant. Shea was well aware of where I stood on the subject of a physical relationship. "What is so wrong about Shea?" I demanded to know. "It was good of him to come to you first before we go out tomorrow."

Mom laughed sarcastically. "That boy is dangerous, Sara," she insisted. "I won't have you anywhere near him. Going out with him is out of the question. No." She shook her head.

"Dangerous?" I scoffed. "Shea has been nothing but kind and decent to me," I insisted, repeating my words of praise. "He helped me get my job!" I exclaimed. "He helped me to settle in at school and to feel comfortable." People no longer stared at me. Only us, now. "I even told him I'm not comfortable with a physical relationship yet, and he is fine with that!"

"Oh, Sara. Don't be so naïve. He's already got his hooks in you. Of course every teenage boy is going to tell you that he's happy to wait. That is until he gets drunk at a party, much like the one he's attending tomorrow night, and decides to force his good, innocent, all too trusting girlfriend into submission."

Was my mother on something? Where had this person come from? She was usually the most kind, loving and supportive mom around. I loved her to pieces. She would do anything for me, and anything for her patients.

But where did this hate for Shea come from? Was it him, or was it boys in general?

"I'm not naïve," I snapped. "And I'm going out with Shea. You can't stop me."

I could not believe where this conversation had gone. I was not this girl. I was not the rebel who flouted her parents.

But my mom wasn't this person either. She didn't just blow up without a good reason. Fear of teenage pregnancy just seemed too far-fetched.

"You are my daughter, and what I say goes," Mom said firmly. "I would never do anything that wasn't for the benefit of your safety."

"My safety?" I exclaimed. "What are you talking about? Do you think Shea is going to hurt me?"

"Yes!" cried Mom. "He is dangerous, Sara!" she insisted.

"In what way?" I challenged, folding my arms across my chest. If she replied with teenage boy hormones, I was actually going to lose it more than I already had.

But Mom didn't say anything. She just stared at me with a lost, fearful expression. We stood silently for a few moments, just staring at each other, processing what the other had said.

"Shea is important to me," I said slowly, after a while. "We are going out tomorrow night, and any other night that he asks. I want you to actually get to know him, Mom. He's a good person. He loves his family. He looks after his mom and his sister. For some reason, he cares about me, too."

"It's too late," whispered Mom. "I should never have brought you back here." In a move that floored me, she started to cry, and she came over to hug me. She held onto me so tightly that she was starting to restrict my lungs. But I didn't move.

"Mom," I whispered. "It's okay." Was she afraid of losing me? Was this some crazy reaction to her thinking she was losing me? Shea and I weren't getting married. We were just going on a date. I still had another year of high school, and then college. I had years before I would even start thinking of marriage.

I was an only child. And she had been widowed young. Maybe this was why she had reacted so insanely. She didn't like Shea because he was a threat to our relationship. But he wasn't. She would see that.

Mom let go of me and turned back towards the door. "I'm just going to go to the market, Sara. We need juice. We're out." And she grabbed her keys and left.

In seconds, Shea was behind me, hugging me comfortingly. "I'm sorry, I'm sorry, I'm so sorry," he whispered in my ear remorsefully.

I burst into tears and turned into his chest, promptly soaking his nice shirt with my crying. "I mean, what the hell, right?" I cried emotionally, my voice cracking.

"I shouldn't have come over. I didn't think she'd react like that. I'm so sorry, Sara," Shea continued to apologise. "I didn't expect her to feel that way."

"She doesn't," I insisted. "She's just afraid of losing me. She doesn't know you from a bar of soap. She can't judge you. She's just trying to stop me from leaving her. It's just been me and her for so long. You pose a threat to her is all."

But that didn't make it any better. Mom and I weren't okay. And I wasn't okay with that. I didn't know how to make it better. Well, I did, but I wasn't about to stop seeing Shea just to put Mom's fear of losing me to rest.

The fact of the matter was that just because I might grow up and get my own life someday, it didn't mean that I was lost to her. She was my mom. I was always going to need her.

"You haven't changed you mind, have you?"

I wiped my eyes with the back of my hand so that I could see clearly. "No, of course not."

Shea wiped some lingering tears away with his thumb. "It will be okay," he promised me. "I'll win her over. I'll show her I'm not dangerous or anything."

I wasn't hungry anymore. Instead, I just wanted to go upstairs to bed. I changed into my comfortable, old pyjamas and climbed in beside Shea, who was waiting for me with open arms. As terrible as I felt, his embrace was truly comforting to me.

With his spare arm, Shea opened up my Netflix on my laptop and chose a light-hearted sitcom in an effort to cheer me up. Instead, I watched the little clock in the corner of the screen, waiting for my mom to come back home as it got later and later.

At quarter past eleven I heard the front door open. Shea was dozing off beside me, but was quickly alert when he heard the noise, too.

"Hide!" I hissed, slamming my laptop closed and throwing back my blankets.

Shea leapt out of my bed and dashed into the closet, closing the door on himself. I quickly smoothed over his side of the bed so it looked like I had been the only person in here. No sooner had I done that, I heard my mom's footsteps approach my door.

Mom opened my door quietly, in the same manner that she did when she thought I was asleep. Mom had always checked on me before she went to bed, ever since I was a baby. Being a doctor, she was well aware of all sorts of scary things that could happen to babies in their cribs. She had never broken the habit.

When she saw that I was awake, she opened my door fully and came inside. Mom's eyes were red and swollen, like mine were. She had been crying. Mom came and sat down on the edge of my bed. I pushed my laptop away to give her room.

"I know how you're feeling, honey," Mom told me quietly. "It's exciting and confusing and altogether a little nuts."

Well ... yeah. That was it exactly.

Mom touched my cheek affectionately and exhaled. She looked so sad. To see her like this, in a way I'd never seen her before, was just heartbreaking. "One day, in the very far off future, you will have your own daughter, and you'll understand what it's like to love someone more than your own life. Every decision I have ever made for you, and for us, has been to protect you."

"I know, Mom," I told her.

She smiled. "No, you don't. And that's okay." She exhaled again. "I went for a drive to organise my thoughts. I know that I can't keep you away from Shea. I know that's impossible now. But I have decided that I have rules."

Rules. I could deal with rules. Rules were better than her blanket banning him from my life.

"Shea is not to be in this house when I am not here," Mom said firmly. "I understand that I work late, but if he wants to come over, it can be for dinner or something when I am home."

I knew immediately we would be breaking that one. I understood the purpose for that rule, but I was perfectly capable of protecting my own virtue. "Okay," I nodded.

Mom smiled. She was glad I accepted that one. "Okay, next," she paused awkwardly. "I want you on birth control."

My face dropped and again I felt the type of humiliation that made me went to crawl underneath my covers and never come back out again. Why did Shea have to hear all this?

"But Mom," I started to protest, but she held her finger up.

"No buts," she retorted. "I'm not stupid. I know what happens when you're young and in love. It is by no means a free pass, or my permission, but I would rather protect you than live in denial."

Thank God Shea couldn't see me right now. My cheeks were burning. "Fine," I whispered.

"Curfew. You've never had one before because you haven't need-ed it. But I want you home by ten-thirty every night. No exceptions or you're grounded."

Curfew. Okay, that was an easier conversation than birth control with my mother while my almost-boyfriend was hiding in the closet. "Okay, that's fine."

Mom nodded. "Okay, good. My last rule is the most important one."

More important than birth control?

"You are going to a four-year college after high school," she said firmly.

I frowned. I knew that.

She could see my confusion. "If the best school you get into is across the country, then you'll go there," she continued. "You are not to jeopardise your future over a boy, do you understand?"

"Mom, we've only known each other for four days," I said quietly. College was important to me, and it was probably even more important to my mom. She had a baby while trying to get through college and med school. She wanted my life to be easier than hers. I think that's what any good parent wanted for their kids.

"Promise me, Sara," Mom insisted.

I didn't know what was going to happen with Shea. Like I said, it had only been four days. We weren't even official or anything. It was hard to imagine that a year from now, when I was filling out applications and choosing schools, that I would be basing my choices on a relationship. Be it God, or the fates, or damned destiny that had a hand in whatever I was experiencing with Shea, if I chose to go to college in Timbuktu, then it shouldn't matter. "Okay, Mom," I agreed.

She was satisfied with my answer. She touched my cheek again and then stood up from my bed. "I just want you to know you have power in a relationship, Sara. You can choose to do whatever you want. To leave, if you want. You're not tied. It's not permanent. You don't have a tattoo."

I understood where she was coming from, but what a weird direction to take that in. Okay, yes, I didn't have a tattoo. I probably wouldn't get one anytime soon. My pain tolerance was pathetic, anyway. I then thought of the awesome white line tattoo of Jamie's name on Cece's chest. I guess that was pretty permanent. They wouldn't want to break up.

"I love you, Sara." Mom leaned over and kissed my forehead. "More than you could ever comprehend."

I exhaled. "I love you, too, Mom."

Mom left my bedroom and closed my door. Shea didn't leave my closet until we heard her bedroom door shut. Shea sat down on the bed next to me in silence.

We both didn't have anything to say for a moment. That was a lot to take in and process.

"Hey Mom, meet Shea. Nice to meet you, Shea. I'm Amanda. Welcome to our home. How was school today?" I murmured, mimicking the conversation that I hoped might happen, even in the slightest chance.

"Look, if I've learned anything over the past few years, it's that parents who give a crap are good parents," Shea said plainly, "even if what they want pisses you off."

CHAPTER 9

Considering that I was part house cat, I really didn't know that much about football. Mom and I watched trashy reality shows on Monday nights instead of the games.

And I never attended the games of my high school in New York. I wasn't a player or a cheerleader, and I really had no idea what I was watching, so I saw no sense in going.

Football, it seemed, was a religion in Providence. All businesses closed early. Even the police station was shut down for a few hours which I wasn't even sure was legal. Every man and his dog were flocking to the stadium at Providence High School to see our team take on Newtown.

By the time Shea and I got there, all the student spots were full, taken by parents and town members. We were just lucky that Shea had his senior spot reserved. People were parking nearly a half mile away.

I was initially shocked by the sheer size of the crowd that was gathering in the stands. The massive stadium lights were on, and the perfectly kept ground was on show. Students, parents, and all other adults were wearing school colours of some description. I could already spy Cece and the squad down on the field, doing an incredibly choreographed routine to a song I had just heard playing on the radio.

The cheerleaders were kicking and flipping and doing all sorts of contortion that I found thoroughly impressive. Cece stood out, of course. Her smile was the biggest and brightest, and she was also the most powerful tumbler. She flipped at lightning speed, causing the crowd to erupt in cheers.

"Cece is so good at that," I said to Shea as we climbed the bleachers to take a spare seat.

"She's a bit of a show off," murmured Shea in reply, rolling his eyes. "I keep telling her to calm down her stunts ... you know, so she won't hurt herself, but she doesn't listen to me."

"Ha!" I cried. "The first person not to." I grinned at him. "But she is seriously so talented. She could probably get a cheer scholarship to college if she wanted to."

Shea nodded. "That's the plan," he confirmed. "Oh, yeah!" Shea cried, suddenly standing up and clapping as the football team ran out onto the field. The entire crowd followed suit, and I got up to cheer on my school, too.

I mean, I didn't really pick up the rules, but I cheered when Shea cheered and cried out in annoyance when Shea did. Shea found it really amusing.

Our school ended up winning by a field goal, as Shea called it, which meant that the party at Zoey's house was going to be even bigger than we thought. By the buzz of the people in our class, it seemed as though every junior and senior student was going, and if you were dating anyone younger than that, they were going, too.

Cece claimed me after the game with a huge grin on her face. "Hey, you two!" she cried. "Don't you look good together?" Cece winked at me and I blushed.

"Cece," Shea said in a scolding tone.

Cece shrugged her shoulders.

"Cece, I can't believe how talented you are," I remarked, changing the subject. "I wish I could dance like that."

"You probably could. Never know, could be in your blood," Cece encouraged. "Natural athleticism and flexibility."

"Of which I have neither," I retorted jokingly.

"Keys," Cece demanded, holding out her hand. Cece had come to the game with Jamie. Shea would go to the party with Jamie and we would take Shea's truck.

Shea sucked in a breath. "Now, she's a stick," he said delicately. "I swear to God, if I hear you grinding the crap out of my baby, you will be sleeping outside."

Cece laughed as she snatched the keys.

The plan was for Cece to come back to my house to get ready for the party. Mom might be a little more comfortable and accommodating if she saw me leaving with a girl and not Shea. Shea would meet us there.

Cece grabbed my hand. "Okay, let's go back to yours and get beautiful. See you later, Shea."

I only had time to wave at Shea before we disappeared into the crowd.

Cece unlocked Shea's truck and opened her door. As I opened mine, she said, "So I put a bunch of dresses in the back of Shea's truck this morning. I wasn't sure what you had. Do you have a bathing suit?" Cece started the truck and it roared to life. She didn't have much trouble putting it in gear. I wondered if she grinded the gears just the annoy Shea when he was around.

"A bathing suit?" We would be swimming?

"Zoey has an amazing pool. We always end up swimming. Fair warning though, if you're going to puke, do it before you get in the pool. You don't want to spend your Saturday morning fishing your own vomit out of the filter. Trust me." Cece shuddered, obviously speaking from experience.

Gross. I would be editing that little detail out of what would be said to my mom. I had never touched alcohol before, and I could guarantee that my mother would sniff it on me like a bloodhound if I did.

"Things seem to be going pretty well between you and Shea, though, huh?" she mentioned as she drove. "I mean, he's been sleeping out the last few nights ..."

I looked out the window. "Things aren't like that. My mom would freak. We're taking things slow." He hadn't even asked me to be his girlfriend yet. I wondered if I'd read too many romance novels. Did guys even do that?

"You are so cute, Sara," Cece murmured. "You're just right for him. He hasn't been this happy in a long time."

I smiled. It was nice to have Cece's seal of approval.

A short drive later, Cece pulled into my driveway, parking behind my Jeep. Cece jumped down from the driver's seat and collected her bag of things from the back seat. We walked together to my front door and I opened it with my key.

Mom was sitting in the living room, a cup of coffee in hand, and a magazine on her lap, though I could tell she wasn't focussed on it. She was still upset from the day before. We had hugged it out last night, but the wounds were still raw. It was a good idea that Cece was here and not Shea. Though she was crazy beautiful, Cece looked like a normal teenager in her cheer uniform.

"Hi, Mom," I said delicately.

Mom looked up from her magazine. She smiled at me tentatively and her eyes flicked to Cece. "Hi, hon. Who is your friend?"

"It's nice to meet you, Dr Bryant," Cece said warmly. She was such a confident person. She marched right into our living room and shook my surprised mother's hand. "I'm Cece Braverman. Sara and I have Spanish and English together."

"Braverman?" Mom shook Cece's hand and recognition filled her face. "Cecelia? My, last time I saw you, you were about this big." Mom held her hands out to the size of a loaf of bread.

Cece's smile disappeared from her face, and for the first time I saw sadness in her usually sunny face. "My dad was the only one who called me Cecelia," she replied quietly.

"I heard about your father. I'm sorry," Mom said sincerely.

"Thanks, Dr Bryant." Cece adjusted her bag.

"The bathroom is at the top of the stairs if that's where you girls are going to get ready." She pointed to the stairs. Cece and I went to leave, but Mom caught me. "Just a minute, Sara," said Mom.

Cece looked at me, before I nodded for her to keep going up.

Mom furrowed her eyebrows. "She is Shea's younger sister," she stated.

"I know," I replied. "She's my friend. She's the one I told you about on my first day of school. Cece is really nice, I promise."

"Sara, that family ..." she trailed off.

I was taken aback. I could understand her apprehension towards Shea. But Cece? She was a girl, she was my age, and she was so sweet! What could be the issue? "What about their family?" I demanded to know.

My mother's green eyes narrowed. She didn't want to say anything, but she was holding back. "Just be careful," she said intensely, holding onto my upper arms. "And broaden your horizons. Don't just make one friend."

What was her problem? She hadn't been this judgemental in New York!

I didn't ask, though. I didn't want to start another fight. I didn't want to risk her changing her mind about letting me go to the party. "Well I might make another tonight. We are going to Zoey Eckhart's party." However, I couldn't see Zoey and I becoming chummy anytime soon.

"Eckart?" Mom repeated. It was another name that I could tell she recognised. Maybe it was their parents Mom had an issue with. Maybe they had all gone to school together and not got along. Mom shook it off. "Remember your curfew. Past ten-thirty and you're grounded, you hear?"

"I got it," I replied, before disappearing up the stairs.

I went into our small bathroom and gasped. Cece had already covered every available space with beauty products. The shower curtain was pushed back and the rail was being used to hang up several very revealing outfits.

Cece didn't seem fazed. She had already wiped her face clean with a wipe and was reapplying her makeup. She looked like an expert as she blended her eyeshadow perfectly.

I stood next to her in the mirror and felt thoroughly plain. Even with a half-applied face, Cece was stunning. Everything about Cece was perfection. Nobody ought to be that good looking. Her brother suffered from the same affliction. Me, on the other hand, I was normal. Pale skin, breakouts, pigmentation, acne scarring, shadows … and that was just my face.

"I can't believe your cheekbones aren't contoured," Cece commented. "Do you know how hard I have to work to give myself cheekbones," she said as she used a brush to chisel out her cheekbones.

Me, good cheekbones? I turned my face on an angle and saw that I did have naturally defined cheekbones. I'd never really admired them before.

"Pick something to wear," Cece instructed as she started to apply blush to her cheeks. "I brought over enough options for us both to choose something bomb."

I tentatively started to flip through the dresses that were hanging up on the shower rail. The dresses were all short and would be especially flattering on someone with a figure like Cece's. The dresses all had some sort of cut out, usually on the midriff where one's abs would look amazing. I did not have abs. I wasn't even sure if I had them under the little layer of belly fat I had.

"Cece, I'm not sure these will suit me," I murmured, my voice lacking confidence. "Or fit me."

"You're a six, right?" Cece checked.

I think we were both different size sixes. "Yes," I admitted.

"Me, too. All those are sixes. Choose one. You'll look hot in them all."

I bit the bullet and chose a black dress, the only one that didn't have cut outs. It was a short dress covered in some sort of shiny material. Upon feeling it, I realised it was latex. Oh, dear God. I couldn't pull that off.

Just as I was about to put it back, Cece squealed excitedly. "Oh, my God. You will look incredible in that!" she exclaimed.

"But it will be skin tight! Everything will show!" I hissed, embarrassed.

Cece frowned. "What are you hiding? A third nipple?" She shook her head and rifled through her bag. Pulling out something small and black, she threw it at me.

I managed to catch it, despite my poor reflexes. It was a black bikini. A tiny black bikini. No more than a tube top and bottoms that looked little more than a thong.

"Put those on, under the dress," Cece instructed, as she started to pull off her cheer uniform. She was not embarrassed at all to undress in front of me as she selected a red bikini from her bag.

Of course, I wouldn't be embarrassed if I had a figure like hers. I decided to stop being a coward and I quickly changed as well. Putting the bikini on was easy. Getting into the latex dress required some serious contortion. Cece helped me to pull the dress up and over my chest. It was a little tight, and she struggled with the zipper momentarily. Much to my humiliation, my breasts were a little big for the dress, and so I had the best cleavage I had ever had.

Cece slipped into a red strapless dress with midriff and hip cut outs. She looked damned incredible. I just felt fat. Once we were dressed, Cece sat me down on the edge of the bath and she started to apply makeup on me. She buffed in foundation and powder, filled in my brows, and created a smoky eye look to complement my outfit.

"I'm so jealous of your cheekbones," murmured Cece as she applied blush and highlight to my cheeks. Selfishly, it made me feel a little better that Cece envied me for something. She finished off my look with lipstick, mascara, and a spray that was meant to help makeup be waterproof.

Cece and I were different shoe sizes, something for which I was relieved. She had planned to put me in some dangerous looking stilettos. Luckily, I didn't own a pair of heels like that, so I wore my black Chucks, much to Cece's chagrin.

When Cece was finished, I couldn't believe my reflection. I actually looked pretty. I had never seen myself look like this. I didn't know I could look like this. My eyes were my favourite part. The smoky eyeshadow made the green of my eyes stand out brilliantly. Could she come and do my makeup everyday?

"Wow, Cece, thank you so much!" I exclaimed, inspecting every detail of her work.

Cece giggled. "I just can't wait to see Shea's face."

I blushed. I couldn't wait either. Though I couldn't help the tiny thought of insecurity that reminded me that I wouldn't ever look like this again, not unless Cece came and helped me.

"Now, come on. Let's get going or else Shea will send out a hunting party looking for you." She grabbed my hand and I laughed.

We both made our way downstairs, Cece's stiletto heels making more noise than my Chucks, which caused Mom too look up. Her eyes immediately widened.

"Oh my goodness, don't you girls look beautiful!" she remarked. She abandoned her magazine and walked over to us. That was when she noticed the latex of my dress, and the fact that I was nearly falling out of it. Perhaps I ought to grab a jacket. "Sara ..."

"Doesn't she look amazing, Dr Bryant?" asked Cece excitedly. "About time Sara stops hiding that bod under her clothes."

My hand immediately went to the cookie pouch I called a stomach. I wouldn't exactly call it a "bod".

I think Mom noticed my insecurity. Instead of telling me to change, she kissed my forehead and told me I was beautiful. I smiled at her, and Cece dragged me towards the door.

"Now, is there adult supervision at this party?" Mom cried after Cece.

"Oh, of course!" Cece promised over her shoulder.

"No alcohol, Sara!" Mom warned. "And home by ten-thirty!"

"Bye, Mom!" I waved at her, and we were out the door.

When we were safely out of ear shot, Cece giggled. "Zoey's brother is twenty-one. He buys the beer. He counts as an adult, right?"

I playfully slapped Cece's arm as we climbed in Shea's truck.

Chapter 10

I didn't know that Providence had gated communities, but it did. Cece drove us into an exclusive looking estate that contained enormous mansions concealed by large trees and concrete walls.

We hadn't even driven a hundred feet into the estate before I could hear the party.

"Zoey and her brother, Kyle, pay off the neighbours," Cece explained.

"Don't Zoey's parents care that they have a hundred teenagers at their house?" I wondered out loud.

Cece laughed. "No. Zoey's parents love that their house hosts all the gatherings. It makes them feel important. They're obsessed with status. It's sickening. But they were close with my parents, so I suppose we've always got to put up with them."

That just seemed weird. How could throwing a house party give people status?

"But at the end of the day, we get the free beer and a cool party house." Cece parked Shea's truck behind another expensive looking car on the street. "And I didn't have to kiss anyone's ass to get it." She smirked.

We both climbed out of the truck and started the walk up to the house. I felt like we were parked a half mile away, what with the dozens of cars lining the street. I was now extra grateful for my sneakers.

Each house seemed to get bigger than the last. When we finally came to the source of the music, my jaw dropped. Through the large, wrought iron gates, was a three-storey white plantation house. But while the façade of the plantation was kept, that being the traditional columns and large windows, I could see through the windows and open doors that the interior was entirely modernised.

Cece pulled me by the hand through the front door of the mansion and my astonishment only grew. Everything was open and huge. I could see through the entire house, right to the open louvre doors that led out onto a large deck. The house was all timber, metallics, and glass. Everything looked new and expensive, yet every surface was filled with bowls of snacks, red plastic cups, and bottles of who knows what.

There were people everywhere. I only recognised a handful. The music was blaring through a speaker system, and there were gyrating bodies all around me. Cece still had hold of my hand as she pulled me through the crowd to the kitchen.

The modern kitchen boasted a mammoth marble island, and there were currently half-naked girls covering nearly every inch and guys did body shots off of them. Cece merely leaned over a few to grab some new cups and a bottle of vodka.

"I don't want any!" I cried over the noise. "My mom will kill me!"

"Are you sure?" Cece shouted back.

I nodded. Cece poured a few shots worth of vodka into her cup and then filled the rest of soda. She poured me just the soda. Once we had our drinks, we made our way outside onto the deck. I was grateful for the temperature change. All those bodies made it unbearably hot in there. Not that the deck was any less empty.

Deck was really a poor description of the impeccably landscaped outdoors of Zoey's house. There was a huge, sprawling timber deck that was littered with expensive lounges, tables, and bench seats. In the centre of the deck was a gorgeous looking infinity edge pool that just seemed to drop off into the rest of the extensive garden.

We heard the sound of a smack, and we both realised that someone had just slapped Cece's ass. Cece turned around to punch the asshole when she realised it was Jamie. She still hit him, only playfully. Then she proceeded to stick her tongue down his throat and I knew that my companion was no longer going to hold my hand during this party.

I felt shorter than anyone. I wasn't wearing heels, and every guy here seemed to be over six foot. I tried to crane my neck to see if I could find Shea, but I just kept getting bumped and then bumping into people. I managed to make my way to a balcony, fenced by glass which gave the appearance of being invisible. I was standing next to a large pot plant and hiding in the corner.

"I am so lame," I cursed myself.

"I don't think you're lame," came a male voice from behind me.

I jumped and turned around. I immediately knew that I didn't recognise him. I hadn't seen him at school. He looked a little too old to be a high school student anyway.

Everything about him looked expensive and designer, down to his perfect fade haircut. He was tall and lean, and his blue eyes were appraising me hungrily. "In fact, I think you're pretty hot." He stepped towards me with an air of territory about him. I stepped backwards but I couldn't go anywhere. My back was touching the glass of the balcony.

He extended his hand and ran his knuckles down my bare arm. I flinched away.

"Aw, come on. Don't be like that. You can't walk into my house looking like that and not expect a little attention. What's your name?"

I could have vomited. This parasite, who could only be Zoey's brother, thought it was okay to encroach on a girl's personal space because of how she was dressed? Had he not been watching TV lately? That was not okay.

Adrenaline coursed through my body as I brought my knee up and into his groin. Kyle doubled over in pain and fell backwards into a table, knocking over several drinks that were subsequently dumped on him.

"My name is Come Near Me Again and I'll Cut It Off," I hissed. I turned around to get as far away from the letch as I could, but I walked directly into the hard chest of another guy. My reaction was to immediately throw him off me, but I recognised his scent a second later. Instinctively, I wrapped my arms around him for comfort.

"I was about to throw him off the balcony but I could see that you had yourself covered. Remind me never to cross you," Shea murmured into my hair. "However, there are just some things that I need to be made clear." Shea positioned me behind his body before he stood over Kyle. Kyle looked up and gasped when he saw Shea. "You even look at Sara again and we are going to have a serious problem," he spat.

"I didn't know she was Sara," stammered Kyle. "I wouldn't have tried if I knew it was her."

Kyle was genuinely afraid. Good, I thought. What a pig. I hope Shea scared him straight.

"Let me rephrase that," Shea said intensely. "You approach any girl like that again and we are going to have a serious problem. You're on the borderline of sexual assault, you absolute asshole."

Shea turned away from Kyle and took my hand, pulling me back into the crowd. When we found a pocket of space, he turned back to look at me, cupping my face with his hands.

Amongst all the noise, the people, and the chaos, my world stopped when Shea looked at me like he was. I saw such tenderness, concern, and ... well ... love in his eyes. My heart swelled at the thought.

"Are you okay?" he asked me.

I nodded. "Cece made me wear the dress."

"Not an excuse for him to behave like a freaking predator," Shea said firmly.

I smiled. "I'm glad you feel that way. I hope he won't be attacking anyone else tonight."

Shea smirked. "I think he'll be sitting his balls on some ice for the rest of the night, don't you worry." He laughed to himself. "By the way," he added, ducking his head down to my ear. "I love the dress." He practically purred the words, and a shiver went down my spine.

I found myself wrapping my arms over my stomach self-consciously. "Cece said you would. I think it is awful tight. I feel a bit exposed." Silly, really, to feel exposed in this dress when I had a tiny bikini on underneath it.

Shea could see the insecurity on my face. "Sara, I've said it once, and I'll keep saying it until you believe it. You are not of this world. I don't think you have any idea of how beautiful you are to me. Now, please, have a little fun."

And whenever he said those words, I believed them. I relaxed a little and tried to let myself enjoy the party. We moved around the different sections of the house together. There were games of beer pong, there was a keg stand on the other side of the deck, alcohol was flowing, and the music was loud. Shea didn't drink anything, though, and when I asked him why, he told me that he was driving me home before curfew. He wasn't putting me at risk by drinking.

We danced together on the dance floor that had formed in Zoey's living room, and I found myself feeling flushed, hot and bothered moving so closely with Shea to the beat of the music. He didn't take his eyes off of me, and I found it difficult to look away from him.

I wanted to kiss him. I wanted him to kiss me. But not here. Not in front of everyone.

At around nine forty-five, we found Cece and Jamie out by the pool. They had both changed out of their clothes and were wearing their bathing suits. It was then that I noticed Jamie had a matching tattoo on his chest, in the same script as Cece's, though this time it said "Cecelia".

I found it sweet, yet peculiar, that two people as young as them would gamble on their relationship like that. But, I supposed, when you know you know.

I wondered, if everything worked out, sometime down the road, if Shea would get a tattoo of my name.

As we talked, I started to notice a lot of the other party-goers. Guys who were shirtless, girls who were wearing bikinis. A lot of them, not all, but a lot, had tattoos on their chests. Not large, intricate designs of tribal ink or anything, but simple, fine, white line tattoos that simply read a name.

I remembered Cece telling me that she couldn't remember the name of the tattoo parlour where she had hers done. But wasn't it weird that so many people would have the same tattoo? Or at least, done by the same person. Why would so many of them tattoo their girlfriend's or boyfriend's name on their bodies? Was it like a mass dare or something?

"Why do so many of you have the same tattoo?" I asked the group, interrupting whatever conversation they were having.

Cece giggled, clearly drunk. "Because when you've got a hot piece, you need to mark your territory!"

Shea suddenly scooped me up and jumped in the pool. I didn't have time to scream before we hit the warm water. He took me under for only a few seconds before we resurfaced again.

I forgot my questions and proceeded to jokingly berate him for ruining my makeup. Shea and I couldn't keep our hands off of each other. He stripped off his shirt straight away, and I loved to hold onto him, to feel the warmth and the strength in his body as he held me. His hands, never roaming so far as to push me, but still made me feel butterflies in my stomach.

We were so close, our foreheads touching, our lips only an inch or too apart. I could feel his breath on my face. He was breathing quickly, just as quickly as I was. My heart was racing. I'm sure he could feel it. We were staring at each other so intensely, so deeply that we could easily see into each other's souls.

Holy shit, this was some real, intense stuff. My heart was pounding in my chest. I felt like I was going to throw myself at him right here in this pool, in and amongst the twenty other people frolicking about.

"I need to pee," I suddenly said.

Shea, taken aback, said, "What?"

I immediately scrambled out of his arms and he let me go immediately. "I've got to pee. I'll be right back." I swam to the edge of the pool and pushed myself out. I didn't dare look back at Shea, though I wagered I could pick his expression. "You're such a coward, Sara." I was running from what I was feeling. I was running because, Goddammit, this was frighteningly intense.

I was dripping all over the floor, though I'm sure water was better than the beer and other liquids that were currently present on Mr and Mrs Eckhart's floors. I didn't actually have to pee, so I decided to run out the front of the house for a few minutes to catch my breath, before going back inside and finding Shea again.

There were still people around in the front yard, so I went outside the iron gates and out onto the street. It was finally quiet. Or at least the music was slightly quieter here. I placed my hands on my hips as I paced back and forth for a bit. I concentrated on my breathing, slowing it down, and subsequently my heart.

Shea wasn't going to hurt me. He wasn't going to pressure me. I wanted him to kiss me, didn't I? Of course, I did. Just because it would be my first kiss, I didn't need to be a big chicken about it.

"Big night?"

I practically jumped out of my skin. I hadn't heard anyone approach, and yet all of a sudden, a large, intimidating man was standing before me, leaning against Zoey's gate. He wore only a pair of cargo shorts, showing off his muscular, tattooed chest. This man was covered in tattoos and piercings. He didn't look to have a clean piece of skin left. The largest piercing I saw was the spacer in his right ear, making his ear lobe appear as though it was the size of a golf ball.

"Um, yeah," I replied. "Just needed some air."

"Me, too," he replied. Had he been at the party? I hadn't seen him. But then, I hadn't recognised a lot of people, and there were easily a couple of hundred here. "I'm Lex," he introduced himself.

"Sara," I replied.

Lex came off of the gate and approached me, though not with the predatory prowl of Kyle, but one of ... curiosity. As he walked, he looked me up and down, appraising me. As he came closer, the light of the street lamp showed me his features properly. He was a lot older than me. He looked to be at least thirty, and he really had no business at this party.

"You're not what I expected," he commented.

My heart, which I had all but controlled a minute ago, took off again. I didn't feel safe. This man was a stranger, and he had just said something completely strange. I wanted to scream for Shea. I had my knee ready to take down my second attacker of the night.

"I don't know you," I told him firmly. "You must have me confused with someone else."

Lex laughed lightly. "I know you don't know me, Sara." He shook his head. "But I –"

"What the fuck are you doing here?"

I practically got whiplash as Shea pulled me away from Lex and positioned me behind him once more. I placed my hands on his back and exhaled the breath I had been holding. I was safe. But Shea wasn't, I worried. Who the hell was this guy?

"Be seeing you, Braverman," Lex taunted. "Be seeing you both." His cool eyes flicked to me.

Who the hell was this guy? Did I know him? I was certain I had never seen him before. He had the sort of unique appearance that you didn't forget. But he knew Shea. Is that how he knew me? Or knew of me?

Wait, did he just threaten me? Threaten us?

Lex disappeared down the dark street and Shea immediately took me in his arms, pulling me close. I was pressed up tightly against his chest, so tightly that I could feel his rapid pulse against my cheek. His face was pressed into the top of my head. He was matching his breaths to mine, though mine were erratic as it was.

"Shea, who was that guy?" I asked fearfully.

"I'm so sorry you had to see that," he apologised quietly. "You don't belong in the middle of my family drama."

"Family drama?" I repeated back to him.

I felt Shea nod against my head. "It's bullshit, really," he promised me. "Lex's dad and my dad, well, let's just say he's taken up the family tradition of hating my guts."

The way he had taunted Shea was just creepy. He had taunted me, too. "Did he threaten you?" I asked, pulling my head away slightly so that I could look up into his eyes to see the truth. "Did he threaten me?"

"Sara, Lex is a jackass with daddy issues and a chip on his shoulder. I'm honestly too young to remember what went on back then. But the feud of our parents has become my problem for some reason. I don't want you to worry. Nothing is ever going to happen to you, not while I'm around." He pressed his lips to my forehead and I relaxed a little.

And then I felt even more sympathy for Shea's burdens than I already did. It wasn't just his mom and his sister that he had to take care of. Shea was left with his father's problems, too. I wondered if maybe they could sort it out. If they both sat down to talk, they could agree that the sins of their fathers were not theirs to bear. But I wouldn't broach it tonight. I was honestly still a little too spooked to even think of seeing Lex again.

"Come on, I'm going to have to speed through town to get you home before your curfew. I am trying to make a good impression on your mom, remember?"

CHAPTER 11

Shea didn't let go of my hand as he drove me home, which made driving a stick all the more impressive. He somehow managed to change gears and drive one handed.

He was going between ten to twenty miles over the limit as we went through town. The one benefit of the party was that there were no cars on the road as everyone was at Zoey's.

"Aside from the jackass who won't be named, did you have fun tonight?" Shea asked me as we drove down the main street.

"Oh, yeah, kneeing Kyle Eckhart in the balls was a joy," I joked in an attempt to lighten the mood. I could feel the energy in the cab of Shea's truck. He was still full of adrenaline.

But he did laugh. "You impress me, you know. You do something every day that impresses me."

I cocked my head at him. That was actually a really sweet and thoughtful compliment. I never thought I would be impressive to anyone. I never endeavoured to be. I was just me. And if Shea found that impressive then … God, I hope he kissed me tonight. I wouldn't have the balls to initiate it.

Which was ironic considering I'd practically amputated Kyle's balls only a few hours ago.

"With four minutes to spare," Shea remarked, gesturing to the digital clock on his dash as he pulled into my driveway.

"Will you stay tonight?" I asked him, feeling incredibly vulnerable all of a sudden.

Shea placed his hand behind my headrest and turned his torso towards me. "I wish I could, but I can't tonight. I've got to check on my mom. See to some family stuff." He sighed. "Can I see you tomorrow?" he asked hopefully.

"I made plans with my mom tomorrow," I said regretfully in a quiet voice. "And considering the circumstances, I really think it's important that we hang out so that she can see nothing has changed. Maybe ... maybe you could meet us for dinner? I'll ask and call you if she's okay with it." If Mom could see just how non-threatening Shea was then I hoped she could come around to the idea of me having a boyfriend.

"Sounds good. Hey, if you're not busy on Sunday, would you like to come over to my house and meet my family? I know you've obviously already met Cece, but I'd like my mom to meet my girlfriend."

I felt completely stupid as my heart skipped a beat at the word. Casually, I attempted to ask, "Your girlfriend?"

"Oh," Shea's voice dropped. "I mean, that's what I thought you were. I'm sorry if I've made a mistake." I could tell that Shea really thought he'd put his foot in it.

"Shea, I'd love to meet your mom, as your girlfriend," I assured him.

Even in the dark, I could see that Shea was grinning. "Yeah?" he checked excitedly. "Great, well I'll pick you up at like eleven? You can come over for lunch or something?" Shea suddenly looked back at the clock on his dash and cursed under his breath. "You better get inside, Sara."

It was one minute to curfew. With that, I knew he wasn't going to kiss me tonight. "Right, okay." I nodded and climbed out of his car. I started towards my house, getting halfway up the driveway before something grabbed my arm.

I was suddenly spun around and before I knew it, Shea's lips were on mine. I was almost too surprised to react, having completely dismissed this idea not ten seconds ago. But it suddenly hit me that I was kissing Shea!

His lips were soft and gentle, and he wasn't pushing me to go farther than I was comfortable. One of his hands was on the back of my neck while the other was around my waist, hugging me against his body. I began to move my lips with his, praying that I was doing the right thing. Shea seemed to guide me as I felt all sort of butterflies in my stomach.

Except they weren't butterflies, they were freaking rampaging elephants as I fell completely under Shea's spell. I was in his arms and I felt as though I belonged there. He was mine and I was his and this was how it was meant to be. Love at first sight. Fate. All that crap. It was real and it was meant for us.

I didn't know how much time had passed when Shea broke our kiss. I certainly wasn't the one who broke it. I was practically panting, though my humiliation was lessened when I saw that Shea's shoulders were rising and falling quite quickly, too.

"Sweet dreams, Sara," he whispered, before turning back around to get into his truck.

I walked in the house in a daze. I barely noticed that mom was sitting in the living room. The TV wasn't on. She didn't have a book or a magazine. She was just waiting for me.

"Well," Mom said, with an edge to her voice, "he's punctual."

"Huh?"

"Have you been drinking, Sara?" Mom demanded to know. "You look drunk."

I suppose I was a bit. "No, Mom," I promised. "I didn't drink anything."

She seemed to accept my answer. "So, how was the party?"

"Um, yeah, good." I nodded. I mean, the time I spent with Shea was great. Everything else was really subpar. Stupid, pervert Kyle, and Lex, the guy who Shea said he had family drama with. He seemed like a total creep. I hoped I wouldn't see him again. "Zoey's house is super nice. We went swimming for a bit."

"I noticed the hair," Mom noted. "You'd better go and wash your hair. You don't want the chlorine to damage it," she warned.

I nodded again. I went to the base of the stairs before turning back towards her. "Hey, Mom."

Mom looked up at me, although I could see that her green eyes were glassy. Oh, my God. Was she about to cry? I couldn't ask her about Shea coming for dinner now. Instead, I went to her and hugged her tightly. She wrapped her arms around me even tighter.

"Thanks for letting me go. It means a lot," I whispered.

Mom let out a half laugh, half sob. "Go and wash your hair," she said, rubbing my back affectionately.

I couldn't stop thinking about the kiss. Not while I was in the shower. It took the water turning cold for me to realise the conditioner had been in my hair for nearly a half hour. The kiss was on my mind as I dressed in my pyjamas and as I got in bed.

Goddammit, I wanted to do that again. Never in my life had anything felt so right. It felt so right that the time in which we had known each other was fading away. I was losing all concern for it.

Before I went to sleep, I grabbed my phone and send Shea a text. I was trying to be funny, and flirtatious, both of which I had little experience in.

As far as kisses go, that does make my top ten.

He had to know that was my first kiss. I surely wasn't that good at it.

My phone vibrated seconds later with his reply.

Only top ten, huh? Well, my goal is now to crack the top five.

I laughed. I loved his sense of humour, but I was secretly glad I could look forward to another kiss. I quickly typed back my reply.

I don't know. That's a tough field to beat. Will take some serious practice.

Challenge accepted. I've got to go, babe. Family drama, you know. I'll speak to you tomorrow x

Shea seemed to have a lot of that. Family drama with his mom. Family drama with Zoey's parents. Family drama with Lex. I knew it was none of my business, but I wondered if he would ever tell me. He seemed to want to keep me out of it, at least, that's how it seemed when he reacted so negatively to Lex being at the party.

Shea was so used to carrying burdens by himself. I hoped, maybe, one day he might share them with me. These broad shoulders had to come in handy sometime.

Night x

I fell asleep dreaming about that practice.

In the midst of a deep sleep, I started to dream that I was hearing voices. Two voices specifically. Shea's and my mom's. They seemed clear to me, as though they were speaking close in proximity to me.

They seemed to be arguing. A foreshadowing perhaps.

"I will not have my daughter around you and your lot," my mom hissed. Why did she have to be angry in my dream? Why couldn't she be happy and accepting? "You need to leave her alone."

Shea's voice was quiet, and he sounded tired and hurt. No. I didn't want him in pain. I felt my subconscious reach out to him, but like always, when you're dreaming, you can never touch.

"You know why I can't do that," Shea's voice replied.

"Well, you can damn well try," Mom shot back. "She's not safe with you!"

"I can protect her," Shea growled. He sounded angry now.

Stop arguing! I willed my subconscious. Make up! Be friends! Be happy.

But it didn't work. Mom scoffed. "You can't even protect yourself!" she retorted. Her voice was like acid.

Shea didn't say anything. Where had I got that thought from? Why on earth would I think that Shea couldn't protect himself?

"Not many people would ever dare speak to me like that, Dr Bryant," Shea said after a moment of quiet.

"I'm a mother, Shea." Mom's voice had calmed during the silence. She sounded just as intense, but not as emotional. "You'll understand when you have your own daughter one day just the lengths you will go to protect her. Sara isn't like you," she said slowly, emphasising the last word. "She isn't," she insisted. "You know it, and I know it. So you know she isn't safe with you, with any of you. You need to leave her alone. You know it's the right thing to do. If you care about her the way you say you do, then you will do this. She is not safe, and it is clear by the state of you that you're out of your depth. Deal with it in your own way, but for God's sake, leave my baby out of it!"

I couldn't understand where my subconscious was pulling this argument from. My imagination was running wild, dreaming up all sorts of nonsense for my mom to be afraid of.

Shea didn't speak again for a while. I think I drifted in and out of the dream, occasionally hearing Shea sigh, suck in breaths and grunt strange noises, but eventually I heard him utter, "Thank you," to my mom. I didn't hear anything else.

My dream shifted after that, back to imagining the next time I would get to kiss Shea. I hoped it would be tomorrow.

When I woke up the next morning, I didn't feel rested. That dream I had was lingering in my head, bothering me. I knew it was just in my head but I wanted to quickly text Shea. I didn't like the idea of him feeling or sounding hurt, even if it was just in my subconscious.

Good morning! Sorry if I wake you. Just wanted to let you know I was thinking of you x

I hit send before I realised what a textbook, cliché girlfriend I sounded like. I never thought I would be one of those people who sent sappy good morning texts but yet here I was.

Shea always replied instantly to my messages, so I waited a moment for him to reply with something similar. But the little dots telling me he was typing didn't appear.

Weird.

I'm going to ask my mom about tonight. I'll let you know what she says.

Great, now I'm a double texter.

Still no dots. No reply. I checked the time and saw it had only just ticked past eight. He was probably still asleep. No need to freak out, Sara.

I shook it off, put my phone in the pocket of my sweats and slipped into my robe. I then trudged downstairs and was greeted by the comforting scent of bacon. Mom was cooking breakfast. She never cooked breakfast.

She had cooked a hell of a lot more than that. As I came over to the counter I could see that she had been to the market. She had bought all kinds of fresh fruit, yoghurt, she had made oatmeal and pancakes, and was in the midst of frying eggs and bacon.

"Wow, Mom, what's all this?" I remarked.

Mom was fully dressed, perfect makeup applied, and not a hair out of place. She smiled warmly at me. "Morning, hon," she chirped. Wow, she was in a good mood. Maybe it was a good time to ask about dinner tonight. "Just thought I'd commemorate our first week in our new home by breaking in the kitchen."

"You hardly broke in the old kitchen and we lived there for twelve years," I jested.

Mom laughed. "Just trying some new things. I'm in a good mood today."

Oh my God, she was humming. She really was in a good mood.

"So, what movie did you want to see today? Is there anything out that you'd like to see?"

I really didn't know what was out. The last month of my life had centred around moving and the last week had been pretty consumed with all things Shea. I pulled my phone out of my pocket and quickly noticed I still didn't have a reply from Shea. I brushed it aside and pulled up the website for the local theatre.

While we ate breakfast, Mom and I discussed the three options the local theatre had for us and decided on the action comedy. Neither one of us liked horror movies and Mom didn't like sad movies so the romantic drama was out.

These pancakes were the fluffiest I had ever eaten. Mom quickly confessed she had bought those from Sally's, but she had managed to fry the eggs herself. After breakfast I checked my phone frequently as I helped her to clean up the kitchen.

"Expecting a call, hon?" she asked me.

"It's Shea," I replied truthfully. "He usually replies to me straight away but he hasn't yet. I don't know. He could still be sleeping." My phone told me it was approaching nine-thirty.

"Boys, you can't rely on them," she said flippantly. Just as I was about to tell her Shea wasn't the type to just blow me off, she clapped her hands and said, "Come on, let's get ready. I'll tell you what, we'll drive into Newtown and go to the salon there. It's so pretty, I've thought so each time I've driven past it this week. We'll get blowouts and then go to the theatre there."

Mom practically ran up the stairs like an excited child. What had gotten into her this morning?

I decided against testing my mom's mood until I heard from Shea. By the time I'd showered, dressed, and had time to dig around in my boxes for my makeup bag, he still hadn't messaged me back.

I didn't want to be worried, but this was unusual for Shea. He had told me last night that he had some family drama, but I still didn't really know the details. I decided to text Cece. She could at least tell me he was still passed out in his room and hadn't had a chance to text me back.

Hey Cece, just wondering if you've heard from Shea this morning? He isn't replying to my messages and I'm a bit worried. Let me know.

I added a couple of smiley face emojis to my text so I didn't sound completely like a stalker girlfriend and then shoved my phone in my jeans pocket.

I found Mom waiting for me on the landing, a bright smile still plastered on her face. "Ready to go, hon?" she asked excitedly.

I nodded. I placed my hand on my back pocket just to double check I still had it and couldn't wait to feel it vibrate with a text message. Not knowing was freaking me out.

We both grabbed our purses and Mom grabbed her car keys and we both settled into her Mercedes. The engine purred to life and she switched the radio station over to a chipper pop song.

Mom sang along to the radio as we drove through town. I couldn't help but practically press my nose against the glass as I looked for Shea or Cece or anyone I recognised who could tell me that Shea was okay.

It was only now occurring to me that I didn't have his address. I couldn't drive to his house and see him. I shuffled awkwardly in my seat as I pulled my phone out from my back pocket. I checked my reception and even sent my mom a smiley face emoji just so I could check that my phone was actually sending my messages.

My text flashed up on the touch screen in her car, and she smiled. "You're cute," she commented.

But neither Shea nor Cece had replied. I was just about to message Zoey on Facebook when Mom pulled into a parking spot outside a fancy looking salon. I hadn't noticed that we were no longer in Providence and that we were now in Newtown.

Mom was right. This salon was nice. It was all white, with a fancy, calligraphy sign on the window offering services for ladies. We climbed out of the car and walked inside and were immediately greeted by a friendly receptionist.

The salon looked a bit like a hotel. The white tile on the floor was reflective, and the chairs looked to be all white leather. The mirrors were gilded with silver, and there was a selection of gossip magazines on the tables before each station. The only thing that ruined the ambience was the scent of acetone in the air from the manicurist who was working at the back of the salon, although the receptionist had tried to cover the smell by burning a vanilla candle at her desk.

"Good morning," she greeted kindly. "Do you have an appointment?" She looked like she belonged into this environment. Her blonde hair was coloured, toned, and highlighted to perfection, and her makeup made her look like she was a fifties pin-up girl. I wished I had the talent to line my lips like hers.

I didn't know if you'd need an appointment here. It wasn't that busy.

"No," replied my Mom, "but my daughter and I were after a blowout if you have the space?"

"Your daughter?" repeated the receptionist in disbelief. "Oh, my, I could have sworn you were sisters."

She wasn't sucking up. We got that a lot. Mom took care of her skin. Having me super young also helped.

Mom laughed lightly, and politely. "You're too kind."

The receptionist led us over to two empty chairs, and allowed us to put our purses down, before taking Mom over to the basin first to wash her hair. I sat down in the comfortable chair and stared at my phone for what felt like the hundredth time this morning.

A few minutes later, the receptionist returned with a cup of coffee for me. I looked up at her and smiled. But she frowned. "Boy troubles?" she guessed.

I nearly scoffed. "How did you know?"

"You have that look. We've all had it before," she said knowingly.

I spied my mom with the stylist. Her hair was still being pre-rinsed, and she couldn't possibly hear me over the spray of the water.

"It's my boyfriend," I admitted to the receptionist. I now wished I knew her name. I then realised that was the first time I had ever referred to Shea as my boyfriend out loud. "We had this really special moment last night, and we were texting back and forth after, but this morning I've heard nothing. He usually replies to me straight away." I sighed. "I'm this close to messaging his ex-girlfriend just to see if she knows anything."

"Oh, honey, don't do that," the receptionist gasped. "Boys don't over-analyse things like we do. They reply to a text three hours after they received it and don't give it a second thought. Meanwhile, we're spending those hours stressing that they're not interested anymore."

I mean, I was certainly over-analysing. But I didn't think that he wasn't interested anymore. I mean, he was interested! I couldn't doubt that.

She could see the stress and confusion on my face and smiled at me comfortingly. "I once had a boyfriend who would make me feel all sorts of butterflies, and then would suck with the communication. Like because we had talked in person, the texting didn't matter. We would make verbal plans, and he didn't get why I would text him to confirm or anything like that. So I sat him down, and I told him that if he left me on read one more time then he could forget about seeing my nice underwear again." She winked and I blushed.

"When did you guys break up?" I wondered.

"We didn't," she replied. "I married the idiot." She held out her left hand and showed me her twinkling wedding ring on her perfectly manicured finger.

I knew she was trying to make me feel better, but I couldn't help but know that Shea wasn't like that. All this week he had been replying to me instantly. And then nothing today? It just didn't make sense.

To not even have a reply from Cece was really worrying me.

"Thanks," I said gratefully. Even if her situation couldn't help me, I appreciated the effort. At that moment, another customer entered the salon and she left to serve them.

I decided to call him. Screw it. I tapped on his number and it started to ring. And ring. And ring. Eventually, I heard an automated voicemail box. I hung up before leaving a message.

Hell, I was already a double texter, I might as well be a double caller as well. I called again, but this time the call didn't ring out. The call ended after two rings. I pulled the phone away from my ear in shock. Oh my God, did he just reject my call?

Shea was awake alright. He was awake, and he'd rejected my call. He didn't want to speak to me.

That stung. The really freaking hurt, way more than I expected. What possible explanation could he have for kissing me last night, flirting with me the way he did, making me feel all sorts of things, and say all sorts of things, and then just ignore me today? Where the hell did he get off?

My brain involuntarily took me back to a conversation I had had with Cece this week. The part specifically where she told me that she and Jamie had only lasted three hours before having sex. I mean, I know Shea told me that it didn't matter to him, but what if ...?

I shook away the thought. No, I had to think better of him than that.

By that time, another stylist had come to collect me and she took me over to the basin. I shoved my phone back in my pocket and tried to forget about Shea while my hair was washed.

Chapter 12

I didn't hear from Shea again on Saturday. He never replied to my texts. He never called me back. Not even Cece texted me back.

And it took all my willpower not to message Zoey to ask if she had seen Shea at all today.

I tried my best to put on a happy face for my mom. Today was clearly important to her. We got blowouts, we saw the movie. I wasn't concentrating, but I made sure the laugh when she did. She then took me out to lunch at this little Italian restaurant that she told me she had been frequenting for lunch.

By the time we'd walked along the main street and shopped in every little boutique that Mom pulled me into, it was nearing dinner time. Mom asked if I wanted to find a restaurant for dinner, but I opted for fast food on the way home. She obliged me.

It was clear that Shea wasn't going to be joining us for dinner anyway.

"Are you okay, Sara?" Mom asked me quietly as we drove back towards Providence.

"Yeah," I lied.

"You know you can tell me if something's wrong," she urged.

I stole a glance at her, but she was looking at the road. "It's Shea," I admitted. "He hasn't talked to me all day. I don't know, I'm just a little worried." Little was an understatement.

For a split second, I could had sworn she smiled. But it was gone so fast I was questioning whether I'd really seen her do it. "Oh, honey," she said sympathetically, "teenage boys are never reliable. Best to wait for college to meet someone. Someone mature, a pre-med, or a pre-law student?" she suggested.

I mean, I knew she wasn't Shea's number one fan, but she had sure given up on him quickly. It pissed me off. "Mom, a little support would be nice," I snapped.

"I am being supportive!" she retorted, huffing. "I'm telling you that you shouldn't worry yourself over a silly high school boy when there are bigger and better things to look forward to in your future!"

I wasn't going to get the kind of support I wanted from Mom. Unless I was in the mood to bash Shea for being a member of the male species, she wasn't the person to talk to. I needed a girlfriend to talk about my boyfriend problems. But Cece wasn't answering either.

It was incredible how I had gone from such a big high last night, to feeling so flat and miserable today. I freaking hated this. Shea had honestly better hope something had happened to him because he couldn't be this much of a jerk on purpose.

I immediately took that thought back. I felt horrible and guilty for it.

When Mom pulled into a drive through, I mumbled my order for a cheeseburger and I held our food on my lap as she finished the drive back to our house. But I wasn't really hungry.

Mom was still acting like today had been the best day ever. She put our food on plates and flipped through the DVR before settling on something to watch. I placed my phone on the arm of my chair so that I could see it if a message popped up. I didn't have the sound on. I didn't want Mom saying anything if she heard my phone chime.

I practically jumped out of my skin every time an email came through for some website I was subscribed to or if a new show had been added to Netflix. And disappointment filled me every time when I realised it wasn't from Shea.

When the show finished, I took my plate to the kitchen and excused myself, offering my mom a thank you for our day out. She smiled at me warmly, before selecting something else to watch. I went upstairs and changed into my pyjamas and climbed into bed.

I needed to put my phone away before it drove me crazy. But I needed to send him one last message.

Hope your day was good. I missed hearing from you. I hope everything is okay. I'm here if you need me. I'll see you tomorrow at 11 xx

I hadn't forgotten about his invitation to meet his mom. He had invited me only yesterday. I would be ready to go at eleven, and ready to listen to whatever explanation he had for today.

I didn't sleep well. I didn't have the same dream as I did the night before, but I still didn't sleep that great. I woke up just after eight o'clock, and I didn't feel rested.

And surprise, surprise. There were no messages on my phone. Only junk emails.

I jumped in the shower to wake myself up, but all that did was give me time to think about yesterday, Friday, and today. What would I do if it really was over? It had barely started. How could I be this anxious, this much of a mess, when it had barely started?

In frustration, I pulled on a pair of yoga pants and my sneakers, as well as a sports bra and a tank top. I decided to go running. I never ran, but I thought that focusing on not dying while exercising might take my mind off of things and help eleven o'clock come faster.

Mom wasn't up. Her door was still shut when I walked past. I shoved a house key in my bra and my phone in the waist band of my yoga pants and took off out my front door.

I was so unfit. The only time I ran was during mandatory gym class. I was fortunate to have the kind of metabolism that didn't punish me to the extent that I needed to exercise regularly, but that didn't mean I shouldn't.

I left my street and ran down the beach. I tried to concentrate on my breathing, the sound of the waves crashing on the beach, and the feeling of the sand underneath my feet. The cool sand hadn't dried since the tide had gone back out, so it was still pretty compact under my feet. It helped my speed, so I didn't look like an unfit elephant while running. At least, I hoped I didn't.

I pushed myself. Hard. I sprinted for ten seconds, and then slowed, then sprinted again. I ran until I felt like I was going to vomit my stomach up. My heart was thumping a million miles an hour. My head was going even faster.

I think I stopped breathing, and I blacked out before I even hit the ground.

I heard voices, I think.

"... protect ... watch ... saw ... faint."

Male, deep, Shea.Shea was here. I tried to say his name, but my mouth wasn't working.

I couldn't make out what my mom was saying. But her tone was angry. It reminded me of my dream the other night.

I slipped back out of consciousness and I couldn't hear anything else.

I felt something cool on my forehead. I blinked a few times and my vision focused. I was in my living room. Mom was sitting beside me with a concerned look on her face. She was dabbing my forehead with a cool cloth.

"Oh, honey, you're awake!" she exclaimed. "I was this close to taking you to the emergency room."

I tried to lift my head. I didn't have a headache. I was just really foggy.

"Here." Mom handed me a glass of water. "Next best to IV fluids."

I obediently took the glass and drank thirstily. "What happened?" I asked her.

"You passed out on the beach," she told me. "You're dehydrated. Did you drink much yesterday? I've been racking my brain but I can't remember if I saw you drinking anything. Not even the coffee at the salon."

I remembered running. I didn't think I remembered passing out. I finished my glass of water and Mom poured me another from the pitcher she had on the coffee table. "Where's Shea?" I asked.

I immediately looked to our kitchen and dining room, but he wasn't standing there. Had he gone outside?

Mom frowned. "He was never here," she replied.

No, that can't be right. "I heard him," I insisted. "I came to for a bit, and I heard his voice." I was certain of it.

Mom shook her head. "No, hon, you must have been dreaming."

I wasn't dreaming. Shea and Mom had been talking. Arguing, even. They sounded just like they did in the dream I had the other night. Well, then … maybe I had been dreaming?

"Then how did I get here? You can't have carried me here all the way from the beach!" I was getting emotional. I had been certain I had heard Shea's voice. I had been certain he was here, for me, and everything was okay. Shea had to have been the one who found me on the beach and brought me back home.

"Oh, Sara, you've seen those videos online of those moms who can lift cars off of their children. I went looking for you after you weren't answering your phone and I found you down the other end of the beach," Mom said fluidly. She rubbed my arm comfortingly. "You've had a hard start to the day, hon. Just rest, drink your water. I want that pitcher gone before half twelve."

Half twelve? "What time is it now?" I asked her.

Mom check her watch. "Eleven forty-five," she replied. Smiling, she got up, and went into the kitchen. I heard her filling up the coffee pot with beans.

I stared at the glass of water in my hands. I can't have dreamed that. I sounded so real. I spied Mom out of the corner of my eye flitting about the kitchen. She wouldn't lie, would she?

I didn't want to call my mom a liar, but I wasn't crazy. I hadn't imagined Shea being here. I wasn't concussed. I didn't have a head injury she could blame hallucinations on.

The argument I heard today sounded just like the argument I dreamt on Friday night. But it got me wondering, what if it hadn't been a dream? What if there really had been an argument between my mom and Shea on Friday night?

I found myself going over the words my mom had used in my "dream". She accused Shea of being dangerous. She didn't want me around his "lot". Was that supposed to be his friends? Did she think he was in a gang? Mom kept emphasising I wasn't like him. Like what? He's a guy and I'm a girl?

I went over and over the words she used in my head, and the only thing that made sense to me was that my mom had beat him down to the point where he wouldn't come around anymore. I didn't want to believe it, but it could explain everything.

I kept watching her out of the corner of my eye. Something was sticking out to me in and amongst the dozens of theories that were now swimming around in my head.

Mom knew something.

Mom knew something about Shea that she didn't want me to know. The way she had been berating Shea said more than it just being a simple fear of teen pregnancy. She was genuinely worried for my safety.

Something else was sticking out to me. She had said, "You can't even protect yourself!"

What was that supposed to mean? Why would she say something like that?

My head, like it had been on the beach, was racing a million miles an hour. Why had Shea been at my house at that time of night? What reason would he have to speak to my mom at that time if were not an emergency? And what kind of emergency, what kind of desperation, would take him to my mom in the middle of the night?

She was a doctor, too, and not just my mother.

Had ... had Shea been hurt?

I looked over at my mom again, and she had disappeared into the laundry room. For the first time in my life, the person I trusted most was not my mom. She was lying to me, and I was going to find out what about.

I threw off the blanket that she had covered me with and grabbed my car keys from the table near the front door. I was already out the door and in my car before I heard Mom yell in protest.

I couldn't help but cry as I drove. What the actual fuck had happened to my life in this past week? Everything seemed so simple in New York. I went to school, I got good grades, and I was all set for getting into a good college. I had a great relationship with my mom, and we were a team.

And now, after moving to her home town, everything had gone to shit. Mom had changed. I had changed. I had learned there was more to life than college prep and homework. Meeting Shea had stirred something inside of me that I hadn't known was there. I was opened to a whole new world of experiences that I had previously shut myself off from.

I wasn't about to let my mom take that away from me without a fight.

It took me driving past Sally's to realise that I had no idea where I was going. I only knew one address from Shea's group of friends, and I started towards Zoey's house without hesitation.

Zoey's house, or mansion, looked much different in the daylight. Or rather, much cleaner when there wasn't cups, vomit, and food littering their front yard. I parked in front of her gate and was grateful when I found that it was unlocked. I quickly jogged up to her front door with no shame and knocked loudly. I then realised that there was a doorbell by the pot plant on the porch. I pressed it, and a loud, traditional chime sounded.

A few minutes later, an older, yet still beautiful woman answered the door. She had to be Zoey's mom. Her hair, like Zoey's, was bleach blonde. Her makeup looked like a professional had applied it, down to the eyelash extensions which gave her a very youthful appearance. Her clothes looked to be designer, and they clung to her fit figure well. What made me certain she was Zoey's mom was the look of disapproval on her face as she looked at me.

"Hi, Mrs Eckhart," I greeted politely.

"Do we know you?" she sniffed.

"Uh, no, you don't, but I go to school with Zoey. Is she here?"

Mrs Eckhart nodded. "Yes, she is. Who are you?"

I then realised I hadn't introduced myself. "My name is Sara. Sara Bryant. I just moved to town with my mom."

Recognition flooded Mrs Eckhart's face. She knew my name. I wondered if Zoey had complained about me to her mom. But Mrs Eckart's expression didn't stop there. She actually looked nervous. I couldn't be sure, but it looked like nerves to me.

"Actually, Sara, Zoey just stepped out. I'm sorry but you need to go now." And to my shock, Mrs Eckhart closed the door in my face.

I stood on their porch for a few minutes astounded. Was I not allowed to be there? Had Zoey told her parents that she didn't want to see me? Why on earth would she be that specific? I took a few steps away from the house and then looked back at the upstairs windows.

Zoey was watching me from the centre window, not even pretending to have "stepped out" as her mom claimed. She had a blank expression on her face as she looked down on me.

I wasn't expecting Zoey to have all the answers and be my best friend. I was just hoping that she would be able to point me in the right direction, or at least give me a clue as to what the hell had gone on since the party.

Something was going on, and I was determined to find out what.

I didn't know where Shea and Cece lived. I didn't know where anyone else lived, and it was fruitless to be driving around for the rest of the day going nowhere. I decided to confront them at school tomorrow and demand to be told what was going on.

I was pretty sure Mom was lying to me. Shea wasn't talking to me. Neither was Cece. Mrs Eckhart seemed nervous in my presence. I had had enough, goddammit.

Until I had spoken to Shea, I wasn't going to confront my mom with my suspicions. The last thing I needed was to be wrong and to implode my relationship with mother. We had been as thick as thieves for seventeen years. I couldn't wreck that on the off chance I was wrong.

That didn't make me any more pleasant to be around, though, when I got home. Mom immediately scolded me for leaving the house without telling her. I listened to the lecture for a few minutes before going upstairs to my room.

I literally didn't have anything else I could do except study. Everything else was up in the air, and everything else seemed so much more important than a book that was written a century ago.

I tried to concentrate on my homework, but my mind kept taking me elsewhere. I tried to think of which was worse: Mom lying to me, or Shea blowing me off. The thought of Shea taking off with someone else after how close we had become hit me like a punch in the gut. I hated the thought of him suddenly losing interest and ditching me. It just didn't seem right to me. I couldn't imagine it. Well, of course I could imagine it, but with how I felt when we kissed, how I imagined the stars aligning, the Fates singing the hallelujah chorus, I couldn't imagine that Shea would be the type to just ditch me without a good reason.

Which brought me back to my mom. And honestly, if she was lying to me, even if it was to protect me, I knew that it would hurt more. Mom had never lied to me. The last lie she had told me was about Santa Claus. Mom had always been transparent with me.

She let me know when she was struggling financially, especially when she was making it through med school and her residency. I learned to go without some weeks and adapt. She was always honest about her ambitions and her fears for me. How many times had she stressed that I was not to get pregnant, and that I was going to a four-year college?

This honesty allowed us to have good times. It allowed us to be closer than most mothers and daughters, I thought. I didn't want her to lie to me, and I couldn't shake the feeling that there was more to her reasons for not liking Shea.

I pretended to study when Mom came up to check on me, and later on in the evening, she brought me up a chicken salad sandwich for dinner.

"How are you feeling now, Sara?" she asked, feeling my forehead.

"Fine," I replied. "Shea still hasn't texted me." It was the truth, but I wanted to see if I could elicit a normal response from her. Prove me wrong, Mom, I willed.

Instead, she clicked her tongue and shook her head. "Well, at least you know now you can stop wasting your time and focus on your studies," she said positively. "He was never good enough for you, anyway, Sara," she assured me.

"Okay, well, I'd better get back to it." I gestured to the open book I was pretending to read. She took my hint and left, closing the door behind her. A tear rolled down my cheek and feel onto the book, the pages soaking up the moisture. I grabbed my phone as a sob escaped my throat.

Please. I don't know what's going on but I need you. I think my mom is lying to me and I need you.

I cried as my message went ignored again. No matter what my mom said, how could he not come to me when I was feeling like this? If he needed me, I would be there in a heartbeat.

I turned my face into my pillow so that my sobs were muffled. I fell asleep shortly after.

CHAPTER 13

I woke up the next morning to an empty house. Mom had left a note saying that she'd had an early consult so I was left alone with my thoughts.

Once again, I slept like crap, and so I looked like crap. I tried my best with makeup but not much could hide bloodshot, sleep deprived eyes and bags that looked like freaking balloons.

Despite how I felt, I was excited to go to school. I wanted to speak to Shea. I wanted to pounce on him and not get off of him until I had answers. I hated this past weekend. I hated it with every fibre of my being. I hated feeling helpless, and worthless, and goddamn lied to. I needed Shea to tell me the truth because my mom sure as hell wasn't going to.

So long as Shea was ignoring me, Mom thought it was reason to celebrate.

I barely nibbled on an apple before I grabbed my book bag and keys and headed to school. I didn't realise it was so early, but I was one of the first cars into the lot. I took one of the closest parking spots and waited. I was watching the entry drive way in my rear-vision mirror, just waiting for Shea's black truck to pull in.

It was nearly eight-thirty when I finally saw Shea's truck pull into the lot. My heart leapt out of my chest as I threw open my door and grabbed my book bag from the passenger seat.

Shea parked across the lot from me, and I was dodging and weaving between cars to make it over to him as quickly as I could. But I stopped in my tracks when I saw that it wasn't Shea who climbed out of the car. It was Cece and Jamie. Where was Shea?

Disappointment filled me, but I then realised that I could still get answers from them about Shea. I would also demand to know why Cece hadn't bothered to reply to any of my messages over the weekend, as well. I wasn't in the mood for niceties.

I adjusted my book bag on my shoulder and marched over to them. When they saw me coming, they exchanged a questionable expression before both of their eyes returned to me.

I immediately noticed that Cece seemed really off. She was usually so chirpy and bright, but she seemed so solemn today. Even the way she was dressed was different. She usually wore tank tops, or something revealing her athletic figure. But today she was wearing dark sweats and an oversized grey hoodie. She honestly looked like she had been to a funeral according to the expression on her face. What the hell was going on?

"Hey!" I called out, as soon as I was in earshot. "What the hell happened this weekend?" I demanded to know. "Shea hasn't spoken to me all weekend. You weren't replying either." I thought back to Mrs Eckhart slamming her front door in my face. "Even Zoey's mom refused to talk to me. Seriously, what the hell? Is Shea okay?" Why wasn't he at school, anyway? Why was Cece driving his truck?

Jamie took Cece's hand and he squeezed it comfortingly, however, he didn't meet my eye.

"He's okay, Sara," Cece told me quietly. She stole quick glances up at me, but like Jamie, she wasn't meeting my eye.

My stomach was in knots and panic started to fill me. What was actually going on? What the hell was wrong with them?

Jamie pulled on Cece's hand and she started to follow him towards the main school building. Cece looked like a different person. It was almost as if someone had possessed her body, as though she was reading from a script.

I was dumbfounded for a minute before I continued after them. "Wait!" I cried. "Cece, what's wrong? What the hell is going on? You're not telling me something!"

"He's fine!" Cece insisted, her voice still off. "You had better get to class. We're running late." Cece and Jamie took off then, walking at such a pace that helped them to disappear into the crowd of students all filing into the school.

I wanted to cry. I wasn't to burst into tears and sob right there in the parking lot. Something was going on that they weren't telling me. Something was going on that they didn't want me to know.

I hated this. I hated not knowing. I hated feeling helpless and useless. As I looked around me desperately, trying to find the face of one of Shea's friends so that I could beg them for information, I noticed that half the students were deliberately avoiding my eyes. People were diverting around me, purposefully avoiding me.

What in the actual hell was going on?

I couldn't give up on Cece. She was my friend. She had to tell me the truth. I took a few deep breaths and composed myself, ducking into the school and hurrying towards my locker to grab my books for Spanish.

As I walked through the halls the same thing kept happening. People were moving away from me, like I smelled bad or something, deliberately altering their course to avoid crossing paths with me.

I walked into the classroom and looked for Cece at our usual table at the back. But she wasn't there. It took my two seconds to see that she was sitting beside Liza at another table. They were deep in conversation. Either that or they were trying to appear deep in conversation to avoid me.

Well, it wasn't going to stop me. I walked over to their desk and cleared my throat.

Cece looked up at me, though her expression told me that she hadn't wanted to. She honestly looked like she was in pain.

"You need to tell me what is going on," I instructed firmly. "Shea isn't talking to me. You're acting weird. Half the school is treating me like I have bad BO or something. Seriously, Cece, you're my friend." There was a begging tone in my voice. Hell, I was begging.

Cece looked at Liza who was behaving just as oddly. Liza's shoulders were tense as she avoided my gaze. "Sara, I'm not ... I can't explain, I'm sorry," she mumbled. She then turned her body away from mine, dismissing me.

I couldn't believe my ears. Cece wasn't going to say anything further. I retreated back to my seat and pretended to listen through Spanish. But really, I struggled to take my eyes off of the back of Cece's head.

Something weird was going on. Something bad, I feared. And they were all tongue tied by it. Was it illegal? Was that why it was so secretive?

This suddenly felt so much bigger than my mom merely not liking Shea as my boyfriend. There was something bigger going on. And they were all in on it. It made me wonder if my mom was aware of this, too.

Shea wasn't at school for some reason. Half the population were pretending as though I didn't exist. I needed to find out the reason for this before I went crazy.

Cece completely ignored me in English, as well. I sat by myself and thought up creative ways of trying to find out Shea's address.

I daydreamed through the rest of my classes, or rather I watched as people continued to ignore me. Even some of the teachers seemed to be avoiding my eye, but that could have been my imagination. I think by the time I got to lunch, I was feeling paranoid.

Shea's table, sans Shea, was full as usual, but there was no invitation for me to join them. Their heads were all down, and they didn't seem as cheerful or enthusiastic as they had been last week.

I decided to sit by myself on a small table down the back of the cafeteria. This was how I had expected it to be last week as the new girl anyway. I just hadn't expected for everyone to treat me as though I had freaking leprosy.

I picked at my macaroni and cheese as I mindlessly flipped through social media. I found myself checking Shea's socials like a stalker, but he hadn't posted anything new online. I was so engrossed in what I was doing on my phone that I hadn't noticed someone join me at my table.

When I saw a large figure in front of me, I jumped, nearly dropping my phone in cheese sauce.

I recognised him from the game on Friday night, and the party afterwards. He was on the football team, and he wore a letterman jacket just in case you'd forgotten. He looked like a guy who spent an awful lot of time on the weight machines in the gym, and he was really large for a teenager, but I suppose if you want a scholarship, you've got to work hard.

His face was youthful and cute, and his green eyes were actually meeting mine which was a nice change from today. "Hey, sorry, didn't mean to scare you," he greeted after I'd quickly composed myself. "I'm Josh."

"It's okay," I replied. "I'm Sara."

"I know." He grinned. He had a really cute smile, with deep dimples on either side of his cheeks. "So you and Braverman, what happened there? Are you guys over already?"

I was taken aback by his question. Was that what people were thinking? I suddenly realised how it looked. I had been practically attached at the hip with Shea and his friends last week, and now here I was sitting alone like a loser who'd just been dumped.

Dumped. Wow, that word was frightening. Did it apply to me? Was this how people got dumped nowadays? I mean, I had never been broken up with before, but was this how it happened? Did guys just stop texting you and then tell all of their friends to pretend like you don't exist?

I shook off the thought. Shea and my mom had fought. That was the one concrete thing I was certain had happened. There had to be a better explanation for all of this.

"Um." I didn't really know what to say. Shea had called me his girlfriend on Friday night.

And now I was being shunned.

"I don't know," I replied honestly.

Josh smiled at me. "Hey, whatever went on, someone as pretty as you shouldn't be eating alone."

So, if I were ugly, I should be eating alone? Jesus, Sara, don't be such a cynic. He's literally the first person who's willingly talked to you all day!

I just smiled at him in return for his attempt at a compliment. Josh tucked into his burger and I made another attempt at my macaroni and cheese.

After a while, I found myself enjoying Josh's company. He was as normal a guy as I had ever met. He chatted about his interests, mainly about football, and I did my best to follow along. He told me about the game this week, their opponents, and their likelihood to win. Josh explained that he played the role of Left Tackle, which is why he needed to be so big and strong. I really didn't know what a Left Tackle was but I took his word for it.

I really could have talked about football with Josh for hours if it meant someone was talking to me. Who would have thought that having someone look you in the eyes after a day of being ignored would feel so good?

"They're a weird bunch, though," Josh commented near the end of lunch, nodding over to Shea's table. "Always sticking together. Sometimes it's like this whole school revolves around them. Around Shea." He shook his head at the ridiculousness.

I didn't say it, but I completely agreed with him. The whole school seemed to follow them. They were all certainly avoiding me today.

I looked over to the table, which I had been avoiding up until now. Cece's head was in her hands, and Jamie was comforting her, along with Liza and Francesca. She really looked miserable. I felt the urge to go over and comfort her, but my sense held me back. The whole table's attention was on Cece ... except for Zoey. Zoey was glaring daggers at me, as per usual.

Well, at least I wasn't being completely ignored by them.

"Zoey hates me," I murmured. I noticed Josh frowned when I mentioned Zoey. A mixture of emotion filled his face before he shook it off.

"Zoey's nuts," he stated simply.

I couldn't help but laugh. It felt nice. "Bad experience?"

He rolled his eyes. "I transferred here from Newtown High sophomore year and we were immediately crazy for each other. Like insane."

I could form a mental picture. I resisted gagging.

"But before it could go all the way, Zoey pulled the plug and jumped on Braverman."

Okay, now I had an even clearer mental picture. I wanted to burn the image from my brain. I was immediately reminded of all the Facebook pictures of Zoey and Shea together. She had dumped Josh for Shea?

When I got over my nausea, I could see that Josh was actually quite affected by what had happened. He didn't look like a hormone crazy teenager who missed out on having sex with a hot girl.

Zoey had really hurt him. How anyone could have genuine feelings for Zoey was beyond me, but it seemed that Josh had at one point.

I stole another glance over and she was still wishing me dead with her eyes. Was she ... jealous?

But I found that I could empathise with Josh. I could empathise with how I was feeling over the weekend, with how I was feeling right now. Cast out, and completely cut off.

"Do you have a girlfriend?" I wondered curiously. I was honestly curious to know if Josh had managed to find someone after Zoey.

Josh ran his hand back through his blond hair cockily, albeit jokingly. "No, but I'm always shopping." He winked. "Look, I don't know what's going on with you and Shea, but that doesn't mean we can't be friends. I know what it's like to be the new kid."

My first impression of Josh had been completely wrong. He seemed like a genuinely nice guy who was actually interested in including me. And I was not in a position to turn down friends. "Thanks, Josh. I appreciate it."

"A bunch of us are going down to the beach tonight for a bonfire. We know this guy who buys us beer. You totally don't have to drink, but it will be fun." He smiled kindly. Josh had a nice smile. Sweet and sincere.

The last thing I felt like doing was going to a party filled with rowdy teenagers, but what was my alternative? Hang out with Mom while she went on and on about how boys, mainly Shea, suck? Sit at home wondering if Shea and I were over before we'd even really begun? Sit at home and fixate over what the hell was going on between Shea and Mom and Cece and the whole damn school?

I then realised that for the last few minutes or so I hadn't been freaking out and obsessing over what was going on with Shea. It was the first time since Saturday that my brain had had a break. It actually felt a tiny bit relaxing.

"You know what?" I decided after a moment. "Sure. I'll be there."

I was going to find out what was going on. I was determined to get to the bottom of it. I needed to find out what was going on with Shea, and I needed to find out if my Mom was hiding something from me.

But I couldn't handle being in this damn school if I was going to spend the rest of the semester being ignored and treated as though I don't exist. If people actually wanted me around, then I was going to be hanging out with them.

For my own damn sanity.

Josh grinned. "Sweet. Eight o'clock," he told me. "You can't miss us."

"I do have something to do before I come. I wonder if you can help me?"

He furrowed his eyebrows. "I can try," he offered.

"You don't happen to know where Shea lives, do you?"

CHAPTER 14

S hea's house wasn't at all what I imagined it to be. I mean, I wasn't exactly sure what I imagined, but after seeing where Zoey lived, I wasn't expecting a tiny bungalow in the middle of wood and farmland.

Shea lived about a half hour drive from the beach, which made me wonder how he had managed to get home from my house and beat me to school the other day. He must've driven about a hundred miles an hour.

I tried to put on a strong and determined face as I marched up the steps to his front porch. I took two deep breaths before I knocked on the door.

I didn't have to wait longer than ten seconds before the door was opened. Through the rusty screen door, I could see Shea, and all my anger and frustration over today melted away. He was okay. He was safe. Everything would be alright.

Shea pushed open the squeaky screen door so that I could see him clearly. When I looked at him properly, I gasped. His face, his usually handsome, flawless face, was covered in yellow, aging bruises. His right eye looked swollen, but healing, and it appeared as though it might have been swollen shut at some point.

I didn't understand. These bruises looked like they could be a week old, or more. I had only seen him on Friday night. I quickly shook my confusion away. Shea had been hurt. I had had a suspicion about that, and I was right. Was this why he and my mom were arguing the other night?

I finally found my voice as I cried out, "What happened to you? Are you okay? I have been worried sick! Why didn't you tell me this happened?" in one breath.

Shea didn't invite me into his house. Instead, he stepped out onto the porch with me. He was wearing a plain, white t-shirt and a pair of loose sweatpants. I had never seen Shea in anything so daggy, and so not form fitting. I wondered if this was for comfort or if he wore this because of other injuries. I could remember wearing only sweats as an adolescent when I got my appendix out as I hated pressure on my stitches.

"Sara, I'm sorry," he said quietly.

"What are you sorry for exactly?" I demanded to know. I wanted to know his crimes specifically so that I could confirm some of my suspicions.

Shea reflexively reached up to run his fingers through his hair but winced and put his arm back down by his side. Pain. Quicker than anything, I was behind Shea, searching for wounds. I had no qualms with lifting up his shirt in my search, but Shea caught my hands before I could see. I still felt something beneath his shirt that was not his skin. It felt soft, like a bandage.

"Don't," he said firmly.

I sighed exasperatedly. "Shea, seriously. This isn't a joke to me. I have been worried all weekend. You don't show up at school today and Cece is treating me as though I've got an infectious disease. In fact, that's how half the school is acting. And then I see you like this! What happened to you?" I asked desperately.

"Sara, I'm sorry," he said again.

I felt the urge to punch him. But it seemed as though a lot of that had been happening this weekend. I felt anger course through me, and tears fill my eyes. I hated that I was going to cry. I wasn't upset, I was frustrated. I didn't want to seem hysterical when I was trying to be serious.

"I know you fought with my mom. I know she told you to leave me alone. She said some things that makes me think as though she's hiding something from me. As though you're both hiding something from me. I want to know what it is."

Shea's face didn't betray anything. "I haven't spoken with your mom, Sara."

I felt steam erupt from my ears as he told me such a blatant lie. "Don't you dare lie to me!" I seethed. "Tell me what happened to you!"

Shea sighed. "I'm a guy. We get in fights."

Was he serious? Did he seriously just blame this weekend on being a teenage boy? I had a feeling I knew who the fight was with. I decided to bait him, to see if I could extract the truth from him. "Well, maybe Lex will tell me the truth," I threatened. "He seemed awfully keen on getting to know me at the party. Perhaps I should call him. I'm sure people know him. It is a small town."

It did the trick. Fury filled Shea's brown eyes and he clenched his teeth and let out a growl. He grabbed my upper arms and pulled me close. His grip wasn't enough to hurt me, but it was enough that I couldn't move. I didn't feel unsafe. I knew his reaction was protective, but it was exactly what I needed.

"You don't know what the hell you're talking about," he growled darkly, his face only inches from mine. "Lex is not someone you gossip with. He is dangerous. Do you understand me?"

I glared at him. "Do you know what? I've heard that word used a lot this past week. Namely from my mom describing you. So long as someone in this godforsaken town has wits enough to tell me the truth, I don't give a damn how dangerous they are."

I saw several emotions flash through Shea's eyes. Sadness, fear, desperation, and always fury.

"Sara," he struggled, "you've got no idea who you ..." he trailed off.

"No idea what?" I pressed. "Goddammit, Shea!" I cried. "If you don't tell me what is going on, so help me I will find Lex and ask him!"

His protective grip on me tightened. "Lex is not coming within a hundred miles of you," he promised me quietly. Shea flicked his eyes up, looking into mine directly. "Sara, something is going on. Something I can't tell you about."

"Why?"

"Because I can't," he reiterated. "I need you to stay out of it, okay? I know that being in the dark is frustrating, but it has to be this way. I don't want you in any of this, okay? And I know that if you knew, there are only two possibilities for your reaction."

I didn't think it was possible to be more confused than I already was. Shea was speaking in riddles and I couldn't deal with it. "What are you so convinced that I will do?"

"You will either be in the thick of it, which I can't have, or you will leave, and I can't have that either," he said simply. "So my only option, for now, is to leave you in the dark, and to keep my problems away from you."

"Shea, if this is about what my mom said I –"

"It's not about your mom, Sara," Shea interrupted.

Like hell it wasn't. "I heard her say that I wasn't like you. What does that mean?" That I wasn't in a gang? Was Shea in a gang?

Shea actually smiled down at me. "You aren't like me. Be glad of it. You have opportunities that a lot of people I know don't have."

What? Like my mom could afford to send me to a good college?

Shea released me and took a step back. "I'm sorry," he said again. "Please, just stay out of it. Go to school, work, do your homework. Everything will be normal, and I will deal with my problems. I promise things will get better."

Was he seriously asking me to sit on my hands and wait for him? Did he seriously just tell me to do my damn homework? Who did he think he was, my father? After essentially telling me nothing about what was going on?

"Was that what today was all about? Everyone ignoring me? You're trying to keep me out of it?" I felt the tears coming back and I fought them hard.

Shea nodded begrudgingly. "I thought it would be easier to keep you out of it if you weren't speaking to any of ... my friends."

"But Cece is my friend. She wouldn't just shut me out. Why the hell would Cece agree to that?" I demanded to know.

"Because I told her to," Shea said simply. "I am her older brother," he added.

No. Nope. This was ridiculous. I was not going to let this charade, lie, or whatever it was, ruin my day any longer. Mom was lying to me. Shea was hiding things from me, and he had already lied to me this afternoon. They didn't want to tell me the truth? Fine.

"I have to go. I have a date."

Okay, it was childish and immature, but the reaction on Shea's face made me feel slightly better, which was nice considering how I had been feeling for the last three days.

I could have sworn Shea's eyes turned black, almost animalistic, but in a split second, they were brown again. I must've imagined it, I told myself.

"You have a what?" Shea spat.

I didn't reply. I turned on my heel and marched back to my car. I heard Shea momentarily pause behind me before he followed me. As I opened the driver's side door, he caught it, blocking me from getting inside.

"Sara," he appealed.

"Shea," I replied bluntly.

"You're not dating." The way he said it was like he had decided for me. The decision was made. Shea was in charge. What he says goes. Well, that just pissed me off.

"Maybe you can boss your sister around, andhalf the school, but you can't tell me what to do," I snapped. "Get out of my way. I want to go and spend some time with someone who isn't lying through his teeth." I clenched mine as I spoke.

Shea conceded and released my door. I could tell that he was trying to hide his emotions from me, and the small amount of pleasure his pain had brought me was quickly evaporating. My stupid conscience, and my stupid heart, didn't want to hurt him.

Tonight wasn't even a date. There was going to be other people there.

Why did I have to be crushing on Shea? Why couldn't I have a thing for a football player like Josh who would let me wear his letterman jacket like we were in a 50s movie?

"Bye, Shea," I said quietly as I climbed into my car.

Shea stepped back from my car and I started my engine.

I wondered at what I had actually achieved as I drove away from Shea's house. I looked at him in my rear vision mirror. He hadn't moved. He was still standing out front, watching me leave.

The tears that had been threatening began to fall as Shea faded into the distance. He was okay. At least I knew that. He had been in some kind of fight, with whom, and for what purpose, I still didn't know. But he was alive.

Shea was also involved in something big. Something that was so bad that he didn't want me involved in it. In some backwards, masochistic way, he was trying to protect me. But I didn't need protecting. I needed my boyfriend to communicate with me and not blow me off.

Speaking of being blown off, I had learned that Cece and half the school population where ignoring me at the behest of Shea. How freaking messed up was that? Was being shunned supposed to make me less determined to find out what the hell Shea was caught up in?

What pissed me off even more was that Cece would even go along with it. If Shea had told me to stay away from my friend, I wouldn't have listened. I wouldn't do that to a friend.

I was then suddenly reminded of how Mrs Eckhart had behaved towards me when she had found out who I was. She immediately didn't want anything to do with me. At first I had believed she was just being rude because Zoey didn't like me. But was she involved in this somehow too? Did Shea's shun order extend to the parents of his friends?

What eighteen-year-old had that much influence?

Lastly, I had come to the conclusion that whatever Shea was involved in, my mom knew what it was. She had claimed I wasn't like Shea. He was dangerous. He needed to stay away. What was Shea supposedly like?

Was he a damn gangster or something?

I shook my head and dismissed that ridiculous idea. Shea lived modestly. Weren't gangsters rolling in illegal money? What the hell could it be?

I got home just before six. To my surprise, my mom's car was in the driveway. I then fished my phone out of my book bag and saw there were half a dozen missed calls from her, and a bunch of texts asking where I was.

As I scrolled down my notifications, I noticed I had nothing from Shea. I wasn't surprised, but I was regretfully disappointed.

I cut the engine and climbed out of my car. The front door was practically pulled off the hinges before I got a chance to fish my keys out of my bag.

Mom's green eyes were wide, but filled with relief as she assessed me, checking me for injury, I was sure. "Oh, Sara, where were you?" she cried, pulling me into a hug.

I felt a kind of indifference to my mom. Something had changed between us. Not the love. I knew she loved me, and I loved her, but the trust wasn't the same. She was lying to me and had been lying.

It made me wonder what other lies she had told me, what other false truths I had fallen for.

But the idea of confronting her, of shattering this bubble that we still had, brought bile to my throat. If I was right, everything was gone. Our relationship would be forever changed. Everything I knew would be altered. Mom was the only person I had. It had always been the two of us, and if I lost her? Well, the idea was simply devastating.

"I went to see Shea," I replied honestly.

I saw anger flash across her face before she quickly composed herself. "You went out there?" she asked in disbelief.

"You knew where he lived?" I retorted.

"Don't change the subject," she snapped. "Sara, you need to let this go!" she insisted. "He's not talking to you. He's not worth your time."

"He had been hurt, Mom." I folded my arms across my chest. "Shea's face was all bruised, and I'm fairly certain there's an injury on his back." I recalled the softness underneath his shirt that I believed to be bandage. Deep breath, Sara, I told myself, and followed my instruction. "Did you know anything about it? Did you help him?"

It would explain why Shea was here in the middle of the night. If he couldn't go to the emergency room, he might have sought out my mom. What sort of conflict would prevent him from going to the emergency room? Goddammit, I wanted to know what was going on.

Mom recoiled from me and a look of shock appeared on her face. "What?" she gasped. "Of course not. But that only strengthens my resolve. You see, a boy who gets into fights is not the boy for you."

I rolled my eyes. "Mom, please," I begged. Tell me the truth before I call you out for lying, I internally pleaded. "Did you help him when he was here the other night?"

"He wasn't here," Mom said firmly, furrowing her eyebrows angrily.

Damn it. "He was," I replied softly. She wasn't going to tell me the truth. She would rather lie through her teeth than tell me the truth. Like someone else I knew. "I know he was. I heard you arguing. I know you're lying to me about something, Mom. I'm going to find out what it is. But you could tell me, and I would try to forgive you."

I was being sincere. She was my mom. Of course I would forgive her. But she had to meet me half way. If I had to work this out on my own and she continued to lie to me then where would that leave us?

"Sara," Mom began seriously. "You need to listen to me."

Holy crap. She was going to tell me. I mentally prepared myself for whatever it was. Gangs, thugs, drugs, anything. I mean, there was no possible way I could prepare myself for those things, but at least the notions had entered my brain before they escaped her mouth.

Mom put her hands on the sides of my arms and looked into my eyes. "You are not like Shea, okay?" she said slowly. "You need to stay away from him."

My heart sank as I shook off her hands. "For God's sake, Mom!" I exclaimed in frustration. "What the hell is that supposed to mean? I'm not like Shea?"

Mom chewed on her bottom lip nervously. "I mean that you are practically a different species!" she cried. "You, my darling, are going places! You are smart, and good, and kind, and you'll go to college and make a life for yourself! Shea is going nowhere. His life is in this town with his people and that is all he will ever be."

I felt like punching something. We seriously had not just come back to the college argument. "Mom, so help me, if you don't tell me the truth about ... everythingthen I am never speaking to you. You can forget college. I will work until I can afford my own apartment," I threatened.

Mom flinched. I knew I'd hit a soft spot for her. But she didn't say anything. She didn't say a word. She just stood there and stared at me sadly. Whatever it was, whatever she was hiding, it was more important for her to keep it from me than it was to have open honesty with her own daughter. Even if it meant sacrificing our relationship.

I turned on my heel. I wasn't about to give her any more time to obliterate what was left of our trust. I stomped upstairs and immediately climbed in the shower. I didn't turn on the fan, letting the steam fill the bathroom.

And I cried.

I cried for Mom.

I cried for Shea.

I cried for the life I knew before now.

I cried for New York.

I cried for my plans. My simple life plans.

I cried for my past.

I cried for my future.

What the hell had just become of my life? How could it all just suddenly turn to crap? What had I done in a previous life to deserve this?

Chapter 15

Mom called after me as I left the house but I ignored her. I kept my word. I would not be speaking to her until she decided to come clean.

Josh had been right. I couldn't miss the bonfire. As soon as I stepped down onto the beach, I could see it not two hundred yards from my house. The bonfire was built high, and the smoke was billowing up into the night sky. I could see dozens of teenagers dancing and drinking around the blaze, and I could hear the club music being pumped from someone's speakers.

I wondered how long it would be until an annoyed neighbour called the cops. I set off towards the bonfire, trudging through the sand. As I got closer, I heard my name being called from one of the grassy dunes.

I immediately turned my head towards the voice and squinted at the dark figure. I saw him stand, and come closer to me, eventually revealing himself in the light being thrown off of the burning bonfire.

You didn't really forget a face like Lex's. I honestly didn't know what to do. I had heard of the fight of flight response at school, but was there such a thing as freeze? My legs didn't move as I stared at Lex, trying desperately to ascertain as to whether or not he was a threat.

"You look terrible," he commented as he reached me, standing about three feet from where I was standing. "Bad day?"

Something about his casualness calmed me a little. Maybe I was overreacting. I mean, Shea's family drama with Lex didn't really concern me, right? I knew nothing about it, obviously.

"Gee, thanks," I said sarcastically.

Lex chuckled. "I mean that in the nicest possible way," he assured me. "No Shea tonight? I wouldn't have thought he'd leave a girl as pretty as you to fend off the rowdy teenagers." He nodded towards the bonfire.

Little did Lex know that he'd just hit a sore spot for me. "Why are you here?" I countered. "Have a preference for teenage parties?" I mean, it was now two that he had shown up to.

"No," he said, laughing, "not really my scene. If I want to party, I throw one of my own. I just make a little extra cash on the side buying booze for kid parties," he said, shrugging. "The economy, you know," he added, I'm sure in response to my expression.

I then realised that Lex was Josh's connection for beer.

I stilled in shock as Lex reached his tattooed arm out to me, brushing a damp piece of my hair out of my face and tucking it behind my ear. What the hell? Just as I was about to ask him to keep his hands to himself, mainly because he was like, thirty, and he did not have my consent, Lex sighed, and said, "He really did leave you alone. I didn't think he would do that. I would've thought he would treat his Luna with more care and respect than that."

I was bewildered and confused by Lex, and I was feeling thoroughly uncomfortable and out of my element. The way he was talking didn't make any sense. It was as if ... I don't know, like he knew things about me. But then, he had gotten my name wrong. "Luna?" I repeated. "My name is Sara."

Lex laughed again, this time, it was at me. "You've really got no idea who you are, do you?"

What the hell was he on about? Why did it seem like Lex, of all people, knew something about me? What was there to possibly know? I was a junior with an excellent GPA and rotten luck with boys. I was exceptionally ordinary.

But then, everything had been turned upside down in my life in the past few days. I had no idea who I was, according to Lex. Well, who the hell am I then? Just as I was about to demand an answer to that very question, I felt a large hand wrap around my upper arm and pull me away, so quick that I almost got whiplash.

By the time I was able to focus on the person who had just manhandled me, I recognised him as one of Shea's friends, Matt. Matt had the build of a line backer and the stare of killer by the way he was glaring at Lex. Where the hell had he come from? And why the hell was he grabbing me?

I really needed to stop keeping my outrage and questions in my head.

"Stay behind me, Sara," Matt instructed intensely, putting his hand up to stop me approaching him. His legs were apart, and his body was squared to Lex's, as though he was ready to pounce.

Lex just laughed. "Please. I don't fight puppies," he scoffed.

"Shea knows you're here. I would disappear if I were you. If he finds you here with her then you won't get off so easy."

I saw Lex's eyes flick down to his wrist, which is when I noticed that he was wearing a black brace. It looked more technical than just a crepe bandage, as though it might have been fractured.

Lex had been the one to hurt Shea.

"What did you do to Shea?" I demanded to know. "Why were you fighting?"

Lex grinned. "Ask your boyfriend. Maybe he can fill you in on what you've missed over the years. I'll see you again, Luna. You can count on that." Lex then took off down the beach and disappeared into the darkness.

Matt rounded on me. "Are you hurt? Did he touch you?" he asked intensely.

I recoiled from Matt. He had barely spoken to me, and I him, in the last week. What the hell was he doing here? Why was he talking to me anyway? Wasn't there some sort of ban on that? How did Matt even know I was here?

"No," I snapped. "What are you doing here?"

"Party," Matt replied coolly. "Just happened to see you and Lex and I thought I would help out."

"Do you think I was born yesterday?" I challenged. If one more person told me a lie today I thought I might hurl them into the ocean. "Why were Shea and Lex fighting?" I asked tensely.

Matt shrugged his shoulders. "I don't know. Male hormones, I guess."

I felt myself start to shake as I seriously doubted my ability to toss six-foot five Matt in the sea no matter how I wanted to. "Do you know what Lex was talking about?" I tried again, still wanting the truth more than anything.

I saw conflict and panic momentarily cross Matt's face, which was quickly replaced with relief as a figure came towards us, jogging down the beach from the direction of my house. He didn't need to come into the light for me to know it was Shea.

Shea and Matt shared a strange nod before Matt disappeared and Shea stood before me. Shea looked a mess, even worse considering the bruises on his face. But now he was shirtless, wearing only a pair of khaki shorts, and I noticed that his torso was covered in little bruises and healing, or already healed, cuts. In the light of the fire, Shea was glistening with sweat. His chest was rising and falling rapidly as he caught his breath, as though he had run the half hour drive it would take to get here.

His brown eyes flicked over my body, and he shared a similar relief when he saw that I was perfectly fine.

Physically.

Emotionally, I was a damn wreck.

"Are you okay?" he asked me quietly.

My eyes flared. "No, I'm not okay, Shea," I spat angrily.

"Lex didn't..." Shea couldn't even finish his sentence as he began to shake with anger.

"No," I snapped. "I feel like I'm going out of my mind!" I cried. "Everything has gone to shit! Everybody is lying to me! Everybody is keeping secrets from me! Even Lexseems to know things about me that I don't know."

You've really got no idea who you are, do you?

What could he mean by that? Who am I?

I suddenly realised that Shea didn't have a shirt on. Quicker than he was ready for, I flitted behind him, and my suspicions were confirmed. Shea had an injury on his back. A freaking big one. Threefreaking big ones.

Down the entire length of Shea's back, he had been cut, sliced, by something sharp and jagged. The cuts were parallel, messy, and they looked incredibly painful. But they had been stitched. Hundreds of little sutures were fixed into his back to hold the cuts together, and they were protected by a clear bandage.

I would bet every dollar I had that this was why Shea was at my house the other night. Mom sewed him up.

I cupped my hands over my mouth as I gasped, and Shea spun around to shield me from the sight.

Tears filled my eyes. This wasn't just a punch up. If Lex had tried to stab Shea then he ought to be in jail! It was freaking attempted murder! What the hell kind of family drama would lead to such a crime!

"Sara –" Shea started, but I interrupted him.

"God help me, Shea, if the next words out of your mouth are a lie then I will never speak to you again," I threatened.

Shea recoiled slightly but nodded. "I'm okay, I promise," he said, choosing his words carefully. His eyes were so soft and sad as he spoke. "I swear to you, I want to tell you what's going on, but I want you as far from this as possible. I am going to keep Lex away from you, I promise you that."

"Why?" I demanded to know. "Maybe he might tell me what's going on." Lex might be … I don't know, bipolar or something, but he seemed like he would be more willing to share. But then, I wasn't so eager for a third encounter after seeing Shea's back.

Shea's eyes narrowed. "That's not funny," he snapped.

"I'm not laughing," I retorted.

"Sara," Shea said softly.

"Sara!"

We both looked up when we heard my name being called from the direction of the bonfire. Josh was running over towards me, a dopey grin on his face, as though he was already three beers in.

Shea tensed, but I smiled. "Hey!" I greeted. "I was just coming over."

When Josh reached us, he appraised Shea, confused. "Braverman, it's like fifty degrees." He laughed, as he gestured to Shea's lack of clothing. Josh then put his arm around my shoulders, and I knew that Shea wanted to hit him.

"I don't get cold," Shea snapped as he glared at Josh's arm.

"Okay, well there's beer in the keg if you're interested. C'mon Sara, we're roasting marshmallows." Josh pulled me towards the bonfire and I went willingly. My head needed a break. "More like incinerating them," Josh continued. "The fire is too hot. They just burn." He laughed, and the ease and the simpleness of this con-versation about marshmallows had quickly become the best part of my day.

Josh sat down with me and a bit of driftwood. His cup of beer was wedged in the sand and he quickly returned to it, all the while handing me a stick and the bag of marshmallows.

I recognised a lot of the people here. Most of the football team, a handful of cheerleaders, I saw the lacrosse team, and the basketball team, and the girls' softball team. Pretty much every sport was represented. And all of them, when they saw me, at least smiled in greeting.

None of Shea's friends were here, and I was glad.

I pushed a marshmallow down onto the stick and held it just close enough to the flame for it to toast. I did actually want to eat mine, and I saw the collection of marshmallow ash in the embers of the fire.

I stole a quick glance over to where I had been standing with Shea, and I saw that he was still there, only now he was sitting down on the sand ... watching me. No, actually he was watching Josh.

"What's up with you and Braverman?" Josh asked, repeating the conversation we had earlier today in the cafeteria.

My marshmallow was now perfectly toasted. I pulled it off of my stick and it melted into a gooey mess in my hand. I did my best to eat it as gracefully as possible.

"Nothing," I said, licking my fingers. "We're not together anymore." How could we be when all there was between us was lies and secrets?

"Does he know that?" Josh nodded over to him.

I could have sworn I saw Shea's shoulder blades tense at the comment. But he couldn't possibly hear us from where he was sitting. "He was the one who ended it," I replied. It was entirely Shea's decision to ruin whatever was blossoming between us.

"Oh, I'm sorry."

"It's okay." It most certainly was not okay, but I didn't want to talk about it anymore.

I changed the topic of conversation to marshmallows, and Josh and I had a wonderful time lighting them on fire. We danced to the music, I even had a sip of his beer, which I hated, and by the time it was around midnight, the bonfire was being extinguished and people were starting off home.

I had a really good time with Josh. He was so normal, and the drunker he got, the more entertaining, normal, and funny he was. He really made me laugh when he realised he had a calculus quiz in the morning, and he quickly asked me desperately what calculus was. Something told me he was going to get an F on that one. That's what happened when you partied on a Monday.

"Do you want me to take you home?" Josh asked, his words slurring slightly.

"No, that's okay," I replied, smiling. "I live just up there. Are you going to be okay getting home?" I wouldn't let him drive. If I had to, I would go and get my car.

"Oh yeah," he chuckled. "Garrett's the tee-tolater," he assured me.

I was glad there was at least one person who was sober.

Josh hugged me goodbye in a platonic way. It wasn't romantic between us. At least it wasn't on my end, but I thought that he felt the friendship between us as well. I hoped that he could be my friend. I needed one.

As people began to leave, I noticed all the plastic cups that had been left on the beach, and I couldn't leave them. I decided to gather them and put them in my trash when I got home. I began to stack them in my hand, finding a new one every two feet or so.

I wasn't alone. He didn't leave. I knew he wouldn't leave. Shea began to help me, gathering the cups on the other side of the bonfire.

"This doesn't make up for ... everything, you know," I reminded him quietly.

"Hey, fourteen billion pounds of trash end up the ocean each year. I'm just thinking of the dolphins," he said defensively, but I could tell he was trying to be cute.

I wasn't having it. I cleaned up with him in silence, and Shea didn't try to be casual again. We walked back to my house together and placed the cups in the trash. I would look up local recycling programs tomorrow to see if there was anywhere locally that took number six plastic and if there was, then I would rescue them from the trash.

I knew Mom would be waiting up for me. I was now well past curfew and I knew she would try to punish me. If she wanted me to obey her rules then she ought to be more honest with me.

"Will you be seeing him again?" Shea asked me as we stood on my porch. His voice sounded really vulnerable, and I could tell that seeing me with Josh had really bothered him.

Well, you know what had bothered me? Seeing hundreds of stitches in his back without any context, or without him even telling me that he'd been hurt.

"Yes," I replied. He didn't know that it wasn't going to be romantic. I knew I was being childish, but I felt like I earned it.

Shea pursed his lips and nodded. He was doing his best to mask his emotions. "I can't ... I can't ... bring you into this. It's not safe for you."

I huffed in exasperation. "Do you know what? I am sick of people telling me what is and isn't safe for me. I am not a child. I am old enough to decide for myself." Shea flinched and I sighed. "I know that you care about me. I know my mom loves me. But all you're doing is hurting me by lying to me. If you're so worried, just tell me what I need to be afraid of."

"You don't have to be afraid," Shea promised me, responding almost immediately. "I will protect you," he swore.

Somehow, I couldn't be afraid. I couldn't let myself be scared of a threat that I was unaware of. I couldn't be scared when I felt such anger, frustration and exasperation towards the people who were supposed to care about me more than anything.

Shea wasn't going to tell me anything. He was trying to keep me out of whatever this was, but he was woefully failing. He thought that if I didn't know then I would be safe in the dark, or at least that is what I'd deduced from our cryptic conversations. But all he was doing was fuelling my determination to learn the truth.

I turned around, grabbed the spare key from under the eave and let myself into the house without saying goodbye to Shea.

Chapter 16

S ure enough, Mom was sitting in the armchair, cup of coffee in hand, wearing a disapproving expression on her face. She was wearing her robe, and her face was scrubbed free from makeup.

"Saraphine, no matter what happens between us, that is no excuse to be out until after midnight!"she scolded. She set her coffee on the table and stood up, placing her hands on her hips. "I have been worried sick!"

Good, I thought. I stalked past her and stomped up the stairs loudly. When I got to my room, I slammed my door. I knew they were both childish acts, but what else did I have? I wouldn't be talking to her until she told me the truth, anyway.

I stripped off my clothes and changed into my pyjamas, quickly climbing underneath the covers before I realised that I needed to brush my teeth. Groaning, I climbed out of bed and darted across the landing to the bathroom. Mom was behind me in seconds as I squeezed the toothpaste onto my toothbrush.

"Sara," she appealed firmly. "No matter how angry you are about my decisions, they are still mydecisions to make while you are still a minor and living under my roof. You are my child, whether you like it or not, and every decision I have made for this family has been to ensure that you have a safe and happy life. I understand that moving to Providence has forced you to encounter certain complications, shall we say, that I had not believed we would face, but it is no reason to freeze out your mother and give me the silent treatment."

You want to bet? I felt like saying. Instead, I just brushed my teeth, looking at only myself in the mirror, and not meeting Mom's eyes.

"I love you, Sara," she told me sincerely. "More than my own life. I hope you understand the capacity of a mother's love one day. Then, and only then, will you understand the decisions I have made for you." With that, she left me, and my icy resolve melted a little.

Goddammit, I knew she loved me. I loved her, too. She was my mom. I loved my mom. But the lies! The dishonesty!

I spat out my toothpaste and retreated into my room.

Standing before my bed, and looking at my window, I thought about how Shea had been here with me for two nights. It was a huge deal for me, but it felt right, and it honestly felt like I would be doing it for a long, long time. It was like being hurt all over again Shea knowing how I felt about such intimacies and him going and doing this to me.

It was like he was showing he cared in a completely "I don't give a crap" kind of way.

I slept terribly again. The bags under my eyes were becoming my face's newest permanent tenants and I was starting to break out from the stress I was under. I hated that I had the skin type that showed exactly what was going on in my life.

I half-heartedly covered what I could with concealer and powder and got ready for school.

Mom was already gone, but she had left me a coffee in a travel mug and some banana oatmeal. The bananas formed the shape of a heart in the bowl and I had to roll my eyes. If she thought some sliced fruit was going to make me forget what she did then she had another thing coming.

Still, I was hungry. I quickly had a few bites and a few sips of coffee, before grabbing my work uniform from the laundry and leaving for school.

I didn't wait in the parking lot today. If Shea showed up, I didn't care. I was two pissed to say a kind word to him. I took my books to the library which I found was open. There were a few other students, mostly seniors, in the library studying, and so I found an empty table and opened my English book.

I had neglected my homework over the weekend through sheer preoccupation with boys. When did I become thatgirl?

About the time you looked into Shea's chocolate brown eyes, my subconscious told me.

"Shut up," I said under my breath as I forced myself to concentrate on what I was reading.

I studied up to the first bell, my distraction technique working so well that I was nearly late for Spanish. I had to book it, and I raced into the classroom just as Señora Gomez was about to take attendance. She raised a disapproving eyebrow at me as I immediately started towards the back of the classroom to my usual seat, and I stopped abruptly when I realised that Cece was back there, too.

Cece looked terrible, too, but for Cece, which meant that she still looked like she belonged in Sports Illustrated, but with a sad look on her face.

I considered sitting somewhere else, but there were no empty desks. Even the seat beside Liza was taken by someone who had been absent yesterday. I sighed, adjusting my bag on my shoulder, and I made my way to my seat.

Cece turned her body to me as soon as I sat down and she grabbed my hands in hers. "Sara, I'm so sorry!" she whispered, but the expression in her voice was sincere and regretful.

However, I wasn't in a sympathetic mood. "Oh, you're allowed to talk to me today, are you?" I replied sarcastically.

Cece pursed her lips awkwardly. "Sara, you don't understand."

So I had been told. Many, many times. "Enlighten me," I snapped quietly, before responding to my name on the roll call.

Cece looked so conflicted and torn. Torn between telling me the truth, and no doubt following her brother's orders. Who does that? Who so loyally does what their sibling tells them to do? I mean, I know I was an only child, but siblings were rarely this obedient, right?

"I don't always agree with what my brother says, Sara," Cece admitted quietly.

"Well then, why did you go along with it?" I hissed. "You completely blew me off! You're supposed to be my friend."

"Because I hadto!" Cece snapped back, her frustration evident. "What my brother says goes, okay?"

"No, it's not okay!" I shook my head in disbelief. "It's not the fifties, Cece. We live in the twenty-first century." Did Shea really enact such a 'the man is the head of the house' mantra in his household? Man, that would never fly with me!

"I know that! Of course, we do," she huffed. "It's not the same thing, its –" but she cut herself off and closed her mouth, as though she was about to say something she wasn't supposed to. "I'm not allowed to tell you. I cannot disobey, okay? I just wanted to say I was sorry. I'm sorry about yesterday. You are my friend and it killed me to be like that. I told him I didn't want to, but he made me. But don't be angry with him, if you knew ... oh, Sara, things would be so much easier if you knew."

I had been trying to say that for the past four damn days. "Tell me," I urged Cece. "Don't worry about Shea. He doesn't have to know you told me."

Cece smiled sympathetically. "It doesn't work like that," she replied. "I wish you could figure it out." Her eyes widened suddenly with excitement. "Oh my God, figure it out, Sara!" she whispered, grinning. "Figure it out. If you find out on your own then there won't be any secrets." She grabbed my arm hard. "You have to know. Just think, it's staring you right in the face!"

At that moment, Señora Gomez called on Cece for an answer as she noticed we were talking in the back row. Cece managed to effortlessly reply in Spanish and Señora Gomez continued her lesson.

Cece began concentrating then and taking notes from the lesson. I, on the other hand, got to thinking. Could I really figure this out?

I had already considered the obvious. Gangs, drugs, illegal activities. But it couldn't be that obvious. And something told me that if my mom knew Shea was into anything illegal that she would have turned him into the police immediately. No, this was something different. Something big.

I kept looking at Cece beside me. She looked so normal. Well, as normal as someone who ought to be a Victoria's Secret model ought to look. She was perky, and cheerful, and nice ... when she wasn't following her brother's orders to treat me like crap.

Who does that? In fact, a whole lot of people followed Shea's instruction to treat me like crap yesterday. I was not going to be over that until I got an apology from him, ^but it got me thinking. What sort of power did a guy have that made him that influential?

It was almost like magical mind control or something. I was leaning towards the or something.

Shea didn't come to school all week. I didn't know if he was avoiding me, or if he was still recovering from what had happened over the weekend. Cece only told me that he was at home with their mom.

Shea's ban on speaking to me had extended to the entire posse of followers that he had. People weren't avoiding me, but I still wasn't comfortable enough to sit with Shea's friends knowing that they were in on a secret that I didn't know. Not even Cece could persuade me to eat lunch with them.

So I spent more time with Josh. Sometimes we ate with his friends, and sometimes we ate alone. It was nice to see that not all high school footballers were clichés. Josh was a good, normal guy, with the same college aspirations as me. His family were hard up, he had confessed to me in private, and so it was vitally important for him to secure a scholarship to pay for college. Josh studied hard, maintained a solid 3.5 GPA and he trained every other day for football.

I found myself really enjoying Josh's company. It was welcome distraction to the train wreck my life had become.

I enjoyed working, too, to take my mind off things. Sally was just as kind and friendly to me, something that I had been appre-hensive about considering how Shea had spoken to her, but she seemed normal.

When I wasn't ignoring my mom, at work or studying, I was trying to work out what the hell this big secret was. And I wasn't any closer. I had gotten to the point where I was considering hypnotism as a possible answer, and that's when I knew that I was getting no-where fast.

"Are you coming to the game tonight?" Josh asked me on Friday. We were eating alone today, which meant that I had the familiar sense of daggers being sent towards my head from the direction of Zoey. If it were possible, I think she was trying to make my head explode with her mind.

I had no intention of spending the night in with my mom. I had half expected her to crack. After not getting a word from me in days, I couldn't believe that she was sticking to her guns and not telling me.

"I'm still not entirely sure of the rules," I admitted. Shea tried his best last week to help me but ... I stopped myself. It seemed like a lifetime ago, and it was hard to believe it was only a week.

Josh grinned. "We score, you cheer. You'll get the hang of the rest. The party is at Zoey's again tonight, too."

If I showed up with Josh, there would be more than one person there who would be very pissed.

"Are you okay hanging out at Zoey's?" I asked him curiously.

Josh shrugged. "I don't really see her. I mean, she's usually hanging all over Braverman ... but that stopped when you arrived." Josh's voice was very monotonous, giving nothing away, but even then I could see that it bothered him.

I wondered if Zoey ever got off her high horse whether she and Josh could be happy together? I mean, what was wrong with Josh anyway? He was smart, and cute, and he had ambition. What more did she want?

She couldn't really be so materialistic that Josh was too poor for her, could she? Though, I couldn't really put much past Zoey. I really hoped something as horrible as that couldn't be true.

Did she really want Shea that badly? Shea was ... a lot of things. But now I was wondering as to whether I really knew him at all.

"So, will you go?" Josh pressed.

I nodded. "Sure."

I did as Josh told me to. I cheered when we scored. Which unfortunately wasn't very often.

With two minutes on the clock, our school was down by sixteen points, and the attention of the crowd seemed to have shifted towards the after party, which sounded like it was going to be even bigger this week. Everyone wanted to forget tonight's performance.

"Enjoying the game?"

I jumped as the seat on the bleachers beside me was suddenly filled by a large figure.

I had to do a double take when I saw Shea. When I saw him on Monday, his face had been healing, but now, only a few days later, it was like nothing had happened. Did bruises really disappear that quickly, and that flawlessly? Goddammit, he was handsome. I found myself distracted for a second after not having seen him in so long. I momentarily forgot that I was monumentally angry with him.

"What are you doing here?" I snapped when I finally found my voice.

"This is my school, isn't it? I always come to the game," he retorted, an ounce of cuteness to his voice, as though he was trying to break through my hard exterior. It wouldn't work.

"Where have you been all this week?" I asked nonchalantly, turning my attention back to the field.

"Helping my mom," he replied, his tone quickly saddening. "She's, um, had it tough this week. Me being hurt and all, she took it pretty hard." The seriousness in his tone told me he was telling the truth, which felt nice to receive for once. It also meant that Cece had been telling me the truth.

"Shouldn't your mom be taking care of you when you're hurt?" I wondered. Or I could have helped, if you hadn't been such a jerk.

"Mom took care of me my whole life. It's my turn now," he said defensively, his voice suddenly sharp.

I flinched a little, and I could tell that I had hit a nerve with my careless comment. I brought my eyes back to his. As I looked into their brown depths, it still felt strange to me how comfortable and right I felt with Shea, even after everything that had happened. The stupid, romantic part of my brain just needed him, and hoped that he needed me.

Shea closed his eyes. "Sorry," he apologised, "I don't mean to snap. You couldn't have known ... I don't want to ..." Shea sighed. "I've missed you this week, Sara," he said, settling on his words.

And the logical part of me knew that this wasn't fair. "You missed me?" I repeated. "You put me through what is probably the worst week of my life and you missed me?" For Christ's sake, my mom and I were not even talking. I'd experienced ostracism. Shea had been hurt. Badly.

I wondered how his back was. I wanted to ask if he was in any pain but my pride stopped me.

"I know, I know." He sighed. "I get that this sucks, Sara, but –"

"No," I snapped, cutting him off. "No buts." I got up from my seat on the bleachers and stood in front of him. "I don't know what kind of martyr game you're playing with me, but I'm over it. I let you in!" I hissed. "I told you things, I was vulnerable with you! I let you sleep in my freaking bed. You've made me feel like a complete idiot. A complete cliché who falls for the guy who simply doesn't care enough to throw the girl a bone." My voice was so low, yet so angry, it felt like ice escaping my throat. "You don't get to show up when you want, and tell me, or not tell me things, and decide for me. You're not my father, and I'm not a child. If you want any kind of relationship with me going forward, then you had better pray for some honesty next time we talk."

Shea stared at me, stunned. His lips parted, but no words came out.

The game had finished sometime during our argument, and people started filing out of the stands.

"Josh will be waiting for me." I didn't wait for his response. I simply spun around and moved with the crowd out of the stands.

I was already having second thoughts about the party as Josh and I pulled up to Zoey's house. The party looked so much bigger than last week, with people spilling out onto the street clutching red cups of who knows what.

Again, I was reminded of the fact that only a week ago, Shea and I were together at this party. Cece had done my makeup for me and had dressed me in something completely daring. But tonight, I was with a friend, and I was comfortable in jeans and a cardigan.

"Let's have some fun, Sara," Josh urged. "I'm super depressed about losing tonight. Help me feel better." He grinned, winking at me, before motioning for me to get out of his car.

I rolled my eyes and followed him into the party. We weaved our way through the sea of people on their way to being drunken messes. The music was so loud that I could barely hear the greetings of Josh's friends as we arrived. His friends were gathered in Zoey's grand entrance foyer, sitting and standing around the stairs with drinks in their hands, and it looked as though they had stolen a few bags of pretzels.

I couldn't really engage in the conversation as I was struggling to hear them, so I found myself looking around the large, open plan rooms that was the ground floor of Zoey's house. There had to be at least two hundred people in this room alone. There were so many bodies that I was getting too hot for my cardigan. I quickly removed it, hanging it over the staircase, leaving only my plain tank top.

I noticed a lot of people stealing glances in my direction. A lot of them looked confused or curious, exchanging frowns and unspoken thoughts with their friends as they made judgements about me.

Of course, I knew I could be completely paranoid, but after this week, people staring seemed like a normal occurrence.

I couldn't see Shea. I didn't even know if he would be coming. He hadn't been at school all week, so I doubted it. But Cece would probably be here. Zoey was her friend after all. I didn't like how things were with Cece. Things hadn't been normal all week, but especially now that she had told me to figure things out for myself. Every time she saw me, she kept looking at me with expectation.

I didn't understand why she couldn't just tell me.

"Do you want a drink?" Josh yelled in my ear, the sheer volume of the music meaning I could only just hear him.

Did I want a drink? Screw it. I've had a tough week. I nodded, but then followed Josh through the crowd of people to choose what I wanted. I didn't have a lot of experience with spirits, but I wanted to have some say over what I used to get trashed for the first time in my life.

As we reached the kitchen island, we were confronted by dozens of bottles. All kinds of alcohol that were opened and had pourers attached. It looked like a professional bar. Josh seemed to know what he was doing as he grabbed a cup and started mixing a drink. I followed suit, deciding that pink drinks had to be safe for my first proper drink. I grabbed a cup myself and filled it a quarter of the way with raspberry soda. I then grabbed a bottle of vodka and filled up the rest. I didn't really know much about ratios, but I hoped it would taste okay.

I brought the cup to my lips, the scent already burning my nose, and just as I was about to drink, the cup was snatched from me.

"Are you insane? You'll end up in the emergency room with a virgin stomach like yours," Shea snapped angrily in my ear. I hadn't noticed him approach me, or enter the party, but it was hard to miss him now. Anger seemed to increase his size, and his furious eyes were directed at me.

Shea took my drink and immediately tipped it out down the sink.

Irritation, frustration, and utter fury filled me. What gave him the right to just show up and boss me around when it suited him? "Leave me alone!" I screamed at him, though I could only just barely hear myself. I seized the bottle of vodka, not bothering about a cup and quickly disappeared into the crowd, hoping to find my way back to Josh's friends.

I didn't get far, however. I was suddenly pulled into a room I hadn't noticed was off the kitchen, and the door was shut behind me. The music was muffled slightly. I rounded on Shea, and just as I would about to go off at him for interfering, I realised that he hadn't been the one to grab me.

Zoey stood before me, having dragged me into what looked like her walk-in pantry, looking utterly pissed off. She was completely dressed up and looked like she belonged on a runway. I felt thoroughly underdressed next to her. Zoey's fists were balled at her side.

"What is wrong with you?" she spat.

I recoiled. "What is wrong with you?" I countered. "What did I do to you?"

"You ... you skip from one guy to the next!" she accused angrily, her eyes flared. That was rich, coming from her. "You have Shea all over you, he is freaking obsessed with you!" she cried. "And yet you still need to bed hop to Josh!" Her voice sounded like what I imagined venom to taste like. Oh my God, she hated me.

"Why should you care if I spend time with Josh?" I shot back, deliberately trying to provoke her into admitting feelings for him.

It was obvious that was why she was pissed off with me today andhad been all week. Josh liked Zoey, too, for some odd reason.

I mean, of course, she was beautiful. But I had yet to see any endearing features in her personality.

And in that moment, I though Zoey was going to slap me. But she didn't. She looked like she so wanted to, but couldn't, and I wondered if Shea and his strange hold over people had anything to do with that.

"It's not cute to be a slut," Zoey seethed after a minute. She was practically shaking with rage.

"It's not cute to slut shame," I retorted, frowning. "Come on, Zoey."

Zoey recoiled, and she actually looked like she was going to throw up. Okay, it wasn't cute to bait her like this. I couldn't let her think that I had slept with Josh when it was so obvious that she liked him. I was not that girl.

"Josh has feelings for you, too, you know. If you like him so much, then just tell him. I think he would take you back, no matter what happened between you in the past," I offered softly.

Zoey recoiled again, but this time, she looked a lot more vulner-able. Her anger immediately softened, her eyes widened, and her sneer disappeared. "What did he say to you?" she asked, an edge to her voice.

"Not much," I admitted. "But he did tell me that it was you who suddenly went cold on him, and then you were all over Shea the next minute. He sounded quite upset when he told me that," I said honestly.

Zoey did her best to mask her emotions then, putting on the cold, hard exterior that she seemed to reserve especially for me. "If you sleep with him, I'll cut you," she threatened.

"Why don't you sleep with him then, if you like him so much?"

Zoey laughed, a snarky, facetious laugh. "You wouldn't understand." She shook her head, but then stopped, "Well, I suppose you would. My parents want a better pedigree for me."

What a bitch. Pedigree? What the hell was this, a dog show? What was so wrong with Josh? Was he not rich enough for Zoey's snob parents?

"Well maybe you aren't good enough for Josh," I snapped angrily, before pushing my way out of the pantry and back into the party. I was immediately assaulted by the sheer volume of the music and the scent of alcohol and sweat in the air. I was disoriented for a minute, before I spotted the staircase and made an effort to get back over to Josh and his friends.

"Sara!"

Shea was doing his best to manoeuvre through the crowd to get to me, and that was the opposite of what I wanted. I couldn't take another lie. If he was as obsessed with me as Zoey claimed, then he wouldn't have treated me like crap.

"Leave me alone, Shea!" I shouted at the top of my lungs, just as the loud song finished, and just in time for everyone on the lower floor of Zoey's house to hear me.

Shea stared at me as two hundred people stared at us. I didn't know whether to feel liberated, embarrassed, or just plain miserable.

"Dude, Luna's gone cold!" a drunken voice slurred.

Luna? I wasn't sure who said it, but that was the second time someone had called me that. First Lex, and now this person. That couldn't be a coincidence, could it? What, or who, was Luna?

I managed to avoid Shea for the rest of the night, or perhaps he finally got the message and left me alone. Although I constantly felt his eyes on me, he didn't approach me again. When I managed to get him out of my mind, I was able to enjoy myself with Josh and his friends.

I got my hands on a beer and we toasted to the team's loss that night and for the hope of a win next Friday. I danced, I sang along poorly to the songs I knew coming from the speakers, and I drank a bit more, to the point where I was feeling a little lightheaded. I had never been drunk before. Was this what it felt like?

The next thing I knew I was being helped into the cab of a car as my attention kept dropping in and out. I would have been scared had I not recognised the scent of the person helping me. I knew Shea's cologne.

My head felt heavy as I leaned back on the headrest. I did my best to turn it to the left to look at Shea in the driver's seat. He was staring straight ahead at the road. His face, his neck, his shoulders, everything looked very tense.

"Are you angry with me?" I asked, amused, though my words coming out a little slurred.

"No," he replied calmly.

"I think you are," I laughed. "That's rich considering how you've treated me. I ought to take a Louisville slugger to both headlights or however that song goes."

"I didn't cheat on you," he scoffed, as though the idea was ridiculous. "Perhaps I ought to take a slugger to your headlights, huh? Josh was too drunk to take you home, though, so I don't consider him to be a very responsible choice in boyfriend." I heard the ice in his voice though, even as he was trying to be light and casual.

"Josh is just my friend," I tiredly confessed. "He and Zoey like each other but won't do anything about it. Or she won't. I don't know why."

"Zoey?" repeated Shea, sounding shocked. "Zoey and Josh?"

"Yeah," I confirmed. "I don't know what her problem is. He's a nice guy. She said something weird about her parents wanting a better pedigree or something." My eyelids were starting to feel very heavy as they fluttered closed. Oh my God, I was tired. I don't even think I drank that much, but Shea had been right. I had a virgin stomach.

"Hey, Sara," I head Shea say quietly.

"Mm," I mumbled.

"I'm sorry for everything I've put you through. You can't know how it kills me to cause you any sort of pain. I promise, I'll do better. I want to be the kind of boyfriend you deserve, and I want to give you a life free from anything that can bring you pain. I'm trying, I promise you."

I was too tired to concentrate on his words. I couldn't process them or even hear them, really. Sleep was the only thing I could focus on, and the soft rumble of Shea's truck lulled me into an easy slumber.

CHAPTER 17

y phone chimed.

My eyes flickered open and I was quickly blinded by the sun that was streaming into my bedroom. I hadn't closed my curtains last night.

Ugh, since when was the sun so bright? I shielded my eyes with my forearm and felt out onto my nightstand for my phone. The first thing I found, though, was an aspirin and a glass of water. I wondered who had left those for me.

Shea had brought be home. I remembered that. I didn't remember getting into bed, though, so he must've helped me after I fell asleep in the car. I hope my mom was asleep when we got home. We might not be talking right now, but I did not want an alcohol lecture.

I quickly took the pill before taking my phone in my hand.

I saw that I had been tagged in something online. I quickly opened my Facebook app to see that one of the guys from school had uploaded a video from the party. It wasn't just me that was tagged, but a whole group of people. I clicked on the video and watched as the camera was sloppily spanning around the room, capturing the party goers, the drinking and the music.

I saw myself near the kitchen as I quite loudly told Shea to leave me alone.

"Dude, Luna's gone cold!" The microphone had managed to pick up that drunken slur, and I immediately remembered thinking the term was odd, considering Lex had called me a Luna before then. It couldn't be a coincidence, could it? What sort of nickname was Luna?

I mean, I knew it was a baby name that was semi-popular at the moment. But it wasn't like Sara was anything close to Luna. I had to use any clue I could find to work out what the hell was going on. Maybe this was nothing, but maybe it was something.

I was more awake as I opened up the web browser on my phone and typed in "Luna meaning". I was immediately offered results explaining the meaning of the baby name, but that didn't seem significant enough for me. I abandoned the site and kept scrolling until I found something interesting.

I clicked on a dictionary website that gave me an intriguing piece of information.

Luna was the alchemical name for silver.

Even more interesting was that Luna was the Roman Goddess of the moon. The moon personified.

I followed this trail and opened at least a dozen pages that kept offering me the same few words. Luna, lunar, silver, and lycan. That last word I wasn't familiar with, and so I searched it.

And that's when I knew I was insane. It was like googling your symptoms when you felt sick. You only made things worse and you scared yourself.

Well, I was about to have a freakin' nightmare.

"Lycans, commonly mistaken as werewolves," I read, "are not servants of the moon, but are a more advanced species that can control their transformations at will. A lycan transforms into a bigger specimen of wolf, and is typically stronger than a werewolf, with senses more superior than any other creature. Lycans rarely live away from a pack, and follow a specific chain of command, similar to other animal pack hierarchy." I looked up from my phone and frowned. "What the fu –" I checked the website that I was looking at and saw that it referenced mythological species.

But my brain was already racing. The crazy, unnatural, illogical part of my brain was considering this, even though every fibre of my being knew that this was insane.

But reading was this was like driving past a car crash. I just couldn't look away.

"The leader, commonly referred to as an Alpha, commands total obedience from their pack. Disobedience is unheard of, and their social makeup is part of what makes the lycan superior to other species."

My mind, which felt completely independent from all coherent thought at that moment, immediately flashed to my conversation with Cece in Spanish. I could vividly see her struggling with her secret, battling against her want to confide in me, and being physically incapable of doing so. She simply couldn't.

"Their superiority as a species is further demonstrated by their heightened speed, strength, sight, hearing, and sense of smell. Lycans are able to use their skills to defend their territory, their pack, and their mate."

Shea was fast. I had noticed it many times. He lived half an hour away from school, and yet still beat me there after going home from my house. I wracked my brain, trying to think of evidence of Shea being fast, or strong, but I was just feeling overwhelmed at the thought as I continued to read this manifesto of crazy.

"Lycans are monogamous, and mate for life."

"Whoa," I gasped, and threw my phone away, it landing on the end of my bed.

At that moment, there was a knock on my door, and my mom entered the room with a cup of coffee in her hand. She was wearing her robe, but it looked like she had been awake for a little while.

"Thanks," I said, as I accepted the coffee. I needed one after what I had just read.

"Sara, we need to have a talk about last night," she said seriously, sitting down on the edge of my bed.

"I had a really shitty week, Mom. I just had some fun with my friends," I told her as an excuse. But I knew that wouldn't fly.

I could tell that she was really biting her tongue. She wanted to blow up at me. She was a doctor. I would wager a hundred bucks that she had pictures of alcohol affected livers on her phone right this minute. But at risk of us not talking again for another week, she was trying to be cool.

"You need to have your wits about you with these people, Sara. It's too dangerous to be vulnerable like that," she said calmly.

Dangerous. There was that word again. Mom was obsessed with how wrong these people were for me. How wrong Shea was for me. She had forbidden me from seeing him, for Christ's sake! She had been convinced he was the devil incarnate out to do me real harm. And it had come from nowhere.

Like she knew already what the impossible was.

Oh my God, my own brain was freaking me out. This wasn't possible, was it? This was the stuff you saw in movies, and you read about in books. You would see this stuff at sci-fi conventions, not in your own backyard! Magic, the supernatural, freakin' lycans, were the stuff of fairy tales. Or nightmares.

"I know, what an asshole Shea was keeping me from harm by bringing me home safe. We really ought to have him arrested," I muttered sarcastically.

"Sara," Mom said in a warning tone.

She couldn't know, could she? Who knows this sort of stuff? Who on earth is actually aware that this could even be possible? My mom is a doctor. She was a woman of science. She believed in facts. She was a staunch atheist, after all. Entertaining the thought that my mom could believe in any sort of magic seemed unnatural.

But Mom had grown up in this town. She had known all these people once upon a time. Was this a town secret? Did everyone know but me? Surely she couldn't keep something this crazy from me?

It then suddenly hit me that I was not only considering the fact that Shea could run really fast, but that he could transform into some kind of wolf beast. What the actual fuck? What the hell kind of crazy was this? It was nuts. People couldn't just turn into animals like they could in the Harry Potter universe.

"Do it again," she warned, "and you're coming with me to meet some patients in alcohol-induced liver failure." With that, she stood up, and left my room. I was still in the middle of my freak out that I hadn't much registered what she'd said.

Before I knew what I was doing, I had already tapped on Shea's number in my phone and I was calling him. He answered on the first ring.

"How are you feeling?" he asked.

What a loaded question that was. "Um ... pretty ... awful, actually," I managed to respond. My hangover was forgotten. I honestly couldn't feel my alcohol headache. The pounding in my head was over imagining a person actually growing fur.

"Shea," I whispered. Was I going to ask him? Would he laugh at me? God, I was hoping he would laugh at me so that everything I was freaking out about would be just in my imagination. "Can you come over? Right now?" I chickened out. But then I realised he would just have to laugh at me in person. I still hoped he would.

"Yeah, of course. I was on my way to see you anyway. I thought I could take you out for a greasy breakfast. Bacon is the only fix for a hangover. That and not getting drunk in the first place."

"Okay," I whispered and hung up the phone. I mindlessly got dressed, and my window opened as I was dabbing concealer under my eyes.

"Didn't think your mom would be any more my fan after last night. Figured the window was my best bet," Shea joked.

I could see him in the reflection of my mirror. Damn, he looked good for a Saturday morning. I looked and felt like crap, which was quickly becoming my usual. Don't be a coward, Sara. Just ask him. The worst he could do is laugh.

No, the worst he could do was confirm that all your crazy conspiracies are true.

"Did you want to get breakfast now or –"

"Lycan," I said, interrupting him.

Shea stopped talking immediately and recoiled in shock.

I sucked in a breath and turned around to face Shea. He honestly looked like I had just sucker punched him. And just like that I knew it was true. This utter insanity, this crazy conspiracy that I had stumbled across on the damn internet was true.

"I'm sorry, what did you just say?" he coughed out.

"You heard me," I whispered. He had heard me. He knew exactly what I'd said. He knew I knew.

Chapter 18

You know when you're little, and you dream about fairy tale worlds, and wish that they're true. You see these magical places on television and you just know that life is bliss there. You'll meet Prince Charming. You'll have some great dresses to wear. So what if there's a few monsters. The heroes will get them in the end.

Well, turns out that it's all true, except there are no castles, and people can turn themselves into giant dogs at will.

And I had one standing in my bedroom, right in front of me.

I didn't know whether to be afraid of him. He didn't look very frightening right now, considering I had just sucked all the air out of his lungs with one word. But knowing what Shea could do, it scared me. I think anyone would be scared. That was normal, right? Who I am kidding? Nothing about this is normal.

"How did you find out? Who told you?" Shea asked angrily once he had regained some of his composure. I was immediately reminded of Cece. Obviously everyone in Shea's controlwas sworn to secrecy.

I blinked. "I think what you meant to say is, "Oh, Sara, I'm so sorry for lying to you. Let me explain everything and help you not to be scared of me.""

The word scared seemed to snap him out of his anger completely. And for the first time I saw him move faster than I'd ever seen anything in my life move. In less than a millisecond, he was by my side, holding my hands in his. I fell backwards at the sheer speed in which he had moved, but I didn't fall. Shea was holding me, rubbing my arms, and whispering that it would be okay.

"You never have to be scared of me, Sara. I would die before letting anything or anyone hurt you," he told me intensely.

But I could see the truth in his eyes, and for some reason, I calmed down a little. I felt my heart relax and I wasn't breathing such shallow breaths. And then I remembered reading about lycans and monogamy. They mated for life. Could ... could Shea really feel that way about me?

I mean, we had barely been on a proper date. For most of the time that we had known each other, I was being ignored. How could he know? Did I know? Did I feel that way? I wasn't so sure.

I liked him, for some crazy reason, despite all this. But mating? The word just sounded weird. How could that even work? I was just a normal person.

"I can hear your heartbeat," he said quietly. "It often picks up around me, which I like very much, but you're calmer now."

Let's pretend thatwasn't entirely embarrassing. "Why didn't you tell me?" I asked him, looking up at him vulnerably.

Shea smiled slightly. "This isn't exactly first date conversation. Or second date."

"Shea," I said impatiently.

"I've never had to have this conversation before. Everyone I've ever socialised with, my friends, my family … girls, they've all been like me, they've all already known."

Cece turns into a wolf. Zoey turns into a wolf. Oh my God.

"It wasn't my intention to keep this from you forever. I just wanted to keep you out of it while we … sorted out a conflict."

"Lex," I deduced. He must be a wolf, too.

"He is a very dangerous person. Very volatile and unpredictable, and with a huge grudge against me and those I protect," Shea said firmly. He led me over to my bed so that we could sit down.

I kept a few feet between us and I could see that Shea noticed, but he didn't push me.

I had so many questions that I didn't know where to start.

"Can I ask how you figured it out?" Shea asked. "Or did someone tell you? I gave the order to keep you in the dark, so if someone did tell you, I need to know. Was it Cece?"

"Nobody told me," I rebuffed quickly. "I just pieced it together. Lex called me something, and someone said the same term again last night, so I searched it online. I basically followed a trail from Luna to lycan and went with the crazy theory."

I still wasn't entirely sure what a Luna was, and how I was one, considering I was not in any way, shape or form a lycan. I was a normal, ordinary teenage girl from New York.

"I guess I didn't realise how smart you are," Shea murmured, though looking impressed.

"What is a Luna?" I couldn't help myself.

"A Luna is our term for the mate of the Alpha. She is the female leader of the pack. A matriarch of sorts," Shea explained carefully.

Alpha. I had read that. He was the leader. Shea was the leader. I tried to make it make sense in my head, but it was all still a jumble. "I just don't understand how this is at all possible."

"I know it must seem surreal and unbelievable. You're not alone in your reaction. Every human that has ever found out about us has reacted in the same way. We are an evolved species, just like humans, and just like every other mammal. Our genetic makeup allows us to manipulate our DNA and shift into another form. As we have evolved over the millennia, we've gained control and are able to blend in with society seamlessly."

It felt like something you would learn about in a biology lesson. It sounded completely logical. The way Shea explained it made it seem perfectly normal that people could just manipulate their own DNA.

"Holy shit, Shea," I said, exhaling.

Shea laughed lightly. "I know. Holy shit."

"Alpha," I said, pulling whatever words I could recall from the internet. "You?" I wasn't meaning to speak in one-word sentences, but it was all the words that my brain was sending to my mouth.

Shea nodded. "Yes, I am Alpha. My father was before me, and I was thrust into the role when he died a few years ago, like I told you." He paused for a second. "The chain of command is very important for our strength as a pack. I am the leader, and I am obeyed. It might seem ... archaic, but it's how it has always been. Every order, every decision, is for the safety of the pack, and the people who are in my care. I take my role very seriously."

I could tell. Shea seemed very dominant when he was speaking about being Alpha. He was a leader.

"But I don't understand why they would call me a Luna. I mean I'm not ... I can't ..." It suddenly occurred to me that perhaps I wasn't the Luna. Perhaps someone else was meant to be the Luna. Someone that was a lycan and could lead alongside Shea. I mean, of course there was. That wasn't me. There was no way I belonged in that world.

But Shea smiled at me reassuringly. "Calm that heart of yours, Sara."

I hadn't realised it had picked up again. I did my best to control my breathing to calm myself. It was still completely embarrassing that he could hear my heartbeat.

"When I was a kid, my dad used to read to me from "The Iliad". Have you heard of it?" he asked me.

Weird way to change the topic of conversation, but okay. I nodded. I had learned about it during eighth grade when we had studied ancient history.

"I still remember asking my dad these questions when I was a kid. I couldn't understand our ways by watching movies and getting ideas about the world from them. We were so different. Even the way we loved was different. We would see the fickleness of human love on TV and in books and on the magazine shelves when we would go grocery shopping.

"But seeing the people, the relationships around me, it was hard to grasp. As a kid, I couldn't imagine growing up and falling in love. I saw what my mom and dad had, and it grossed me out, but I still wanted to understand it, and my dad referenced "The Iliad" of all things." Shea laughed as he remembered. "He told me about Helen of Troy, and how she was said to have a face so beautiful, that it launched a thousand ships. A thousand. When

Helen was taken by Paris, her husband, Menelaus, launched a thousand ships and started to the Trojan War to bring her home to him. My father described the love that you felt for your mate could only be mirrored in mythology, and not in the human reality. One day, he told me, I would love someone so much that I would launch a thousand ships for her."

His words were beautiful, impassioned, and freaking confusing all at the same time. Was he talking about me? I still wasn't sure if it was even possible for someone like him to love someone like me. How would that work?

"I didn't understand it, the lightning bolt moment, until I saw you. My parents, Cece, all described it as being hit by lightning. You're paralysed as your world is quickly consumed by the person designed specifically for you.

"It isn't the same for humans, I don't think. Humans have been mated with lycans before now, and have lived completely happily, but their feelings can change. Not always, but it happens. Humans are not a naturally monogamous species. They try to be, but they can fall out of love as quickly as they can fall into it. Humans can leave. Human have the power to brutally destroy a lycan. But it doesn't change for us. We only get one."

Oh my God, he wastalking about me. As I looked at Shea, for the first time I saw him in total transparency. He was being completely honest with me, bearing his soul, and sharing his heart.

I stood up from my bed and went over to my window as I process what he had just said to me. I was it for him. I was his person. I was his mate. Shea loved me. Shea was biologically programmed to love me for the rest of his life. God, that was overwhelming.

Was it weird to find it overwhelming? Wouldn't most girls love to find out that someone loved them? How often did it happen?

"Tell me what you're thinking," Shea urged quietly. "Your pulse can only tell me so much."

"You've got to give me a minute, Shea," I whispered.

I didn't want to dwell on this. I didn't want to get distracted by this. I mean, we had loads of time to figure this side of things out, didn't we? There was still so much I didn't know. So much I wanted to know. I honestly hoped my mom wouldn't walk in right now, because I would not know how to explain this.

"Hey, Mom, my sort-of boyfriend is a real-life teen wolf. Do you care if he stays in my room?"

Holy shit, Mom! It was a theory I had. My mom knew. Mom thought Shea was dangerous. Mom hated Shea from the second she knew who he was. I spun around. "Does my mom know about you?" I demanded to know.

Shea nodded immediately, still being honest. "Yes, she does."

My heart, stomach, and pretty much all my other organs dropped. Mom knew. How the hell could my mom know this? This wasn't something you just know. How long had she known about this for? For how long had she been keeping this a secret from me?

"How?" I demanded to know.

Shea shook his head. "That's a conversation that you need to have with her. I can't tell you everything."

He was still keeping things from me. "Yes, you can," I snapped. "She helped you the other night, didn't she? She lied to me about that and said that you were never here. She lied right through her teeth. How many times has she done that?"

"Your mom has her reasons, and like I said, you need to take that up with her. That side of things is her responsibility. Yes, she helped me the other night. I was injured during an altercation with Lex. Usually we heal pretty quick, but he got me pretty bad. Our usual doctor, his daughter is pregnant and lives out of state, so he was visiting her. But I needed help, and I knew that your mom knew about us, so I went to her for help."

I was momentarily stunned at the image of two giant wolves fighting. I remembered seeing the slashes on Shea's back, and I now realised that they were from claws. The thought of such violence, and such mortal danger, was terrifying.

What were they fighting over? What kind of disagreement would warrant such violence? I mean, it was freakin' grievous bodily harm, wasn't it? Was there some sort of supernatural police that you could contact? The Winchester brothers? Magic 911?

But I made myself focus. Mom knew. Mom knew, and she didn't tell me. Mom was keeping secrets from me. Mom had lied to me repeatedly.

CHAPTER 19

I marched out of my bedroom with purpose, and Shea followed me. I knew mom would blow up about that, but I had one hell of a retort.

Mom was downstairs in the living room. She was sitting on the couch with her coffee, watching breakfast television. She looked up at me when I entered the room, and her eyes widened when she saw Shea following me.

Her head snapped towards the door, and then back to Shea. She was quickly piecing things together, and I could see her blood boiling as she glared at Shea.

"What the hell are you doing upstairs?" she demanded to know of Shea.

"He was being honest with me," I shot back, folding my arms across my chest.

"Honest?" she repeated, furrowing her eyebrows. "What are you talking about? What did you tell her?" she asked Shea in disbelief.

"He told me," after I figured it out, "that he is a lycan. I know that you knew, Mom. What I want to know is why you lied to me about it." I still couldn't believe that those words were coming out of my mouth, or that this was a possibility, let alone my reality.

All the blood drained from my mom's face. I had never seen her look so pale as, I'm sure, all kinds of crazy, dreaded thoughts were passing through her head.

Instead of apologising, or explaining to me why she had kept me in the dark about something as big as this, she instead turned to Shea, and asked accusingly, "Why would you tell her that? Why would you involve her in this? I thought you were supposed to care about her!"

"I do care about her," Shea snapped. "Sara figured it out and I wasn't going to lie to her anymore. She has a right to know."

"I don't believe this. I didn't think this would be a problem. She turned sixteen and nothing happened, and I thought everything would be okay." It was like Mom was talking to herself rather than either of us.

"Mom, what are you talking about?" I asked firmly, and yet fearfully. I couldn't shake the feeling that there was still a hell of a lot more about this world, for want of a better word, that I didn't know.

Mom's head snapped to me, and she looked at me with fear and shame. I had never seen those emotions on my mom's face before. It was so unsettling that I just wanted to comfort her. Mom didn't always have it together, but right this moment she looked like she was disintegrating.

"Sara, please sit down, honey," Mom urged, motioning towards the couch.

I didn't feel like passing out on the hardwood, so I took her advice and sat down on the couch. She sat down on the same sofa but left the middle cushion between us.

I could see Shea from the corner of my eye sitting down on the bottom step, knitting his fingers together and leaning his arms on his knees as he watched us both.

Mom took a deep breath. And then another. And then another. She took a good couple of minutes as she looked like she was in deep thought, thinking of how she was going to break whatever it was to me.

I tried to keep my mind blank. If I didn't, I knew it would race ahead and I would only make things worse. Surely what she was going to tell me couldn't shock me more than my boyfriend being able to turn into a giant dog.

"I was sixteen when your daddy first asked me out," she told me calmly.

I recoiled slightly, not expecting the conversation to turn to my dad. We rarely talked about him. Mom didn't like to, anyway. I didn't know whether to be glad about learning things about him, or fearful about what I might learn.

"I said no," Mom continued. "I was too focussed. I was a smart girl who had places to go. I wasn't meant to stay in Providence. But Ronan persisted, and I found myself falling in love with him. He was a senior and I was a sophomore. My naïve heart liked the attention. The years that followed were some of the best, and worst, of my life. I loved your daddy with my whole heart, and he loved me. But I had to sacrifice a big part of myself to be with him, and it was a sacrifice I was willing to make at the time.

"I stayed in Providence after high school. Something I never thought I would do. My parents thought I was crazy, and they kicked me out because of it. But Ronan asked me to marry him." Mom smiled slightly, a nostalgic, sweet smile, and I found myself with tears in my eyes. She had never spoken of him like this before. "And before I knew what I was doing, I was an eighteen-year-old bride who thought I had it all figured out. I didn't need college. I didn't need my parents. I didn't need anybody but Ronan, because he loved me, and we would make it work."

Maybe, maybe Mom's objection to Shea had nothing to do with the lycan thing. Maybe it was because of her life with Dad. I still didn't know how she knew about lycans, but she just really wanted me to have a different life, and easier path into adulthood then she had had herself.

"But I wasn't happy. I wasn't myself. And your daddy knew it. He helped me enrol in the community college so that I could get my degree, and still stay close to home. And I was okay for a while. I was studying, flexing my brain in an environment that wasn't a North Carolina high school.

"Ronan supported me whole-heartedly. That was always the wonderful thing about him. Your daddy loved me unconditionally. Anything I wanted, he would go above and beyond for me. Anything bad I could do, every fight, he had already forgiven anything that I could ever do. The way he looked at me, God, it was like he would dive in front of a bullet for me." Mom shook her head as she sighed. "But there were always secrets. Things he wouldn't tell me. Things I couldn't know. If ever I asked a question, asked him where he was going of a night time, he would just kiss my forehead and tell me not to worry.

"I thought he was having an affair."

My heart dropped, and I saw Shea's shoulders stiffen as he heard the change in my pulse. Oh my God, I had never even considered that Dad could have cheated on Mom. The way she was talking about him, it sounded like ... kind of what Shea described, but an affair?

"I watched him for months, disappearing off into the woods, and it just made me angrier, and angrier. Who was he meeting? Did I know her? Was there some sort of cabin that I didn't know about where he met her?

"So, one night, I did a shot of tequila and I followed him. It was completely stupid and dangerous to go wandering in the woods by myself. I only had a flashlight, but anything could have got me in there. And something almost did. All I remember seeing is this enormous, black, furry beast. I heard it growling, I could see its teeth in the light of my flashlight. And then I heard myself scream. I ran for my life, I ran faster than I ever had, and I remember my foot catching on a root. I tripped and I knocked myself out.

"When I woke up, I was in our bed, and Ronan was taking care of me. He asked me what I remembered, and I told him what I saw. And then Ronan told me his secret, one that he had kept from me for the four years that we had been in a relationship. He told me that he wasn't human."

I was fairly certain that my heart was flatlining. My breathing stopped, and I didn't know how to start again. Everything inside me dropped as the realisation hit me. I felt like I was being assaulted with bombshell after bombshell. Things that I shouldhave known, should have realised.

Oh my God. My dad was one of them. My dad was ... my dad wasn't human. My daddy.

"Sara, honey, breathe," Mom urged. "You're turning red."

I forced myself to suck air into my lungs. It felt like acid.

"Do you want me to stop?" Mom asked.

"No," I whispered, my voice hoarse with emotion.

"I tried to be okay with it, as okay as I could be. Ronan brought me into the pack, as he called it. There were so many people, and they were all completely normal, and they treated me like a beloved family member. I did like them. I even made a few good friends. I really liked Karen Braverman. She had a little boy named Shea," she said, eyeing Shea, "and she was a few months along with her second child. Karen's friendship really helped to normalise everything for me. I didn't feel like we were Ronan and Amanda Bryant anymore. We were different. But seeing Karen, and seeing her as just a normal mom, helped me to feel like I could be okay with everything, even though it was just utter insanity to think that this all existed.

"It wasn't long after finding out about your daddy that I realised I was pregnant with you. Ronan was so excited. Beyond excited," she remembered fondly. "And for a while I thought we could be just like Shea's family. If she could raise a happy baby in this world, then so could I. Around that time, Ronan started to tell me about some issues he was having with a rival pack. Their Alpha, his name was Kurt, I think, was particularly aggressive. I don't remember exactly what the conflict was, but all I do remember is Ronan coming home night after night with injuries, really frightening cuts and slashes. It was escalating. The anxiety that I felt was overwhelming. I was scared all the time, for my husband, and for my unborn baby. But he was never scared, and I had never seen him happier than on the night you were born. He called you his angel, his gift from God, and that's how we picked your name." A tear fell from Mom's eye.

"When you were born, everything changed for me. You became the love of my life. I would have died before I let anything happen to you. I still would. And when your daddy, in the midst of all the violence that was going on with the other pack, presented you to his pack as his heir, I have never been more scared of anything in my life. In that moment, I saw you, my precious, perfect, innocent baby, being maimed and ripped apart by vicious creatures. I saw your whole future in that moment, and I didn't want that for you. I wanted you to be as far away from that life as possible."

I wasn't entirely sure how much of this information I was absorbing in this moment, and how much of it would hit me later. But what did occur to me was the terrifying realisation that my father, my lycan father, called me his heir.

Did that mean that I was ... one too? My heart started to race. I had never felt any different to how I felt now. I felt normal. But was my normal ... lycan?

Mom grabbed my attention back as she continued. "The love I have for you gave me the strength to break your daddy's heart," her voice cracked with emotion. "That was the hardest thing I've ever had to do in my life. But I couldn't raise you there. I couldn't put you in harm's way. I couldn't let you be groomed for a life of violence, a life where you didn't have any other option but to put yourself in danger."

She didn't describe how she broke my dad's heart, and I didn't think I wanted her to. Shea told me that it wasn't the same for humans. They could leave. Lycans couldn't. He would have only ever loved my mom.

"I transferred colleges and we moved to New York. A little while later I heard that both he and the other Alpha had been killed in a fight." Mom's voice was so delicate as she spoke those words, and I knew that she had grieved hard. She played with this thin gold wedding band that she still wore on her left hand.

I, however, had never learned the circumstances of my dad's death. Mom had only ever described it as an accident, and I assumed that she meant a car accident. But to learn that he had been killed?

I felt bile rise in my throat as I thought of Shea in that same position. Shea had been severely injured by Lex. God, what might happen?

"I raised you as best I could, Sara. I wanted you to have what I didn't. Ronan told me once that the first shift happens when you turn sixteen. I was fully expecting to have this conversation with you then. But you didn't change, and I realised that you have more of me inside you than I thought. Somehow, you didn't inherit that gene, and I felt such relief. I thought that I didn't have to worry about you any more than a mother would normally worry about her teenager. That's the only reason I even accepted this job. You weren't a lycan. You could go to school and still be a normal girl and have normal experiences. I just didn't count on you ... I just didn't count on Shea."

Mom trailed off, and I realised that she had reached the conclusion of her tale.

Holy. Shit.

I felt like my brain was imploding inside my head. Everything that I thought I knew was wrong, and yet, everything she said made sense. Every lie, every lie she'd ever told me was bubbling into my head.

Mom had always told me that we'd moved to Bedford when I was two, after Dad died. But by the sounds of it, I hadn't been very old at all.

I didn't have much information about my dad to compare, but I was strangely glad to know what I now did about him. My dad loved me. My dad wanted me. He wanted our family. I didn't even know what he looked like. Mom didn't have any pictures. Did I look like him at all? Did I behave like him at all? But I knew that he loved my mom and he loved me.

And Mom took me away from him. She took us both away from him.

"Humans have the power to brutally destroy a lycan," Shea had told me.

And then I burst into tears. "Oh my God, you destroyed him, Mom," I shakily accused.

How could a person, in that much pain, possibly think coherently, or make decisions properly? I wondered. My mind, as it was tending to do, started to race. Mom said that she had found out he had died only a little while after. He couldn't have been in his right mind. It had to have affected him. He wouldn't have died otherwise. He wouldn't have.

Chapter 20

"Sara!" Mom said emotionally, as she tried to close the gap between us.

But I jumped up. "No, I need some time to think," I sniffed, before running for the front door and grabbing my purse as I did.

I heard voices behind me, but I focused on trying to find my keys. I cried, and could barely see through my tears, as I fished through my bag to find them. But I couldn't find them amongst the junk that I hoarded.

I cried in frustration as a wave of sobs hit me. I honestly didn't know what I was feeling. All I knew was that I was feeling. It was overwhelming and overstimulating, and I just wanted to cry and scream, and throw things.

Shea's arms were around me then. Their sturdiness was comforting, and I tried to control my breathing as I leaned into him. I tried to match my breaths with his, which I found nearly impossible. I sobbed and hiccoughed and let out these uncontrollable wails as every pathetic emotion escaped out of me.

"My dad is dead," I whispered, after standing in my driveway with Shea for I don't know how long.

I honestly didn't think I'd ever said those words out loud. And I had certainly never felt them. Before today, my dad was honestly no more to me than a sperm donor. I knew nothing about the man. He had died and I didn't remember him. Mom hadn't let me remember anything about him.

But I suddenly felt like I had lost him today. A father who loved me, who wanted me, and proudly showed me off to all his friends. A father who loved my mother, and he would only ever love her. Would I have called him Dad or Daddy? Mom called him my daddy, and that freaking hurt my gut.

"Did you know?" I asked Shea, already knowing the answer.

I felt him nod. "Not the whole story, but the gist, yeah," he confirmed quietly. "You couldn't hear that from me, though, Sara," he added softly. "That had to come from your mom."

I knew he was right, but it didn't change how I felt. I didn't want to ask, but I knew that I needed to know. "Do you know how it happened? How he died?"

"The conflict your mom was talking about, with the Alpha named Kurt?" he reminded me. "His name was Kurt Hale. His scouts attacked a member of our pack. They might have been drunk, or just plain stupid, but it started an all-out war. It was violent, my dad told me, and messy, and plain dangerous. He told me your dad wanted to settle things, just him and Kurt. They were alone, and they killed each other."

I flinched at his words, and Shea's grip on me tightened.

"It didn't end there. It hasn't ended. Kurt's son, well, you've met him."

Lex, I realised.

"That is why he is so dangerous. He's out for blood. Cold-blooded revenge. Lex knows who you are, and I'm afraid he's ... that's why I wanted to keep you away from it all. I thought if you were completely oblivious, and Lex could see that, then he would keep taking his fury out of me, and not you."

My father and Lex's father killed each other. It just didn't seem like a real thing that could happen. Like a goddamn duel that happened in the Old West where everybody just watched on the street. That was not justice. That wasn't okay. They couldn't be a law unto themselves. Deaths went unanswered for. Deaths happened unnecessarily.

My dad was dead, and he didn't have to be.

"Why would your pack let that happen?" I asked Shea, my voice still uncontrollably emotional from crying. "That's just barbaric. It's still barbaric. Where is the law in this?"

What if Shea and Lex did the same thing? Oh my God. What if Shea and Lex did the same thing?

Before Shea could even answer me, I latched onto the front of his shirt, holding the fabric in my fists. "Don't you dare fight him alone like that," I ordered. "Maybe some humans are fickle, I don't know," I cried. The jury was still out on my mom. "But I know I'm not. If you died, Shea ..." my voice cracked.

"Hey," Shea said soothingly. "I've got no plans to go anywhere, okay?" he assured me, pressing his lips to my forehead. "I've waited a long time to love you, Sara. God knows I'm not going anywhere."

I cried. I cried because I didn't know what else to do. Maybe my body was shutting down. Maybe I didn't know how to process complex emotions. Maybe I just couldn't handle finding out my boyfriend, and my father, were of a different species, and that my mom knew, and my dad died, and Shea loved me, all in one day.

"Come on. I want to show you something." Shea took my hand. We walked together past my Jeep, and towards his truck. I wiped my face with my sleeve. Shea fished his keys out of his pocket and he unlocked it, opening my door for me.

I climbed inside and tried to breathe calmly, inhaling the comforting scent of Shea's cologne. The driver's side door opened, and Shea climbed inside, before firing up the engine.

I quickly realised that he was taking me towards his house, as we were headed out of town. Shea tried to distract me as we drove. He tried to keep the conversation light-hearted, answering my curious questions, rather than letting me dwell on the painful ones.

I was grateful for the change of topic.

"The tattoos," I asked. "Is that a lycan thing?" There were just too many people with tattoos, the same kind of tattoos, for it just to be a coincidence. "I know you don't have one, but a lot of people do."

"Uh, yeah," Shea laughed awkwardly. "The tattoos are a lycan thing," he confirmed.

"Why don't you have one?" I asked curiously.

"Um," he trailed off.

Shea seemed a little embarrassed. It amused me a bit. It felt good to be amused and not overwhelmed.

"We don't really understand the tattoos. They just happen. Although with us being able to manipulate our DNA, I suppose we are able to manipulate our skin as well. I don't know. We don't exactly have a pack geneticist to explain these things to us. We don't really call them tattoos, anyway. We call them marks."

"Marks?" I repeated.

"Yes. To humans, they look like tattoos, which is a good cover, but to other lycans, they basically just say, back off, this one is taken."

I thought of how many tattoos I had seen at Zoey's party that night. All of them were taken, they had mates. I glanced sideways at Shea and wondered why he didn't have one. I mean … I was his mate, right?

I had to admit, seeing my name on his chest would be a little bit romantic.

"I can see you looking at me. Enhanced senses, remember?" Shea reminded me.

"Well, why don't you have one yet?" I bit the bullet, asking him. "Does it not work if I'm not a lycan?"

Shea chuckled. "No, it works either way. I'll get one. You won't. Though, I am a little bit disappointed at that fact, I have to admit."

That didn't answer my question. "Do you have to go to a special tattoo artist or something?" I pressed.

"No, like I said, they're naturally occurring," he replied. He kept his eyes firmly on the road, and I noticed him tense a little. What wasn't he telling me?

"Yeah, but howdo they naturally occur?"

"Hey, look at that, we're here," Shea remarked, sounding relieved as his house came into view.

I huffed. I would get it out of him eventually.

Shea and I climbed down from his truck and walked up to the front door of his house. I wondered if his mom was home. I hoped I would be able to find a mirror before I met her. I probably looked like a complete mess. I was still hungover from last night, and I had been crying like crazy.

Shea used a key on his keyring to let us into his house. We were immediately met by a mirror in their small entryway. It hung above a buffet table that housed a collection of family photographs. I smiled when I saw pictures of Shea and Cece when they were younger. They were pictured with who I could only assume were their parents. Shea's mom looked young, and cheerful. And his dad looked strong, noble and protective. Shea looked exactly like his dad. Same olive toned skin. Same russet brown hair. Same dark eyes. He would still be handsome even when he was older.

Then I caught sight of the frightful face his handsome son had brought into the house. I looked worse than I thought. My skin was red, blotchy, and completely broken out. Maybe that was the alcohol … or the stress. My eyes were still bloodshot and puffy, and my nose was red from it running. My hair was a mess, and even though I was dressed, I looked like I had just fallen out of bed.

Standing next to Shea, I rolled my eyes. "Is looking like a demigod a lycan thing, too? Because I think you make me look uglier than I am. Or maybe I am just constantly having a bad face day."

Shea laughed. "Hey, if that's your theory, then you're part demigod, too," he countered. He was still holding my hand, and he brought it up to his lips, kissing it. "I think you need glasses."

"I have acne," I murmured.

"So does everyone," Shea retorted. "You should see Cece's mess in our bathroom. She has this electronic brush thing that like scrubs all the skin off her face. I don't know exactly, but long story short is that we all have things we're insecure about."

"What are you insecure about?" I asked him. I would honestly be shocked if he could point out a flaw in himself.

Shea's face softened. "I don't know if it's an insecurity, but I do feel insecure about you and me," he admitted. "It's just not the same for humans. It isn't and that's not your fault. But that's what I'm scared of. You have the power to completely destroy me and you don't even know it."

Why did I just whine about a couple of zits? My mouth opened, but I didn't know what to say.

"I love you andyour zits," he told me, though he couldn't hide his smile when he said the latter. "You are very beautiful, and if you don't believe me, just ask the two hundred guys I had to threaten on your first day of school." He winked at me, before leading me away from the mirror.

I followed, dumbfounded. Shea led me into his living room, which was quaintly decorated with eclectic furnishings, nothing matching. The far wall was lined with sturdy timber bookcases, littered with what looked like volumes of thick texts, combined with popular books, and photographs.

Shea went directly to the bookcases, kneeling down on the floor and he began sifting through what looked to be large scrapbooks, or maybe photo albums. When he found the one he wanted, he pulled it from the shelf, and stood back up.

He brought it over to one of the couches and we sat down together. He laid the large scrapbook across both of our laps. When he opened the first page, I was immediately amazed.

Mom had tried scrapbooking for a minute when I was in elementary school, but after she'd dropped beads all over the floor, and gotten glue all over her clothes ... and spent two hundred dollars on supplies, she gave up.

This, though, looked professional.

The first page was Shea. I knew because beautiful, baby blue letters were glued at the top of the page, spelling out "Shea Robert Braverman". There was a picture of him on his mom's chest, all bloody and new, as well as a cleaned up one in his cradle. His tiny hospital bracelet was attached to the page, as well as his mom's.

"Let's just skip the pictures of me looking like a potato," he joked.

He flipped the page, and his mom had made a similar one, only this time on pink paper for baby Cecelia Marie Braverman.

The next few pages were filled with cradle pictures of Shea and Cece, combined with firsts, like their first baths, their first smiles, them crawling, and walking.

Then Shea reached another page, another birth page. It took me a second to register what I was looking at.

"My mom saves things," Shea uttered quietly.

Pasted onto the page, surrounded by decorative beads and ribbons, was a yellow birth announcement card, complete with little duckies.

My heart lurched in my chest as I read the words.

Ronan and Amanda Bryant

are thrilled to announce

the safe arrival of their beautiful baby girl.

SARAPHINE JO BRYANT

Born September 21, 2001.

6lbs 11oz

20 inches.

Just seeing my parents' names written like that filled my eyes with tears. I had never even seen my dad's name written before, let alone seen it combined with my mom's, like any other ordinary married couple.

I started to cry again. Because I read the word "their". Their baby girl. Belonging to twoparents. A mom and a dad. A daddy who was thrilled to announce that his daughter, Saraphine Jo Bryant, had arrived safely.

Glued down underneath the birth announcement was a picture. A candid. It was a picture of two parents, filled with love, as they held their baby.

Mom ... she looked so young, so tired, but so pretty. She was lying in a hospital bed cradling me.

And next to her ...

I had to wipe my eyes.

Next to her, sitting beside her on the bed, was my dad. His hand was cradling my head, and he was looking down at me with such wonder. His other arm was wrapped around Mom.

This was the very first time that I had ever seen what he had looked like. And he looked nothing like I had imagined.

Like Mom, he was so young. His face was youthful. He would have only been in his early twenties. His hair was dark, though it wasn't as dark as Mom's, and his eyes, from what I could see, were light. He was smiling so widely, and I could see he had dimples in his cheeks. I loved them. He looked broad, and strong, a protector, even in his youth. I could see that by the way he was holding us both.

"Oh my God," I whispered.

"I thought you might've wanted to see him," murmured Shea. "My dad was your dad's Beta. His second. Mom made these pages for him after he died, to help him remember his best friend. We looked at them together sometimes. I remember asking him where you went. There was something about your name, it always stuck in my mind. Maybe, subconsciously, I knew you would be important one day."

Shea flipped the page, and sure enough, there was another picture. One of my dad and Shea's dad. They stood together, smiling at the camera. The picture was taken down at the beach, and I wondered if that was the same beach that we lived by, and if we have ever walked the same path.

They were both only wearing swim shorts, and their tattoos were proudly on show. "Karen" was across Shea's dad's chest, and there it was, Mom's name, "Amanda", was on Dad's chest.

They both looked so young, young enough that they looked as though they could be seniors in our school. It was so strange to see him this way. I had always pictured him older, wiser-looking.

But to see him this young just broke my heart even more. That was no age to die. His life, his whole life, was ahead of him. A life with Mom and me, if only she hadn't been so scared.

He seemed so familiar to me. My heart, it felt, longed to know him.

"Ronan loved fishing but couldn't catch a darn thing. Pickles and peanut butter on toast were his go-to snack. And he was loyal to a tee. There wasn't anything that he wouldn't do for his girls, his pack, and the community," Shea told me, as though he was recalling a conversation that he'd had with his own father.

I honestly didn't know how to feel. I felt a combination of anger, subsequent guilt, and painful longing.

But I mainly felt grief. I finally had a dad I could see, that I knew things about, and I had lost him senselessly.

CHAPTER 21

"I really wish you would have told me, Shea," I whispered after a while. I remembered him asking me about growing up without a dad on our first date, while we were talking down on the beach. And as I shared something deeply personal with him, he had known who my dad was, and what had happened to him.

"I wanted to, Sara. Believe me, telling you everything was what I wanted to do. I just thought I was doing the right thing by keeping you out of it. I hadn't counted on you being smart enough to work it out on your own." Shea paused and then frowned. "That was supposed to be a compliment."

I managed a small smile. I ran my fingertip over the page, outlining his smile with my nail.

"It wasn't my place, no matter how much I wanted it to be," he uttered quietly. "Your mom needed to tell you."

"I understand that," I uttered. "But I still can't help but feel lied to," I admitted. "Your heart was in the right place, but you lied to me." I watched as Shea's face fell from hopefully apologetic, to shameful. "If I am supposed to be this important person in your life, then I want complete honesty from you. My dad," my voice cracked, "he waited four years to tell my mom the truth. If he had been honest from the start, then maybe ... maybe, she wouldn't have taken me away from him. Maybe," goddammit, more tears, "maybe, he would still be here."

I was still feeling all kinds of confused with regards to my mom. She was not innocent here. She had lied to me for seventeen years. She had kept me from knowing about this man, this real person, my daddy, who loved me and wanted me.

"Sara, your mother was a frightened, twenty-year-old girl who had just found out monsters were real. Couple that in with pregnancy, and all the fears that come with that, I probably would have made the same decision were I in her shoes."

Shea and I both turned to the entrance of the living room. Standing there was a woman who could only be Shea's mom. What caught me immediately were her eyes. Her large, brown eyes, that were so incredibly sad. She was pale, and very slender, and probably the same height as Cece. Her hair was an ashy blonde, though there were sporadic greys, and it looked thin and wavy. She wore comfortable house clothes, sweatpants and a long-sleeved t-shirt, the sleeves only emphasizing how thin her arms were.

She looked like life was incredibly hard for her, and she looked on the wrong side of thin. I could see exactly why Shea felt the need to look after her.

This woman had lost her soulmate.

I then began to register exactly what she'd said to me.

"Mom, this is Sara. Sara, this is my mom, Karen," Shea introduced softly.

Karen managed a smile, as she walked into the room. "The last time I saw you, Sara, you still smelled like a newborn." Karen sat down on the armchair that was adjacent to the couch we were sitting on.

"It's nice to ... see you again, Mrs Braverman," I replied politely.

"Karen, please," she insisted. "Shea and Cece have talked about you constantly since you and your mother arrived back in Providence. I'm glad I could finally get to see how you've grown up. And you have done, beautifully."

"Mom," Shea hissed, but I quite enjoyed this change. His mother was embarrassing him. This was normal.

"Thank you, Karen," I said gratefully.

"I know this must be a shock for you. It would be a complete shock to anyone who wasn't born into it," she said with understanding. "But I don't want you to be too hard on Shea, or your mother. Both of them only want what is best for you.

"I knew your mother. Amanda and I were friends. And I have never seen anyone more afraid, and more completely out of their element than I had when your father brought Amanda into our pack to meet us all. He had wanted to for years, but he was afraid, and for good reason, it turned out.

"Amanda tried so hard to be a part of us. She really did. But she was a kid herself, with her own issues, and on top of that, she had found out that she was pregnant. Knowing that she was going to be a mother brought Amanda clarity, I think. The decision to protect your child above anything else is second nature to a mother. She did what she thought was best for you."

But how could taking me away from my father be what's best for me? "I understand where you are all coming from. I know that my wellbeing was at the forefront of all your minds, but it would have been nice to be consulted," I said quietly. "I don't want anyone deciding what is best for me. I decide." I stood up from the couch and took a deep breath. "Shea, can you take me home, please?" I asked.

Shea nodded and stood silently, an expression of apprehension on his face.

"It was really nice to meet you, Karen," I said sincerely.

"You as well, Sara. I hope to see you again soon," she replied, following us out to the front door.

The car ride back into town was a silent one. I could tell that Shea was tense and nervous. He had done something wonderful this afternoon, in showing me my dad, but he had also revealed yet another untruth. He knew who my dad was all this time.

I got it. I knew he was trying to protect me. Just like Mom was trying to protect me. But at the end of the day, they were still lying to me. Mom's lie ... Mom's was way worse.

Mom had lied to me my entire life. Starting from giving me wrong information about my father's death. She had told me he had died when I was two. From what I had learned, it sounded as though he had died shortly after I was born.

She had let me believe he was little more than a sperm donor by neglecting to tell me anything about him. She hadn't told me that she had been the one to leave him. She hadn't told me that he had wanted a family, or that he had been excited to be my dad.

And perhaps the biggest lie of all was that my DNA was ... well, I wasn't entirely sure what the hell was in my DNA. I certainly couldn't transform into a creature, but what would she have done if I had been able to? Leave meas well?

I knew that was ridiculous, but really, my Mom had a lot to answer for.

And Shea? I stole a glance sideways at him. His eyes were firmly fixed on the road. His arms were tense, and his hands were firmly placed at a ten and two o'clock position. I could tell that it was killing him not asking me questions or knowing what was going on inside my head.

I didn't even know what was going on inside my head.

Shea pulled up outside my house, and I saw that my mom's Mercedes was still there. She hadn't left. Shea cut the engine, and let his arms drop to his sides. I heard him exhale.

"Do you want me to come inside?" he asked softly.

"No," I replied. "I think it's best if Mom and I talk alone."

Shea nodded.

"I honestly think I'm okay with the lycan thing," I told him after a moment of silence. I didn't know how that was the easiest part of today to get over, but it was. "It's the lying that's really bothering me."

"I'm sorry, Sara," he said sincerely. "I don't know how to make it okay but to apologise."

In one day, I had both gained and lost a dad. This was mostly because of my mom's lies, but Shea had known. I knew his heart had been in the right place, and I knew it was Mom who needed to be the one to tell me, but it was still bothering me.

"Shea, you've got to give me some time to get my head around this, okay?"

He swallowed loudly and nodded, before turning to me. "I just want you to know that I'm not a monster, Sara," he said, his eyes filled with vulnerability.

It's not the same for humans, I repeated in my head. He must be so afraid right now. And that didn't sit right with me. "I know you're not, Shea," I assured him. I undid my seatbelt and leaned over, settling a soft kiss on his cheek. I heard him suck in a breath. "I am so grateful for what you showed me, for what you shared with me." I leaned back and said, "Just let me figure this out with my mom, and I will see you at school on Monday."

I had started off today feeling frightened of Shea, and unsure of what the hell he could do. But just by the look in his eyes, I could feel the intensity of his feelings for me.

Shea wanted to love me. Just as my dad had wanted to love my mom. And she had shattered his heart because of her fear.

I knew I wasn't in love with Shea yet, but I knew that I could never do to him what my mom had done to my dad. I was in possession of Shea's heart, quite literally.

I knew I would forgive him a lot quicker than in the time it would take to forgive my mom.

I climbed out of Shea's car and I made my way back inside, pausing to take a deep breath before I went through the front door. My heart was hammering. Shea, who was still parked outside my house, could no doubt hear it.

As soon as I crossed the threshold, I was hit with the scents of lemon and bleach. Mom had been cleaning. In the short time that we had lived here, I had never seen it look so tidy. Everything was straightened, and even the cushions on the sofa had the professional cuts in them to make them look staged.

She must have been going crazy.

I left my purse by the door as I heard footsteps coming down the stairs.

For the first time, ever really, I saw my mother look less than perfect. Her clothes were grimy. Her hair was messy. She was wearing no makeup, or, it had smeared off while she had been busy about the house. Her look was complete with rubber gloves and a bottle of industrial strength cleaner.

"Sara!" she said with relief when she saw me. Upon closer inspection, I could see that her makeup had come off through crying. Her mascara had run, and she had wiped it away with her hands, leaving a greyish black cast on her cheeks.

She quickly abandoned the cleaning agent on our coffee table and peeled off her rubber gloves.

Sniffing, she said, "I thought I had better give this house a proper clean as we haven't been too concerned about keeping up with it."

Mom was a wreck, and all I wanted to do was hug her. Damn it. I crossed the room and wrapped my arms around her, hugging her tightly. I had barely even touched her since we had fought about Shea, and it felt momentarily good to have some semblance of normalcy.

Mom cried. I think this was what we were doing now. Crying a lot. She hugged me hard, stroking my hair.

"You smell toxic," I muttered into her shoulder.

She laughed through her tears.

"I love you, Mom. But I'm still so mad at you," I added.

Mom pulled away and wiped her eyes with the sleeve of her sweatshirt. She nodded. "I know, I understand, Sara."

"I don't think you do," I replied. "I understand where you were coming from. You were trying to protect me. I get that. But in doing that, you took my father away from me. You took me, and you, away from Dad. He loved us. He wanted us. And, as if that wasn't bad enough, you never told me a thing about him! You let me believe that he was little more than a sperm donor. Someone we didn't need to bother mentioning. And the only thing that I knew about him was a lie. He didn't die when I was two. He died shortly after I was born!" I didn't mean to become so exasperated, but I couldn't help it.

Mom put her hands up defensively. "I know, I messed up, Sara. I'm not perfect, and I never claimed to be." Tears welled up in her eyes. "I know I lied. I took you away to protect you. But I lied to protect me." She ran her fingers through her hair as she tried to stay calm. "Talking about your daddy today has brought it all back to the surface. I grieved. I grieved hard. There were days when I could barely pull myself out of bed, but I knew I had to because I had a baby who needed me! I loved that man with everything that I had, and ..." her voice cracked as she put a finger under her nose, her lower lip wobbling, "and I put my grief and memories, both good and bad, and my love for him in a box a long time ago. I locked it up tight to protect myself, so that I could be the best mother I could be.

"When I left Providence, when I left Ronan, some part of me didn't think it would be for good. I didn't know I would never see my husband again. I didn't know my baby would never know her father. And when I got that news," Mom trembled, "I felt like I had died, too. So, no, I couldn't tell you about your daddy, because I wasn't strong enough to re-live it over and over again. And I know that it's terribly selfish of me, Sara, and I'm sorry. I'm sorry, honey."

I saw a different side to my mom right in that moment. It was like she had become a widow in the space of a few moments. She suddenly reminded me of Shea's mom. But my mom never needed me to take care of her. At least, not in the dependent way. She had pulled herself together, masked her pain, and had gotten on with our lives. She had masked it so well, that I never knew she felt anything sad at all.

"I chose paediatric oncology because I wanted to protect the children of other frightened mothers and fathers, parents just like me. In my mind, and in reality, I had made you safe, and I wanted to help others do the same thing."

Oh my God. Now I felt like a terrible person for holding a grudge. Was this something that I just needed to get over? Everything logical inside me was telling me no, but I knew that this situation wasn't logical. That went out the window the minute I found out mythical creatures were real.

My mom was human, in every sense of the word. She made mistakes. She wasn't perfect. And she protected herself, which was the natural human instinct. But she also raised me by herself, while dealing with unimaginable grief.

I was proud of her, even if I didn't agree with her on every decision she had made for us.

I thought, like Mom, this was going to have to be something that I dealt with on my own. I couldn't ask her to bring up any more painful memories, as that would just be punishing her. What was done was done, and nothing, no amount of arguing or apology, was going to change that.

I hugged her again, this time in a nurturing, soft manner. She received it whole-heartedly, crying into my shoulder. "I love you, Mom," I whispered.

"Oh, I love you more, sweet girl," she replied with emotional conviction.

I hadn't forgiven her, but I couldn't punish her. This would be my burden.

CHAPTER 22

om and I spent the day together on Sunday, without our
phones.

On a normal day, she had the tendency to check up on work on weekends even though she had them off. The beauty of working in a clinic meant that she had set hours, and on call doctors took care of any emergencies, but being the concerned person that she was, she couldn't help herself.

I, like any other teenager, probably would have spent the day texting my friends and talking to my boyfriend, but I didn't. I sent Shea a good morning text to reassure him and then I left my phone in my room.

It was important to Mom that we have time together, binge watching whatever trash she found recorded on the DVR and eating food that contained approximately forty-three different preservatives. In her mind, we were starting fresh.

In mine, I was starting the long road towards forgiveness, adjusting to my new normal, and accepting that my life had taken this path without any of my knowledge.

Mom didn't mention Dad, and I didn't bring him up, but I did notice an addition to our collection of family pictures on the mantle when I came downstairs this morning.

My mom had about every class picture framed and displayed them proudly. Couple those with annual mall Santa pictures, vacation shots, and a picture of us at Mom's college and med school graduations.

The addition, however, didn't feature me for a change. It was of my parents. It seemed weird to even think of them as a plural. But I had parents, it was a thing now, and my dad was acknowledged in this house. The picture was their wedding photo, and I just about cried when I saw it.

I had waited for Mom to got to the bathroom to practically leap on it, to study it in great detail for the two minutes she would be gone.

They looked so incredibly young. Mom was rocking the late 90s off the shoulder ball gown, while my dad looked incredibly handsome in what was probably his prom tux. Their smiles practically touched their ears as they looked at the camera, while holding onto each other. They looked like high school sweethearts, and nothing could ever break them apart.

I had quickly retrieved my phone for a second, snapped a photo of them both and had set the picture as my wallpaper. My phone would have to be unlocked for anyone to see it, so there was no way Mom would know. I just wanted them with me, as lame as that probably sounded.

Mom ordered in take out for Sunday night dinner, and we finished watching a show where the couple all got married when they first met each other. I actually got super into it, but I suppose anyone would if they'd watched seven hours of the show in a row.

When it was time for bed, as we both had school and work in the morning, Mom thanked me for the day.

"It felt nice to just hang out with you, Sara. We haven't done that in a while."

"It was nice to hang out with you, too, Mom," I replied with a small smile.

"I promise, the truth from now on, okay? I won't ever lie to you again." With that, she kissed my cheek and retreated into her bedroom.

I went in the other direction and wandered into my own room. I picked up my phone and checked my messages and social media.

I only had one message from Shea, responding to my text this morning. I had a feeling he was trying to restrain himself.

On the other hand, I had elevenmessages from Cece. Now that I knew, it seemed she was desperate to talk to me. Something told me we wouldn't be learning much in Spanish in the morning.

I replied to them both, before noticing something on my pillow that hadn't been there earlier when I'd come to grab my phone. It was a CD case.

"Saraphine" was written on the front, in handwriting I didn't recognise. I put my phone down on the nightstand and picked up the CD case. Underneath my name was a yellow post-it. In my mom's handwriting was "play me x".

I opened the case to see a blank DVD, so I immediately grabbed my laptop and opened the disc drive. I placed the DVD inside and waited for it to pop up on my screen. I clicked on it immediately when I saw the notification, and a video started to play.

A shaky camera was directed at a bassinet. The baby was me. I recognised myself from the infant pictures my mom had of me.

"Holy shit," came a male voice from behind the camera. "Oh, fuck," he cursed again. "Don't listen to me, Saraphine!" he pleaded, a hand appearing on screen as he attempted to cover one of my ears.

This was my dad's voice. I was listening to my dad's voice. My jaw was wide open with shock. But in a weird way, I felt like I already knew his voice. Maybe in some way, I'd committed it to memory.

The camera fumbled a little more as he appeared to be setting it up on a tripod, the lens pointing towards my bassinet.

"Amanda!" he called, but in a hushed voice so as not to wake me. "Honey, how do you attach this thing? Oh, never mind, I got it!" And just like that, the camera steadied and the picture wasn't all over the place anymore.

I heard Mom laugh. "Are you okay?" she asked from somewhere in the room. "Don't you dare break that thing," she warned humorously.

"Why, you going to spank me?" he teased.

"Jesus Christ!" Mom cried. "When Saraphine watches this she's going to think her parents are perverts." All of a sudden, my mom appeared on screen. She was standing behind my bassinet, bending over and looking up into the lens. She looked so incredibly young. She was only a couple of years older than I was now. "We aren't perverts," she assured me, and I couldn't help but laugh. "Alright, I'll leave you to it. I've got tonight's Charmed taped, so I'll go watch that and then it'll be time for her nine-thirty feed. I love you, baby."

"Love you more, hon."

I was going to cry. I was going to cry over hearing my parents talk to each other.

Her Southern accent was much more prominent then than it was now. She sounded like a regular Southern Belle.

Mom kissed me in the bassinet, then left us alone in the nursery.

Then my dad appeared on screen, taking a seat behind the bassinet, one hand resting on my blankets. He looked just like he did in the photos that Shea had. Incredibly young, and cheerfully happy.

His eyes were light, like I thought. A beautiful, bright blue. His dark hair was a remnant of the late 90s, early 2000s, floppy era, but it suited him. When he smiled, it was so big that it made his eyes crinkle. He smiled big at me.

"I'm just a bit of a pervert, but only for her," he informed the camera, well me, holding up his thumb and index finger to show me the tiny amount. "Your Mommy is so damn pretty it ought to be illegal." He sighed and looked down at me with a mesmerised expression. "Where to start, angel?" he asked. "I'm not very articulate. Is that the word? Mommy's the smart one. I really hope you're smart like her. If you get my brains, college won't be much fun."

He looked up at the camera again, looked up at me again. "I wanted to make this video because I want to remember every second of this time with you. Remember how I'm feeling right now, though I don't think I'll ever forget how much I fucking love you. Shit!" he cried. "I've got to get a handle on my cursing. Mommy will probably hit me with her car if your first word is "fuck"," he laughed. I laughed, too.

"Fuck it," he continued. "I'll figure out how you bleep out the cursing like they do on TV. Do you know how goddamn cute you are? I never thought I'd hear the end of Robert harping on about how gorgeous his daughter, Cecelia, is, but my daughter is the fucking cutest. No competition," he bragged.

"Tell you what, I'm going to get you into those Baby Gap commercials. Those kids are fucking trolls compared to you." He looked upon me with such love that I got the air stuck in my throat.

"Okay," he continued, "so I wanted to make this video for you, too." He looked back up at me. "I want this video to sit on the shelf next to Mommy's Tom Cruise movies," he rolled his eyes, "Fucking Jerry Maguire, kid, I swear. "You had me at hello," and she's crying. Somehow me telling her she had me at mustard stain on her shirt doesn't work the same magic." He laughed again. "Anyway, I'm getting side-tracked. I want this video to be where you can grab it every time you hate me.

"When you're pissed off at me for grounding you for staying out past curfew with your boyfriend. Or for when we're fighting because I fucking know the jerk isn't good enough for you. Or for when you're not talking to me after I've criticised your shitty driving after a lesson. Or for when I catch you sneaking one of my beers. Or for when I catch you cursing after you've heard it from me. Or for when you get a bad grade. But let's face it, you can blame Mommy for that one. She'll be on you for your grades." He grinned. "This video is for you to watch every time you hate me, to remind you that I love you.

"I thought becoming a dad would be the scariest thing in the world. But it isn't. You are my child, my flesh and blood, and loving you is like breathing to me." Exhaling, he looked down at me again, playing with my fingers with his index finger. "You're so sweet and innocent, Saraphine. You bring me a kind of joy that I didn't know I could feel. I love you so much that I'm scared I'll fuck it up."

He shook his head. "I will fuck it up," he corrected himself. "I will fuck it up so many times, Saraphine," he said, looking back at the camera. "But don't you ever doubt that you are so damn loved. Mommy and I love you as big as the world.

"So, if you're watching this, and you're fifteen or something, and you're pissed at me for cracking it at you for mouthing off at Mommy or dating that dipshit I know you'll be dating because like mother, like daughter," he winked, gesturing to himself, "first, take it easy on your old man. I'll be old then. My temper will probably be shorter. Second, know that I fucking love you, angel, and everything that I do, or have done, or will do, will be for you and Mommy.

"I will love you every damn day of my life. I am counting every one of my blessings for you, and I am so grateful that I've got a while before I've got to buy you a prom dress, or get you a car, or walk you down the aisle and give you away at your wedding." He seemed to pale a bit. "Shit," he said to me in the bassinet. "Stay little, okay? Do you know what goes through a guy's head at prom? Because I fucking do. And we fucking did it. Now way in hell you're fucking doing that."

And for the first time in my life I was embarrassed by my parents.

And then his expression changed to that of disgust. "Oh, Jesus, Saraphine. What is she feeding you, expired Mexican food?" he cried, blocking his nose. "I think you just diarrhoea-d on your new romper. How do I turn this thing off?" He came up to the camera, and I could see the pattern on his shirt as he tried to find the off switch. "Amanda, how do I –" and the screen cut to black.

I closed my laptop and wiped my eyes with my sleeve. I laid down and stretched out my legs. God, how I wished things were different. I wished that Mom had never left. I wished that Dad was still alive. I wished, I wished, I wished. But, to use my Dad's words, my Mom fucked up. I was watching that video while feeling all sorts towards my Mom, and it did give me some perspective.

But it also gave me something else. It gave me my dad. He had been gone nearly as long as I had been alive, but I had him in a sense. I had his words. I certainly had a sense of his personality. I had a vision of what he and Mom had been like together when things had been good. And I had a clear vision of how it would have been to grow up with him.

I picked up my phone and dialled Shea. He answered on the first ring.

"Sara?" he sounded concerned.

"Hey." You could tell in my voice that I had been crying.

He was immediately alarmed. "What's wrong? Are you okay?"

"Yeah," I answered, actually surprised. "I'm okay. I'm the most okay I've been in a while." I rolled onto my side, facing my other nightstand, and I saw that Mom had made another addition.

It was the same hospital picture that had been in Karen Braverman's scrapbook, but it was framed in beautiful, white wood.

I smiled. "What did you do today?" I asked.

CHAPTER 23

M om had a seven o'clock patient, so she was gone by the time I managed to pull myself out of bed on Monday.

I nibbled on a bran bar and sipped a coffee while I quickly finished off my homework that I had seriously neglected over the weekend.

In fact, sitting at my kitchen counter with my algebra notes in front of me on a Monday morning seemed pretty normal. I was actually relieved considering the weekend that I'd had.

I didn't want anything to be weird. I didn't want anything to be difficult.

I could only imagine what awaited me at school. Cece, first up, in Spanish. I could already see her bouncing in her seat as she waited to hear everything. But thinking of Cece made me smile nostalgically for a bit.

Her father, Robert, had bragged about her to my father, Ronan. They had both claimed that their daughter was the prettiest. It made me happy to know that after everything, I was friends with someone that I would have grown up with had I been allowed to stay in Providence.

And Robert had been right. My dad had just been biased.

I packed my bag, checked that I had all my homework, and made sure my phone was set to vibrate. Shoving it in the back pocket of my jeans, I gave my appearance the once over in the mirror by the front door, before grabbing my keys.

As soon as I opened the front door, I noticed Shea's black truck parked on the curb outside my house. He was leaning against the passenger side door, waiting for me.

I stared for a moment. Shea looked ridiculously good looking today. I mean, he always looked handsome, better looking than any boy I knew back home in Bedford, but today, oh my God.

He wore a tight pair of black jeans, rolled up at the ankles, and a pair of expensive looking sneakers. His t-shirt was white and plain, but tight on the arms, hugging his bulging biceps, which were flexed as they were folded across his chest.

I think what made me notice his appearance so much this morning was his confidence. He had a renewed, confident smile on his face as he looked at me, it only widening as he saw me leave the house.

My heart fluttered. Holy shit. That boy loved me.

I felt like I was seeing with 20/20 vision today or something. There were no secrets. Shea knew me, and I certainly knew Shea. I could see him properly. I could see how he felt about me. It was written all over his face. I could see that through the macho, confident high school senior was a good, decent brother and son who cared so deeply about his family.

Shea bounced off the side of his car and came over to me. I realised I hadn't moved from the front door. He was grinning at me, the skin at his eyes crinkling adorably. I loved his brown eyes. They were so warm and comforting.

"It almost sounds like you've seen something you like, Sara," Shea said, tapping his ear.

I snapped out of my lustful trance and embarrassingly realised that he could hear my heart palpitations. Blushing, I turned away, making sure I had locked the front door, checking again twice to avoid facing him.

"Hey," Shea said softly, his arms snaking around my waist from behind as he met me at the door. "If you could hear mine, you would know that it's doing the same thing. You have noidea how you affect me," he muttered in my ear.

The warmth of his voice sent a shiver down my spine. As much as he made me feel as though I was out of my comfort zone, I enjoyed confident Shea. I didn't like to make him feel insecure, and our conversation last night had obviously made him feel better about my feelings for him.

I needed to be confident, too. I wanted to be confident. I spun around in Shea's arms, facing him, and I looked up to him. "How do I affect you?" I asked him.

He smiled devilishly, appreciating my forwardness. "Let me count the ways," he murmured. "Your scent is always the thing that hits me first. It fogs up my brain to the point where you are the only thing that I can focus on. You smell ... fresh, like the rain. It's different, and it suits me perfectly." Shea suddenly pressed his lips to my neck and inhaled. I shivered again. Shea then placed his hand underneath my chin and brought it up. He stood back to his full height and looked down at me. "And then when I finally see you, it's your eyes that get me. They're so big, so green, and they betray your every thought most of the time, which I enjoy. I can't look away. Nature won't allow it. Eyes really are the window to the soul. Yours are so pure and innocent. I want your eyes to see me, the good and the bad. Because I feel that when you're looking at me, you understand me. To be seen by you makes me want to be better for you." Shea's thumb ran over my bottom lip, which dropped slightly. His eyes dropped to my lips for a moment. "And when you speak to me, when you talk to me, when you say my name, you truly have me under your spell. I would do anything you asked of me, Sara."

My traitor heart kept flip-flopping, which caused a smile to tug at the corner of Shea's mouth.

I wondered if I would ever understand the mate thing. Would I ever have the capacity, as a human, to reciprocate? All I knew for sure was that Shea was incredibly important. He spoke so well, so vulnerably and honestly about how he felt, and I truly adored it.

While I still had a few seconds left of my confidence, I stood up on my toes and kissed him. I closed my eyes and felt a true connection with Shea. We fit together perfectly, and he responded to me enthusiastically. He held me tightly, one hand around my waist, the other cupping my cheek.

I was startled by my phone, causing me to pull away.

"Your ass just vibrated," he uttered humorously, not breaking eye-contact with me.

I blushed as I pulled my phone out and saw this it was a message from Cece. "It's Cece," I told him. I opened the message to see a funny countdown to Spanish.

Shea rolled his eyes. "I hate my sister sometimes."

I laughed.

"Come on. She wanted to be the one to drive you this morning. She's excited to gossip with you." He shook his head, but led me towards his truck, keeping an arm around my waist. "There is one more thing about you that affects me," he added.

"What?" I asked.

"You're super hot," he said casually.

I gaped at him as we walked.

Shea just grinned and kissed my temple. "Damn. I still think about that latex dress you wore to Zoey's party," he teased, but I could tell by the huskiness of his voice that he was being one hundred percent serious.

I managed to casually laugh, but it made me feel quite vulnerable to hear of him talking about me in that way. I mean, I know I had just majorly checked him out only five minutes ago, but to hear of him talk about being sexually attracted to me made me feel like a fish out of water.

I knew I wasn't ready. I wasn't fully comfortable. I still hoped he was okay with that.

Shea, probably hearing my panic, didn't say anything, and I was grateful. He opened my door for me before jogging around to the driver's side and climbing in.

"I get that this is a lot to comprehend in such a short amount of time."

I was wrong about the not saying anything. I swallowed loudly.

Shea smiled at me and tilted his head. "Sara, you are the most important person in my life now. You always will be, no matter what happens. You don't have to be nervous about anything with me."

I appreciated him really trying to settle me. It was very sweet, and I knew he was speaking truthfully, but that didn't make me any less nervous.

Was I being dumb? I mean, the last person to see me naked was when I was young enough to still need bathing by my mother. The thought of being so … exposed … was terrifying.

I wasn't even going to start my thoughts on the differences in our, er, experience.

Shea drove us to school and parked in his senior spot. His friends had already all arrived, and were casually leaning against their own cars as they waited for Shea. It occurred to me that they were all probably lycans, too.

I knew Matt and Lucas, but there were a few other boys, and their girlfriends, or perhaps their mates, hanging around that I wasn't familiar with. I had seen them around, but I didn't know them.

Shea cut the engine and we got out of the truck. I was imme-diately greeted by a collection of "Luna!" cries. Shea took my hand and brought me over to where his friends were convened.

No sooner had I corrected them all, instructing them to call me "Sara", I heard my name being called behind me.

I turned around to see Josh walking towards us. He was looking between Shea and I with a confused expression on his face. I realised that the last that Josh had seen of me was me screaming at Shea on Friday night at the party, and here I was on Monday morning, holding his hand and seemingly back together with him.

Shea noticed where my attention had gone, and he seemed to instinctively hold onto me tighter. I supposed, as humans were so fickle, anyone would seem like a threat to him.

"I'll see you at lunch," I told him quietly. Shea released my hand and I walked over to Josh.

"I mean, I thought you were hungover. I didn't realise you were getting back with Braverman," Josh said to me, surprised, as I met him in the middle of the parking lot.

"I was hungover," I confirmed. Probably the worst hangover anyone has ever had. "But Shea and I sorted things out over the weekend."

Josh frowned. "Are you sure you want to be with him?" he asked, sounding genuinely concerned. "At the party you seemed pretty convinced that you wanted him to leave you alone. Sara, seriously, if something's wrong, you can tell me. These guns aren't just for show," he said, flexing his biceps.

I rolled my eyes, embarrassed. "I cannot believe you just said that. But I do appreciate the sentiment, no matter how lame you are. I promise, Shea and I sorted everything out. We're okay."

Josh seemed to accept that. "Okay," he nodded. "Well, I'm happy for you. At least one of us got laid this weekend," he said, putting his arm around my shoulder as he led me towards the school building.

I was watching Shea, who promptly froze as Josh put his arm around me. I knew he heard what Josh had said, and if looks could kill …

"Ew, Josh," I scolded. "Feminism, hashtag me too, respect for women," I snapped, shrugging his arm off me. Shea relaxed a little as we walked past.

"Hey, I have the utmost respect for women," he said defensively. "They just freaking hate me. Well, one does in particular," he soured.

Let me guess.

"You're a girl, right?"

I raised my eyebrows. "Gee, let me think."

"You know what I mean. Seriously, what is with the mood swings?" he asked exasperatedly. "Not long after you left, Zoey freaking attacks me, pulling me into a bedroom and we're full on hooking up."

I really thought I didn't want to hear this.

"Like, this girl is incredible. I can't even describe what it felt like to be with her."

Please don't.

"And before I know it, she's rounding on third, and then she slaps me! Like full on bitch slaps me, and storms out." He threw his arms up in the air. "What's with her? Am I crazy to think that it could work for a second before she decides she hates me?"

Graphic imagery aside, I understood why he was asking for my advice. I couldn't exactly imagine the football team being very understanding. And I needed to remember that Josh actually likedZoey for some strange reason.

It was like a lightbulb went off in my head. Some strange reason. All of Zoey's threats and jealousy surrounding Josh. Josh's confusion over her. Zoey's glaring daggers at me anytime I spoke to him.

Josh was Zoey's mate. And Zoey, I thought, was in denial.

"She'll come around," I assured him, knowing that I was certainly right. Zoey wouldn't be able to stay away forever. "Give her some time to get off her high horse. You could always make her jealous. That certainly would get a reaction." I knew from experience.

Josh laughed. "That's the thing though. I don't really want to date anyone else. It's weird. Like I don't find other girls attractive anymore. The thought of actually dating or being with anyone else just feels wrong. And yet the one girl I could actually see myself with treats me like a freaking leper. I sure can pick 'em."

"If you want, you can use me to make her jealous," I offered. Provoking Zoey into revealing and acting on her true feelings was probably going to be the only thing that worked. "She already hates that you hang out with me. She'll see us at lunch."

Josh grinned. "Might just take you up on that. Alright, I'll see you at lunch." Josh then jogged off into the school building.

I checked the time on my phone and realised that I needed to get inside as well. I turned and waved to Shea, who was still watching me, disinterestedly listening to his friends. I offered him a reassuring smile, letting him know everything was okay, and he smiled back at me.

I quickly made my way to my locker, collected what I needed for my first classes of the day, before making my way to my Spanish classroom. The bell rang just as I crossed the threshold, and I could hear students being collected for tardiness behind me. I breathed a sigh of relief, before I saw what was awaiting me in the classroom.

Cece was practically vibrating, she was so excited. Something told me I wasn't going to be learning any Spanish today. I shuffled between the desks and hurried to my seat before Señora Gomez scolded me.

"Hi, Cece," I said knowingly as I sat down.

Cece grabbed a hold of my hand and pulled me into a tight hug. "Oh, Sara!" she whispered. "I can't tell you how glad I am that you know. I swear, I swear that I wanted to tell you. But you know why I couldn't."

"I get it, Cece," I assured her. "It's okay."

Cece beamed. "I'm so happy for you and Shea. He's been a total mess. But this is it, now, right? You're one of us!"

Before I could respond, Señora Gomez barked our names and demanded our attention. I turned my focus to the whiteboard as Señora Gomez was teaching us our new verbs.

One of us. It was hard to imagine myself as one of them. I wasn't one of them. Not really. And yet, as soon as I had got out of the car, Shea's friends had called me "Luna". It was a role that I knew nothing about, and it was a role that felt entirely out of my comfort zone. It wasn't just like trying something new, it was being a part of a close-knit, worlds-apart community that had their own set of rules and hierarchy.

Shit.

CHAPTER 24

The bell rang, and I told Cece I would see her in English. I quickly ran into the girl's bathroom and called Shea. I needed to communicate. I couldn't stew on these fears and questions I had, and would no doubt keep having as I further understood their world.

As always, Shea answered on the first ring. It was something that I was quickly coming to love about him. "Sara?" he breathed.

"Ihavetogotocollege," I blurted out all in one go.

"What?"

I took a deep breath. "I have to go to college, a four-year college," I said, slowing down my words. "Not just because my mom would drag me to one, but because I want to. College is important, and I might get into one out of state, and I want that to be an option for me. I don't know what you expect of me, or need from me, but I need you to know that."

"You're going to college," Shea replied quietly, but confidently. "You're too smart not to. I don't know what Cece said to you, but you have no obligations to our pack. You are my mate, but you are also human. I couldn't make you do anything that you didn't want to. I would never do that."

I wondered if my mom had had this same conversation with my dad. She stayed in Providence after high school to be with him. Had he told her not to go?

"No matter what you decide, or where ever you decide to go, I will be in the front row cheering like a lunatic when you get that diploma. My burdens aren't yours, Sara. I don't get to choose. I could never take your choices away from you."

Shit.

But this time, it was a good shit. As in shit, Shea could be so incredibly selfless. And in turn, I felt so incredibly stupid. Shea was not going to hold me back. Just like my dad would not have held my mom back if they'd managed to communicate properly.

And just like Shea wanted more for me, I wanted more for Shea. To not have choices at eighteen? That wasn't right. That wasn't fair. The world was supposed to be at our feet at eighteen.

We were silent on the phone for a minute or two, and I already knew I was late for English. But I didn't feel like going now. I had never skipped a class in my life, but I really couldn't force myself to care about prose right now.

"If you could be anything, Shea, anything in the world, what would it be?" I asked him quietly.

"I would be the kind of man his family can depend on," he replied effortlessly. "The kind of man that a college educated young woman could respect and love."

I caught sight of my reflection as he said those words, and I saw my pure reaction. The touched emotion was written all over my face.

"I love you," I whispered, without realising the words had escaped my mouth. They came naturally, and my heart realised them before my head did.

I loved Shea. Maybe I was delusional in convincing myself that it was too soon, that I wasn't ready, that I wasn't there yet. But I was. I had been for a while. Maybe I had been from the start. I loved Shea, and I didn't think I would ever stop.

I heard his breathing stagger on the other end of the phone as he heard my words. It made me smile uncontrollably. I loved him. I loved him. I couldn't stop my brain at this point.

"Braverman!" I heard a voice bark in the background. "Is that a cell phone?"

Oh my God, Shea was in class. I didn't think he would answer if he was in class. Then again, I was supposed to be in class, too.

"Sorry Mr Barry, my girlfriend just told me that she loved me so we're kind of having a moment," Shea told Mr Barry unapologetically.

I, on the other hand, was mortified for him.

"How nice," replied Mr Barry sarcastically, as the students in the background cheered. "Tell me more about it in detention. Cell phone," he demanded.

"Shea, I'm so sorry!" I cried.

Shea just laughed. "Don't be. Nothing can ruin my mood today. I love you, too." The call ended.

Smiling, I put my phone in my back pocket and went over to the basins to check my appearance before I went back out into the hall. The acne that had reared its ugly head on Saturday was still there, but it didn't look as angry. I had been able to cover the blemishes this morning and they didn't look too bad. I tucked some loose hair behind my heads and sighed.

I was then suddenly startled when one of the cubicles unlocked and someone emerged. I hadn't thought to check if I was alone in the bathroom when I had come in to call Shea. I momentarily panicked, trying to remember if I had said anything that would give his secret away before I realised that it was Zoey.

Zoey, with what seemed like her permanent sneer facial expression, glared at me as she came over to the basin to wash her hands.

"I understand you know our little secret now," she muttered. Zoey raised her eyebrows and looked at herself closely in the mirror, using her index finger to make sure her eyelashes were still curled.

I didn't say anything. I merely nodded.

Zoey looked away from herself and turned to me, placing her manicured hands on her perfectly proportioned waist. "Well then, now that you understand how he feels about you, not sure why," she said the last part under her breath, "I would suggest you show a little more respect to Shea by not whoring around with other guys," she snapped.

Now knowing what I did not about her, I merely smiled. Zoey was jealous. And she was just too damned proud to admit that Josh was for her.

"What I do, and who I choose to do it with, is none of your business," I retorted, deliberately trying to sound coy. "Humans, after all, are not monogamous." My words hit her like a slap in the face, and she recoiled, her eyes flaring furiously.

Zoey reached out her hands in pure rage, as though she wanted to strangle me, but she pulled her hands back as she clenched her teeth. "You are lucky I have self-control," she spat. "I swear to God, if

I see you and your whorish smile anywhere near ..." she closed her eyes and took a breath. "I will not be accountable for my actions."

But I could see that Zoey wasn't in control. She was the least controlled that I had ever seen her. Her jealousy was making her go out of her mind. I thought about just telling her that I knew Josh was her mate, and offering her empathy, but something told me Zoey would just throw it back in my face.

Zoey's interests were also not those that I was looking out for. She was screwing around with my friend, and I owed him loyalty before her. She could threaten me all she wanted. Until she actually made the decision to accept Josh as the decent guy he was, then I couldn't give two hoots about what she said to me.

Zoey wasn't the type of person who could be told. She needed to get there herself.

So I merely smirked at her, before leaving the bathroom.

I studied in the library until my next class, and then continued on with my normal schedule.

When lunch came, I made my way alone to the cafeteria, and stood in line for whatever unidentifiable special was being served today. As I was counting the ones I had in my purse, Josh came up next to me.

"Hey," he said excitedly, looking around for Zoey. He spotted her almost immediately, sitting at Shea's table beside Cece. Shea was there, too, watching us with idle curiosity.

I smiled at him. I loved him. I still couldn't get over it.

"Zoey cornered me in the bathroom during second period today. She's going absolutely crazy," I informed him. We made our way up to the servery, choosing a few things to put on our trays before paying for our food.

"Okay, she's looking," whispered Josh, almost inaudibly.

Just as I was about to offer him my tray to carry, all in effort to make Zoey jealous, I was surprised by Josh suddenly in my face, crashing his lips to mine.

It took me a second to realise what was happening, but Josh was kissing me. I didn't have a chance to push him off of me, because that was already happening.

Shea was beside us in a second, pulling Josh away, and looking positively lethal while doing it.

"What the fuckdo you think you're doing?" he seethed. Shea seemed to grow a foot as he stood between me and Josh.

Josh, who was a left tackle, was just as tall, and if not more muscular than Shea, but he looked intimidated. I needed to defuse this. Before I could even get around Shea, he had shoved Josh, causing him to drop his cafeteria tray. The sound and the commotion had quickly drawn all attention to us.

Shit, shit, shit. Shea was going to knock Josh out and then get suspended or something because of me. I knew this wasn't a normal reaction. This was a lycan thing. A territory thing. And I could have been all pissed off being thought of as property, and I would later, but right now I needed to make sure the damn cops weren't called.

"Shea!" I hissed, grabbing his arm and pulling him away.

Shea barely noticed. He shoved Josh again, and this time he fell onto a crowded table, sending their lunches flying everywhere. Students were now covered in spaghetti and milkshakes, and the tension was quickly rising.

"Shea, he didn't mean anything by it!" I tried again but he ignored me. He was getting angrier, and angrier, his body shaking with rage.

Cece was next to us now, trying to calm down her brother, and to my surprise, Zoey had run over, and had inserted herself between Shea and Josh. She wasn't glaring at me, but Shea.

She looked fierce, and strong, and utterly territorial. "Back. Off," she said firmly through clenched teeth.

Shea paused, though his anger had in no way diminished.

Teachers suddenly flooded the cafeteria. Students were dispersing and trying to get away from the fight, but Shea, Josh, Zoey and I were all caught up in it, and immediately sent to the principal's office.

We were seated on the sofas in the office while we waited for Principal Baynard to arrive from a meeting. We were alone in the office. Shea and I were sitting on a small loveseat, while Zoey and Josh occupied the two armchairs.

The office was covered in school memorabilia, trophies, flags and ribbons. It was an entirely spirited, cheerful space. Anything but like the meeting at the moment.

Shea was still furious. I hadn't had the chance to explain. And nothing could really be said considering Josh was ignorant of everything.

It was hard to tell who Zoey was angrier at. Shea or me.

Me. It would always be me.

"I don't know what the fuck goes on in your locker room, you jackass, but kissing a girl who didn't ask for it is fucking assault," Shea finally spat.

Josh glared at Shea. "Oh, and shoving me across a cafeteria isn't, caveman?" he retorted.

Good one.

"I think we can all agree if Sara had just kept her slutty hands to herself, none of us would be in this mess," muttered Zoey.

I rolled my eyes. "And I think we can all agree if we had just been a little more honest with ourselves, we wouldn't be in this mess, huh Zoey?" I snapped impatiently.

Zoey's eyes narrowed.

"Watch yourself, Zoey," Shea said angrily. "You speak like that about Sara again and we're going to have a problem."

"Hey, don't talk to her like that," Josh said defensively. "You're not the boss of her."

Shea laughed ironically. I squeezed his thigh to get his attention. He looked down at me and I gave him a look that told him to shut up. "And I thought nothing could ruin my mood today," he murmured to me.

I shook my head. This was all such a big misunderstanding. And it was Josh's fault. How he thought kissing me was a good idea, I didn't know. But Shea didn't need to be such a caveman. And Zoey needed to put on her big girl panties and admit that she liked Josh.

The office door opened and Principal Baynard walked in. He was wearing a suit that looked to be one size too small for him, and an expression that looked like my mom's whenever she had too many balls to juggle. I was guessing we were the last thing that he wanted to deal with today.

His eyes first settled on Josh. He sighed defeatedly. "Hackett, if you're suspended, you can't play. What the hell did you do?"

"Nothing," Josh said defensively. "I should not be suspended. I get suspended, I will lose any chance at a scholarship!"

"Nothing?" laughed Shea. "He was sexually harassing my girlfriend. He's lucky I didn't do worse."

"Is that a threat?" Josh turned on Shea.

I could kill Shea. You know what, fuck it. Nobody was losing their scholarship, and words like sexual harassment were not being thrown around over some stupid misunderstanding.

"Principal Baynard, let me explain," I pleaded.

"Go ahead, New Girl," he allowed tiredly.

Okay. "Josh likes Zoey, and Zoey likes Josh, but she can't admit it because her nose is stuck up so high in the sky that she can tell if it's going to rain tomorrow. Josh and I are friends, and I am dating Shea. Zoey keeps messing Josh around, so we thought it would be a good idea to make her jealous in order to provoke her into admitting her feelings. I thought that meant Josh carrying things for me, but Josh obviously thought that meant kissing me. Josh kissed me in the cafeteria which Shea saw. Shea got angry and behaved terribly, but nobody was sexually harassed, and nobody ought to be suspended."

Principal Baynard blinked a few times as he absorbed the information, I just gave him. "Oh, I don't get paid enough for this. Behave like second graders again and I'll send you back to elementary school. Hackett, you keep your nose clean. I don't want you missing any games. Miss Eckhart ... give my regards to your parents."

And their bank account.

"Braverman, we've given you a lot of leeway because of what's gone on at home these last few years, and we haven't needed to speak to each other. Something like this happens again and you'll be suspended. And New Girl –"

"Sara," I interjected.

"Sara, you get one of my players in trouble again and you'll be suspended, too."

I frowned. Was that even legal?

"Get out," he ordered, pointing to the door.

All four of us then filed out of his office, past the front desk, and out into the main school foyer. We all stood facing each other, not entirely sure what to do next. I wanted to yell at Shea. I wanted to yell at Josh. I wanted to yell at Zoey. But we were silent.

Shea broke the silence first but uttering one word to Zoey. "Him?" was all he said.

Zoey barely moved her jaw, but that was as good a nod as he was going to get.

I took Shea's hand and led him away, leaving Josh and Zoey by themselves. Shea and I walked around the corner to an empty corridor and waited to give them privacy. Shea sat down on the ground and leaned against a locker. I stood in front of him.

"Shea, seriously," I sighed.

"Sara, you're not marked," Shea retorted, before screwing up his face. "Or I'm not, and … it's just a biological reaction that I have to any threats when we haven't … when you're not …"

"Shea, you can't blame behaving like a caveman on genetics." I paused, looking down at his twisted facial expression. "What?" I asked softly, sitting down beside him.

He turned his head to me, his dark eyes boring into mine. "I told you that I felt insecure about you and me. I told you that," he said quietly. "You can't know what it meant to me to hear you say that you love me. But the fear is still there. You're out there, able to fall in love with anyone, and there's nothing I can do about it." His voice was low and vulnerable. "Seeing Josh today, seeing him kiss you," he shuddered, "it was just an epic reminder of how temporary this might be. I'm sorry for behaving like a jackass. I'll apologise to Josh when I don't feel like killing him anymore."

I leaned over and kissed Shea softly. He reciprocated just as tenderly. "I told you I love you and I meant it. You know this is very new to me, and I don't say it lightly. You need to start feeling a bit more secure, because I doubt a cop is going to be as forgiving as Principal Baynard if you lose it at some guy on the street. You're eighteen. Legally an adult. I have no desire to participate in any conjugal visits." I was trying to make him laugh and I succeeded.

He smiled at me.

"You told me that the tattoos are marks," I recalled our conversation from Saturday. "I want you to tell me about them." He had avoided this purposefully.

Shea nodded. "They're naturally occurring," he said, repeating what he had told me before. "You are officially mated as a pair once the mark appears, and it will only appear after you ... uh ... mate essentially." Shea pinched the bridge of his nose. "I feel a heightened level of threatened because we're not properly mated, and I'm not pressuring you, I promise I'm not, it's just how it is."

I felt really stupid then. How had I not put that together? It was really obvious if you thought about it.

"Say something," he urged.

I stole a glance at him, and he was staring at me worriedly. I knew he didn't want to freak me out. But it was hard not to be freaked out when all of this was so new.

"I understand the principle," I said carefully.

"You understand the principle?" he repeated, raising his eyebrows. "That's all you've got to say?"

"Why is it so bad that Josh is Zoey's mate?" I asked, changing the subject. "I understand he is a human, but so am I. What is the difference?"

"Sara," groaned Shea. "I get that sex is an awkward thing for you to think about, but you've got to be able to tell me what you're thinking, and how you're feeling." Shea slouched against the lockers.

A shiver ran down my spine as I thought of how to answer his question. My only answer would be that I wasn't ready. I didn't know when I would be ready. I didn't know how I was supposed to feel. But I was guessing that embarrassed and self-conscious weren't the emotions you were supposed to feel when you were ready.

As if fate was listening, the bell rang, and movement began to sound as people left the cafeteria and were on their way back to their lockers.

"I'll see you later," I whispered, and I kissed his cheek, before jumping up off the ground and hurrying away. I was a total chicken, I knew it.

Chapter 25

"**M**om, I need to ask you about something."

Mom was standing at the sink, rinsing off our dinner plates. She was still wearing her work pants and a button-down shirt, but she had unpinned her hair, allowing it to fall down her back. She had had a good day today, which was why I was hoping that she wouldn't freak out when I asked her this question.

Mom turned off the faucet and turned to face me, simultaneously drying her hands on a dish towel. "What the matter, hon?" she asked me.

"How do you know when you're ready to have sex with someone?"

Mom's green eyes widened to the point when I could no longer see her eyelids. Her jaw dropped, and her face paled. She looked as though she went through about six different sets of emotions before she was able to compose herself enough to answer me.

"Sara, have you ...?"

"No!" I answered quickly. "No, I was just wondering."

Mom breathed a sigh of relief. "Well, I suppose if I'm talking as a woman, and not your mom, then I would say that you're ready when you can fully trust that person, trust them with your whole self. You love them, and the person you're with brings out the very best in you.

"But as your mom, honey, don't rush into anything. And don't feel pressured at all. Take it from someone who knows. With Daddy and I, it was a whirlwind. We rushed everything, all the firsts. So much so that it was a blur a bit of the time. I wish we had waited and made things a little more special than they were.

"And as your doctor, sex leads to kids and diseases. Are you ready to be a mom? Are you ready for routine STI testing? Labour, crying, night feeds, cracked nipples, stretch marks, excess skin, a teenager who asks you terrifying questions?"

Mom was barking scary words at me rapidly. But she had answered my question. Did I fully trust Shea? Did he bring out the best in me?

I thought so, but my apprehension told me that I wasn't sure yet.

Mom sighed. "I meant what I said about birth control," she said, referencing an earlier argument that we had had about Shea. "I understand it's different. You feel different. The connection isn't normal. But pregnancy is. I'm making you an appointment." Mom then wandered off, no doubt in search of her cell phone.

Great. I had that to look forward to.

I did the same thing. I had purposely left my phone in my bag upstairs. I had been avoiding speaking to Shea after everything that had happened today. As soon as I checked my phone, I saw that I had a missed call from Shea, and a text message asking me to call him when I could.

As soon as I saw that, I could feelthe restraint in him. He had wanted to check on me, but he wasn't allowing himself to in order to keep pressure off of me. I needed to put him out of his misery and stop punishing him for his nature.

I also needed to stop being such a wuss, as my nerves were directly affecting his insecurities and I didn't want that.

I tapped his number and he answered on the first ring, like always.

"Sara," he breathed, though sounding hesitant.

"Sorry it's so late," I whispered. "I've been thinking a lot about what happened today."

"Yeah?" he murmured fearfully.

I gulped. "Sex is a really awkward thing for me to talk about because I am so new to all of this. And you're right, I need to communicate better. I'm really good at keeping my thoughts to myself."

"Yes, you are," he replied.

"I'm not ready yet," I said firmly. "But I promise to tell you when I am."

"That's okay, Sara," he assured me. "You know I will do whatever you ask, whatever you say."

I smiled. "I know."

"Sara."

"Yeah?"

"I love you, you know." His voice was soft and calm. Constant.

"I know. I love you, too," I breathed.

The next few weeks of our relationship could only be described as flawless. I was deliriously happy, and well aware that I was blissfully in the honeymoon period of my first real relationship.

Shea was an amazing boyfriend. He picked me up every day for school, he bought me thoughtful gifts, even if it was just a coffee from Sally's I appreciated it. Shea often sat in one of the booths at Sally's while I worked doing his homework, just so we could spend a little more time together between customers. He was also really attentive to my mom, who I believed was warming up to him little by little. He never uttered the word "lycan" and he tried to make her feel as comfortable about him as possible. And occasionally he would sleep over. Though Mom didn't know about that last part.

We hadn't done anything more than kiss, but I was feeling more and more comfortable with Shea by the day. He was so good to me that I honestly wondered what I could bring to the relationship. Shea had assured me that I brought everything just by being with him.

Shea hadn't really spoken to me much about what he was going through in the pack. There would be times when I could tell that his mind was elsewhere, and when I asked him, he brushed it off as nothing.

I wondered if, like my mom, he was afraid of scaring me off if he told me too much. I wanted to assure him that this wouldn't be the case, but I wasn't entirely sure if that was true.

My mother was one of the strongest women I knew, and yet, this had been too much for her. What would it be like for little old me?

But it was now late November, and I hadn't heard anything further about Lex since my last encounter with him. I hoped that meant that he would be staying away, or finally giving up whatever vendetta he had against Shea and me.

In the world of high school, late November meant it was time for the big away game. The entire football team, football staff, cheerleading squad, and half the student body were all getting on busses and in their cars and travelling to Charlotte.

That meant hotel rooms.

I was rooming with Cece, but I wasn't entirely sure if that meant that we would be sharing a room for the entire night. Shea and Jamie were also rooming together. Cece was sworn to secrecy, but she told me that she could get Jamie out of that room if I wanted. I hadn't decided yet.

It was Thursday. The entire school was abuzz with excitement for the game the following night. All students with written permission were excused from school the next day in order to make the three-and-a-half-hour drive to Charlotte.

It took a ton of convincing to get my mom to let me go, but now that I was on birth control, thanks to sitting through a disturbing slideshow of gonorrhoea pictures curtesy of her colleague at the clinic, she was confident that I would be responsible.

"I am so excited. I haven't been on a trip in forever," Cece excitedly gushed as we stood in line in the cafeteria.

"We're going to watch football in Charlotte, Cece," I said, bringing her back to Earth.

Cece cocked her eyebrow. "Alright, Little Miss Manhattan, we aren't all as well travelled as you."

I laughed. "Try Little Miss Upstate New York."

"Jamie wants to take me on a road trip this summer. See the Grand Canyon. I just hope everything is finally over that we might be able to get away for a few months," Cece said anxiously. It was the first time I had heard their situation mentioned in ages.

"Is everything alright?" I asked.

Cece pursed her lips. "You get the gag order thing now, right?" she asked me.

Shea had asked her not to say anything to me. I nodded. I would ask him, no matter how scary the outcome.

Cece shook off the sudden solemnity. "Do you own nice underwear?" she asked me randomly.

I immediately blushed and prayed that nobody could hear. Shea was in the cafeteria and could no doubt hear our conversation with his super sonic hearing. "Jesus, Cece," I hissed.

She rolled her eyes before taking out her phone and quickly firing off a text.

My phone buzzed.

I can easily get rid of Jamie from Shea's room. Do you own nice underwear?

Do I look like I only wear grannie panties? I fired back, hoping it would come with as much sass as I intended. Not that I often inspected my underwear drawer, but I didn't think that I had horrendous taste.

Cece snorted in humour. I have heaps, still with tags. Let me know if you want me to bring anything with me.

I momentarily considered her offer before realising something. Do you really want your brother to be seeing your underwear?

Cece froze, before dramatically gagging and laughing. "Okay, that's a firm no."

Cece was very blasé about this sort of thing, and I actually appreciated it. She calmed me and helped me to not make such a big deal out of it. Of course, I knew it was a big deal, but if I always thought of it that way then I was going to go insane with anxiety.

We paid for our food, and as we were walking over to Shea's table, I noticed Josh sitting by himself, scrolling on his phone.

Josh and Zoey were not together. The whole drama with the fight a few weeks back had only made things worse. Zoey, I thought, felt embarrassed that she had put herself between Josh and Shea. She had shown an actual emotion and was now trying to cover it up. Josh was miserable, and was constantly bumming out his friends, which was why he was by himself a lot.

I had tried to convince Shea to talk to Zoey, but I got a firm no in response. He wasn't going near Zoey and her emotions with a ten-foot pole.

Walking past Shea with my tray, I kissed him on top of his head, before continuing on to Josh's table. I felt Shea's eyes on me, but they weren't in such a jealous rage as they had been before. He knew that Josh wasn't a threat thanks to Zoey.

"I swear to God, if I play like shit again tomorrow like I have been for the past few weeks, I can kiss that scholarship goodbye. There are going to be college scouts at this game, Sara, and all I can think about is the spawn of Satan." Josh held his head in his hands.

Josh had played really poorly the last few weeks. Or, at least, according to Shea he had played poorly. Football was all still running and falling to me.

"My folks can't afford college tuition. If I don't get a full ride I might as well drop out now and become an exterminator." Josh's father owned his own small extermination business.

Zoey had really messed with Josh's head, all because she couldn't put on her big girl panties and admit that her mate was a human. She was now going to actually mess up his life because she was such a coward.

I knew Zoey would come around eventually. It would be against her nature to stay away forever. But in the meantime, she was screwing with my friend and I was over it.

I leapt up from the table in a huff and abandoned my food. I marched over to Shea's table, my eyes set firmly on Zoey who was nibbling daintily on a kale salad.

"I need to talk to you," I said, glowering at her.

In a dramatic fashion, Zoey dropped her fork and stared up at me. "Can't. Busy," she said, smiling a fake smile.

"You don't, and I'll tell Josh your dirty little secret," I threatened, earning the attention of everyone on the table. I chanced a glance at Shea, and he was watching me curiously.

Her eyes flared with anger and resentment. "Bitch, don't push me," seethed Zoey.

"Zoey," snapped Shea.

Zoey reluctantly conceded and stood up from the table. I walked out of the cafeteria and looked around, before selecting an empty classroom in the same hallway and making my way inside. Zoey followed me silently and slammed the door behind us.

I turned on her and tried to make my voice as fearsome as possible. As fearsome as a seventeen-year-old girl could be to a person who could transform themselves into a wolf. "You are screwing up Josh's entire life," I spat accusingly.

Zoey winced as I hit the one nerve I knew she had. "You don't know what you're talking about," she retorted.

"I know my friend," I shot back, "and I know that he is stressing about how the hell he is going to get into college when all he can think about is you."

Zoey didn't say anything this time. Her facial expression hardened as she glared at me.

"Josh is talented!" I stressed. "He is sweet and kind, and a decent person who had a great shot of getting a full ride to a four-year college. But you're messing with his head and affecting his performance when you could just be with him and be happy! I don't understand it, Zoey! What is wrong with you?"

Zoey snapped. "What's wrong with me?" she seethed. "Your little mind couldn't even begin to comprehend me, us, and our way of life!"

"Enlighten me then," I challenged. I would be stunned if she could justify being such a bitch to Josh.

"My family is one of the oldest pure lycan families on the continent. Eckhart lycans came over on the freakin Mayflower. Eckharts have mated into packs all over the country, and my parents expect nothing less than an influential pairing."

Okay. Maybe I was a little stunned. Had I really just heard her use the term "pure lycan"? Was that ... was that a little racist? I mean, the only thing I could equate it to were the purebloods in the Harry Potter series. Were her parents supposed to be the Malfoys of the lycan world?

That explained why she had been so attached to Shea. She didn't really care about him, but her parents were forcing her to mate powerfully.

"We aren't meant to mate with humans," Zoey continued. "Humans don't have the capacity to love and understand one of us." Her eyes looked me up and down. "Just look at your mother," she added coldly.

I bit back a nasty retort. I was doing this for Josh, and not myself.

"Josh is just like any other teenage boy. Full of hormones that make him feel things that aren't real. And when he goes off to college next year, he'll forget all about me and screw the first sorority girl he sees." Right there. I saw Zoey crack. It was only for a split second, but goddammit I saw it. She didn't believe this crap. She wasn't some human-hating lycan supremacist. She was afraid of getting hurt. Zoey was hurting inside. Really hurting.

Oh my God, I was feeling sympathy for Zoey. "Do you believe that I would hurt Shea?" I asked her.

Zoey shrugged her shoulders. "Like mother, like daughter," she replied curtly.

I rolled my eyes. "Josh will love you if you let him," I said insistently. "I mean, you reel him in, only to treat him like he's a leper the next minute and you're still the only thing he can think about. At some point, Zoey, you've got to decide what you want and take it. You don't have to be afraid. You could be really happy if you wanted to be."

Zoey's eyes began to water, and she immediately turned away from me and looked out the window. I watched her focus on her breathing as she tried to stop herself from crying.

The door to the classroom suddenly opened. Josh, full of confidence and determination, marched into the classroom and quickly assessed us both, softening when he saw Zoey in her state.

"I don't want you fighting my battles for me, Sara," he told me, though offering me a grateful look. "Zoey, look, I know that I'm not good enough for you. I'm not super smart, I'm not rich, I'm not as good looking as some of the guys you hang out with, but goddammit, I will treat you the way you deserve to be treated," he appealed to her. "I know some part of you, deep, deepdown underneath your frosty, ice queen surface, cares about me. You wouldn't spend so much of your time going out of your way to treat me like shit if you didn't. I care about you, too. A whole damn lot."

Zoey, who hadn't looked away from the window to this point, slowly turned her head and looked at Josh. The expression on her face was nothing short of vulnerability.

I wanted to slip out of the classroom quietly to give them a moment, but then I didn't want to draw attention to myself and ruin whatever was about to happen.

"You will neverbe able to comprehend just how much I care about you, Josh," Zoey said quietly. She walked over to him calmly, stood up on her toes and kissed him softly, before leaving them both alone in the classroom.

Josh just looked at me with a bewildered expression on his face. "Fuck it," he said, after a minute of silence, throwing his hands up in the air. "I'm over it. I've got a game to prepare for and a scout to impress. I'm not going to let a flaky girl ruin this for me." He stormed towards the door before turning back to me. Just as I was about to appeal to him to give Zoey a chance, as much as it pained me, he said, "Could you please remind me of this the next time I'm whining to you about how much I like her?"

I smiled. "Sure."

CHAPTER 26

The way Cece was gushing over our room, you would have thought it was the Plaza. In reality, it was the first taste of freedom that Cece Braverman had ever had.

In my reality, it was a crappy hotel room that ought to be put under a blacklight.

Cece dumped her duffel bag on the squeaky spring bed closest to the window, before throwing open the thick, mustard coloured drapes. "Oh, I just love Charlotte," she squealed, taking in the view of the parking lot.

I couldn't help but smile. I guess I had been fortunate. Living exactly forty-seven minutes away from the culture hub that was Manhattan for most of my life had perhaps spoiled me.

I smiled as I texted my mom letting her know that we had arrived safely. Mom immediately replied back with a text asking for curious pictures of our room. I knew she just wanted to see if Shea was there. I rolled my eyes and snapped a picture of our beds, the old desk with a bible sitting pride of place, a sad looking antique armoire, one of Cece by the window, and I quickly ducked into the bathroom to take a picture. Though decidedly more modern than the bedroom, the bathroom was still a classic reflection of the eighties.

"Oh, Sara, we all needed this. A getaway. All Shea can think about when we're at home is looking after Mom. And then we're all thinking about the anniversary. Being away is such a good idea."

"What anniversary?" I wondered if it was the anniversary of her father's death. That ought to be very hard on Shea and Cece's mom.

Cece suddenly pursed her lips and looked guilty, as if she had revealed something she shouldn't have. "Well, actually, Shea hasn't forbidden me from saying this detail. The anniversary of Lex's father's death … and yours … is November seventeenth. Sunday. It's always a day filled with conflict. I wouldn't be surprised if Shea wants to stay here with you over the weekend to keep you away."

I knew I should have registered the more important detail of that revelation, that being Lex's impending outburst, but I had just found out my father's death date. November seventeenth. How many November seventeenths had I let pass without knowing its significance?

"Come on," Cece encouraged. "We've got a few hours before we need to get ready for the game. I want to see some of the city."

Cece and I met up with Shea and Jamie. And although the boys both wanted to visit the NASCAR museum, we ended up at the Carowinds amusement park with most of our class.

Screaming my lungs out on half a dozen roller coasters helped me to forget. I didn't think about November seventeenth. I didn't think about Lex. I certainly wasn't thinking about my nerves. I was just having fun with my boyfriend like a normal teenager.

We screamed together on the rides and I held on to Shea for dear life as we went down the drops. We laughed at our ridiculous expressions on the on-ride pictures and we ate all kinds of deep-fried food.

As we were leaving the park to return to the hotel to get ready for the game, Shea kissed me. He kissed me deeply, holding onto me tightly. Feeling as carefree as I had in a long time, I kissed him just as passionately, smiling as I did.

My heart raced as I looked up into his eyes. Shea's eyes were wide, excited, and happy. I didn't think I'd ever seen him without his usual wariness. But I loved seeing him without it. I loved seeing him happy.

But as we sat together at the game, even in and amongst the atmosphere and excitement, the significance of Sunday crept back into my head.

"Shea," I said, capturing his attention.

Shea groaned as something happened on the field that he obviously didn't like. He looked at me. "Yeah?" he furrowed his eyebrows.

"Tell me about the seventeenth."

Shea stiffened, and his wariness returned, and I wanted to kick myself. He exhaled before nodding, and then said, "The seventeenth is the anniversary of the fight," he replied. "The date that both your dad and Kurt Hale were killed. Lex ... he ... he is always a little more unpredictable on the seventeenth. He's always antagonistic. Taunting, picking fights, causing trouble, but the seventeenth always sets him off."

Lex honestly sounded as though he was stuck in the anger stage of grief and had never left. What on earth was he honestly hoping to achieve? He couldn't bring his father back. "What does he want?" I asked in quiet disbelief.

"Justice," replied Shea, "or whatever his definition of justice is. He can't ever get it. He can't accept that it was a fair fight that ended badly on both sides. Because he knows you're in Providence, the seventeenth just makes me worry even more."

I laid my head on Shea's shoulder and he put his arm around me, before kissing the crown of my head. "I wish you would share some of these burdens with me," I murmured. "You shouldn't have to bear them alone." I needed to suck up my own anxiety.

"I appreciate that," he replied sincerely, but in a tone that told me that he wouldn't be sharing them with me. And I could hear why in his voice.

I looked up at him. "You won't scare me," I assured him, convincing myself at the same time. "If I haven't run off by now, then I won't ever."

"It's bad karma to make promises you can't keep, Sara," he said, smiling sadly.

Just as I was about to offer a retort, Shea leapt up out of his seat along with half the stadium as they hollered and heckled at a decision made by the referee.

I sat with Shea's words for the rest of the game, offering appropriate cheers and groans when necessary. I snapped out of my inner thoughts when Shea informed me that Josh was playing very well, which I was thankful for seeing as there was a scout at this game.

But after everything, Shea really didn't hold out any hope for me. Was he really so convinced that humans were these vapid creatures? I wasn't like that. How could I convince him that I loved him?

Providence ended up winning the away game by three points, which was cause for massive celebration for our school. Of course, the teachers kept us at the hotel, but there were students every-where, in and out of rooms, which made it impossible for them to keep track of us all.

I knew what I wanted to do. It had been on my mind all day, all week even. And I couldn't think of a better way to convince Shea that I was all in, and that I wasn't going anywhere, and that he could trust me.

My own room had been quickly occupied by the sounds that were coming through the door, so I couldn't go inside and change, in hopes that Cece had perhaps brought something nice for me to wear in the end, but I wasn't about to interrupt. It didn't matter. I was just me.

I swallowed, taking a deep breath, and found every ounce of gumption that I had within myself as I set off towards Shea's room. I walked past several rooms that had students falling in and out of them. I saw people making out, and I could smell the alcohol that some had managed to procure.

Holy shit! Josh and Zoey. His door had just slammed closed, but they were together.

I kept moving.

Jamie had mentioned earlier today that he and Shea were in room 1228, which was significant as that was his birthday. I followed the signs as they directed me towards those numbered rooms. This corridor was just as loud, as most of the senior boys where roomed here.

I watched as the shiny silver numbers climbed higher and higher as I made my way down the hall. 1220, 22, 24, 26 ... and 1228.

My heart was hammering in my chest. I could do this. I could do this, I kept repeating to myself. I was so nervous, and I had never felt more vulnerable or exposed in my life, and I hadn't even knocked on the door yet. The enormity of what I was about to do wasn't lost on me. I just wanted Shea to understand how much I loved him, and how he didn't need to worry about me.

Before I could even knock, the door swung open. I assumed that he could hear my heartbeat from inside. Shea frowned as he looked down at me, which hadn't been the reaction I was expecting. He then stuck his head out into the corridor and looked both ways.

"Did you walk here by yourself?" he demanded to know.

Odd question. "Yeah."

"Goddammit, Cece," he cursed under his breath. "She's supposed to be watching you tonight."

Because that wasn't creepy. But I knew why he was worried.

"Are you going to make me stand out here all night?" I asked, trying to make my voice sound as confident and as smooth as possible.

Shea snapped out of his annoyance and softened, opening the door wider for me.

I walked past him and closed my eyes to control my breathing and my pulse just as soon as he couldn't see my face. But, of course, he could hear it. My pulse was erratic as I kept up the nerve to go through with my plan. I had never been more nervous in my life.

"Sara," he murmured, placing a large hand on my upper arm and turning me to face him.

I gulped.

Shea scrutinised me intently, surveying my every micro-expression with his inquisitive brown eyes. "What's wrong?"

"It really bothered me, what you said earlier," I replied, surprised at the conviction in my voice.

"What did I say?"

"That I shouldn't make promises that I can't keep."

"Oh," Shea said, exhaling. He ran his hand over his jaw as if he was pondering what to say next.

I didn't want him to explain anything to me. I didn't want him to tell me that I was human, and my feelings weren't the same. I didn't want him to justify himself. I didn't want him to do anything. I had come here to show him how I felt. To show him that I trusted him. To show him that he could trust me. To show him that he could believe me when I told him that I loved him.

With every bit of confidence that I had in me veins, I stood up on my toes and kissed him. I took him by surprise, so much so that he staggered back a little before recovering his footing. It only took him a second before he was reciprocating, deepening the kiss.

My heart took off as I felt his mouth open, and his tongue moving with mine. My hands, which never ventured anywhere other than around his neck when we kissed, travelled down his torso to the hem of his t-shirt.

Shea responded enthusiastically, helping me to remove his shirt, barely breaking our kiss. His fingers knotted themselves in my hair, his other hand on my back as he held me close. My hands bravely travelled across his chest, feeling the unnatural strength in his muscles. The heat was unlike anything else.

Shea moved to kiss my neck, and murmured, "Sara, are you sure?" in my ear.

"Yes," I confirmed, in an embarrassingly out-of-breath voice. "I want to show you that I love you, that you can believe me when I say I won't leave."

And just like that, Shea stopped. He pulled away from me, though his eyes were wild. My heart immediately dropped, and I felt a sense of humiliation creeping in. All the confidence I had mustered was quickly flying out the tiny hotel room window, and I felt like a stupid girl who didn't know anything.

"Sara, I don't want you to prove anything to me. You shouldn't be doing this to prove anything to me."

I felt like the biggest fool. All sense of rational thought escaped me as I just felt like the biggest idiot there ever was. I had just majorly put myself out there and I had been slapped in the face with rejection and embarrassment.

"I need some air," I stammered, quickly moving towards the door.

"Let me come with you," Shea offered.

"No!" I cried out immediately. The last thing I wanted was for him to comfort me about this. "Just give me a minute!"

And I ran. I sprinted down the hallway, barely breathing. I was too impatient to wait for the elevator, so I opened up the door to the stairwell and ran down them, taking them two, three at a time. I pushed open the heavy emergency door and let myself out into the parking lot.

The cool November air hit me straight away, and I filled my lungs with it. My mind was still racing too fast for me to coherently process what had just happened. All I could concentrate on was the constant feelings of humiliation and dread that were currently taking up residence in my very soul.

And because I didn't know what else to do, I started to cry. Had I not been a complete idiot, and been sobbing erratically, I might've heard the footsteps behind me. But I didn't.

I only felt a prick in my neck before my world went black.

Chapter 27

I was cold. I was hungry. And I really needed to pee. And I needed an aspirin.

Those were the feelings that came to the forefront of my mind as I regained my coherent thoughts. My head felt like it weighed two hundred pounds, like it was a mammoth effort just to lift it up. It was leaning against something hard behind me. I was against something.

The air smelled fresh. I was outside, hence why I was feeling so cold.

And my neck really hurt. I went to lift my arm to feel for any wounds, but I couldn't. My hands were bound. I blinked my eyes, letting in the light for what felt like the first time in ages. I squinted as my vision focused.

I was in the woods. What the hell ... how did I get here? Panic immediately set in as I realised that I was in a bad situation. Something had happened to me that was beyond my control. I struggled, realising properly now that I was tied to a tree. I had been taken, full on Liam Neeson taken, against my will and brought to the middle of nowhere.

My head snapped around as I panicked, looking for any markers, any signs of a trail, any campfire smoke in the distance. But aside from this clearing, the woods were so dense that I couldn't see anything.

The sun was rising. That meant that east was where the sun was, right? Not that it would do me any good knowing where east was if I had no freaking clue where I was. Was I still in Charlotte?

Holy shit. Someone had taken me against my will. Someone had tied me to this damn tree. Was I going to die?

Thinking about my own mortality made me freeze. I felt as if adrenaline was paralysing my body as I panicked, all sorts of horrible things flashing through my mind.

"Good morning."

I gasped in fright as a figure appeared in the clearing, making his way out of the dense forest. He was dressed for the weather, wearing a thick jacket, jeans, and heavy looking combat boots. I could see his tattoos poking out from the neck of his shirt. Lex was staring at me in a dark, disconnected way. He approached me, cocking his head as I recoiled, leaning as far back into the tree as I could.

He honestly looked like he had snapped. The almost evil blankness of his expression was practically sociopathic. I knew right this minute that I was the farthest thing from okay. Lex had snapped. He had taken me from safety as part of his warped mission for justice.

I was trembling. I could feel myself shaking, almost to the point where my wrists were getting burnt from the friction of the rope that was binding my wrists.

I was completely alone. I had no one to depend on but myself, and I needed to make myself safe.

"Lex," I said, my voice insane hoarse. "I haven't done anything wrong." I coughed, clearing my throat.

Lex's face cracked into a smile as he laughed. "I know you haven't, Sara. You're a by-product of a war you didn't start. Just like I am."

Okay, so I couldn't deflect blame off of myself. I searched my rapidly deteriorating brain for a plan B. "You need to let me go. You're holding me against my will. It's illegal. If you let me go now, I won't tell anybody what happened."

Lex just laughed even harder as he crouched down in front of me. He looked at me with his cold, icy eyes, cocking his head again, as if I were simple. "And what your father did wasn't illegal?" he challenged. "My father was only defending his pack and his territory. But your father couldn't just back off. He took it too far, and he murdered him!"

"My father is dead, too!" I retorted. "I don't know what happened, Lex! I didn't even know that lycans existed until about a month ago! Up until then I thought that my dad died in a car accident."

"You don't know?" Lex asked in disbelief. "Seventeen years ago, a member of your father's pack tried to abduct my mother. My father set out to remind the Providence pack just where their border was, and your father took it too far. He started a war, and he ended it by killing my father."

I didn't know what to do with this information. I didn't know if it was true. There had to be more to the story. But what did he want me to do? "Lex, what can I do?" I asked him. "We are not our fathers."

"What can you do?" he repeated, looking me right in the eye. "You, Sara, are going to end this conflict once and for all. You are the rightful Alpha of the Providence pack. You are the Luna, the mate of the current Alpha. You're the linchpin. If you're out of the picture, the pack disintegrates. The Providence pack will answer for what they did, and I will assume control."

Holy shit, he was going to kill me. He was actually going to kill me. I was going to die. Today was my last. My life didn't flash before my eyes as it did in the movies. All I could see was Lex.

Fight. Freeze to fight. Adrenaline was coursing through my body. My pulse was practically a hum, with no individual heartbeat. This person in front of me stood between me and living. I had to keep myself alive.

I was sitting on the cold, damp ground, with only my hands bound. I immediately brought my knees up to my chest and kicked my feet towards Lex's groin with all my might. Lex fell backwards as he yelped in pain.

"Fuck you, you psycho!" I screamed as I struggled and wriggled, fighting my restraints. I only had seconds before he would recover and resume whatever plan he had to end my life. I was scratching the hell out of my arms as I pulled against the tree.

Lex, gasping, fished into his pocket and brought out a switchblade. I heard the blade flip up as he released the safety. "You crazy bitch," he said, staggering to get back onto his feet.

I kicked my legs, bringing up dirt and tufts of grass as I did, but I couldn't pull my arms free. My instinct was to protect my torso as he came towards me with the knife. I tucked my chin against my chest, closing my eyes as I kicked blindly, cursing and swearing with every breath that I had left.

I was fighting. I was trying. But I was thinking of my mom. I was thinking of Shea. Of my dad. I was thinking of the people that I loved most. My last thoughts couldn't be of fear.

"Alexander!" cried a voice from across the clearing.

We both stopped and looked around, Lex still holding the blade as he did. A man had joined us in the clearing. He was holding both of his hands up in a calm surrender. He looked between Lex and I worriedly, eyeing the blade with apprehension.

As he drew closer, walking carefully as he did, I was able to get a clearer look at him. I felt like I had seen him before. His face sparked my memory, but I couldn't quite place it. He looked to be about forty years old, his hair dark, but longer than most men his age, and his facial hair was neatly kept. He was tall, and looked very fit, with a lean, muscular build. His eyes stood out to me early, being of a brilliant blue. The same light colour as Lex's but not nearly as cold.

I had seen him before. Where had I seen this man before?

"It can't be," Lex said in disbelief.

Lex knew him. How on earth did I know someone that he knew as well? I felt like I had met him back home in New York.

"Alexander," he said again, this time he was not twenty feet from us. His hands were still raised in a steady, calming way as he approached us.

It was then that Lex snapped out of his utter shock. He jumped back from me, turning the knife around on the stranger.

"Your fight is not with her," he said calmly. "Not with Saraphine."

I froze. I had heard my name spoken like that before. I had heard my name said in his voice before. I had memorised that voice. I had memorised the way he said my name. I had watched that video a dozen times. Two dozen.

But it couldn't be. It was impossible.

But it was. Underneath the facial hair, and the years on his skin, I could see the baby-faced man who was in my mother's wedding picture. I couldn't believe it.

"How?" growled Lex, his voice now rocky with fury.

"I will tell you everything," he promised, "but you need to let Saraphine go first. Nobody needs to get hurt today. Not her, and not you." He sounded like a cop, like a hostage negotiator on TV.

Lex's head snapped. "You killed my father! How the hell are you alive?" he demanded to know icily.

"I will regret what happened between your father and I until my dying breath, Alexander," he promised sincerely, "but that fight was only going to end one way. I want to explain myself to you, but I cannot do it while you have a knife to my daughter."

Even though my heart was already racing, it probably sounded like a hum right now. He'd just confirmed it. Somehow, my dad was alive, and he was standing here. He'd found me. I couldn't believe my eyes. It was like the drugs that Lex had given me were causing me to hallucinate. But it was real.

This whole insane ordeal was real.

Lex's knife hand hesitated as it slowly dropped to his side, but he didn't drop the blade. He was standing with his back to me, so

I couldn't see his face, but I could only imagine it from how rigid he was.

"This conflict started because your mother's mate was a member of the Providence pack," Dad revealed slowly, carefully, his hands still out with a sense of calming Lex.

"Bullshit," sneered Lex.

Dad shook his head. "No, this is true. I don't know the circumstances of how your parents came to be together, but they were not mates. When your mother found hers in my pack, she tried to take you and join me." His voice was deeper, stronger than it had been in the video, aged like he had. He spoke with such authority and influence, yet he was still calming and sincere. "Your father wouldn't allow it. He had her mate, my friend, murdered to keep her in submission."

Oh my God. This sounded like the freaking Godfather or something.

"I retaliated," continued Dad. "Irrationally at times. But I got to a point where I couldn't take any more loss." He did his best to maintain his tone, but I could hear the pain in that sentence. "It would be just Kurt and me. We needed to end it." He shook his head. "I didn't want it to end that way. I promise you."

My father and Lex stared at each other for several moments.

Both of their heads suddenly turned, and they looked off into the distance. They could hear something that I couldn't. Something was coming.

I felt it before I heard it. The ground began to tremble. That was then followed by echoes of growling and snarling, rapidly getting louder and louder as it drew nearer.

Lex's head snapped back to my father's. "I don't believe you," he snarled, before turning to me and smiled. I didn't have time to react, to scream, or to do anything. He raised his right hand so quickly that I couldn't really see it. He released his knife, sending it hurtling through the air in my direction.

A searing pain burst across my abdomen, which quickly rippled across my entire body. I sucked in a breath, and then another, as pain quickly overwhelmed me.

I heard my dad cry out, but the sound was muffled. The sounds of the woods were beginning to sound like TV static. All I could hear was my rapid, shaky pulse thundering in my ears. As my vision started to blur, I saw dozens of enormous creatures spill out of the wood into the clearing.

Lex disappeared, himself exploding into a giant creature before running off. I watched as the wolves, almost in slow motion, sprinted off in pursuit, though one gigantic creature remained behind. I heard the unholiest of howls escape from its mouth. He was in pain, dire, extreme pain. And I felt it, nearly as completely as I felt my own.

"Go!" said my father, in a muffled cry. "I've got her!"

He came into my vision, blurred as it was. "Daddy," I mumbled, the rusty taste of blood on my tongue.

"Saraphine!" was the last thing I heard him say before I drifted from consciousness.

Chapter 28

Four Years Earlier

Mom pulled up out front of John Adams Junior High School. There was a huge banner strung across the front of the building welcoming everyone to the science fair that was being held today in the gym.

I sat, completely nervous, with a cardboard box filled with my materials to present my energy project. I had rehearsed my project over and over. I had made Mom buy about twenty back up light globes from Walmart as a precaution in case nineteen of them didn't work. My posters were decorated with enough glitter to land an airplane. I just didn't want to embarrass myself.

"You'll be fine, Sara," Mom assured me, tucking a piece of my hair behind my ear. "You know this project backwards and forwards. And so what if you don't win, you still learned something, and we need more girls in the science fields."

I knew I wasn't going to win, although a five-thousand-dollar bond from the state for a college fund was a wonderful prize. I just wanted to get through my presentation without barfing.

Mom leaned over and kissed my temple. "I wish I could be there," she said regretfully, "but I've got to get to work. Text me when you're finished and tell me how you went. I love you."

I swallowed. "Love you, too, Mom," I rasped, lisping over my words thanks to my retainer. I carefully got out the car in the drop off line and juggled my bag and my box of materials. I turned around and smiled as Mom drove away. As soon as she was out of sight, I put my box on the floor and quickly took out my retainer and popped it in its case and slipped it inside my pocket, ready to be put back in when she picked me up. No way was I facing seventh graders talking like my mouth was full.

I picked up my box again and made my way to the gym, which had been set up with hundreds of tables and chairs. Students were already setting up their projects, some of which I knew would be winning contenders.

I found my science teacher to ask where my table was. Mrs Brady directed me to a dozen sheets that had been taped to the wall of the gym. I, along with several other students, studied the sheets to find where my table was.

Bryant, Saraphine – 18

I found Table 18 on the map that was also taped to the wall and found my table a few minutes later. Setting my box down, I pulled out my project posters and began to organise them. My project was to study how chemical energy can convert into electrical energy by way of powering a light globe with a potato.

My posters described the flow of electrical energy through a simple circuit. They explained why sometimes a light globe need-ed more than one battery to light up. I also studied into the history of electricity and electrical engineers and how they have developed the technology that we use today.

I assembled three different electrical circuits, all exhibiting different voltages, inserting the zinc nails and the pennies into the potatoes, before testing the globes. When I was confident that all three globes were working, I took the wire off to save it for my presentation. Once I was set up, I took out my notes, and rehearsed what I was going to say in my head.

Our teachers stopped us all as the first bell went, announcing that the judges would be starting to move around the fair, and that once we had been assessed, we would be free to roam around and check out other experiments.

I had seen a few of my friends earlier, but due to our names being on opposite ends of the alphabet, their tables were far from mine. I wanted to check theirs out at some point.

The fair was open to parents, and so many of them were wandering around, and the super-competitive ones were hyping up their kids' projects. I had a few linger over mine before moving on to a project where someone had built a freakin' robot.

One of the dads did stop at my table though, lingering hesitantly as he looked at me, and then at the information over my shoulder. I didn't recognise him, but then with three hundred kids in the gym and their six hundred parents, why would I?

He was younger than a lot of dads here, with fashionably unkempt dark hair, and a five o'clock shadow. He was very tall, and very fit, as though he enjoyed going to the gym. The idea made me shudder. He was dressed very smartly, with a button-down blue shirt, and black fitted pants. The sticky label on his chest told me his name was Ronan.

"Saraphine?" he asked, reading off the label on my table. His voice was deep, and it had a slight Southern twang to it. He kind of reminded me of my mom's accent.

"Sara," I corrected.

Ronan smiled. "Ah, well I have a little rule I go by where I call people by the names their parents gave them."

Okay then. "Saraphine is kind of a mouthful," I replied.

"I'm sure it means something really pretty, though," he offered, shrugging. He approached my table and started to read my project, looking thoroughly intrigued.

"Are you here seeing your kid's project?" I asked.

He nodded, while reading, before meeting my eyes. "Yes, I'm here to see my daughter."

My phone buzzed as he was reading, and I saw that my Mom had sent me a picture of her. She was sitting in traffic but was giving me a cheesy smile while giving me a thumbs up. She'd captioned it, "Cheering my girl on in traffic!" I smiled, letting out a soft chuckle.

Ronan furrowed his brows. "Something funny?"

I nodded. "Just my mom," I said, spinning my phone around to show him the picture.

He reacted quite strangely, tensing and swallowing hard. Before I had the chance to ask him if he was okay, he said, "I bet she's real proud of you."

"Yeah," I agreed. My mom was my biggest cheerleader. I knew she was very proud of me.

The judges then rolled around to me, seeing as my name was at the beginning of the alphabet. Ronan hung back but stayed to watch my presentation. Taking a deep breath, I began the speech that I had rehearsed so many times.

Thankfully, the light globes didn't falter, and all three lit up like they were supposed to. I was able to successfully demonstrate how chemical energy turned into electrical energy using a potato battery. I also didn't stumble over any words thanks to sneakily removing my retainer.

"Well done, Sara," commended Mrs Brady, as the judges made intimidating notes on their clipboards. "I can see you've put a lot of time and effort into this project. You can now go around and have a look at other projects if you like."

I let out a sigh of relief as I disconnected the wires from my potatoes. "You're a very smart girl, Saraphine," Ronan commended. "I'm sure both of your parents are very proud of you."

He offered me a prideful smile before turning away and moving off, no doubt to look at his own child's project.

Hmm, I thought, he was friendly.

CHAPTER 29

"Ow," I moaned, though my throat was blocked, filled with a tube that was pumping my lungs for me. As soon as I realised that I could breathe by myself, I began to cough and struggle against it.

People fluttered around me as the tube was hurriedly removed from my throat. The air that subsequently filled my lungs burned my throat on the way down. I coughed and spluttered as I tried to get my breathing normal. A tube was immediately then put across my face, taped to my cheeks, as I breathed the oxygen through my nose.

"It's alright, Sara," said a voice I didn't recognise. "You'll be feeling quite out of it for a few minutes, just calm your breathing."

"Sara," another voice whimpered. That was Mom. Mom was here.

"Mom!" I sobbed, suddenly bursting into tears. I felt like I couldn't control my emotions as the sobs came over me.

I blinked, my vision quickly clearing. I was in a small hospital room with monitors and wires connected to and coming out of me every which way. An annoying beeping sound was monitoring my heart rate, which explained the pinching of the clip on my index finger.

As I regained my coherency, I began to feel a dull ache in my abdomen. I remembered everything. I had been stabbed. I had been stabbed. Lex had stabbed me. Lex had deliberately plunged a blade into me to kill me. And my dad ...

"Daddy!" I cried out, anxiously searching the room for him, but Mom and I were alone with the nurse. Dad wasn't here, and neither was Shea.

"No, baby, it's Mom," Mom calmed me, furrowing her eyebrows in confusion.

I focused on her face, and saw how terrible she looked, which was hard for someone as pretty as my mom. Her eyes were red and swollen and her cheeks were streaked with tears. Her hair looked like it hadn't been brushed in days, and her clothes were wrinkled from being slept in.

"I'll go get the doctor," the nurse told my mom.

Mom cradled my face in her hands and she cried. "It's perfectly normal to cry after anaesthesia," she assured me. "Oh, baby, you scared me to death. I don't know what I'd do without you. Do you know what happened to you?"

I did. I knew exactly what happened to me. I wasn't exactly sure how I was feeling about it at that moment, but I knew what had happened. But I wondered if Mom did. I hadn't hallucinated my dad, had I? He had been there. I was sure! What's more is, I was certain I'd met him before. I remembered where I had first placed him. I had seen him, talked to him even, at my seventh-grade science fair. He had been there, too.

But ... but wouldn't he be here? Wouldn't Shea be here?

I decided to play dumb to find out what she knew. "No, what happened?" I rasped.

"Oh, honey," Mom sighed, "I knew, I knew they were dangerous. But the look on Shea's face ..." she trailed off, shaking her head. "You were taken from Charlotte by one of them, a man with a grudge against your ... your daddy. He brought you back to Providence and attacked you. Shea managed to find you and he got you to the hospital in time. You needed a transfusion because of the blood you lost, and you're now missing your spleen, but you should make a full recovery with a scar for your troubles. I'm grateful for him, despite everything. I think it's helped me to understand the connection. How he was while you were in surgery, I've never seen anything like it. I was terrified to lose you, but Shea ... he was dying."

"Where is he?" I asked.

"I'm not sure, hon. He was here all day and all night. As soon as we found out you were okay, he left. I think he blames himself. I know he thinks I blame him. I might have said so," she admitted.

"Mom!" I groaned croakily.

Even though I now knew Mom's version of events, she hadn't mentioned my dad, and she was under the interpretation that Shea had found me. I definitely hadn't hallucinated him. I was ninety-nine percent positive. The one percent had me questioning though.

At that moment, the doctor, who introduced herself as Dr Morgan, walked in with a tablet, and began to flick through my chart. She smiled at me reassuringly as she began to check me over and ask me the necessary questions. Once I had told her what year we were in and who the president was, she was satisfied I was coherent. She took my vitals and checked my incision site before ordering some more pain medication.

The nurse returned and injected a solution into my IV. Not too long after the ache of my wound completely dulled.

"Rest, Sara," Dr Morgan ordered. "You've had quite the ordeal. The police will be wanting to speak to you when you're up to it."

She and the nurse both left.

"The police?" I repeated.

Mom nodded. "We're obligated to report this type of injury, sweetheart. Just be honest. That man drugged you, and he attacked you in the middle of nowhere."

It would be the truth. I would just leave out the back story. "Mom, you need to call Shea. I want him to come." We had not left things in a good place when I had run from his room in Charlotte, and to have been subsequently snatched from the hotel, I needed to talk to him.

Mom nodded. "Okay, hon. I'm going to run down to the cafeteria to grab some food and a coffee, and I'll call Shea when I'm there." She leaned over and kissed my forehead, brushing the residual tears from my eyes. She stared at me for a moment, as if she was memorising how I looked, before she left me alone in my room.

I looked down at myself now that I was alone. I was lying in a hospital bed, my abdomen wrapped in gauze and bandages, because Lex had attempted to murder me. I still didn't think it had hit me yet. I had come close to dying. How do you even comprehend your own mortality like that?

I had seen lycans for the first time through my panicked haze. These huge wolves had been in that clearing and they had chased after Lex. What had happened to him? How on earth was there going to be justice for this? Could you even put a supernatural creature in a human jail?

The annoying beeping seemed to get quicker and quicker as I panicked inside my head. My heart right about stopped when I heard that all too familiar voice say my name. My full name. The name my parents gave me.

"Saraphine," he said softly.

I looked up to see my very real father standing in the doorway of my hospital room. He looked like he hadn't slept in days either, which made me wonder as to what day it was.

But I hadn't imagined him. He was alive, and he was here. "Daddy," I breathed, smiling with relief. It was strange. This was the third time that I was seeing this man in my entire life, and yet I felt like I knew him. I felt like he belonged to me. And knowing what I did about him, I knew he loved my mother and me to the ends of the earth.

"I've been waiting seventeen years to hear you call me that, Saraphine," he murmured, though his voice was shaky and nervous, and he offered me a reserved smile as he approached my bed. He placed his hands on the bed rail and looked over me, scrutinising me, memorising me, just as Mom had.

"I thought ... everyone thought ... Mom thinks you're dead."

"I've got a story to tell, I know," he conceded, nodding. "And I will tell you everything as soon as you're well, I promise."

It felt surreal that I had only got to know this man a few weeks ago, and I have grieved him. I felt his loss keenly. But he was here, and he had been alive all this time. Where on earth could he have been? And how on earth did he find me in that clearing?

He walked around the side of my bed and sat down on the edge, hesitating slightly before he reached out to hold my hand. His hands were much larger than mine, and were quite rough, but they were incredibly warm. I found this to be a very comforting feeling.

"You about killed me a half dozen times these past few days, Saraphine," he said, exhaling. "I have so much to say to you, so much ..." he paused, turning his head towards the door. "Amanda is getting off the elevator."

"How do you know that?"

He offered me a sad smile. "I know," was all he said in reply. "I had better go. Amanda has had enough shocks to last her a lifetime. She doesn't need me adding to it."

His excuse sounded weak, as though he was trying to make up a reason to avoid seeing Mom, and I immediately knew why. I had fought with Mom about it. I had been so incredibly angry at her for it. Mom had rejected my dad, she had left him, and taken me from him. She had just about taken his heart from his chest and stomped on it. What kind of person could experience that sort of rejection twice?

But I didn't want him to leave, selfishly. I wanted him here, I wanted them both here with me. "Please don't leave," I begged, holding onto his hand. "I don't want you to go." What if he went away again? He had been absent for seventeen years and had only shown himself to me because my life had been in danger. What if he went back into hiding again?

But, instead, he said, "I've never been far, Saraphine. I'm not going anywhere."

CHAPTER 30

om stayed with me all the time except when she needed
to eat or get coffee or take a phone call.

She didn't leave me alone long enough for Dad to come back, and I felt incredibly sick having such a big secret. You'd think I'd be used to keeping secrets from my mom after moving to Providence, but this was just too big.

Dad was alive. Her husband was alive.

It had always just been a fact. Something that had happened many years ago. Dad had died. My dad had died. I didn't have a dad. Mom was a widow. But to think that it had all be a lie. He had been alive all this time … and he was only telling me now? What if my life hadn't been in danger, would he have still been in hiding? I had so many questions, and no way of asking them.

I was on the verge of making up some excuse of wanting something from home just to give him the chance to come back when a nurse knocked on the door.

"Excuse me, ladies, but I've got a very handsome young man wanting to visit Sara. Sorry Dr Bryant, but you know the ICU rules. Only one visitor at a time."

Thoughts of my dad left me head when I realised that Shea was here. Embarrassingly, the machine that was monitoring my heart began to rapidly beep. Both Mom and the nurse exchanged an amused expression.

"Can't you shut that off?" I pleaded.

The nurse conceded and came to switch the machine off. "Just while your boyfriend's here," she told me, as the humiliating beeping ceased.

She and Mom both left my room, and a moment later, Shea was standing in the doorway. But he didn't look like Shea. He looked a wreck. He looked exhausted, and completely shattered, as if he hadn't slept in days. Like Mom and my dad, he too didn't look as though he had changed clothes since I had been brought to the hospital. But as he looked upon me, all I saw was guilt and shame.

I was momentarily thankful that the heart monitor was switched off, as my heart was doing bellyflops. I then remembered that Shea could hear it anyway. I wanted to get out of this bed to hug him, but I had all sorts of wires and IVs coming out of my every nook and cranny. As I hadn't been out of the bed to pee, I was also certain I had a catheter, which I did not want to bring attention to.

"Shea, please come in," I urged.

He obeyed me, placing his hands in the pockets of his jeans as he made his way over to me slowly. As he came closer, I could see the effect of him not getting any sleep. He had dark, dark shadows under his eyes, and the whites were incredibly bloodshot.

He sat down in what had become Mom's chair, tentatively watching me. He looked so uncertain. He took his hands from his pockets and placed them on the edge of my bed.

"You lost your spleen," was all he said. His voice was hoarse, but soft.

My eyes flicked down to my abdomen, and Shea's followed, as I nodded. "The doctor told me it was too damaged to save," I replied.

Shea sucked in a breath. "I ... I've ... I've been trying to research. I can't get myself to comprehend the information. The doctors won't tell me anything because I'm not family ... and your mom ... well, what does that mean for you?" he asked me cautiously.

I had asked my mom this very question once I had wrapped my head around the fact that I was now missing an organ. "Mom told me that the spleen is like a blood filter. I can live without it, but I'm more prone to infections now. I suppose I'll learn to adapt and manage my health a little more cautiously than I did before," I replied.

I hadn't honestly thought much about how my life would change without a spleen. I wondered what sort of infections I might pick up? Would I always be on anti-biotics? I suppose this was the benefit of having a doctor for a mother. Whenever questions popped into my head, I had a walking encyclopaedia.

"Shea," I said softly, taking his hand that had been resting on the edge of my bed. He immediately snatched it away. I frowned. "Shea," I said again, firmer this time, "this isn't your fault. I don't blame you in the slightest. Neither does Mom."

Shea let out a sarcastic laugh. "Not my fault?" he challenged. "I left you alone and now you're missing an organ. You could've died!

You were snatched from right under my nose and I didn't stop it." Shea buried his head in his hands.

I felt annoyed. I was annoyed that Shea couldn't see how completely wrong he was. He had to know that this was all Lex's fault. I wasn't to blame. He wasn't to blame. Only Lex. Lex had been the one to take me. And if he hadn't done it in Charlotte, he would have done it in Providence.

But I forced myself to see it from Shea's point of view. He wasn't thinking rationally. And he wasn't thinking from the perspective of a human. I was his mate. He was biologically programmed to love and protect me, and he felt like he had failed me.

"If ... if I hadn't embarrassed you, if I hadn't sent you running from me, you would have stayed with me." Shea's eyes had become glassy. "I was stupid, stupid letting you go. I was only five minutes behind you when I could smell what had happened. I followed your scent until it stopped, when he put you in a car, and you were gone. You were gone!" A tear escaped Shea's eye and he quickly wiped it away. I wanted to sit up so desperately to wrap my arms around him. "You were missing for thirty-two hours because I was careless, and I don't know how you could ever forgive me, because I can certainly never forgive myself."

"I was missing for thirty-two hours because a man made the choice to take me from that parking lot," I said slowly and insistently. "I'm alive because the people that I love looked for me and found me in time to get me help." Screw it, I leaned forward, ignoring the dull ache and pull of the stitches and bandages and took Shea's hand again. "Are you okay?"

Shea laughed a short laugh, before letting out a sob, quickly burying his face in my hands. I felt his tears and my heart just broke. I loved him so much and seeing this kind of pain hurt more than any knife.

"I'm okay," I promised him. "I'm okay, I'm okay, I'm okay," I kept repeating.

Shea cried for a few minutes, and I kept whispering that everything was okay. I didn't think less of him at all. I knew there was a stigma around men and crying but I thought that was bullshit. I cried all the time. He could, too.

When he had calmed himself down, he murmured to me, "I've always resented my mom a little, not a lot, but a little, for being so depressed after my dad died. But fearing you were dead, thinking you were dead, fuck, Sara, I don't know how she's still breathing." Shea met my eyes then. His brown eyes that were bloodshot, were now red and swollen, too. "I love you."

"I love you more."

"Not possible," he replied with conviction.

I shuffled over in my bed, ignoring the protestations of my surgical site and the wires that were tugging all over my body.

"Sara, stop, you'll hurt yourself!" protested Shea.

I gave him a look that shut him up as I motioned for him to lie down beside me in the bed. He obeyed, very carefully lying down on his side next to me in the bed. We were suddenly very close, but I didn't feel that usual sense of embarrassment that I did when I was this close to Shea. Strangely, I felt an even deeper connection to him. We belonged to each other. It was how it was meant to be.

I closed the distance between us and pressed my lips to Shea's. He was reserved for a moment before he softly deepened our kiss.

"You smell weird," he said, murmuring against my lips.

"Gee, thanks." I fought the urge to laugh as he inhaled dramatically.

"I think it's the morphine," he decided. Shea kissed my hair and inhaled, contently saying, "But your hair still smells like you."

Shea was asleep in minutes, breathing calmly and deeply against my hair, inhaling in the only part of my scent that was familiar. I was on an awkward angle, and were it not for the morphine, I knew I would be in a lot of pain, but I was happy to see Shea finally sleeping, and hopefully realising that I was okay, and that he didn't need to blame himself.

A short while later, the nurse carefully let herself into the room and angrily went to protest what she saw us.

I stopped her. "No, please, leave him," I begged. "He hasn't slept in days." I doubted he'd slept since Thursday night.

"You need to look after yourself, especially after losing your spleen. Any damage to your surgical site and you could develop an infection very easily," she informed me, and I quickly realised that this was something I would now be adapting to.

Shea let out a snore. I thought it was adorable. The nurse was not amused.

"Come on, handsome," she urged, shaking Shea.

Shea quickly roused almost defensively, gripping me instinctively. I flinched when his hand held the crook of my arm where my IV was. He immediately released me and offered me a drowsy, apologetic look.

"Mom trumps boyfriend unfortunately," she told him. "Out you go. Get some rest. You ought to be prettier than you look now."

Shea chuckled as he climbed out of my bed, subsequently helping me to lay back down comfortably. I did feel a release of pressure as I laid back down on my back properly. Shea leaned down over my bed and kissed my forehead, whispering that he loved me.

"My dad," I whispered, looking up at him with knowing. It was still hitting me in waves that he was alive, and here, and Shea had to have seen him in the clearing. Unless I had hallucinated the giant wolf as well.

"I got it," he whispered back, before following the nurse's orders and departing.

Mom and I had never really cooked anything fancy on Thanksgiving. More often than not it was Chinese take-out as she was too tired from work to spend ten hours cooking a turkey and I hadn't much minded.

So, eating hospital turkey and Jell-O for dessert on Thanksgiving was like a special treat really.

Half the student body of the school had come to see me once I had been moved out of the ICU. Even some of my teachers had come to visit, and they thankfully hadn't brought homework. Cece had been twice. Josh had been, and he hadn't told me anything about his encounter with Zoey. Whether I'd imagined that as well, or he didn't want to burden me, I wouldn't know.

The story was as close to the truth as possible. I was snatched from the hotel parking lot and drugged by a man with a grudge against my father. He had stabbed me and I was saved by Shea back in Providence. A warrant was out for the arrest of the man that I had described.

I honestly still didn't know the full story. I didn't know what had happened to Lex. I didn't know if there could be any kind of justice for someone like him. Grief sometimes puts you over the edge. I hadn't had the chance, or the guts, to ask Shea.

Shea hated having the credit for saving me. He still believed that he had been the one to lose me in the first place no matter how I tried to convince him otherwise. But he was coming around to believing that I wasn't angry at all. He and I both knew that it had been my dad who had found me.

Mom still had no idea. I didn't know how to tell her. I didn't know if I was supposed to tell her. I hadn't seen my dad since he had been in my room the other day. And now we were sitting here in the hospital ward flicking through Black Friday sales on our cell phones as if her not dead husband wasn't in the same building.

Mom refused to leave my side. She had taken to moving in and had used her pull as a doctor with hospital privileges to get a cot put in the same room with me. Shea had been to our house to grab changes of clothes and toiletries, and Mom had vocally forgiven him.

I was healing well. I was slowly being weaned off of the strong stuff and being introduced to good old Tylenol for the pain every so often. There had been no infection. Considering my risk was higher with no spleen, this was a good thing. All I would have for my troubles is a nasty scar and the knowledge that someone unhinged had put it there.

CHAPTER 31

I was released from hospital two weeks to the day of my kidnapping. I thought I had been ready to go home much earlier but Mom insisted on monitoring me for much longer. I had no idea how good our health insurance was, but it had to have been for such a stay. I also thought that some of the doctors and nurses were scared of her to go along with it.

Nobody could get between a mama bear and her cub.

Mom and Shea both helped me inside the house, which looked oddly comforting with our stuff still strewn across the place as though we had only been here yesterday. I was set up on the couch with a blanket, tea, some snacks, and the remote.

It was the first week of December. I had already missed a lot of school and it was only too easy to fall behind. I was going to try and get my mom to let me go back on Monday. We would see how that went.

She, much to her dismay, could no longer get any more time off of work. She had used all her sick leave and hadn't been working long enough to rack up much in the way of annual leave. So that

Friday morning, she set off to work, with strict instructions for me to check in every hour with my temperature.

Oh yeah, I also had a thermometer handy.

I made Shea go to school as well. It was even more important for him to go as he was a senior. He promised to come by right after school.

And then, for the first time in what felt like forever, I was alone. The house was quiet. It felt odd to suddenly not hear the annoying beep of the heart monitor, or the nurses chatting away outside my room about hospital gossip.

I turned on the TV for some noise and began to flick through all the shows that had been recording over the last two weeks. I settled on my favourite soapy drama and clicked play.

I wasn't five minutes into the show before there was a knock at the door. I was surprised, but then not so, when my first instinct was fear. Anxiety began to rise inside me as I didn't know who was behind the door. It could be anyone. I was alone and vulnerable.

I stopped breathing as my heart sped up, my eyes flicking around the room for some sort of weapon to defend myself with. What if it was Lex? Oh my God, how the hell was I supposed to defend myself against him?

But my fears were quickly quashed seconds later. "Calm down, Saraphine," came the comforting, deep voice of my dad. "It's your dad."

I breathed a sigh of relief two times over. Not only was I safe, but my dad had come back to see me. I knew why he'd had to stay away. But I'd hated it.

Carefully I made my way off of the couch and waddled over to the door. I took a deep breath before turning the handle. I swung the door open to see him standing before me. Now that I was standing before him, I could appreciate his height and size. I really had inherited my height and build from Mom. He was probably about six and a half feet tall and he clearly looked after himself. He didn't look like most dads with their thinning hair and beer gut.

He looked down at me with the same look of parental adoration that mom did. I thought back to his words in that video and I knew how much he loved me. I had a dad. I had another parent. Two parents who loved me to pieces. Jesus Christ, this actually felt like the damn lottery.

"Daddy," I whimpered, before throwing my arms around him. The stretch pulled at my abdomen, but I didn't care. I was hugging my father for the first time in my life.

Dad seemed to read my mind, lifting me up as his arms wrapped around my waist. "Oh, baby girl," he said softly, in a content voice filled with relief. I felt him place a kiss on top of my head.

The level of security I felt by being hugged by my dad was something incredible.

After a minute, he put me down on the ground, before cradling my face in his hands. He just smiled with sheer wonder. "You are so beautiful, Saraphine," he said fondly.

I couldn't help but wince as I managed the pain, and even though I smiled through it, Dad saw it.

"You shouldn't be standing. This is my fault, I'm sorry. Let me help you."

We came to sit down on the couch together, and Dad looked around the room. I watched him stop on the pictures on the mantle, and I was sure with his eyesight that he could see them as clear as day.

"Ignore the braces," I murmured, referencing those awkward junior high days.

"All part of growing up. You must've got my shitty dental genes. I needed braces, too," he replied humorously before stopping himself. "Sorry about the cursing. I've always had a bad mouth."

I laughed, more delighted by learning that I'd inherited something from him. "I don't care," I assured him, before sighing. "Daddy, where have you been all these years?"

He placed an arm over the back of the sofa and turned to face me. "I've never been far, sweetheart," he promised, "and I will tell you everything you want to know."

"Okay," I agreed. "Why did we all think you were dead?" I asked bluntly.

Dad pursed his lips shut and thought for a second. "I need to explain the context first," he started. "I don't know how much your mom has told you. I don't know how much you know about me or my kind, or anything really."

"I think I know enough."

Dad nodded. "Well, it all started when I first saw your mom. Well, when I saw her for the second time. I'd always known Amanda. I thought she was crazy pretty. I was older than her, and we ran in different circles. She kept to herself. She was very smart. Very smart. Going places. Not like me. She was still in eighth grade when I turned sixteen." He spoke with such reserved sadness. Like he had been practicing speaking about Mom. Goddammit, I could hear the raw pain still. "When we turn sixteen, it's like a second puberty. We are able to shift for the first time, and we are able to realise our mate when we see them. I knew it was her. From the second I saw her I knew. It was like I was seeing her clearly for the first time. But we were both still kids and there was no way she was ready for the sort of relationship that we are capable of.

"So, I waited. I was crazy in love with this girl, but I waited. I was friendly to her. Tried to make her see that when I eventually asked her out, I wouldn't be such a horrible guy. So, when I did finally ask her out two years later, she was eating a hotdog in the cafeteria, and mustard had dropped onto her shirt. It was adorable. And she said no." He rolled his eyes at the memory. "I think I just kept annoying here until she gave in. And what we had was amazing.

"We are always told that humans don't have the same capacity to love as we do. It's not the same. But Goddammit, I thought it was. I thought she loved me just as much as I love her."

It didn't escape me that he used the present tense when talking about loving my mom.

Dad closed his eyes and pinched the bridge of his nose. "But she didn't. Couldn't. I know a lot of it was my fault. If I could go back and do things differently, I would." I assumed he was referring to keeping Mom in the dark about his secret identity. "We'd been together for four years. Got married, said vows before God that I meant with every bit of my soul, and we'd had a beautiful little daughter. I was blind ... blind to her fear, her unhappiness ... and she took you, and left me." His voice cracked and I immediately reached out to him, taking his hand in mine. I didn't know what to make of this story, or Mom's. Hearing it from both of them, it was like they shared the same pain, but not together.

And then Dad stiffened.

"What?" I asked.

Looking to the door he said, "Your mother came back."

Shit. How the hell was I going to explain this?

Dad went to get up from the couch, as though he was going to slip out the back door. I seized his hand, stopping him. No. This had to happen, no matter the fight it would cause.

"Stay!" I begged.

"Saraphine," he said in a pained voice.

"Stay!" I insisted again. "It won't be as bad as you think." I resisted the urge to cross my fingers.

Not two seconds later, I heard Mom's keys in the door. She pushed open the door and came rushing inside, holding her hands up in a flustered way as she ran over to the kitchen counter.

"I'm not here!" she cried. "I just forgot my cell. I'm not checking up on you, I promise." She stood with her back to us as she flicked through her phone momentarily before shoving it in her back pocket. "But while I'm here, Sara, I want to check your –" as she turned around, she froze. Her eyes locked with Dad's and all blood rushed from her face. I had never seen someone literally pale before.

I looked at Dad, and he was staring at her intensely, a whole mixture of emotions on his face. "Amanda," he whispered.

Mom's eyes then rolled back into her head as she passed out.

CHAPTER 32

In one moment, Dad had gone from sitting beside me on the couch, to cradling Mom in his arms, catching her before she had hit the floor. In that action, in the way that he held her, I could see just how much he still loved her.

It was while holding my mom that I noticed his left hand. Just like Mom did, he still wore his wedding ring.

Dad stood up, adjusting Mom in his arms and he brought her into the living room, sitting her down on the opposite end of our couch very gently. I helped by grabbing a cushion and using it to support her head.

"Do you have any smelling salts, Saraphine?" Dad asked.

I wasn't even sure what those were, but I knew we had some essential oils from when Mom went through a meditation phase for a week. But I couldn't pinpoint where they were. Probably in a box in our garage with the other junk that we had carted down from New York.

Instead, I shook her, grabbing hold of her upper arms. "Mom!" I shouted. "Mom, wake up!" I didn't know if this was bad or not, but the only doctor in the room was unconscious.

Dad joined in, clicking his fingers at Mom's ear. "Amanda, can you hear me?"

Mom came to a few seconds later. Her green eyes shot open, and darted between the two of us, before fixating on Dad. She completely stiffened as she stared at him in utter disbelief and shock.

Dad was still kneeling down beside her. "Deep breaths, Amanda," he instructed calmly.

"I ..." Mom stammered. "I ... I don't understand ... how?"

"I was just explaining what had happened all those years ago to Saraphine," he replied.

Mom's eyes flicked to me. "Sara ...? You knew about this?" she asked, still evidently in complete shock.

"Not until recently, Mom," I assured her, though I knew that was still bad.

"Well, what happened?" Mom demanded to know, gaining a little more gumption. "I don't understand. How are you alive?"

Dad stood up and walked the few feet over to the mantle to look at the pictures there more closely. "When you left me, Amanda, and took my baby away from me, I just about wanted to die."

His words sent an undeniable chill down my spine. I stole a glance at Mom and saw that she, too, was frozen still.

"That sort of rejection for my kind ... well, I've learned to endure the pain."

I felt like he was substituting pain for another word. Probably something like agony, or total anguish.

"The next month or two are honestly a blur. I think I repressed them, blocked them out. It was the darkest time in my life." His voice was strained, but calm. We were listening to every word. "I remember the tensions with Kurt's pack coming to a head, and there was a fight, just him and me. I had nothing to lose." He exhaled, stealing a glance at Mom. "Not anymore. The next thing I knew, I was waking up in a pool of blood. A lot of my own, a lot belonging to Kurt. My body was torn to shreds, but I had landed a fatal blow on Kurt."

I could see how haunted he was by this memory. I wasn't fully sure I understood properly, to know what it was to duel, to fight, and to kill in their world.

"I was bleeding out, and I remember hearing scavenging animals surrounding us. Somehow I managed to shift and run. Trudging and stumbling until I came to a hospital miles and miles from Providence. The doctors wrote it off as an animal attack. I nearly died from the blood loss. An infection nearly caused blood poisoning shortly after. But the good docs managed to save my life. What was left of it, anyway.

"I had no ID. No next of kin. They didn't know I had a wife, a daughter, a family. I was a John Doe. When I was finally released, I went back, though I had no idea how the hell I was supposed to lead. And when I got back, I saw my funeral. They thought I had died in that field alongside Kurt."

"And ... and you decided to let them think that?" Mom whispered.

Dad nodded, looking at her with a sort of fearful tenderness.

"And ... and you decided to let me think that?" she asked, her voice becoming frankly extremely pissed.

Dad sensed her shift in tone. He stiffened defensively.

But Mom continued. Knotting her fingers in her hair, she seethed, "You fucking asshole, Ronan!"

I flinched. I don't think I'd ever heard Mom curse like that before.

Standing up from the couch, she yelled, "How could you do that to me?"

"You left me!" Dad hissed, anger filling his eyes. "Quote I don't want you anywhere near Saraphine orme unquote!"

"I didn't mean that!" Mom shouted, tears filling her eyes.

"Well it sure as hell looked like you did when you packed up your stuff and took my baby out of the state!" Dad retorted.

They were both breathing heavily, their shoulders rising and falling rapidly as they stared at each other. Mom looked so angry and so confused. Dad looked to be a mixture of fury and hurt.

And there I was, trying not to draw attention to myself so that they could get out what they needed to say.

"I grieved you!" Mom exclaimed after a moment, "I don't think I ever stopped grieving you. My husband, the father of my daughter, died.But you weren't really dead ... Ronan, how could you do this? How could you let me, let us, believe that you were dead?"

Dad faced Mom properly, squaring his shoulders and opening his arms, as if to show honest body language. "You broke me, Amanda," he said quietly, "you fucking destroyed me. I was a twenty-some-thing year old kid whose world imploded on top of him, and at my lowest point, I didn't have my wife, and I didn't have my baby. The two most important people in my life were gone, and you said the words, Amanda, you said that you didn't want me to be anywhere near you or Saraphine. For a human, that would be catastrophic, but for someone like me?" He shook his head.

"No!" Mom retorted. "Don't you dare blame me for this! I was a kid, too! I was a scared kid with a baby to protect and all that was going on around me was danger!"

"I would have neverlet anything happen to either of you!" Dad snapped. "Don't you get it? Don't you know how I feel about you?"

"You were showing Sara off to everyone saying that she was your heir!" Mom shot back. "How is that not putting her in danger?"

"I was proud!"Dad exclaimed. "I had a beautiful, perfect kid, and I was showing her off to my friends! And yes, whether you like it or not, she is my heir!" Dad suddenly stopped. "Wait, was that it? Was that why you left me?"

Mom's lower lip was trembling, as though she was going to break down any minute. "I can't do this right now. I'm late for work." She began to frantically look around her for her car keys, which were on the floor by the kitchen counter near where she had fainted.

"Amanda, please." Dad reached out to her, coming before her in half a second and taking her hand. "I'm sorry. I'm so sorry." As soon as he touched her, she burst into tears and threw her arms around his neck, hugging him so tightly she might have choked him. He reciprocated immediately, wrapping his arms around her waist and burying his face in the crook of her neck.

Mom was trembling as she cried. "I hate you. I hate you," she kept repeating. But I could tell by her tone that she didn't mean it. She didn't hate him one bit.

I quietly crept off the couch and made my way towards the kitchen to find Mom's phone. There was no way she could work today. Let alone even drive in her current state. I found it on the kitchen floor, near her keys, and by some miracle the screen hadn't smashed. I found her boss' number and made up an excuse concerning me.

She spent all day looking after other's people's kids. Surely one more day looking after her own was permissible.

Seconds after I hit send, I heard my name being cried.

"Sara!" from Mom.

"Saraphine!" from Dad.

They both began to lecture me about being on my feet, and I could help but smile like an idiot. Parents, plural, telling me what to do. I knew this would get old pretty fast, but I loved it.

Dad picked me up and carried me back over to the couch. He set me down gently and Mom adjusted the cushions behind me so that I was comfortable. As they were kneeling down together and fussing, I could help but notice how easily they worked together. Their movement together seemed natural and fluid.

And then Mom suddenly stopped. "Where the hell have you been all this time?" she demanded to know.

I looked to Dad as well. I was curious, too. More than curious, seeing as I was fairly certain we had met once before.

"New York," he replied simply.

Mom blinked and furrowed her eyebrows. "What?"

Taking a deep breath, Dad said, "After everything that happened, I couldn't stay in Providence, I couldn't live in our house, I couldn't see my friends with their mates and their children knowing what I had lost. But I had an obligation so long as I was alive to lead them. And it was an all too easy out letting them believe that I was dead. With the headspace I was in, I couldn't think of anything else to do. I followed you and Saraphine to New York."

He had been in New York the whole time? Was that what he was saying? I suddenly remembered him telling me coyly that he had never been far. Shit, was that what he meant?

"I purchased a fake identity from someone affiliated with my people under a pseudonym and got work as a contractor. I was always good with my hands."

Mom shook her head and held her hand up. "You were in New York?" she checked. "While we were?" She gestured to me.

Dad nodded. "I needed to make sure you both were safe. You two were all I had."

Mom readjusted so that she was sitting down on the floor and leaning back against the couch. She brought her knees up to her chest and leant her head down. "My med school tuition," she murmured, the sound muffled as she hid her face. "I got a scholarship that I never applied for."

"I did really well as a contractor in the city. I wanted to help you."

"And the mortgage for the house in Bedford. I wasn't approved until I got a phone call telling me the bank had reconsidered," she added another recollection.

"I put up the collateral," Dad replied calmly.

"Sara's day care, her school fees … oh my God, I'm such an idiot. There aren't packages and assistance for moms who are students." She pinched the bridge of her nose.

"You're not an idiot," Dad said firmly. "You're always the smartest one in the room. You just needed help."

She turned her head then, staring at him with angry, hurt eyes. "What I needed was my husband."

Dad sucked in a breath. "You told me the opposite, Amanda," he reminded her painfully. "You told me you were miserable. You couldn't go to the college you wanted. You couldn't have the life you wanted if you were with me. I was a danger to you. A danger to our daughter." His voice cracked then, as if the idea of him being dangerous to me nearly killed him. "You left me before any of this happened. You practically fucking gift wrapped the knife as you drove it into my chest. So, I thought I was doing what you wanted while still being near enough to you to satisfy my instinct to protect you. I couldn't show my face to you. I barely survived your rejection once. I honestly don't know what will happen to me when it happens again."

"Stop!" I cried, capturing both of their attention instantly. "If I have learned anything throughout this whole ordeal it's that your family is precious. Losing them is gut wrenching, and getting them back ... well, if that's not a miracle, then I don't know what is." I smiled at my dad, who's expression softened tenderly.

Mom quickly set about composing herself, dabbing her eyes with her sleeve and trying to keep her mascara in place. "You're right, Sara," she agreed, climbing to her feet. "I almost lost you," she gulped, "and your health is what matters. We shouldn't be having this discussion in front of her, Ronan."

Not what I meant.

But Mom suddenly froze, her eyes drawing up slowly to glare at Dad. Oh God, what now? "Wait, you knew the man who attacked Sara, didn't you?"

Dad nodded regretfully. "Yes. His name was Alexander Hale."

Was. A shiver went down my spine. That was my first confirmation. I hadn't had the chance to speak to Shea about what had happened with Lex. But knowing that he was dead left me feeling a little safer, and I didn't know if that made me a bad person or not.

"His father, Kurt, was the man I killed seventeen years ago. His vendetta against the pack came to a head when he set his sights on Saraphine. I thought she would be safe in Charlotte with Shea and Cecelia and ..." he trailed off before taking a breath. "Anyway, I stayed behind to make sure you were safe leading up to the anniversary. When I learned Saraphine was missing, I tracked Alexander's movements, and found Saraphine's scent, which led me back to where it happened. It led me to the clearing. I tried to talk him down. I wanted it to end peacefully but –"

"But instead my daughter was nearly killed by a crazy person with a knife, and now she has no spleen and none of her own blood left in her body!" Mom interrupted furiously.

"Mom!" I pleaded in a rational tone. "He tried to save me. He found me!"

"Something you'd neglected to tell me, Sara," she added sharply. "But I don't care. You were unsafe ... I knew this would happen. This is what I was afraid of!"

Shit, she was blaming my dad now.

Dad laughed knowingly, shaking his head. "Don't you dare act like I put that knife in Alexander's hand," he rebutted. "All I have ever done is watch out for my kid. I did everything in my power to protect Saraphine from harm, and it wasn't enough. And I will live with that. But I got her as fast as I could to the people that could help her."

He laughed again, but with regret and pain. "All I have ever done is try to protect the people around me. I tried to protect Alexander's mother as she tried to join my pack, and I wanted her son to come with her. That caused the conflict with Kurt.

"I tried to protect you, Amanda. First and foremost. I kept you out of it, and I realise I should have been honest, but would it have made you leave me sooner? Perhaps that is very selfish of me, but that's the way our minds work.

"I have loved you, Saraphine, more than my own life, for every single day of yours." He looked upon me with complete sincerity. "I will never be able to make up for the years I've lost, and denied you, and I am so incredibly sorry. It has been the hardest thing I've ever done, not knowing you. I hope that you can find some way to forgive me, and I hope that this next stage of your life, we can build the kind of bond that I have always wanted to have with you." Looking back to Mom, he said, "I am a flawed man, but nobody could ever say that I didn't fucking love my family."

My mom looked so raw. I wanted to hug her, to let her know it would all be okay. I honestly couldn't tell what she was feeling. I didn't know how she felt about my dad. I knew there were still a lot of unresolved issues there.

"I am sincerely sorry for everything that I put you through, Amanda. Everything. Before and after. I wasn't the best boyfriend. I certainly wasn't the greatest husband. You stuck yourself with a dumb kid, and I understand a lot more now why I couldn't make you happy. You deserved a lot better. You deserve a lot better. And for what it's worth, I'm so proud of you, for everything you achieved, and for how amazingly you brought up Saraphine."

I could sense "goodbye" in his tone, and it made me feel suddenly apprehensive. I didn't really know what I expected to happen between them, but I didn't want whatever it was to end.

A single tear escaped Mom's eye and she quickly wiped it away before it could roll down her cheek.

"I think you ought to go, Ronan," Mom said quietly.

My heart sank, and I could see the dread and pain on Dad's face immediately. He was preparing himself for rejection.

"Daddy," I whispered, willing him not to go far.

He offered me a small, sad smile, before nodding in concession to Mom. He leaned over and kissed my forehead, before turning towards the door.

As he went to go, Mom added, "We eat breakfast around eight-ish in the morning on weekends."

Looking over his shoulder, Dad asked, "Is that an invitation?" nonchalantly, though I could hear the hope in his voice.

"What do you want me to do? Spell it out for you?" she chastised self-consciously.

He wisely chose not to push her, probably in fear that she would rescind the invitation. "I'll bring coffee."

"Do you … do you remember how I like it?" she asked nervously.

"I remember."

CHAPTER 33

M om watched the front door for several moments after Dad left. I didn't say anything. I didn't want to interrupt her train of thought.

Finally, she took a breath and turned to me. She blinked, her mouth opening to speak, but she didn't have words. Small sounds escaped as she tried to start sentences, but she couldn't form anything coherent.

"That ... that was your dad ... that was Ronan," she finally murmured in disbelief, as though her eyes had been tricking her.

"Are you okay?" I asked her, already knowing the answer.

"Oh, hon, I don't even know what I am right now." She knotted her fingers in her hair as she sat down beside me on the couch. I immediately wrapped me arms around her and rested my head on her shoulder. Turning her head, she kissed my hair.

We sat together on the couch for a while, quietly considering what had happened. I wasn't sure I still fully understood what had happened between them, and what had happened to my dad, but all I knew was that I had my dad back. Selfishly, I was so glad.

Unselfishly, I didn't know what this would mean for my mom. I didn't know how my dad would cope being around her. I then shuddered at the thought of him leaving. What if being around Mom was too much for him?

We were both startled by the sound of my phone ringing. In all the commotion, it had fallen down the side of one of the couch cushions. I fished it out and saw that it was Shea calling me. I also saw that it was lunch time. Shit. How long had we been here for?

"Hey," I answered.

"How are you feeling?" he asked. I could hear in his voice that he was itching for news. He really had protesting going to school today.

My eyes darted to my Mom, who was still sitting, quite bewildered, beside me. "Um," I paused, but then forgot to finish my sentence.

"Um?" Shea prompted. "Sara, are you okay?" he demanded to know. "I'm leaving. I'm coming right now." I could hear in the background that he was in the cafeteria. I could hear him clambering to his feet, and I could hear the questions from his friends.

"No, no, I'm fine!" I promised. "We're just a bit tired." That was an understatement. "Mom's home with me." I couldn't exactly tell him what had happened with my Mom sitting right next to me.

"Your mom is there?" he repeated. "Are you okay?" he pressed. "Are you sick? Do you have a fever? An infection? Is your incision site red or tender at all?"

Clearly someonehad been spending a little too much time talking to my mom at the hospital. "I'm fine!" I said again with a smile. "I'm not sick, and I've got snacks, and a whole lot of Real Housewives to watch."

I knew it was difficult for him to be apart from me, especially when I wasn't one hundred percent.

"Would it be too much to ask you text me your temperature every so often?" he asked quietly. "I know your mom wanted you to do that, and I've been researching –"

"Shea," I stopped him. "People function completely normally without their spleens," I assured him. "You will be the first to know if I develop a fever. Which I won't."

Shea sighed in a way that told me he knew he was being over-protective. "Is it still alright for me to come by after school?"

"You want to watch Real Housewives with me?" I teased.

I could practically hear the eye roll. "Whatever makes you happy," he replied in good humour.

I heard the bell sound in the background, so I knew he needed to get going. "I'll see you later. I love you."

"I love you more," he replied, before cutting the call.

We hadn't really had a chance to be just us in the past few weeks. Being attached to all sorts of machines and IVs hadn't helped, but Shea had been really concerned about me, and he clearly still was. I was looking forward to when we could get our relationship back on track, and I hoped I wouldn't fully embarrass myself like I did the last time.

"Shea is going to get grey hair if he's not careful," murmured my mom.

"Don't I know it," I replied. Taking a deep breath, I said, "Mom, I'm really sorry for not telling you about Daddy. I promise you I only knew for a little while, and he didn't want me to tell you."

As soon as the words were out of my mouth, I knew I could have phrased them better.

"You are not responsible for your father's sins, Sara," she replied with a reassuring tone. "If anything, I'm the one who's responsible."

"What?"

"We all say things without really meaning them. We mean them in the moment, but not really." Mom looked down at her wedding rings, spinning them absentmindedly. "I am very angry at him. I hate the grief he put me through. But I'm angry at myself as I said some horrible things to him back then. I hurt him, deliberately, in anger, and what I said kept him from being in your life, and in my life." She leaned her head back on the couch and sighed, closing her eyes as though she was getting a migraine.

"Mom, none of this is your fault either," I insisted. "You were just being a good mom. Like you always have done."

She blindly reached for my hand and I squeezed it. "Oh, sweetheart, I shouldn't be bothering you with this. Kids aren't supposed to worry themselves with their parents' problems, and you certainly shouldn't be stressing about any of this. You need to be resting." Shaking her head, she got up from the couch, and went into the kitchen to make us some lunch.

We watched TV together for the rest of the afternoon. Trashy television to distract us. Well, I hope it distracted Mom as it certainly didn't distract me. I kept stealing glances at my mom as we watched. She had always spun her rings mindlessly every so often, but she had not stopped today.

Was it really childish of me to be hopeful? Or had too much happened? Would they get divorced? They were still technically married after all.

Shea must have broken about a dozen road rules as he arrived at my house eight minutes after the final bell would have gone for the day. As soon as he was inside and on the couch with me, Mom left with her purse, muttering something about going to the store.

Shea looked so relieved to see me, and after everything that had happened today, I was certainly glad that I could trust him with it.

"My mom found out about my dad today," I told him as soon as we were alone.

Shea's brown eyes widened in shock. His mouth opened for a moment before he found words. "Shit, how did she take it?"

"Not well ... and well, a little of both," I replied, shrugging my shoulders in disbelief. "Daddy came over after she left for work and she forgot her phone. She found us here together. They fought ... I think that's what you'd call it. It was kind of like I wasn't there. They fought, and talked, Mom cried. She hugged him, and they fought some more."

I rested my head on Shea's shoulder and exhaled. I hadn't realised just how tired I was after today, and I hadn't really done anything except sit on my behind.

"I think my mom and dad are going to get a divorce," I admitted sadly.

I mean, I could imagine up happy endings in my head, but really, who could come back from this? Seventeen years had passed. They were probably completely different people now. That on top of the whole resurrection thing was enough to push a couple to divorce, no matter how much they loved each other in the past. I didn't know if my mom could handle this.

"I'm sorry, Sara," Shea murmured comfortingly. "I hope this is a consolation, but I know your dad is planning on sticking around."

I lifted my head up. "How do you know that? Did he say something to you? Have you spoken to him?"

Thanks mostly to my mom never leaving my side while I was in the hospital, I hadn't had a chance to speak to Shea privately about my dad after I'd asked him to check in on him. Some things could not be communicated via text message.

"Obviously there's a lot of unfinished business and questions from our end," he started, implying that there was a lot of pack drama, "but we understand rejection and how that affects a lycan. Your dad was rejected by his mate, and his child was taken from him. While his actions were extreme, abandonment isn't as ridiculous as you might think amongst our kind."

I wondered how common it really is. I wondered if it was humans that were the ones to reject their mates. I wanted to ask, but I knew it was a soft spot for Shea.

"My dad was the Alpha, wasn't he?" I asked, changing the subject. "Is he joining back up again?"

Shea smiled slightly. "We're not like a baseball team where you can just sign up again when you feel like it," he replied in a slight teasing tone. "But being a blood Alpha does have its advantages. At the end of the day, I'm the son of a Beta. I'm meant to be a Beta. If he wanted to, he could challenge me."

I frowned. "Challenge you? What does that mean?"

"We'd fight," he said simply. "Whomever gets the other on his back first wins."

"What?" I spat. I pulled away from Shea, sitting up on my own and I stared at him. "Are you actually kidding me? All this bullshit started with a damned fight. You really think I'm going to let you fight my dad?" Or let my dad fight Shea, for that matter.

"Sara, it's not like that," he promised me defensively. "Neither of us will get hurt. Besides, your dad hasn't even challenged me yet."

"I don't give a shit!" I retorted. "You're not fighting. I'm saying no."

Images started to fill my head all of a sudden and I started to panic. I could see those giant wolves in the clearing, but them fighting each other. My dad and Shea ripping at each other. Absolutely not. Were they insane? One stray swipe and they could catch an artery. I shuddered at the memory of Shea's back after a fight with Lex. No. Nope. Not happening.

"Sara –"

"No!" I interrupted. "You told me that you would do anything for me. Anything I ask. I'm asking you," more like ordering, "not to fight my dad. Work it out another way. I've had enough fighting and violence to last me a lifetime." Much to my annoyance, my conviction sounded more like an emotional mess. I hated crying when I was passionate or insistent on something.

Shea held his hands up and nodded reassuringly. "Okay," he agreed. "Okay. I won't fight. There won't be a fight," he promised.

Relief filled me as I comprehended his words. I breathed a sigh of relief.

Our conversation changed after that. Shea asked me about how I was feeling, and we got on to talking about school and what was happening there. I prodded for information about Zoey, but he didn't tell me anything about her and Josh being official. I couldn't wait to ask Josh about what I'd seen in Charlotte. But I did hope it wasn't just Zoey getting his hopes up once again.

Mom still wasn't home at dinner time, so Shea ordered a pizza for us.

"You like pepperoni, right? You get that in the cafeteria," Shea checked as he was filling out our order on his cell.

"Hawaiian, please," I requested. "They don't offer that in the cafeteria."

Shea stared at me deadpan. "You like pineapple on your pizza?" he asked me in disbelief.

"Yeah," I confirmed, smirking.

"Well, jeez, Sara," Shea said, running his hand back through his hair. "I just don't think this relationship is going to work out."

I laughed and playfully slapped him. "Shut up! Pineapple belongs on pizza! It freshens it up!"

"Pizza doesn't need freshening up!" he retorted just as humorously, however I could see that he truly did think he was right. "Pizza is perfect just the way it is. Pizza is offended by you."

"Be quiet and order me my pineapple pizza." I grinned.

"Gross. I'm dating a cretin," he murmured under his breath, still smirking. He typed in half pepperoni, half Hawaiian, like it was physically injuring him to do so.

It felt wonderful, just for five minutes, to be arguing about something as stupid as pizza. As if that was the worst thing that had happened to either of us in the past few weeks.

But I couldn't help myself. I had to ruin it. I had to ask. "Shea," I said vulnerably.

He noticed the change in my tone immediately. "What is it?" He put his phone down and edged closer to me.

"Is Lex dead?"

I had been wondering for weeks. And today, when my dad had talked about him in the past tense, I believed that he might have been dead. But I wasn't sure. And I wanted, no needed,to know what happened.

Shea's face dropped as he nodded.

My heart stopped. I honestly didn't feel as relieved as I had felt before. I felt dread. I felt dread rise in me as the enormity of the admission sunk in. Holy shit. Lex was dead. Had Shea killed him? Oh my God. Was Shea capable of doing something like that?

"We chased him all the way to South Carolina," Shea explained quietly after a few minutes. "I was ... I was not alright. When I saw what happened to you ... Jesus, Sara, it's a fucking wonder ..." He huffed. "My pack, my friends, my family, they looked after me, and I hate that the burden was on them. We gave him every opportunity. We tried to stop him, to calm him, to trap him even, but he just kept coming. Even after what he did to you, I didn't want to see him dead. I didn't want it to end that way. All I know was it was self-defence. We took him back to his pack and explained everything. Lex had gone rogue. They were well aware of that."

Shea was quiet for a moment, and I took that time to fully comprehend what he'd just said. It was honestly still surreal to me that this sort of thing could happen. Like it was a recurring nightmare that I was happening, and I would wake up any minute and everything would be normal again.

But this was normal. My normal. My new normal. The world wasn't what I'd thought it was. The supernatural existed in reality, and not just in books and movies. My father was a lycan, and shape shifter, and so was my boyfriend. There was such a thing as mates, and my mom was it for my dad, and I was it for Shea. This bond, which I still didn't fully understand, was something incredibly powerful.

"Everything will be okay, won't it?" I mumbled.

Shea wrapped his arms around me and kissed the top of my head. "You will be okay, Sara. I promise."

While I felt reassured, I did notice that he worded his answer carefully. My parents weren't included in that.

Chapter 34

Our pizza arrived a little while later, and Shea and I bickered over pineapple again. I was full after two and a half pieces and Shea was still hungry, so he begrudgingly sufferedeating my leftover Hawaiian pieces, dramatically acting as though I was trying to poison him.

After dinner, we found a movie to watch on cable and settled into the couch. I rested my head on Shea's chest, not realising just how tired I was after today. My eyes were quickly becoming heavy, and Shea's calm heartbeat was lulling me to sleep.

I must've fallen asleep, because I woke up startled when the front door burst open and Mom practically fell through carrying a dozen shopping bags. Shea and I leapt off the couch to help, but I regretted the sudden movement.

Shea stopped, but I motioned for him to go and help her while I sat back down with a thump.

Shea immediately took the brunt of the burden, carrying the majority of the bags over to the kitchen counter for her. Mom followed him, and I couldn't help but noticed her hair looking shiny and refreshed. It looked healthy and bouncy and –

Oh my God, my mom went and got a blowout.

She began unpacking her groceries, muttering to Shea where they belonged, and I saw her lifting out packages of bacon, eggs, pancake mix, fresh fruits and four different kinds of milk to go with the seven varieties of cereal she had purchased.

I then saw that the remaining bags that weren't groceries were from clothing stores that I had seen in Newtown. She must have just made it before they closed.

A blowout, all this food, and new clothes?

My mom was trying to impress my dad! That wasn't a crazy assumption, right? Holy shit, she still cared about him! I beamed like an idiot, and Shea noticed, giving me a puzzled look.

Once the groceries were away, Mom collected her clothing bags and ducked upstairs. She hadn't noticed my stupid expression. She honestly looked a little stressed.

"What?" asked Shea curiously. "It's weird for your mom to buy food?"

"Mom got a blowout!" I whispered excitedly.

Shea looked at me like I had just spoken Japanese. "What in the world is a blowout?"

"Didn't you notice her hair?" I scoffed.

Shea frowned. "It's ... brown?"

I rolled my eyes and grinned. "My dad is coming over for break-fast tomorrow!" I told him. "Mom went and got her hair done. She's bought all this food. I mean, she bought almond milk! She's trying to impress!" Mom didn't even like two percent milk in her coffee as she thought it tasted like water. "And she's just gone upstairs with bags of new clothes!"

"You're cute when you're excited." Shea smirked.

"Will you help me up the stairs?" I pleaded. "I need to talk to her!"

I had expected him to allow me to lean on him as we walked, but instead Shea whipped me up into his arms and carried me up the stairs with ease. Placing me down safely on the landing, I made my way over to my mom's bedroom.

I knocked on the door and opened it, slipping inside, and closing the door behind me.

Mom was standing in front of her floor length mirror wearing a sports bra and yoga pants, while holding up two very nice blouses up against her. One was a minty green colour, which suited her complexion nicely, and would go great with her eyes. It looked like it was quite form fitting, and wrap around, leaving a low v neckline. The other was black, sleeveless, and more flowy.

Mom dropped the blouses to her side, holding the hangers by the tips of her fingers. She stared at herself, her eyes zeroed in on her stomach as she relaxed it. My mom had a really nice, feminine figure. She was curvier than she used to be, but I thought that came with having a baby. Her stomach was still flat as a pancake, and when she did sit ups every so often, it could be toned.

"I don't know what it is about the freshman fifteen, Sara, but it never leaves your stomach, ass and thighs," she muttered angrily, dropping the blouses on the floor before pulling at the skin on her stomach.

"Mom, what are you talking about? You're beautiful!" I said sincerely. I had never seen her feel self-conscious before. My mom was not a vain person, even though she did look after her appearance like any other person would.

She offered me a thankful look before going back over to the shopping bags on her bed. She fished around before she pulled out this elastic looking tube thing. It looked like spanx but without the underwear part.

"I bought this. The lady in the store said it's supposed to suck in all your fat." Mom sucked in her stomach so that her ribcage was protruding. She stretched the spanx before stepping into it, shimmying it up her thighs and pulling it up over her butt so that it sat around her waist.

My mom was nervous. She was feeling self-conscious. She hadn't seen her husband in seventeen years and she wanted to look good. I was so stupid excited.

"Mom, you look perfect!" I continued. "You don't need spanx. It's not really doing anything anyway."

Mom cocked an eyebrow. "It smooths everything out and sucks in the pudginess. I'm not twenty years old anymore, Sara. It shows." She huffed as she picked up her blouses again and held them up against herself. She impatiently tossed the green one away, murmuring that she needed to lose five pounds before she could pull that one off.

"Daddy isn't twenty years old anymore, either," I said quietly, hoping that she would be less hard on herself if she considered that he was older now, too.

Her head snapped around and her green eyes narrowed. "Men have it easy. They can eat a freaking mango and lose ten pounds. I look at a muffin and it's attached itself to my thighs." Mom slipped the blouse on and started pulling and adjusting it on her frame.

"Trust that man to come back from the damn dead looking ..." she trailed off.

I carefully collected the green blouse from the floor and brought it back to her. "I think you will look really beautiful in this," I promised her. "You're a rockstar, Mom, and it's not because of your looks ... even though you are beautiful. You're a doctor, a very respected one! You're always the smartest one in the room. You're a kickass mom, and you're my best friend. Any man would be lucky to have you."

Mom rolled her eyes and took the blouse from me. But she smiled. "I know what you're thinking, Sara. I can see it all over your face. I don't want you to get your hopes up." Sighing, she said, "Sara, I want you to have exactly the relationship with your father that you want. I won't stand in your way at all."

I knew that. She wasn't a vindictive person. "What kind of relationship do you want with him, Mom?" I knew I was pushing my luck, but I was desperately curious.

A slight blush filled her cheeks as she huffed bashfully. "You ought to get to bed. You need to rest. I'll be in to check your temperature and your abdomen in a bit." She then ushered me out of her room and I met back up with Shea on the landing.

Were I not a total invalid, I would have been bouncing. How had I thought that they would be getting a divorce? They were meant to be!

"Mom and Daddy, sitting in a tree, K-I-S-S-I-N-G," I sang in a hushed voice which made Shea laugh.

Putting his arms around me, he hugged me tight. I nuzzled his check, enjoying his comfort.

"Well, being without you for thirty-two hours just about killed me. I don't know how I would cope without you for seventeen years. I hope for both their sakes they can find some happiness."

Shea didn't stay. Mostly because we knew my mom would be like a helicopter and hover over me throughout the night. I honestly wouldn't have been surprised if I woke up to a thermometer in my mouth.

And it was the first night I'd been alone since … well, since before it happened. Lying in my bed in the dark, completely alone, felt a little more overwhelming than I had imagined.

I felt scared. Not in the way that I thought something bad would happen to me, but because something terrible had already happened to me. I was scared that my innocence had gone. Any little remnant of naivety I had was gone because it really can happen to you.

My pulse began to quicken, my breathing grew shallow, and I felt the adrenaline begin to course through my veins as the panic began to settle in. My heart was hammering. Oh my God, it felt like it was going to explode. I felt my body start to shake as the tips of my fingers and toes went numb. Was this a heart attack? Was I having a heart attack?

I sucked in breaths like crazy as I used all my might to roll onto my side to fish for my phone. My eyes were being blinded by my panic tears, and it was a miracle I could dial with numb fingers, but I was calling Shea within seconds.

He answered on the first ring.

"Sara?" he answered, his voice thick with sleep.

"I'm … having … a … heart … attack," I cried in a breathless, helpless voice.

I heard all sorts of fumbling in the background, but it was hard to concentrate on anything other than the sound of my own organs getting ready to explode. I clutched my chest as I sucked in raspy breaths.

"Sara, I need you to calm down," Shea said slowly, more alert than before. "You're not having a heart attack. You're having a panic attack, okay? You're not dying, I promise you." He spoke clearly and calmly.

I cried out. This didn't feel like a normal panic attack. "My heart!"

"I know, Sara, I know!" he said soothingly. "You need to focus your breathing, okay? Put me on speakerphone, can you do that?"

Even though I was trembling like crazy, I managed to hit the little button that put Shea on speakerphone. His voice was louder now, and not just muffled on the other end of the phone.

"Am I on speaker?"

"Yes," I said breathlessly.

"Okay, good. I promise you this will be over in a minute. Now, match your breathing with mine." I heard him take a deep breath in, so I did my best to copy. Shea then exhaled. My breaths were shaky, but I managed to suck more air into my lungs than I had been. "And again," he instructed, taking a deep breath.

I tried to focus my mind entirely on just that sound. Ignoring everything else, every fear, ever anxiety, I switched it off to focus solely on the sound of Shea breathing in and out. We didn't speak for a while. We just breathed.

My heart began to slow down, eventually beating at its normal pace. My shakes stopped, and I felt tingles in my fingertips and toes. The sound of Shea's deep, even breaths eventually lulled me to sleep.

Chapter 35

A loud snore woke me up. Instinctively, I rolled over to kick Shea but there was no one in my bed. Sitting up, I realised that we were still on the phone. I looked at the call time to see that we had been supposedly on the phone for six and a half hours. Shea was sleeping on the other end.

It took me a minute to remember what had happened the night before. I had experienced an honestly harrowing panic attack. I'd always had recurrent anxiety and I had experienced panic attacks before, but that was absolute hell.

I wondered how Shea knew immediately what was going on, and how he knew what to do. I would ask him when he woke up.

I then wondered if it would happen again. That kind of fear was crippling. It honestly felt like I was knocking on death's door. My poor heart felt like it would literally burst in my chest. How much more could the organ take?

I checked the time on my phone and saw that it was nearly seven. My dad would be here in an hour. Pushing my fears and anxieties aside, I ended the call with Shea and got out of bed to go and help my mom.

I dressed in a pair of yoga pants and a loose sweater. I scooped my hair back into a messy bun and decided that was good enough. I could still only wear loose fitting clothes thanks to my surgery scar. I hadn't seen it properly. Not in a mirror anyway. But I was pretty sure it was a monster. Trauma scars always were. I had never been much of a bikini girl before, but I knew for sure I wouldn't be one now.

I couldn't help but notice that it was particularly painful today. Really painful. But it had been painful the whole time, and maybe the hardcore hospital drugs were just wearing off. Either way, I couldn't bother my mom with this when she would be running around like a madwoman.

As soon as I opened my door, the smell of bacon hit me. I literally started to salivate. I carefully made my way downstairs to see a full-on buffet being assembled before me.

Mom looked like she had been up for hours. She was wearing the mint green blouse, and a perfect face of makeup. Her hair was down, shiny, and healthy looking thanks to the blowout. Based on the half-inch she had lost from her waist line, I could tell that she was wearing the spanx. She looked beautiful, and completely stressed.

"Sara!" she cried when she saw me. "Oh, hon, you should have called for me, I would have helped you downstairs." She came rushing from the kitchen and helped me to one of the stools at the counter.

I got a better look at the counter top once I was seated. She had already prepared three monster stacks of pancakes and looked like she had more batter ready. There were enough fried, scrambled and poached eggs to feed a small army, and she had all sorts of garnishes and fillings to add to omelettes. She was assembling a fruit platter while simultaneously frying bacon. And she wasn't just slicing fruit, she was freaking segmenting it.

"Mom, segmented oranges taste the exact same as sliced oranges," I murmured.

She scoffed. "I know. They just look prettier this way."

"Why are you making the bacon this early?" I asked. "Daddy's not going to be here for another hour." I kind of wished the clock would hurry because I was getting hungry.

"This is just for the pancakes," she explained. "I'll make more closer to eight."

"Pancakes?" I repeated.

Mom flitted back to the frypan, flipping the sizzling pieces. I could see the fat popping in the pan. Ugh, I wanted some. "I used to cut up cool bacon pieces and Ronan would mix them with maple syrup on pancakes. I don't know if he still likes it this way, but he did ... once."

First off, that sounded absolutely delicious. But secondly, the fact that my mom remembered something so trivial as to how my dad liked his pancakes just killed me. It was like I was witnessing a family that was completely different from mine.

I really didn't know much about my parent's marriage or their relationship besides the bits and pieces that they told me. But they were together for four years before it all went to shit. That was a long time to be in someone's company. They had to know things about each other that only they knew.

I adjusted my posture, and resisted wincing as my scar pulled. Shit, that was actually a bad one. I wondered if I could get some Tylenol without my mom freaking out on me.

Before I could, though, Mom gave me a bushel of apples and a potato peeler, because apparently, we peel apples now. I humoured her, and I set to work peeling the apples, letting the task distract me from my abdomen pain.

Mom laid out our never used dining table beautifully. A fresh lot of bacon was sizzling in the pan when there was a knock on the door right on eight. Mom, frazzled, quickly wiped her hands on some paper towel, smoothed out her shirt, checked her reflection in the oven door, took a deep breath, before walking over to the door.

My dad had shaved. He was completely clean-shaven and looked so much more like the pictures I had of him. He was dressed in a pressed, white button-down shirt, and a pair of dark wash jeans. He was carrying a fresh bunch of Gerber daisies, and a tray of coffee.

He remembered Mom's favourite flowers.

Dad smiled when he looked at Mom, albeit kind of nervously. "Good morning," he uttered.

"Morning," Mom replied quietly, opening the door wider for him. "Please, come in."

"You look really nice, Amanda," he complemented cautiously, as though he was treading on eggshells. I knew he had to be shitting himself. How weird was this situation?

But Mom smiled upon hearing it. "Oh, this?" she said nonchalant-ly. "It's just an old shirt but thank you."

I had to stop myself from laughing. She was seriously pretending like she hadn't rushed out to a boutique and spent hundreds of dollars on options for today and spent hours getting ready.

"I saw these and ... well, I know you used to like Gerber daisies. I don't know if you still do, but you did ... and ..."

Holy crap, this was actually too cute.

"I love them," Mom said as she accepted the bouquet. "Pink ones were always my favourites." She turned away from him and brought the flowers over the counter top which she had cleaned off minutes before Dad had arrived. She pulled a vase from the cabinet and filled it with water.

Dad's eyes moved to me and he smiled warmly. He was more confident with me, I thought. "How are you, Saraphine?"

"Hungry," I replied.

He laughed. "Me, too. Smells amazing in here." He walked over to me and kissed the top of my head. "How are you feeling?"

"Fine," I lied. No stupid stomach ache was going to spoil this morning.

"I realised when I was buying the coffee that I don't know how you take yours, or if you even drink it," he confessed. "I'm sure all kids your age are into coffee now. Isn't getting something complicated from Starbucks with macchiatos and almond milk popular now?"

"Bit hard when there isn't a Starbucks in Providence," I replied. "I just like my coffee black."

"Guessed right then," he said, grinning. "Well, I got you a black coffee thinking you could add in milk or cream if you wanted. I know Amanda likes hers with whole milk and sugar. No watery two percent for you," he said, handing Mom her cup.

Mom smiled again as she accepted her coffee.

"Listen, I just wanted to say to you both that I'm really grateful to be invited here," Dad said sincerely. "I know there's been a lot of hurt, and a lot of pain, and I am the root cause of a whole lot of that, but you both will always be the most important people in my life. I hope that I am able to earn back your trust."

As I said, "Thank you, Daddy," Mom came out with, "I put bacon bits in your syrup," which I'm certain was her way of saying you're on the right track.

As we ate, my abdomen really started to hurt. It started burning. It was like someone was holding a curling iron right up against my skin and holy shit, it was excruciating.

I tried to concentrate on my mom and dad's conversation, but I couldn't focus on anything except the pain.

"Sara?" I heard Mom ask faintly.

"Mom, I don't feel well," I managed to mumble.

Mom scrambled from her seat and I felt her cool hand against my forehead. "Oh, Sara, you're burning up!"

"What does that mean?" Dad asked in a panicked tone.

"It means she's got an infection!" Mom cried.

I felt her lift up my sweater so that she could look at my abdomen and she cursed. Was it bad? Shit, what had I done?

"We need to get her to the ER," she said seriously.

"My truck is in the driveway," Dad said, jumping up from his chair and lifting me from mine. "Let's go. I'll drive faster than any ambulance."

I was conscious and coherent, I just couldn't talk for the pain. I started to feel severe chills as the searing hot pain in my stomach grew harsher and harsher. Oh my God, this was really bad.

Mom sat in the back seat with me as Dad sped out of our driveway. "Sara, how long have you been feeling sick?" Mom asked as calmly as she could. Her cool hands were on my cheeks.

"I don't know," I groaned. "Since this morning."

"Are you positive?" Mom pressed.

"I think so."

"Tell me why that's important," Dad demanded to know in a panicked voice.

"Septicaemia is a side effect of a splenectomy," Mom replied shortly.

"How could that happen?" he shot back over his shoulder.

"Blood poisoning can be caused by an infection," Mom said bluntly. "Stop questioning me and drive. She needs IV antibiotics immediately."

Holy shit! Blood poisoning! I had seen enough medical shows to know that wasn't good news. So, a stabbing didn't kill me, but something as stupid as an infection might? "Mom!" I wailed. "Am I going to die?"

"No, hon!" Mom cried, cradling my face. "You're going to be just fine, I promise."

I could still hear the fear and panic in her voice, too.

CHAPTER 36

Dad threw his car in park when we got to the hospital, and as we were right outside the emergency doors, I was sure his park wasn't legal. He wrenched open the back door of his truck and pulled me out, carrying me towards the ER.

I could hear commotion around me, and I was soon placed on a gurney. I could hear my mom spouting medical jargon at the ER doctors. As soon as I was in an emergency bay, I felt my shirt being lifted and my bandages being removed. I immediately started to feel pricks as all sorts of shots started to be pumped into me. A nurse put an oxygen mask on me.

I closed my eyes, trying to solely focus on Mom and Dad's voices. I tried to block out the pain. Pain from my wound, and pain from what the doctors were doing.

If I was going to die, I wanted to only hear their voices.

I didn't feel the adrenaline like I had in the clearing. Maybe you were only allotted a certain amount of adrenaline for one lifetime, and I had certainly eclipsed mine in my short time in

Providence. My body was used to near death experiences. Or real death experiences.

My mind went to Shea. Shea. I loved him. Fiercely. I hoped that he knew that.

Then it was quiet.

I opened my eyes and realised that I wasn't in emergency anymore. I was in a ward. Clearly something had knocked me out. I was connected to a heart monitor again, and I had an IV in my arm with a steady flow of liquid and medication coming into me.

I felt a hell of a lot better. My stomach wasn't burning anymore. I didn't feel cold. I felt okay. That was when I noticed my parents speaking over by the door of my room. They hadn't noticed that I had woken up, and they looked to be having a quiet argument.

I knew I should have let them know I was awake, but I wanted to listen. I closed my eyes and began to eavesdrop.

Mom was crying. I could hear her tears in her voice.

"But seriously, Ronan. What kind of a mother am I? I didn't notice my own kid was in pain because I was too preoccupied with myself."

"Amanda –"

"I was so nervous about you coming over that I spent hours making myself look prettier and skinnier than I really am, all the while my baby has a life-threatening infection! You've messed up my priorities!" she accused emotionally. "I knew this was a bad idea. This is a sign. I can't do this."

I was a millisecond away from sitting up in bed and shouting to them both that I was fine, but my dad responded in an oddly calm voice.

"Do you want to know what I think?" he asked but didn't wait for an answer. "I think Saraphine is her mother's daughter. She's inherited your knack of not letting the people who love her know that something is wrong until it's too late."

Okay, he hit the nail on the head with that one there.

"You're not hearing me," Mom said exasperatedly. "That's your problem, Ronan. You always thought that you knew me so much better than you did. You think I didn't say anything?"

Mom was pissed off at herself. I could hear it in her tone. She was angry with herself, and she was scared, and she was taking it out on Dad.

"I do know you, Amanda," he retorted. "I knew you then, and I know you now. I know you so much that I know you aren't angry at me right now."

"Don't you psychoanalyse me," she snapped.

Dad sucked in a breath. "Understanding you is not psycho-analysing," he shot back. "Just means you've got someone in your corner who gets you."

Mom huffed. "Stop trying to make me feel better."

I heard Dad let out a breathy chuckle. "What do you want then?"

"What do I want?" she repeated. "I want my baby to be okay. And I want her to forgive me for trying to make myself look not thirty-seven and ten pounds lighter when she was in pain the whole time." Mom let out a sob.

"Amanda," my dad said soothingly.

Okay, I had to peek. I opened my right eye a slit and I saw that my dad's arms were around Mom. She was resting her head on his chest. Oh my God, they looked like a real married couple.

"Saraphine is going to be fine," he assured her. Dad kissed the top of her head. "And you are as beautiful as the day I first saw you. You have always been the most beautiful woman in the world to me."

"Oh, you're a liar," Mom whispered. But she tilted her head up, and stood up on her toes, and she kissed him.

I thought that it would be super awkward to watch your parents kiss, but they just looked so perfect together! Like they were meant to be. They only kissed for a second, but they stood there for a moment looking at each other afterward, like it had been a long time coming.

I feigned my eyes fluttering open, as I mumbled, "Mom," to get their attention.

Mom practically pounced on me. Dad was not far behind her as they both started to fuss all over me.

"Sara, oh Sara, how do you feel?" Mom asked desperately.

"I'm okay," I said as I started to sit up in the bed. Dad helped by propping my pillows behind me. "I feel a lot better." That was an understatement.

Mom pressed the call button on my hospital remote to summon someone. Then she went back to fussing over me.

"Mom, I'm fine, I promise!" I said, swatting away her hand which subsequently pulled on my IV. I noticed the saline bag was nearly empty and I really had to pee all of a sudden. I was glad that meant I didn't have a catheter this time.

"No fever?" she checked, feeling my forehead. "How's your pain levels?"

"I'm better," I insisted. "No pain, no fever."

I wondered what time it was, and I wondered where my phone was. I needed to call Shea. I knew that he would be here if he knew I was here. I noticed my clothes were folded in a pile on a storage cabinet and my phone, which had been in my pocket, was lying on top.

"Daddy, could you hand me my phone?" I asked, pointing to it.

He immediately went to my phone and handed it to me. Pressing the home button, I saw that I had a dozen missed calls, and several text messages, all from Shea.

"I need to call Shea," I told them, pressing his number and bringing my phone up to my ear.

He answered on the first ring.

"Are you okay?" he asked anxiously.

"Don't freak out," I said in a warning tone.

"Too late."

"I'm in the hospital," I told him, to which I heard his car keys jingling as though he was racing to his car. "I'm okay! Drive safely!"

"I'm already here, I'm in the lobby," he told me. "I went to your house, and when there was no answer, and both your cars were there, I assumed you'd be at the hospital if you weren't answering the phone. They told me that you had been admitted but they won't tell me anything about your condition because I'm not family. I hate that freakin' rule."

I could hear how upset he was in his tone. I thought that rule was dumb too. So, a distant relative who you don't even know could theoretically find out information about you, but your boyfriend can't?

"The doctor hasn't been in yet, but I had an infection, I think."

"You think? Jesus, Sara, an infection is bad for someone like you. Can I talk to your mom?"

I held the phone out to Mom and she smirked a little. "Hi, Shea, it's Amanda," she said, as she put the phone to her ear. "Yes, she's okay. No fever, the antibiotics are working. Yes, she had a dangerous infection. Cellulitis."

While Mom spoke to Shea, Dad came to me and held my hand. "You really scared me, Saraphine," he told me seriously.

"I'm sorry," I said sincerely. It was a really stupid error in judgement. I knew how bad infections were for me, and I just didn't think. I knew Mom was blaming herself, and the truth was, I didn't want to bother her. But I didn't blame her at all. I was just stupid for a moment.

"I feel bad for the poor kid," he nodded to Mom, obviously meaning Shea. "You being so sick, so hurt these last few weeks, kid's gone through hell. And for someone like him, it's worse."

"I know he worries about me," I replied.

"It's more than that, Saraphine," Dad said knowingly. "The prospect of losing a mate, well, the pain is unimaginable. Trust me." He offered me a small, sympathetic smile.

The on-call doctor entered the room just as Mom was telling Shea my room number. She had her tablet with her and was flicking through my chart. She smiled at me as she checked my IV.

"Well, Miss Bryant, you certainly look a lot better than you did a few hours ago," she said cheerfully.

"I feel a lot better," I replied.

"Well, we've given you something to break your fever which is what is making you feel a lot better, and we've given you some medication for the pain, but the antibiotics to treat your infection will take a while to fully combat the bacteria," she explained. "Now, your file says you were explicitly informed about the risk of splenectomy post-operative infection and signs and symptoms to look out for. Is that correct?"

Both Mom and Dad looked at me like I was a naughty child with my hand in the cookie jar.

"Yes," I confirmed. I didn't really have a good excuse except for that I had a brain fart.

"Right, well, you need to be vigilant, Sara," she told me, tut tutting. "You have what's called cellulitis. Cellulitis is an infection of the tissue under the skin. The lab confirmed it has been caused by exposure to haemophilus influenzae type B bacteria. Now this is a serious infection, Sara, because left untreated, cellulitis can lead to abscesses, necrotising fasciitis, sepsis, multi-limb amputation and death." She spoke so frankly, it felt like she had slapped me in the face.

"Shit," I said in disbelief.

"Yes, shit," she replied, nodding. "Your spleen plays a crucial role in your ability to fight off bacteria, and seeing as you no longer have one, bacterial infections are a very serious matter. I need you to understand that."

"I do," I promised her, before looking to my parents. "I do."

"Good." She began to type a few things into my chart before she checked some of the machines that were attached to me. "Mom and Dad, do you have any questions?" she asked my parents.

"Not at the moment," my dad replied, "but my wife is a doctor, so if I think of anything ..."

Both Mom and I seemed to have the same reaction to my dad referring to her as his wife. We were both a little awestruck.

"Okay, well, don't hesitate to press the call button if you do think of anything. It's important to be Mom first and doctor second in here. I'll be in later to check your vitals again, Sara." She offered us another smile before departing.

The silence that followed was honestly a little awkward. Mom was still a little stunned and Dad didn't know what to say. We were all relieved when Shea suddenly appeared at the door with a nurse in tow, asking if he belonged to us.

Shea, not taking any notice of my parents, breathed a sigh of relief when he saw me. He crossed the room in a second, cupped my face, and he kissed me. I could practically feel his anxiety melting away.

But my dad had to go and be a dad and clear his throat.

Shea pulled away but stayed close to search my face for any sign of harm. I probably looked terrible, but he was used to that. "Are you okay?" he asked me desperately.

I was suddenly thankful that he missed my doctor's necrotising fasciitis and death speech. "Yes," I confirmed. "Just a little infection. I'm fine. They've got me hooked up to the good stuff," I joked, gesturing to my IV.

"She's going to do a much better job of letting us know when she's not feeling well, now, aren't you Saraphine?" Dad arched an eyebrow.

"Yes," I confirmed, nodding.

"Did this start last night?" Shea asked. "I was there, the whole time, you could have told me. Why didn't you tell me?"

"What?" both my parents suddenly asked.

Shea paled, realising how that sounded. "On the phone!" he quickly corrected. "We fell asleep talking on the phone. I was at my house, in my own bed, nowhere near Sara, safe distances et cetera."

I resisted laughing. "I wasn't feeling sick until this morning," I told him. "I should have said something, but I thought it was nothing."

"Sara," Mom said gently, coming to sit beside me on the bed, opposite to Shea. "I'm so very sorry, honey. I should have seen that you weren't okay. I was being horribly selfish."

I looked at my mom deadpan. "Mom, you have never been selfish, ever, not a day in your life. I'm the one who didn't say anything. You have nothing to be sorry for."

I could tell that the fact that I wasn't holding a grudge, or the fact that I didn't blame her, truly meant a lot to my mom. I didn't want her to use this as an excuse to stop herself from living her life, or for exploring what was still there with Dad.

Chapter 37

I was in hospital for another two days for observation before they sent me home with strict instructions to come back if there were any complications. I had oral medication and they gave me a shot just in case.

After that, everything kind of went back to normal. Well, our new normal.

Shea stayed with me every night, coming in my window once Mom had gone to bed. It was becoming our routine and I loved it.

Mom let me go back to school the following week. There was only one week left before winter break, and I knew I would be spending the whole time studying to catch up, but it was so good to see my friends and catch up with everything that I had missed.

It turns out, getting kidnapped on a school trip, stabbed, and having your spleen removed, makes you a minor celebrity in Providence. I had practically spoken to every student and faculty member in one day who all wanted to know how I was doing, or the gory details of my ordeal.

I just replied with, "I'm doing great, thanks."

I finally got to catch up with Josh, who was in a real, public relationship with Zoey. They had gotten together in Charlotte, and he hadn't said anything as he didn't want to rub his relationship in my face when I was going through something horrible.

Zoey had also told him the truth about her, and after passing out, much to his humiliation, he was okay with it. Zoey was proudly still wearing a tube top in December just so that she could show off her new "Joshua" tattoo. Those in the know knew exactly what it was though, and I was happy for her.

That was until Josh told me about the consequence of them being together. When Zoey's parents had found out about her and Josh, they had flipped out. They kicked Zoey out of the house and she was now staying in Josh's room and hiding from his parents.

I knew I wanted to help them, but I had to figure out how.

My dad was around the house quite often now, and I still couldn't quite figure out what was going on between him and Mom. They looked like they were becoming friends again, but they were keeping anything romantic well hidden.

But with Shea there, too, the topic of the pack came up a bit more. It turned out that Shea and his family received a monthly benefit from his father's life insurance policy. However, no such policy existed. My dad had been the one paying.

When Shea had found this out, he felt really guilty and embarrassed, but my dad assured him that Robert would have wanted him to look after his family. Robert and my dad were best friends, after all.

"My mom and my sister are my responsibility," Shea had said, quite vulnerably.

"Your mom, Cecelia, and you, Shea, are my responsibility," my dad had replied. "You're still a kid, and you ought to be one."

It was like a massive weight had been lifted off of Shea's shoulders after that. Shea had always had the burden of looking after his family on his mind. He couldn't do anything for himself, and what life was that for an eighteen-year-old? Of course, he would always be there for his mom and sister, but he needed independence, too.

With my mom's blessing, my dad resumed control of the pack, and Shea took over the role of Beta, just as his father had been. This meant that Shea could have a lot more independence and could even go to college if he wanted to.

I was very hypocritical when I learned this, not wanting him to go away, when I was planning on applying to out of state colleges, but Shea quelled my fears anyway, saying that he liked the option of college, but he hadn't decided what was for him yet.

My question of whether my parents were involved again was answered rather awkwardly one night during winter break when I ran into my shirtless dad on my way to the bathroom at two o'clock in the morning. Seeing the "Amanda" tattoo made me smile, but then it completely grossed me out as we avoided eye-contact and returned to our prospective bedrooms.

Mom tried to awkwardly broach the subject the next morning, but I interrupted telling her I was happy for her. That was the understatement of the century. Nobody wanted to think of their parents doing it, but after the seventeen years apart that my parents had had, they deserved to do whatever they wanted.

After winter break finished, and we were all back at school, I found myself spending a lot more time with Zoey as she was now permanently attached to Josh. And now that she wasn't behaving like she had a mental disorder, I found that I could actually tolerate her.

That tolerance grew to like, and soon enough, I counted her as a friend. So much so that when Josh's parents discovered her living in his bedroom, I found myself asking my mom if Zoey could live in our spare bedroom.

With a little encouragement from my dad, who obviously knew how vile her parents were, Mom agreed, and soon enough, Zoey was now my next-door neighbour.

Zoey turned out to be a pretty good roommate, and a pretty decent friend in the end. It was almost like having a sister. Well, what I imagine sisters to be like. Arguing over bathroom time and who was wearing the other's clothes. Though Zoey insisted she'd never be caught dead in anything I owned, so it was me who was the thief.

But, when we got along, I could talk to her, and she could talk to me. And when Cece was with us, I really felt like I had found friends for life.

Dad moved in with us in March, after he and Mom had been dating for a few months. Mom was honestly happier than I had ever seen her, and Dad just looked like he belonged with her.

So, while they had strict rules about boys in our rooms, both Zoey and I broke them regularly. And the crappy thing about having a lycan for a dad is that his hearing is pretty good. He knew exactly when we had boys in our rooms, but he didn't say anything to Mom.

A few weeks after Dad moved in, Shea took me out into the woods. Everything had been going really great between Shea and I. Being together was honestly so much easier when he wasn't worrying all the time.

"You're not going to kill me, are you?" I joked. "The last time someone brought me into the woods, things didn't go so well."

I was honestly a lot better now, physically and emotionally. I didn't develop another infection. I was now left with a pretty gnarly curved shaped scar on my upper abdomen, thanks to the knife wound, and the emergency surgery. I hadn't let Shea see it, not yet.

But seeing as he stayed with me almost every night, I hadn't had any nightmares either. I did still think about Lex from time to time, but I honestly made a conscious effort to focus on the many blessings that I had in my life instead.

Crap happens. And while my crap was particularly crappy, I wasn't going to wear it like a tattoo on my forehead. I was Sara Bryant, and I had a blessed life.

"Not funny, Sara," snapped Shea, but there was humour in his tone.

"Sorry," I apologised jestingly. "Why are we going into the woods, though?" I pressed.

"You'll see," he replied.

Shea parked his truck at the end of the trail and we began to walk into the dense forest. When my human legs got tired, Shea piggy backed me until we were at least five miles from the trail. When he placed me down, he turned on me, and said, "I love you."

I frowned. "I know. I love you, too."

Shea exhaled. "It's been weighing on my mind for a while now that part of the reason that your parents broke up in the first place is that your mom was afraid of him. I know they're back together now, and that's great, but I don't ever want you to be afraid of me, and I don't ever want there to be a reason for you and I to be apart for that long."

"Shea, I'm not afraid of you," I assured him.

Shea smiled before grabbing his t-shirt and pulling it off over his head.

I never got tired of perving on my boyfriend. Shea didn't mind me checking him out either. He honestly looked a little self-satisfied.

I then realised what he was doing when he unbuttoned his jeans and pulled down the fly. He really didn't want me to be afraid of him. He wanted me to see him. I had only got a glimpse of him in his lycan form once, and I was half-delirious at the time. Honestly, it was all still a little bit like a dream to me that things like this could really exist.

And then Shea took off his boxers.

He seemed very comfortable to be standing naked in my presence, and I could see that he had nothing to be ashamed of, which then caused me to blush and avert my eyes.

Shea chuckled. "It's not seeing me like this that I'm afraid of, Sara."

"I can see that," I murmured. Oh my God, I needed to stop being such a little girl.

Shea and I hadn't taken that next step in our relationship yet, and God knew that I wanted to. I was just such a chicken when it came to initiating anything, and I knew that Shea would never pressure me.

Taking a deep breath, I looked him in the eye.

Shea took a deep breath, too. "Please, don't run."

It was a literal shift. One second he was a human man, and the next there was a large wolf standing before me.

I gasped so hard that it was almost as though I had sucked all the wind out of me. I jumped backwards, as though I hadn't been expecting this to happen.

I blinked a few times as I adjusted to what I was seeing. He was huge. Shea was always a lot taller than me, but as a wolf, he was enormous. Standing on all fours, he was still a few inches taller than me. His fur was a russet brown, the exact same shade as his hair, and his eyes were exactly the same as well. They were larger, and solely looking at me, but I could see Shea in them.

His legs were long and powerful. I could see the strength in his muscles. His fur looked long and soft, and before I knew it, I was reaching out to touch him.

Shea went down on his front legs, as though he was bowing. He lowered his head to me, and my fingers threaded through the fur on his head. His eyes closed. I think it surprised me how soft he was. Not that I had been expecting something. I combed my fingers through his fur, and I felt my own breathing normalise as I grew used to this.

I wasn't afraid, just completely out of my comfort zone.

But this was Shea. I had seen every facet of him. I loved every facet of him. And I knew he loved every flawed facet of me. Honestly, he could have shifted into a tap-dancing monkey and I would still love him every bit that I did.

I leaned over and whispered in his ear, "Shea." His ear perked up. "I love you."

And just like that, Shea shifted back, and he kissed me. I kissed him back passionately. And I knew that I was ready to see my name tattooed on his chest.

Epilogue

August 30, 1 Year Later

I ducked as a volleyball came hurtling towards me, letting out a pathetic scream. Shea jumped in front of me with his fist, sending the ball flying back over the net, landing on the sand opposite to win our team the point.

Shea, laughing, wrapped his arms around me. "I got you, Sara," he said, kissing my temple.

I rolled my eyes but kissed the "Saraphine" tattoo on his chest, before I said, "I'm out. Have fun." I walked off the makeshift beach volleyball court that the boys had set up and I made my way over to wear Cece and Zoey were sunbaking near the cooler of drinks.

I heard Shea cheer along with several of the other guys behind me so I assumed they had scored another point.

I pulled a soda from the cooler and opened the can. There was no beer at this party. Not when my dad could see us from our kitchen window with his super-sonic eyesight. We would have to wait for college next week for that.

I sat down in between Cece and Zoey and sipped my soda.

"Not fun anymore?" teased Cece.

I rolled my eyes again. "I mean, they do have an unfair advantage," I insisted. "They're pummelling volleyballs at me with lycan strength." I was honestly surprised the ball was still inflated.

"That's why we tan, Sara," interjected Zoey, stretching out her long legs. "Make the most of the North Carolina summer before we transition to a New York climate." She grinned at us both before turning her eye seductively to her boyfriend, who had been back home in Providence for the summer.

Josh's natural athletic ability helped him to compete really well with the other guys. I also noticed an addition to his chest as well. Obviously as humans, we didn't develop those tattoos, so at some point during the year, Josh had gotten Zoey's name tattooed on his chest. Seeing that honestly made me feel really happy for Zoey.

Having her boyfriend away at college all year while she was stuck in Providence completing her senior year had been hard for her. Coupled with the natural worry of her kind that humans were pretty untrustworthy when it came to love, it had been rough.

But they had handled it well. And Josh came home on breaks. And we all heard. I did share a wall with her, after all.

Josh had ended up selecting Cornell University in New York as his college of choice. He got a full ride thanks so a spectacular senior varsity season, and he was already a starter for the CU team.

Cece sat up and adjusted her bikini so that nothing was riding up. Do you know how when you usually sit down, your stomach sort of folds, like you've got fat rolls? Yeah, well, Cece's didn't do that. If anything, she had developed even more of a six-pack cheerleading this year.

Both she and Zoey had worked very hard on the squad this year, and their efforts had paid off in securing them partial scholarships to college.

My dad had sold his construction company in New York upon moving back to Providence permanently and had invested the money in property in the city, which was what he was using to fund our college tuition. He was paying my full ride, as not even a 3.9 GPA could help me beat the smart kids in my incoming class. He was also paying the difference in Cece and Zoey's tuition as well, and he wouldn't hear any objection.

Zoey hadn't spoken to her parents since she had been kicked out. There was no way they were helping with anything financially. But she hadn't looked back. Zoey was happier, and nicer than ever, and I honestly had loved having her as a roommate this year.

And Dad had really taken Shea and Cece under his wing this last year. Especially Cece.

"I mean, it's not like it's our last day in Providence or anything," Cece sarcastically complained, eyeing Jamie in particular, who was still participating in the volleyball game.

This was supposed to be our farewell party. Mine, Zoey, and Cece's. Summer had come to an end. We had long since collected out diplomas from Providence High School. We had celebrated homecoming. We had been to prom. I had taken dorky pictures with my parents at graduation.

It was time for the next step. College. Four years.

I sat up as well and cared little about how my stomach rolled. I didn't care much anymore how I looked. I wore my battle scars with pride. I'm sure a lot of people would have been quite self-conscious if their stomach looked like mine. And trust me, I had been.

But this large, arch shaped scar across my abdomen told anyone who saw it that I was a fighter and a survivor. I had survived hell, and I had fought through recovery. I had turned my trauma into something positive.

I studied my ass off senior year, and now I was a pre-med at New York University. I had never thought I would go into medicine, and I was still unsure if I would cut the mustard, but I was going to give it my best shot. I wanted to be on the other side and help people in the midst of trauma like I had been.

I watched Shea as he played, a happy smile on his face, and his happiness made me smile. It was hard to fathom that it would be two years we had been together in October. It honestly hadn't seemed like that long.

And yet, sometimes it still felt like the beginning. I still got nervous. I still got butterflies. But I loved him. I loved the person he was. I loved the person I was when I was with him. And I liked to think that I brought out the best in him.

Shea hadn't gone to college in the end. Things had really settled down after our ordeal with Lex, and we had achieved a sense of normal this last year and a half. After his graduation last June, Shea and a few of his friends, including Jamie, took out a small business loan and started a garage.

They were boys who liked to tinker with their cars, but they knew what they were talking about, and their reach and influence had helped them to drum up quite a bit of business. They were even looking to open a second garage in Newtown in the next year.

I was proud of Shea. I knew he hadn't gone to college because he didn't want to be far from me, but I was still glad he had used his intelligence and his skills to start something successful.

"These four years are going to suck, aren't they?" I worried. Pangs of dread hit me at random times. I was so excited to go to college, but the thought of being away from home for so long just got to me.

"Hell no," Zoey said forcefully. "NYU won't know what hit it."

Cece laughed. "Yeah, college parties have got nothing on what you're capable of throwing, Zoey."

Zoey had been itching to throw a proper party, like the kind she used to throw when she lived with her parents. That was the one thing my parents drew the line on.

"Plus, Josh and I will only be two hundred and twenty-one miles from each other now," Zoey added nonchalantly, though I knew she was wanting to say it more excitedly. She was conscious of both Cece and my feelings.

"And I suppose you've already memorised all the different traffic routes to get to Cornell," Cece mused humorously.

"No, I'm not insane," Zoey rebuffed, though we both knew she was lying.

I sighed and stared out on the ocean. This really was the most picturesque place. It was hard to fathom I had been living here less than two years, but I really couldn't imagine any other place being home.

I was tied here, in more ways than one, and I had come into my own here. I had found my parents, plural, here, I had found friends here, and I had found Shea. But most importantly, I had found myself. I had found my strength, my voice, and my conviction. I had found my confidence and self-worth. I had found my ambition. I knew I would always come back here.

I turned my head towards the houses that were situated along the beach in the distance, one of them being my own. I knew that my dad would be watching me. He, and Mom, had been watching me incessantly, especially these last few weeks. It didn't annoy me, it only made me emotional.

Like me, it was really hitting them that I would be moving away. College was real, and I would no longer be with them every day.

I pressed my fingers to my lips and blew a kiss towards the house. With his vision, I knew Dad would see me. Not a day passed where I wasn't grateful for both of them. I knew first-hand what it was like to go without, and to have both my parents so present in my life, and so completely there for me was a blessing.

Something told me that I would be calling them multiple times a day when I got to New York.

When I turned my head back, Shea was walking over to me, the volleyball game seemingly ending. Without words, he held out his hand to me and helped me up from the ground.

He was looking at me with a sad intensity, an expression that told me he was memorising everything that was about to happen, and I knew then that the volleyball game had been a distraction. Shea didn't want the whole party to be sobbing and tissues.

Though I couldn't promise that wouldn't be how it ended.

He held my hand as he led me up the beach and away from the gathering. We walked away from the main swimming part of the beach, to the rougher, rockier surf, where there were scarcely any locals to hear us, or to see us cry.

Goddammit, here I go. Tears spilled over and I let out a cough and a spluttering sob as I wrapped my arms around him. "I'm sorry," I wailed pathetically.

I was sorry for a lot of things. Sorry for leaving. Sorry to be leaving him. Sorry to need to go. Sorry to cause pain. And then I felt sorry because I wasn't sorry. I wantedto go. I wanted to learn, and stretch my legs, and grow up. Ugh, feelings weighed more than anything.

"Shh," Shea hushed me, rubbing his hands up my back. "You don't have to be sorry," he said hoarsely, the emotion like a frog in his throat that he was going to fight to keep contained. "I don't want you to be sorry. Ever." He brought his hand to my chin and forced me to look up at him. I saw how glassy his brown eyes were and it killed me. "I am so damn, crazy proud of you, Sara," he told me sincerely. "Don't you ever forget that." His voice was almost a whisper as he held himself together.

"But I'm leaving," I whined. Why I said that, I don't know. We were both well aware of the face. My brain just couldn't compute at that moment.

"It's four years," he said, though I sensed he was saying this more to himself than to me. "What's four years in the grand scheme of things?"

I knew he was right. College would probably fly by without me even realising. And then when finals came around it would drag on mercilessly. But in the grand scheme of things, four years was nothing. I would be done with college in four years, and then I would find a med school closer to home.

But I knew I couldn't give up this experience. It was a part of life, and one that I had been planning for long before I met Shea.

But I knew this would be hard for Shea. Tormenting even. I had seen first-hand what Zoey had gone through this last year with Josh away at school. "You know this won't change anything, right?"

Shea knew exactly what I was talking about, and I felt him stiffen in my arms. He nodded once. I knew that if he spoke, he was going to fall apart. I honestly wanted him to, so that I wouldn't be the only blubbering mess, and I could feel like I was comforting him for a change.

"You're stuck with me, you know," I continued, attempting to sound teasing to make him smile.

It worked. Shea let out a laugh as he hugged me once again, even tighter. "Well, crap. Just when I thought I was getting rid of you," he murmured against my hair, kissing my head.

I closed my eyes, enjoying this last little piece of familiar intimacy before I stepped out into the big wide world. But, I thought smiling, as I committed his scent to memory for the thousandth time, I knew where my home would always be.